DEATH OF A KINGDOM

BOOK 6 IN THE SAXON WARRIOR SERIES

PETER GIBBONS

Boldwood

First published in Great Britain in 2026 by Boldwood Books Ltd.

Copyright © Peter Gibbons, 2026

Cover Design by Colin Thomas

Cover Images: Colin Thomas

The moral right of Peter Gibbons to be identified as the author of this work has been asserted in accordance with the Copyright, Designs and Patents Act 1988.

All rights reserved. No part of this book may be reproduced in any form or by any electronic or mechanical means, including information storage and retrieval systems, without written permission from the author, except for the use of brief quotations in a book review. This book is a work of fiction and, except in the case of historical fact, any resemblance to actual persons, living or dead, is purely coincidental.

Every effort has been made to obtain the necessary permissions with reference to copyright material, both illustrative and quoted. We apologise for any omissions in this respect and will be pleased to make the appropriate acknowledgements in any future edition.

A CIP catalogue record for this book is available from the British Library.

Paperback ISBN 978-1-83518-271-0

Large Print ISBN 978-1-83518-270-3

Hardback ISBN 978-1-83518-269-7

Trade Paperback ISBN 978-1-80656-268-8

Ebook ISBN 978-1-83518-272-7

Kindle ISBN 978-1-83518-273-4

Audio CD ISBN 978-1-83518-264-2

MP3 CD ISBN 978-1-83518-265-9

Digital audio download ISBN 978-1-83518-267-3

This book is printed on certified sustainable paper. Boldwood Books is dedicated to putting sustainability at the heart of our business. For more information please visit https://www.boldwoodbooks.com/about-us/sustainability/

Boldwood Books Ltd, 23 Bowerdean Street, London, SW6 3TN

www.boldwoodbooks.com

For my family. Love and support is everything.

PART I

1004AD

PART I

1004AD

1

Beornoth brought the wood axe down hard and split another dry log in two. He paused for a moment, using the sleeve of his jerkin to wipe the sweat from his brow, and then hefted the tool once more in his calloused hands. Another log splintered and cracked in half, and Beornoth added it to the pile. It was early summer in Northumbria, and the sun warmed his broad back. He lowered the axe and squinted up at the pale blue sky and the sheep's-wool clouds drifting lazily overhead. A child laughed beyond the grove as Beornoth worked, where a group of playing children leapt and splashed in the river. Beornoth allowed himself a rare smile. He coughed again, a wracking cough that had shaken his body night and day since winter. Beornoth bent double until the episode ended, and stood, gasping for breath, lungs burning as if scorched by flame.

'Rest for a while, lord,' said Wigs, shifting logs from the pile onto the back of an ox cart. 'We have cheese here, freshly made up at the hall. And ale. It's a fine day. Enjoy the sun.'

'The wood won't cut itself,' Beornoth replied.

'No, I suppose it won't.' Wigs looked longingly at the crock of ale and chunk of cheese beside the cart.

'You take a rest, and I'll cut the wood,' said Gis, spitting on his hands and rubbing them together.

'You'd lop your foot off. Best stick to frightening the crows away from the wheat field with your ugly face.'

'I could lop your head off instead. That would close that mouth of yours.'

'Alright,' Beornoth said, shaking his head. He slapped the axe into a log and left it quivering. 'Open the cheese and ale. Your bickering is giving me a headache.'

Wigs and Gis were Saxon warriors, brave men from England's heartland who had come into Beornoth's service last year amidst a maelstrom of war. Wigs and Gis had helped him fight a Norman enemy, and that conflict had led the trio north to Stag Hall, where Beornoth's friend Brand ruled as a thegn in the shire of Northumbria. Gis, a squint-eyed Saxon with an easy smile, and Wigs teased each other endlessly, but they were good men and great friends. Wigs was a stout man full of good humour, properly named Wiglaf but known as Wigs to his friends.

'If that's not the best cheese you've ever eaten, I'll eat my belt,' said Wigs through a mouthful of the soft, fragrant food.

'I've had better,' said Gis.

'Liar. You're just saying that to spite me.'

'It's true. My old grandmother used to make cheese ten times nicer than this. So you can eat your belt now and wash it down with a mouthful of ale.'

'You, my friend, are what is commonly known as a simpleton. It wasn't so long ago folk would take brain-stunted people like you from their parents as children and throw them off a mountaintop.'

'If it gets warmer this week, Brand should cut the harvest,' Beornoth said to change the subject.

'Are we staying for the summer?'

'Brand has invited us to stay with him. So we could.' Beornoth swallowed a piece of cheese and thought of his wife's grave left untended at his home in Cheshire. He had been away for a year, and weeds would have grown around the cross. He missed the closeness he felt with Eawynn at home, but Stag Hall was a happy place full of the laughter of children. The levity of Brand's hall and lands gave Beornoth peace, something uncommon in his long life spent with sword and shield. The Normans had come to Brand's home with fire and sword last summer, but the family had recovered from the fight quickly, and folk from across the valley had helped repair damaged thatch, walls and fencing.

'We can't stay here forever, though,' said Gis. He unstopped the crock of ale and took a long pull. 'Eating Brand's food and supping his mead. We are warriors. We can't harvest wheat and chop wood for the rest of our lives.'

'Maybe we could join Brand's hearth troop?' asked Wigs.

'They are all Vikings. It's full of them this far north. We're Saxons. This isn't our home.'

'There's war in the south. They need warriors.' Both men glanced nervously at Beornoth and then looked at the grass.

'There's always war in the south. The Vikings have returned, as they do every summer. I will return to Cheshire,' said Beornoth, ignoring their talk of war, though he knew it raged like wildfire south of the Danelaw. 'You will both be welcome there. Ealdorman Alfgar always has a need for stout warriors.'

'Aye, Cheshire,' Wigs replied with no conviction in his tone.

Beornoth's men wanted to ride south where their countrymen fought against the Viking invaders who plagued England's south and east coasts. He understood that need. He had fought Vikings his entire life. Warlords from Jutland, the Skagerrak, Kattegat and the Vik brought their dragon ships south across the Whale Road every summer and had done for a hundred years. They came for blood, glory, silver, slaves and land, and their savagery knew no bounds. Beornoth could almost smell the burning thatch and hear the screams of what it meant to suffer a Viking raid. But King Æthelred had brought this latest war upon himself, and Beornoth shuddered at the suffering the ruler had brought upon his own people. Beornoth had fought the king's men to protect Danes and Norsemen in the Danelaw, and that had cost him his position, his income, and had shaken every belief and principle which made Beornoth the man he was, or the man he had been.

Wigs and Gis ate and drank in silence, uncomfortable because they wanted to ride and fight in the south but would not discard their loyalty to Beornoth to do it. Beornoth was twice their age and had seen enough war to last a dozen lifetimes. He was tired of it and had no urge to march to fight for a king who had picked a fight he could not hope to win. Beornoth's aged body ached every morning, and old wounds in his shoulder, back, legs and stomach hurt in the winter cold as though cold steel still lay stabbed within his wrinkled flesh. Beornoth's hands had begun to twist, knuckles swollen, fingers bent and curling inwards, but he could still wield a wood axe well enough. His hair was whiter now than grey, so that it looked like winter snow melting over the hard, lined crag of his face.

'Beornoth,' called a voice with a heavy Norse accent. 'A rider.'

Beornoth turned at the hip and groaned as his shoulder objected to the movement. Orm, a slim man with long, dark hair worn in two tails hanging on either side of a sharp face, came from the woods and pointed to the southern hills. High on the west-facing slope, a figure ambled down through the heather. A man riding a smoke-grey horse approached slowly. Beornoth squinted, his ageing eyes unable to see the rider clearly.

'Is he armed?' Beornoth asked.

'To the teeth,' replied Wigs.

'Does he carry a sigil?'

'I can't see from here, but he has a shield, a spear and a sword strapped to his saddle.'

'Trouble?' asked Gis.

'Let's find out,' Beornoth replied. 'Gis, fetch Brand.'

Gis hurried into the trees towards the river, where Brand's hall and outbuildings sat beside a fast-flowing river. Orm, who was Brand's oathman, came to stand beside Beornoth.

'Could be a messenger from the ealdorman?' said Orm.

'Let's hope it's not bad news,' said Wigs, and he made the sign of the cross. Orm snorted and touched the pagan hammer amulet hanging around his neck. England was a Christian country, but within the Danelaw many still worshipped the old Norse gods. Odin, Freya, Thor, Týr, Njorth and the rest of the Aesir encouraged their people to war with the promise of an afterlife spent fighting, feasting and swiving in the great halls of Valhalla, Thruthvangar and Sessrúmnir, a heaven reserved for those who died in battle with a blade in their hand.

Beornoth pulled the wood axe from its log, rested it upon his shoulder and strolled towards the rider. Orm and Wigs followed behind. Brand was a Norseman, a Viking, and he was the thegn of Stag Hall. Stag Hall sat within Northumbria, where Beornoth's old friend Thered ruled as ealdorman. Northumbria, like most shires north of Watling Street, the old Roman road which divided England in two and which ran from Lundenwic to the River Mersey, was home to both Englishman and Norseman and had been for over one hundred years since King Alfred had created the Danelaw to make peace with the Great Heathen Army led by the sons of Ragnar Lothbrok.

'He looks grim,' said Wigs as the rider grew closer. His horse picked its way through brush and briar until it reached the valley basin. The horse whickered and shook its mane, and the rider raised a hand in greeting. He was a big man, broad-shouldered and young, with his hair cut close to his scalp and a round face with small, bleak eyes.

'Doesn't look like good news then,' sighed Gis. 'I thought we might have a bit of peace this summer. A rest.'

'You *have* been resting. All you've done today is watch Lord Beornoth chop wood and eat cheese.'

'Exactly. Peace.'

'Who is it?' called a voice in Norse. Brand Thorkilsson came striding from the forest with his thumbs tucked into a thick leather belt, from which hung his bearded axe. He wore his long golden hair in a thick braid hanging down his back, and his beard grew down to his chest, combed to a sheen. His wrists shone with warriors' rings, and his face bore the scars of a veteran warrior.

'We don't know yet, Lord,' Wigs answered.

Beornoth nodded to Brand as the Dane stood alongside him. More men came from the river and the forest to hear what the visitor had to say. Some wore the simple wool jerkins of thralls, and others carried spears and were part of Brand's hearth troop, the band of loyal warriors that the thegn fed and kept in silver and who helped Brand keep law and order across his lands.

The rider reined in and leant forward on his saddle. He wore a leather breastplate, and a shield hung across his horse's back. Now that he was close, Beornoth could see that the shield's leather cover bore three gold crowns on a blue field, the sigil used by the ealdorman of East Anglia in England's south-east.

'I seek Beornoth,' said the rider, his voice gruff. 'Who was once a king's thegn. The man who killed Skarde Wartooth, and Palnatoki of the Jomsvikings. Survivor of the battle of Maldon, victor of the siege of Lundenwic, who men call the Viking killer.'

'I am a simple woodsman,' said Beornoth.

'And I am Osgar, sent by Lord Ulfcytel of East Anglia to see Beornoth.'

'I am Brand Thorkilsson, thegn of these lands,' Brand said, speaking in Saxon. 'Come to my hall, traveller. You are welcome. We have ale, bread and cheese.'

'Thank you, lord, but I must return to Lord Ulfcytel with all haste. Your lands here are peaceful, but I come from the south, where Sweyn Forkbeard and two thousand Vikings ravage our villages, towns and homes. They rape, burn, enslave, steal and eat everything they can get their hands on. I cannot tarry here in your pleasant land whilst my people suffer. Our country is in grave peril, lord, and so Ulfcytel sent me north to seek the only man the Vikings fear. I have a gift for Beornoth, entrusted to me by Ealdorman Eadric of Mercia on behalf of King Æthelred himself. I have ridden many days to find Lord Beornoth, and all the while the Vikings continue their attacks.' The rider dug his hand into a leather pouch and held up a gold ring bearing the dragon of Wessex set upon a bright green stone.

'A fine ring,' said Brand.

'The ring of a king's thegn. There are only ten such men in all of England. Men as powerful as ealdormen, but warriors who answer only to the king himself. Beornoth is one, and the man I serve is another.'

'Forkbeard punishes us for the St Brice's Day Massacre,' said Beornoth. 'The king ordered that slaughter, and Forkbeard's sister died. I know. I was there. So Forkbeard attacks with just cause.'

'Just cause? Does that matter when homes are aflame, when women and old folk lie dead and unburied in ravaged villages, and when our rivers run with blood and bloated corpses?' Osgar's knuckles turned white above clenched fists, and he shook with anger. Beornoth shifted uncomfortably, understanding that rage, sensing the rage that simmered inside himself. Osgar closed his eyes and whispered a silent prayer, mastered himself, and then opened his hard eyes once more. 'Forgive me, friends. We have seen much suffering this year. Just as we have in years gone by. Lord Beornoth.' He inclined his head in Beornoth's direction. 'Normally, I am a man of few words. Excuse my impudence, but I know you are the man I seek. Ulfcytel described you. He has fought alongside you many times, against the Jomsvikings, in great battles, and he has praised your bravery to me at countless campfires. This is your ring, Lord Beornoth, take it up once more, become a king's thegn again and protect our people.'

'I fear you have travelled far on an errand I do not understand. I was a king's thegn once, and yes, I did the things you speak of. But that was before. I have served my people and my land. My family died during the wars, and yet I linger, tired and old with nothing to keep me warm in the night but memories and nightmares. I cannot help you win your war. The king must raise the fyrds of East Anglia, Wessex or Somersaete. We are far away, and my duty is done. One man cannot make a difference.'

'One man can make a difference, lord. If you ride, men will know that the

Viking killer has come to fight the enemy. The Vikings know you, and they fear you. Your presence raises our morale and casts doubt into the heart of the enemy. A legend who can galvanise our men and lend his experience to our cause, to protect those who cannot defend themselves. We need you, Lord Beornoth. England needs you. Your king calls you to arms.'

Osgar tossed the ring, and Beornoth caught it. It was the same ring he had returned to Eadric Streona and King Æthelred when he had resigned his post. Beornoth held it tight in his fist, and memories washed over him like a great sea wave. He remembered fighting Thorkell the Tall on Lundenwic bridge, Sweyn Forkbeard himself coming from the sea like a demon at Maldon with his axe and his malice, his great friend and lord the Ealdorman Byrhtnoth cut down on that dark day along with Beornoth's brothers of the sword. More painfully, he remembered his own daughters' little, shrunken, smoke-blackened corpses. His Ashwig and Cwen, slaughtered in a Viking raid so long ago on the day raiders had captured his wife, cut her throat and left her for dead. Eawynn had survived that horror, only to be cast into a madness which, by God's grace, she emerged from in her later years. Ashwig and Cwen would have been grown women by now, mothers, and Beornoth a doting grandfather. He recalled the smell of their hair, the softness of their small faces, and their laughter as he chased them through green meadows.

Beornoth had dreamed of staying in the north, no longer a king's thegn or a warrior, resigned to a peaceful twilight. He had dreamt of dying at home in Cheshire, beside Eawynn's grave so that he too could rest in the earth beside her forever. Beornoth had longed to be reunited with Eawynn and his daughters in heaven, but as Osgar spoke of Forkbeard, the raids, and how good Saxon people suffered in the south, Beornoth awoke from that fool's dream like a drowning man slapped across the face. Heaven was for the good and the kind, for those who forgive and repent, for folk who turn the other cheek. Beornoth was what he had always been, and war called to him again like death's crooked finger, beckoning, laughing at his foolish dreams. The blade sang to him, the dragon ships snarled at him, and the horror of battle wished to welcome him home, to die where he belonged. On the battlefield.

'Has Forkbeard reached Winchester or Lundenwic?' Beornoth asked.

'Not yet. He camps at Theodford in East Anglia.'

'So the kingdom is not yet lost?'

'Not yet. But we need brave men to fight. We need to mount a resistance, or

Sweyn Forkbeard will destroy our kingdom. He has made no attempt at Winchester, which makes me believe he has not come for conquest.'

'For plunder alone, then.' Beornoth sighed and ran his tongue through the gap in his teeth where, long ago, an arrow had torn through his face. 'To keep his men happy with blood and glory. Denmark and Norway are under Forkbeard's dominion already; he keeps many warriors under his command. How can he pay and feed them without a war to fight? Two thousand men is not enough to conquer England. Even if they are Forkbeard's battle-hardened veterans. Has he asked for the gafol yet?' Beornoth knew King Æthelred well, and his bishops better. They had once paid off Viking raiders with vast sums of silver known as the gafol, and the Danes and Norsemen were like dogs fed scraps after a feast. They kept on returning. Every summer, warships came again for fresh blood and fresh silver to make their warriors rich and burnish their reputations as bright as a honed sword.

'No, lord. But the king and his advisors have already taxed the shires in anticipation of it.'

The ring felt cool in Beornoth's palm. He lifted his head and closed his eyes. The sounds of old battles rang about his head like a bell, and friends lost to enemy blades whispered to him, calling him to war. Beornoth's wife and children were gone. He had lived with Brand through the winter and enjoyed the sound of children playing in the fields around Stag Hall. He could wait to die, tend his garden and listen to the wind. But Beornoth had lived a life of axes, swords, spears, blood and death. He had fought countless times, suffered terrible wounds, won battles and lost wars. Death should have come for him long ago, but if God would not let him die peacefully, perhaps there was another purpose for his old bones. One more war before the end? Death in battle seemed fitting for a man who had seen so much suffering.

'You are right, warrior, I am Beornoth,' he said. 'We shall ride south today.'

As Beornoth, Osgar, Wigs and Gis rode away, Brand, his wife Sefna and their children waved from the hall's stout palisade, and Beornoth's heart burned with sadness to leave the children. Thankfully, the feeling of sadness waned once Stag Hall was out of sight, and Beornoth's heart hardened, returning to the callous it had always been. He rode his great warhorse, Virtus, a roan mare trained for battle in the royal stables, and a gift from the king himself. Virtus meant courage and strength in Latin, the tongue of the Church and of old Rome. Beornoth had received the horse as part of the heriot with his position, along with a sword, seax, shield, byrnie coat of chain-mail armour, a spear and a full-faced helmet whose nasal was shaped like a boar and crested with a plume of black horsehair. Beornoth rode south like a lord of war, a king's thegn once more, and with him rode Wigs and Gis in leather and armed with spears.

'It's a pity Brand and his men aren't coming with us,' said Gis, twisting in the saddle to gaze longingly at Stag Hall, Brand, Orm and the twenty warriors standing beside them.

'It's not their fight,' Beornoth replied.

'It's everyone's fight. If Forkbeard conquers the south, how long before he wants the north as well?'

'You forget, my friend, many of the people north of Watling Street are the descendants of Northmen. A Viking ruler wouldn't be unwelcome in the Danelaw. What difference is it to men like Brand if Æthelred or Sweyn Forkbeard rules?'

'There are Saxon folk here too.'

'There are. Ealdormen Thered and Alfgar are Saxons, but their duty is to protect their people.'

'And to fight for the king whenever he calls,' added Wigs, cheerfully checking the contents of the sack of supplies Brand's wife Sefna had provided for the journey south.

'Then why doesn't he call every warrior in England to march south?'

'Because the ealdormen in the north must also protect the north. Forkbeard will not be the only Viking to raid our coasts this summer. The Northmen smell weakness, they sense opportunity and will pour into our rivers like poison into an infected wound.'

'So we go south to save a kingdom,' Gis said miserably. 'An old man and four soldiers to save England from Forkbeard and his two thousand growlers.'

'Careful. I'm not that old.'

Wigs opened his mouth to offer a smart comment, took one look at Beornoth's face and thought better of it.

'How long until we reach Theodford?' Gis called to Osgar.

'Less than two weeks. We ride hard. Men will rally to our banner when they hear that Lord Beornoth has returned.'

'Do you know Ulfcytel?' asked Wigs.

'I know him,' Beornoth replied. 'A good man. A stout fighter in the shield wall. It seems his star has risen since last we met, but he is a man to be respected. He once led a night raid and trapped half a dozen Viking ships in the East Anglian fens, so he has cunning and courage.'

'At least we don't ride to join a fool, then.'

Beornoth stretched his hands, uncurling the bent fingers and stretching his swollen knuckles. His back ached already after barely half an hour in the saddle, and his chain-mail byrnie felt heavy upon his shoulders. He hoped Osgar was right, and he hoped he could still wield a sword with his old ferocity, or it would be a short and shameful return.

Eleven days later, Beornoth and his companions arrived to find a Saxon army gathered west of Theodford. They travelled south along the old Roman roads, which were still paved in places, and then west through the lowland fens, through sullen villages where fisherfolk sold them food for scraps of hacksilver. Osgar proved to be a fine riding companion, mainly because he spoke little, which suited Beornoth well enough. Wigs and Gis rode ahead of Beornoth and Osgar most days to scout the road and clear away any merchants' carts, flocks of sheep or herds of cows which might block the road. During the long ride, the travellers stopped at the halls of thegns, monasteries and the homes of merchants and wealthy farmers, where Beornoth's ring and the dragon banner of Wessex sewn into his scabbard proved his position as a king's thegn and assured the four companions' food and bed for the night, and hay and shelter for their horses.

'The Danes are in the town?' asked Beornoth as they approached Theodford, emerging from a forest of birch, hazel and alder. They circled south and then north around the wetland fens until Osgar found the meanders of the Ouse river, upon which Theodford sat. The town's name meant 'ford across the river', and Beornoth frowned to see dozens of Viking drakkar warships moored in a wide stretch of the waterway, their dragon-prowed hulls snarling at the land and its people.

'Looks like it, lord,' Osgar replied. 'Though that was not the case when I left.'

A stone church with a wooden cross on its gable end sat outside the town, which was little more than a huddle of wattle and daub houses roofed with grey thatch and circled by a palisade from which broken gates hung from smashed iron hinges. Fire smoke hung above the town in a filthy cloud. It was morning, and women took buckets to the river to collect water, and a bowlegged man led a herd of goats away from the travellers using a length of hazel as a switch.

The Saxon army camped further along the river, where the flatlands seemed to stretch for miles in a patchwork of barley and wheat fields, grazing pastures, low hills, farms and villages split by the roads and hedges which made up their ancient boundaries. Warriors on patrol outside the camp greeted Osgar by raising their spears, and they eyed Beornoth's expensive chain mail and sword carefully, bowing their heads in respect. Tents of leather and greying sailcloth stretched across a riverbank field where men marched through lanes turned to mud by heavy boots, in between stacks of spears, sheaves of arrows, and carts packed with ale barrels, flitches of bacon, dried beef, eggs, cheese and oats all guarded by ruddy-faced warriors in padded wool and leather.

Half a dozen men in mail marched through the camp, and the shortest among them raised a hand in greeting.

'Lord Ulfcytel,' Osgar said. He climbed down from his horse and bowed to the short man.

'Lord Beornoth,' said the man. 'You came. I hope the journey was not too arduous.' He wore knee-length boots, a byrnie which protected him from neck to knee, and a leather belt from which hung a scabbard like Beornoth's own. He had a lined, wind-burned face with a furrowed brow and a long nose broken in some distant fight. His blue eyes shone through his chestnut face, and he was bald except for a ring of hair about his ears and the lower part of his head. He looked more like a farmer or a courtier than a warrior, with narrow shoulders and a pot belly.

'Lord Ulfcytel.' Beornoth climbed down off Virtus and forced himself not to groan or grumble at the aches in his legs and back. He stood straight and took Ulfcytel's forearm in the warrior's grip. 'Looks like you've got trouble.'

'A gentle way of putting it, aye. We've got old Forkbeard himself holed up in the town and his fleet in the river. He's laden with plundered silver and gold, and it's only a matter of time before the king offers the gafol payment and makes Forkbeard rich for the second time.'

'The king paid Forkbeard off once before; I remember it well. And Olaf Trygvasson, and many more. Why hasn't Forkbeard sacked the town?'

'He might yet. I was about to talk to him. Our army is in plain sight, and we've one and a half thousand men here. I doubt he'll want to fight us and risk losing half of his army here in East Anglia. He hasn't taken Winchester or Lundenwic yet. Some men think Forkbeard's just here to raid, but he still will not want to lose many men in a battle if he can sail away rich.'

'Is there food in these parts for him to steal?'

'No. I had my men burn it all a week ago.' Ulfcytel met Beornoth's gaze. He was a confident man, a leader who knew his business. Viking war bands came across the wild North Sea on their shallow-draughted warships with supplies enough for the journey. Once at their destination, raiding and foraging took much of their time in foreign lands. Forkbeard had to feed two thousand warriors every day his army campaigned abroad, and that was a lot of mouths to feed. Ulfcytel was cunning and experienced in war, for no army can fight on an empty stomach.

'Ale or mead?'

'We emptied the ale and mead from every village and town for three days' ride in every direction. No food and no drink other than what we have in camp. Bastards are hungry and drinking river water.'

'Forkbeard won't stay then.'

Ulfcytel grinned and ran a hand down his short beard. 'Hopefully not. He might just sail away back to his own kingdom and leave us alone.'

'Or just sail up another river, perhaps north? Maybe he'll sail around to the south-west and look for easier pickings there.'

'My duty is to protect the people of East Anglia. We are king's thegns, you and I, so we protect the kingdom. If Forkbeard takes his ships elsewhere, then we will follow, but the people and the fyrd of East Anglia shall have peace.'

'Let's go and talk to the bastard then.'

Ulfcytel turned to his men. 'See that Lord Beornoth and his men receive food and ale. Take care of their horses. Osgar, you have done well. Rest now and report to me at sundown.'

'Thank you, lord,' said Osgar, and he took Virtus' reins from Beornoth and led the beast away.

'My men and I are grateful for your hospitality, but first let's go and meet Forkbeard. I haven't come all this way for nothing.'

'Just so.' Ulfcytel grinned, and the two king's thegns set off towards Theodford with a dozen warriors behind them, one of whom flew the banner of East Anglia from a long spear.

'The king has not come?' Beornoth asked as they waited just out of bowshot. Men with long beards and iron helmets peered at the Saxons from the town's palisade.

'No, he retreated to Lundenwic when Forkbeard landed. Though his man Eadric honoured us with a visit. It was he who bade me send for you.'

'I met Eadric before; he was captain of the king's guard then.'

'Well, he's more than that now. Streona, men call him. The Grasper. A weaselly bastard who's made himself as rich as a lord and now calls himself the king's advisor.'

'Does he advise the king?'

'He advises the king on matters pertaining to his own benefit; that much is clear. Eadric's father is Ethelric, you know him?'

'A thegn of Wessex?'

'Aye. A good man, brave. We could do with him here.'

'Why has not the king summoned the ealdormen and their warriors?'

'They must defend their own shires, and if they march here, who will collect the silver the king will eventually pay Forkbeard to go away? You live above Watling Street, Lord Beornoth, and so you know how the northern ealdormen grow distant, less loyal. Would the northern thegns march south if King Æthelred, or Eadric Streona, called?'

'True enough,' Beornoth allowed, understanding that the mix of settled second- and third-generation Vikings, and the northern Saxons, had little love for the king who never ventured north, but sent his tax collectors every year to bleed the shires dry.

'The king has not summoned the Wessex fyrd, nor Defnascir, Somersaete, or any of the western fyrds. Forkbeard could sail to any of those shires within two or three days and left unprotected they would fall like chaff from wheat. We are alone here, save for you, Lord Beornoth, though I wish you had brought more men.'

'Why did the king send for me and not the rest of the king's thegns, or ealdormen who can bring scores of warriors?'

'Your reputation and standing with the Danes. They fear you, and rightly so.'

Beornoth straightened as a score of Northmen came from the town. He imagined the bishops and priests pouring words of peace and payments into the king's ear, whilst all the while his people suffered. Such payments only worked for a year, and then the Vikings came again for more blood and more silver. But Forkbeard had not come to England this time purely for silver. He came for vengeance after the death of so many Danes after the St Brice's Day Massacre. The Vikings came slowly, ambling, talking and laughing as if they strolled to a tavern. The first ten men were monsters, men as tall and broad as Beornoth with long braided beards, axes at their belts, chain mail and faces as flat and hard as sea-battered cliffs. In their midst strode a man of middling height with a round face. He wore a golden torc around his neck and carried a shining war axe. Forkbeard. King of Denmark and Norway, ruthless warlord and master of deep cunning.

'Beornoth Reiði,' Sweyn Forkbeard called in Norse, using the name by which the Vikings knew Beornoth. The Wrathful. The king smiled as though he had met an old friend. 'Is that really you? I thought you would be dead by now.'

'King Sweyn,' Beornoth replied in Norse, and inclined his head out of respect. 'Still alive. You look hale, if not a little hungry.'

Forkbeard laughed. 'I have missed you, Beornoth. Perhaps we should have another contest, riddles again? Or perhaps you could fight one of my champions?'

'My days of fighting champions are behind me, lord king.'

'This is the man who killed the great Palnatoki of the Jomsvikings,' Forkbeard said to his men. 'The last time I saw him, he fought Thorkell the Tall to a standstill on Lundenwic bridge.'

'Is Thorkell here?' Beornoth had not noticed the monstrous war leader who had accompanied Forkbeard when he had last raided England.

'He stays in Norway. There are some troublesome island jarls to pacify, and so he takes his Jomsvikings through the fjords this summer.'

'I am glad he is not here, and I am sorry for the loss of your sister, lord king. Her husband, Pallig, was my friend.'

Forkbeard's eyes twinkled, and he stared at Beornoth for a moment and then at Ulfcytel. 'I heard tell of it. I also heard that it was you who killed the Normans who killed my sister Gunnhild?'

'I did, lord king.'

'Then you have my thanks. This is my son, Cnut.' Sweyn Forkbeard turned and beckoned to a figure hidden by the king's burly champions. A youthful boy stepped out to stand by his father. He was tall and well-made, dressed in leather and wool and wearing a sword strapped to his waist. Cnut had long, dark hair and his father's round face. He lifted his chin and gave Beornoth a pugnacious look.

'Greetings, Prince Cnut Sweynsson,' Beornoth said.

'I have heard of you, Beornoth Reiði,' said the prince, without a tremor of fear or apprehension in his voice, which was no small feat when he found himself surrounded by huge armed warriors standing between two armies. 'Perhaps we shall fight one day?'

'I hope not, lord prince.'

Forkbeard laughed and clapped his son on the back. 'A fine lad, no? I tremble for Midgard when he becomes king.'

'You have come for revenge?' Beornoth tore his eyes from the young prince to ask his father a question, but Cnut's eyes remained fixed on Beornoth. There was cleverness in his face, and confidence in his stance and attitude. He was unafraid, despite the surrounding champions with all their sharp steel, scarred faces, bristling pride and war experience. Beornoth wondered how King Æthelred raised his children. Did he prepare them from the endless war engulfing his country? Did he raise them like wolves, hungry for battle, longing to make the strategic and battlefield decisions that can cause a thousand deaths, make or break kingdoms? Were they prepared to risk their own lives in the fury of war? Beornoth doubted it. He imagined them for a moment flouncing around Winchester and Lundenwic in fine clothes with soft hands, and Beornoth trembled for England. Cnut longed to reach manhood. Beornoth could smell the hunger on him, feel the violence and ambition pulsing from him like heat from the sun. He would grow into a man desperate to make his own legend, driven by the need to conquer and surpass his father's deeds, just as Forkbeard had fought to surpass his father Harald Bluetooth's accomplishments.

Forkbeard smiled. 'I am here, and I am Viking. We sail and take what we wish, unless men can stop us. I like this, England.' He waved his arms around as though appreciating a fine garden. 'I think I shall add it to my empire, or not. Maybe destiny will decide? Your king does not want to meet me in battle, so I shall have to claw him out like a cockle. Do you think the men of England can stop me if I decide to become its master?'

'You can't win a kingdom without food.' Beornoth knew the Vikings from a childhood raised amongst the settled Danes and Norsemen of the Danelaw. He spoke their language, understood their old gods and how Odin and Thor drove their people to war and battle. Many Danes, like Forkbeard himself, were Christians now. Old Bluetooth had converted to the faith after a Christian missionary had performed a miracle in his throne room. The priest had carried a red-hot lump of iron in his bare hands without suffering a burn or wound, or so men said, and that had been enough to convince Bluetooth to renounce the old gods and embrace the new. But even though many Danes now worshipped Christ, they still wore talismans in their hair and left offerings for the forest spirits, sent for wise women to heal wounds and help pregnant women birth their children. Even though the Danes wore the cross, they remained a vicious and savage people who firmly believed the world was their larder to take from what they could. Unless a strong hand could stop them.

'Just so. You have food over there in your camp. Maybe I should take that?'

'Come and try.'

'What does he say?' asked Ulfcytel in Saxon. Beornoth translated, and Ulfcytel crossed his arms. 'Tell him if he leaves Theodford unharmed and sails away, the war is over. We shall not try to stop him. He has grown rich with plunder. Let it be enough. He cannot take Winchester and Lundenwic with so few men and no food. What will his army eat during those sieges if we continue to burn the granaries and slaughter all livestock in his path?'

Beornoth translated, and Forkbeard nodded slowly. 'Bring me forty thousand pounds of silver, and I will go home.'

'Such a sum will take months to gather. What will you eat during that time?'

'You will bring food and ale for my men until the silver arrives, and we shall attack no more towns nor kill any more of your people. I shall give you hostages to show my good faith.'

Beornoth rested his hand on the pommel of his sword, and the Vikings bristled with anger at the threatening gesture. But he was tired of Forkbeard's arrogant air, of the way his champions eyeballed Beornoth without fear. Many Saxons had died as Forkbeard's army hacked and burned their way across south-eastern England, and now he spoke of an extraordinary gafol payment as though it were a pouch of hacksilver. Forty thousand pounds of silver was a king's ransom, a tax Æthelred must drag from his lords and subjects, which would cripple the country for years. Beornoth's shoulders bunched. The time for soft words was over.

'Or maybe I will surround this shithole, pen you inside like squealing piglets. Perhaps I'll burn your ships, starve you, and when you and your men cannot walk because of the shit running down your legs from the river water you have been drinking, I will kill you all. I'd like that. I could take your head to my king and turn your warriors into thralls. I need a man to shovel horse shit back home. Maybe I'll drag you north in chains?' Beornoth pointed at the biggest Viking. 'Or you?' Then at another.

'Let me fight this greybeard,' growled a huge Viking beside Forkbeard. He bore a tattoo of a wolf on one cheek and was so broad across the chest he was twice Forkbeard's size. 'Teach him some manners.'

'I was killing nithing Viking bastards like you back when your mother was whoring her way across the Skagerrak. You couldn't fight your way out of a spiderweb. You attack villages defended by churls, you kill women, children and old folk and think yourself a hero? The champions in Valhalla laugh at your arrogance and piss on your paltry deeds.'

Forkbeard threw his head back and laughed raucously. The big Dane growled and took one step towards Beornoth before Forkbeard stopped him with a touch of his hand. 'Careful, Ulf. Ten years ago, he would have fought you in the Holmgang square, and he would have beaten you just to steal the morale from my army. Now, I doubt he can hold his piss for more than an hour. Drengrs like you don't fight old men; there is no honour in it. We cannot take any more treasure north. Our ships are already heavily laden with silver and gold. We grow tired of raiding, anyway. It's time to go home. I think we shall have a truce. I will leave your hovel of a town alone, Lord Beornoth, and we shall sail away tomorrow. My sister is avenged. Many Saxons have died this last year, so I think your weakling king has learned his lesson.'

Some faces flanking Forkbeard seemed gaunt, Beornoth thought. Big men with pinched cheeks and narrow waists. Vikings were renowned for their size – pulling an oar made a man strong, and lords of warriors ever had the best meat, ale, bread available to their men – and so Beornoth would have expected some of Forkbeard's leaders to have a bit more timber around their midriffs. He took an oatcake from a pouch at his belt and ate it slowly, watching as every Northman's eyes stared at the food, their jaws tense, eyes hungry.

'Lots of honey in this cake, Ulfcytel,' Beornoth said. 'We have so much honey, bread, oats and cheese that even our cakes are fat.' He translated the words into Saxon and told Ulfcytel of the king's offer.

'They won't honour the truce, lying bastards,' Ulfcytel growled. 'They're starving. We should surround them until they rot and then butcher them when they barely have the strength to lift a spear.'

'They have enough men to break out,' Beornoth replied. 'Let them leave. Forkbeard will return to his homeland, and we can have peace, for this year at least.'

'Very well.' Ulfcytel twisted his neck, uncomfortable at coming to terms with the invaders who had ravaged southern England for months.

'A truce, then,' Beornoth said to Forkbeard.

'Tomorrow we shall make the oaths of peace and sail for home. I doubt we shall meet again, Beornoth Reiði. You look like you are on your last legs. Time for you to rest and tell old war stories to small children. Enjoy the sun, for time has caught up with you and heaven beckons. You have been a worthy enemy.'

'As have you, lord king.'

Forkbeard smiled again. He draped an arm around his son, turned on his heel and marched back towards Theodford. Ulf glowered at Beornoth and pushed two fingers into his own throat, threatening Beornoth, before he too turned and followed his king.

'He doesn't look like much,' said Ulfcytel, staring at Sweyn Forkbeard's back.

'He's a savage killer, make no mistake about it. Not all warriors are tall and broad-shouldered.' Beornoth shuddered at the memory of Forkbeard coming from the water at Maldon, axe in hand and fury etched into his bloodstained face. 'He defeated Olaf Trygvasson at the battle of Svolder and won himself a kingdom. He is the son of Harald Bluetooth, so do not underestimate him. I have seen him kill men I knew to be skilled warriors. How many have you seen who are tall and broad of shoulder but have the courage of a kitten, and how many men short and slender who fight with the ferocity of a charging boar?'

'True enough,' said Ulfcytel, himself not an imposing man but renowned for his bravery and war skill. He turned to his men. 'Set double watches all night. Keep the men ready to fight in case they try to surprise us.'

'Yes, lord,' replied a gap-toothed warrior.

'We could just burn their ships.'

'We could,' Beornoth allowed. 'But then Forkbeard and his men would be trapped here.' Beornoth turned the words around and winced at the thought of two thousand Vikings without their ships and with no choice but to fight for their lives, to take a town and make it their own. 'They'd fortify the place, and we would die attacking their walls. Why let them gain a foothold here when Forkbeard can sail away, belly full of slaughter, ships full of silver?'

'It sticks in my craw, Beo.'

'Just let him go.'

Ulfcytel grumbled under his breath and stalked back to camp. Beornoth followed slowly after him. As a younger man he too would have wanted nothing more than to see Forkbeard's precious ships burned and bring sword and spear to the hated Viking raiders. But Forkbeard had two thousand men inside Theodford, and every man a seasoned warrior. Ulfcytel had perhaps four or five hundred warriors who could stand and trade blows with the hard men of the north. The rest of the Saxon force were churls armed with sickles, makeshift spears, clubs, wood axes and flails. There could be no victory over Forkbeard's army, and to drive the Vikings out of England without the crippling gafol payment was a victory in itself.

Beornoth reached camp to find that Wigs and Gis had commandeered a tent, where they were busy making a broth and laying out bedrolls. He sat down heavily on a milking stool and let his men help him out of his byrnie. Beornoth kneaded his shoulder and felt like lying down to sleep for a while. There was a time, he thought, when I would have taken Ulf the Viking's challenge and turned his guts inside out. Beornoth flexed his crooked hands and hoped he could hold a sword with some of his old strength if it came to battle.

2

The Saxon camp grew loud as night fell over Theodford's flatlands. Men drank mead and played knucklebones; others sang bawdy harvesting songs. Beornoth sat with Wigs and Gis watching the stars flit between slow-moving clouds cast in shadow so that they looked like great beasts flying silently across the heavens.

'I don't know why they needed you to ride all the way here if they are just going to let the bloody Vikings sail away,' said Gis, using the heel from a loaf of bread to scrape the last remnants of broth from his iron pot.

'You'd prefer to stand and trade blows with those Norsker bastards?' asked Wigs. 'I would much rather stand on the riverbank and wave them off than have one of those giants try to hack me to bits with his axe.'

'They look like they are celebrating their last night in Theodford. They must have some ale or mead in there.' Gis jutted his chin behind their tent, where Theodford sat beside its ford across the river.

Beornoth cocked his head for a moment and tried to listen above the din in the Saxon camp, but all he could hear were Saxon voices, shouting and laughter. He stood slowly, using one arm to lean and push himself to his feet. Wigs leaned out to help Beornoth stand and then thought better of it when a scowl like thunder creased Beornoth's face. Beornoth turned and looked beyond the tent to where a dancing orange glow pulsed from inside the town palisade. There was shouting coming from the town, and perhaps the glow came from outdoor fires where the Vikings cooked whatever remained of their supplies. A scream pealed out from Theodford like the caw of a seagull searching for crabs on the ebb tide. Beornoth held his breath. More screams, distant, drifting on the wind, full of fear and pain.

'Get my sword,' Beornoth said, fists opening and closing.

'What is it?' asked Wigs, also rising, concern in his voice at the sudden change in Beornoth's countenance.

'Byrnie, sword, seax, helmet and shield. Now. Raise the alarm and fetch Ulfcytel.'

Wigs set off at a flat run whilst Gis fetched Beornoth's war gear and helped him shrug on the heavy coat of chain mail. Beornoth pushed his helmet onto his head, and with its cheekpieces closed, the helmet made his eyes glare from within the heavy iron. Gis pulled on his leather breastplate, slid his seax into his belt and grabbed a spear.

Beornoth strode from the tent, marching through the camp, eyes fixed on Theodford.

'To arms!' Gis shouted to the closest men, who stared at the two warriors in full armour, whilst the rest of the camp ate and drank. 'Spears and shields!'

A man of the fyrd, with wild curly hair and a rough beard, half stood in challenge, and Beornoth kicked him in the chest to send the man sprawling and brutally end any objections.

'Pick up your weapons and follow me,' Beornoth growled, 'or every soul in Theodford shall die this night.'

Hoofbeats thundered through the camp and Ulfcytel arrived on a stallion, armoured and ready for battle.

'What is it, Lord Beornoth?' Ulfcytel said, a spear in his hand and his shield hanging from his saddle's pommel.

'Forkbeard breaks the truce,' Beornoth said, pointing at the town. 'He razes Theodford and will break out tonight.'

Ulfcytel snarled and fought to stop his horse from prancing in a half-circle. 'Burn the ships,' he shouted to his men, 'form up for attack.'

'Give me fifty men to attack them as they leave the town,' Beornoth said. 'You lead the larger force to the river and Forkbeard's ships.'

Ulfcytel nodded and thrust a pot-shaped helmet onto his head. 'You shall have your fifty men. Harry them, Beornoth, and I will kill the whoresons by the water.'

Beornoth flexed his fingers around his shield's handle, and his grip held the heavy linden-wood boards ringed and bossed with iron firm. He drew his sword and closed his eyes, listening to the wailing and screaming as the people of Theodford died. The familiar sound of Viking warfare, blood-curdling and horrific. Flames lit the town in orange and yellow hues, and men came from the gates carrying burning torches.

'Fighting in the darkness is nasty business,' Beornoth said to Wigs, Gis and the men gathering around him. Ulfcytel had sent twenty warriors and thirty men of the fyrd to Beornoth, whilst his own force marshalled closer to the river where they followed its meander to Forkbeard's fleet. 'The enemy is on the move, so there won't be a shield wall. They'll want to reach their ships as quickly as possible, not stand and trade blows with us. So we'll kill them as they come. Stay together. Don't stray. If you stray, they'll pick you off and cut you down, but they won't want to stand and fight fifty men whilst Ulfcytel destroys their only way home. On me!'

Beornoth strode forward with his sword raised, and the fifty men roared their battle cry. Wigs and Gis took up positions on Beornoth's flanks, and Beornoth hoped his aged sword arm would not let him down, that his shoulder could still bear the weight of his shield. Battle lay ahead in the night. Blood, blades and deadly Viking warriors. What if Forkbeard was right? What if he was too old and marched to his death like a fool?

It was too late to worry about that now, for Beornoth led fifty men to kill, hack, slash and rend at the murderous Vikings.

'How many of you have fought before?' Beornoth asked.

'Aye,' said one.

'Fought the bastards twice, lord,' said another warrior, a long-faced man with unfearful eyes.

'I fought beside you before, lord. At Lundenwic,' said an older warrior with a bald head and a greying beard.

'Good,' said Beornoth. 'Then you know what's coming. You men fight in the front with me. We move fast, cut, kill, move on to the next. We aren't trying to stop them from leaving the town, nor are we trying to drive them to the ships. Just kill or maim as many as you can.'

'I'm with you, lord,' said a burly figure weaving his way through the men. Osgar came in a shining helmet and carried a long-handled Dane axe in both hands.

'That's yours?' Beornoth pointed at the enormous weapon, a favourite of Viking champions who fought in the front rank. A heavy weapon used only by the strong, a shield-wall breaker, and an axe to cast fear into the heart of men who faced its wide blade.

'Took it from a Viking once, lord.'

Osgar took a place beside Wigs, and Beornoth led his men forward. He could not see Ulfcytel's men beneath the blanket of night, but so many boots, shields and spears rumbled like thunder as they hurried towards Forkbeard's fleet. The town glowed and shrieked like a dying monster, and Beornoth clenched his teeth. He led his men towards the palisade, praying to God that some of his old strength remained.

'Here we go again,' said Wigs, 'up to our bloody necks in it.'

'If we don't want to push them back into the town, or stop them from escaping, why don't we just let them go?' asked Gis. 'Go back to our beds and let the bastards sail away.'

'Because the dead need vengeance,' Beornoth growled, anger welling and broiling inside him like a cauldron of water. 'We can't burn all their ships, nor can we kill them all. But we can kill some bastards who have slain the defenceless. Kill enough and Forkbeard will return to Norway. So kill the bastards.' Beornoth began shouting, knuckles white around his sword hilt. 'Kill! Kill! Kill!'

They reached the palisade, its timbers rising high and jagged like shadowed fangs. As if in response to Beornoth's statement the clouds opened, and a hard rain pounded, rattling upon helmets and blades, thumping into the grass in fat droplets and there, ten paces away, a line of Vikings tramped from the river-facing gate with heavy boots, shields, fur draped about their shoulders and axes at their belts.

Beornoth's mouth twisted into a rictus of hate. 'Hold,' he shouted to his men. 'Follow me. Do not run. Fyrd men to the rear, warriors to the fore.'

He covered the grass to the Viking line in long strides and bearded faces turned to stare at him open-mouthed and wide-eyed in surprise. Beornoth hefted his shield and readied his sword. The closest man, golden-bearded and blue-eyed, shouted a warning, and Beornoth flicked his sword blade out like a serpent's tongue, all wrist and finely honed sword point. The last inch of steel tore through the Viking's throat and splashed fiery blood onto his shipmates' face, and he flinched just before Osgar's great axe came about in a monstrous, overhead arc and split his head open with a crunch like a butcher splitting a carcass.

The Vikings staggered backwards, their march halted, men stricken by the horror of Osgar's fearsome blow. They drew their axes and turned to face an enemy coming at them from the night. The Vikings had spent months raiding and killing without opposition. They were Viking warriors who laughed at the Saxons' weakness and saw them as sheep and themselves as wolves. But now the sheep had cast off their fleeces, and the wolves now found themselves attacked by warriors come to avenge a summer of burning, rape and slaughter.

An enemy warrior bellowed at his men to form ranks, and Gis thrust his spear at that man's chest. He swayed away from the blade and whipped his axe at Gis' midriff, but the Saxon caught the axe with his shield and stabbed the spear hard into his attacker's eye. More Vikings came to the fight. Beornoth slashed his sword blade across a squat man's eyes and barged another backwards with his spear. Osgar swung his great axe with such power and ferocity that he was as much a danger to his own men as to the enemy. The Vikings shifted away from his twirling axe blade, thick now with blood and gore, and the warriors of East Anglia threw themselves at an enemy they had feared and hated.

Blades hacked, iron chopped into wood and flesh, and men bellowed their war cries. Three Vikings faced Beornoth. They dropped the sacks of booty from their shoulders and drew their axes. Each wore leather breastplates, warrior rings on their wrists and thick chains about their necks. They bellowed to their shipmates to form ranks and face the enemy, whilst ahead of their marching column other Norsemen shouted at men to hurry to the river for their ships were under attack. Beornoth risked a glance towards the fleet, but could see no fire blossoming there, which meant Ulfcytel had either yet to set the fleet alight, or the Vikings held his charge.

Beornoth turned back to the men facing him. There was nothing he could do about Ulfcytel's attack now. Two thousand Vikings were trying to leave Theodford in a long, armed column, and Ulfcytel's East Anglian force must burn as many ships and kill as many of the enemy as possible. Beornoth had come south to kill Vikings, and as the three men facing him came on, he braced his shoulder behind his shield. Before the trio could advance to attack Beornoth as one, Osgar charged into them like a madman and turned their plan to bloody ruin. He howled like a dying horse, axe scything through the night like a demon's claw. Osgar missed the Viking closest to him, but the momentum in his swing thumped the axe blade down into the enemy warrior's foot. He screamed in pain and Osgar barged him backwards with his shoulder. The second Dane swung his axe at Osgar, but Beornoth caught it on his shield and bent low, stabbing his sword beneath the shield's rim to rend and tear at the Viking's groin.

Blood and filth slopped onto the grass, and death filled the night. Wigs and Gis killed the third Viking with deft thrusts of their spears, and the warriors who had advanced with Beornoth charged, emboldened by the slaying of the Northmen they feared so much. The Vikings fell back, unsure whether to retreat to the city or run to their ships, and Beornoth stepped into that confusion. He came at them with his shield raised and sword stabbing with professional skill. Those Danes saw a huge warrior advancing on them from the darkness, a man clad in expensive chain mail, and a full-faced helmet covering his skull in iron. They saw a lord of war with the sword and armour only the most successful warriors could afford. They hesitated, and Beornoth killed them.

He battered a man down with his shield and opened a second Viking's throat with his sword. Beornoth stamped down hard on the fallen man's windpipe and crushed it like a rotten branch. He moved onwards, slowly, efficiently, with Wigs and Gis beside him, three shields together, spears and sword blades lashing out at the Vikings with pitiless brutality.

'He's going to cut one of our bloody heads off in a minute!' said Wigs, swerving away from Osgar's wild axe swings as the Saxon continued to swirl into the enemy, lopping off limbs and scattering Vikings like leaves in the wind.

'He's killing the bastards,' Beornoth growled, 'so leave him to it.'

A dozen Vikings lay dead or dying, and Beornoth's fifty men continued, following the palisade until they reached the open gate inside which fearful faces glared at him from within the town. They were Forkbeard's men who saw their shipmates dying and heard the warnings of an attack on their ships, and they were afraid to run out into the maelstrom and abandon the safety of Theodford's high walls.

'Rally!' called a Viking voice, and Beornoth smiled, for a tall warrior came from the river side of the battle waving a sword above his head. It was Ulf, the warrior who had challenged Beornoth earlier that day. He carried a sword in one hand and an axe in the other. A Saxon charged at him, and Ulf knocked his spear aside with his sword and chopped his axe down hard onto the Saxon's shoulder, smashing collarbone and rending the flesh beneath. He roared like a great bear, and the East Anglian warrior who had fought beside Beornoth once before charged at Ulf. The Viking met him, battering his shield and spear away with his axe and then driving his sword low and hard into the Saxon's belly. The blade cut deep, its point bursting through the Saxon's back in gouts of blood. Ulf tried to rip the sword free, but the weapon was stuck fast in the dying man's insides, so Ulf let him drop, sword and all, raised his axe and bellowed his defiance, rallying men to him, turning slaughter into battle with his strength and ferocity.

3

The enemies who had skulked within Theodford now left the gate and rallied around Ulf, men with shields and spears forming up to make a defence. Ulf kicked men up the arse, pushed others, and roared at the timid men still lingering inside the gate, until a score of men formed a line with Ulf at the centre. If left to organise them, Ulf could quickly bring hundreds of Vikings to bear against Beornoth's small force. Only the panic of an attack at night gave Beornoth's men the advantage. The Vikings found themselves attacked from two sides. In the darkness they could not tell if they faced twenty men or five thousand, it was all blades, shouts of warning and confusion, but in the chaos, Forkbeard had sent his champions to bring order to his army, to organise a disciplined retreat to his ships. Still no fire showed at the river, and Beornoth feared that Ulfcytel's plan had failed. Even if the East Anglians had found themselves thrust back by Forkbeard's experienced warriors, Beornoth had still found an opportunity to kill a boastful enemy.

'Ulf!' Beornoth roared and used a finger of his sword hand to move the cheekpieces of his helmet aside so that the big Dane could see who faced him. 'Your mother was an addled whore, and your father a coward without reputation or honour.'

'Bastard!' Ulf spat. 'I'll skin you alive.'

Beornoth and Ulf charged at one another, two huge warriors towering above the rest, and Beornoth's sword met Ulf's blade with a clang like thunder.

The blow snapped Ulf's sword at the hilt and sent a jarring shock up Beornoth's arm. Ulf swung his axe hard into Beornoth's shield. The force drove Beornoth backwards a step, and before he could recover, Ulf's axe flashed over Beornoth's shield, and Beornoth had to reel away before the weapon opened his gullet. His chest burned with exhaustion, and Beornoth's shoulders suddenly felt like two blacksmith's anvils.

'You are weak. Old turd,' Ulf said, a smile creasing his face. He dropped his broken sword, whipped a knife from his belt and came on again, axe and knife poised before him like great shining claws. The battle raged about them, Osgar, Wigs and Gis leading the Saxons against a Viking column once more fallen into disorder without Ulf to organise them.

Beornoth let his shield drop and winced. He staggered backwards, and Ulf darted at him, sensing weakness, smelling blood. He came to kill a legend and burnish his own reputation bright with Beornoth's death. The axe swung low at Beornoth's knees, and Beornoth lowered his shield to meet the blow, but it was a feint and Ulf's axe lashed out at Beornoth's face, coming fast and sharp as the Viking roared with delight at the prospect of a glorious kill. Beornoth reeled and lifted his shield at the last moment to catch the axe on it. The blade thumped into its linden-wood boards with the power of a horse kick. Ulf struck with the strength locked into his powerful shoulders by a lifetime at the oar and wielding weapons, and the blade sank deep, biting into the timber. Beornoth knelt behind his shield, and Ulf's knife swept over his head so that the Viking's arms crossed, leaving him in an awkward position, off balance and vulnerable. Beornoth punched the hilt of his sword into Ulf's face and stood to his full height.

Ulf gasped, nose broken and twisted, blood pouring into his beard. Beornoth dragged him to one side with his shield, axe trapped in its wooden boards. The knife swept back, and Beornoth let it slip past his midriff and then flicked his wrist so that his sword cut through Ulf's thumb and sent his knife falling to the night-darkened grass. Ulf tried to wrench his axe free, but the weapon would not come. He stared up at Beornoth and, for the first time, perhaps in his entire life as a Viking warrior, a champion of Sweyn Forkbeard and a ruthless killer, Ulf felt fear. Ulf realised he did not face a tired, weakened old Saxon of the race Vikings deemed soft and weak. Beornoth met his gaze, let Ulf look into the pits of his eyes and understand the man he faced.

'Murderer, rapist, thief,' Beornoth growled. 'I am the vengeance for those you have killed, for the women who have wept and the children who have cried.' Beornoth grunted, bringing his sword down hard on Ulf's other hand, severing fingers and bones so that Ulf cried out in horror. He fell backwards, sprawling on the grass, clutching his ruined hands to his chest. He mumbled, horror dragging his features down as he shook his head. Beornoth stabbed his sword down into Ulf's knee with a loud crack as the joint shattered and the Viking champion cried out in unthinkable pain. Beornoth stepped over him and smashed the iron-shod rim of his shield down into Ulf's face again and again until his face and skull turned to horrific pulp.

Beornoth let his shield rest on the grass, muscles and chest burning as it heaved, trying to suck in enough air to calm his breathing. The Danes inside Theodford burst from the town gates and dashed towards the river.

'They flee for their ships!' Gis called, pointing towards the river.

'Let them go,' Beornoth replied, unable to hide the exhaustion from his voice.

'But we have them. We've killed two score or more.'

'Do you want to face a Viking shield wall? Two thousand men with their backs to their ships, fighting for their lives? How many proper warriors do we have? Look at them.' He pointed his sword to the men of the fyrd, who went among the wounded Danes, slaughtering them with wild cuts of their wood axes, scythes and reaping hooks. A Viking warrior charged at them, and a dozen fyrd men fled from his ferocity. Osgar met that enemy warrior, and they traded blows, axes whirling and clanging until Osgar's wild anger battered down his opponent's defence and opened a terrible wound in his belly, cutting through leather armour like it was butter.

'So what do we do?'

'Form up our fifty before the town gates so the bastards can't creep back in if Ulfcytel burns their fleet.'

'Shield wall!' Gis hollered and set off to organise their small force into a shield barrier protecting the open gate.

Beornoth squinted towards the river but saw no fires blazing. He saw torches guttering and twitching in the rain, flickering between shifting figures of men, moonlight glinting off steel. He heard the clash of battle, the cries of the wounded and the shouts of the brave. Beornoth stood, shoulders throbbing, an old injury in his leg stinging and his body screaming at him to stop and rest. He followed the muddy stain two thousand Vikings had left on grass churned by their boots and the rain, a trail littered with corpses, discarded booty and discarded weapons.

Ulfcytel's men had fallen back from the riverbank, and Beornoth found the enemy clambering unopposed on to the long, sleek drakkar warships. They waded out into the shallows, marching up gangplanks or climbing up ropes to board their vessels. Some warships had already slipped out into the deeper water, oars biting into the water made glossy by night. Oars splashed and water dropped from their ash blades like tiny stars twinkling in the darkness. They swept into a wide turn of the river from which Forkbeard's fleet could make for the open sea.

A protective shield wall formed about the retreating army, five hundred shields and spears protecting the withdrawal. Dead Saxons and fallen weapons littered the field around that wall, and before it Sweyn Forkbeard prowled like a great cat, an axe in each fist, staring out at the Saxons, daring them to attack once more and endure his wrath.

Beornoth crossed the flatland and found Ulfcytel amongst his men, his byrnie caked in blood and filth and a wide gash cut through his cheek. The king's thegn pointed and shouted at his men, trying to reorganise and rally the warriors into formation to attack the enemy before they could completely escape from Theodford's riverbank.

'What happened?' Beornoth asked.

Ulfcytel wiped the back of his hand across his rain-soaked brow. He licked at dry lips, eyes flickering about him as men dragged wounded friends back to camp, fyrd men ran from the horror of battle to return alive to their homes and families. 'We did not have enough warriors,' he said. 'At first, we killed many of the bastards, but then Forkbeard arrived and they formed a shield wall. They beat us back and pressed us with a fence of blades. They were too strong. Too efficient. Too experienced.'

'So we let them go.'

'We let them go, and hopefully they never come back. The fire wouldn't bite in the cursed rain. We made it to the first of their ships, but there were guards on board, and they fought us back. Even where we cleared those men, the fire wouldn't take. They saw the torches, and it made them fight even harder. A desperate fight, over in minutes, but we lost many men.'

'Some of our men flee for the hills, lord,' a warrior called to Ulfcytel. He pointed to a hundred fyrd men dashing for the low western hillocks.

'See to the wounded,' Ulfcytel replied wearily. 'Once we've tended to them, we must help the people within Theodford.' Ulfcytel cast his eyes towards the town from which smoke billowed. The wailing had stopped, but Beornoth clenched his teeth at the suffering lying within.

'They will come back,' Beornoth said, staring out at the ships, talking to himself as much as to Ulfcytel.

'Not this summer, they won't.'

'No,' Beornoth allowed. He slid his sword back into its scabbard and hid his trembling hands behind his back. They trembled not out of fear or shock, for battle and blood were nothing new, but from the exertion, the strain of wielding sword and shield. 'But they will return. The Vikings will keep coming back until either they fear us, or they conquer us. There will never be peace in England, not until the strong rule and defend it.'

'Will you stay?'

'I'll stay for a few days and help with the town. But then I shall return home.'

'What about when they come back?'

'Then so will I. I fear that is my wyrd. My fate. I am locked in a cycle of war and death with the Vikings, and God won't let me die in peace. So I will return.'

Ulfcytel nodded grimly, his own experiences forged during a lifetime of war etched upon his face. He reached out a hand, and Beornoth took his wrist in the warrior's grip. Men did their best with the wounded and made piles of the dead. Sunrise came in a crimson wash across the flatlands, and with it came priests who said prayers over the slain and took better care of the wounded.

'We could have beaten them if the ships had burned,' said Gis sourly, as he shared an early morning skin of thin ale with Beornoth, Wigs and Osgar.

'No,' Beornoth replied. 'They would have fought for their lives, and we still would have lost. Better to let them go so our men return to their homes.'

'Apart from those poor buggers.' Gis jutted his chin to where the remaining men of the fyrd made piles of Viking and Saxon dead.

'You fought well,' Osgar said, and the three friends stared at him in surprise.

'That's the first time you've spoken since the fighting,' said Wigs. 'We thought you'd lost your tongue along with your mind. That axe of yours must have killed a dozen Vikings last night.'

'I remember little of it. I should clean myself.' Blood and filth caked his hair, face and armour.

'Go to the river,' Beornoth said, 'and wash it all away. Wash your axe, and with it wash away the faces of the men you have killed. I know that feeling. The numbness, the waiting for the nightmares that will come and haunt you. But you have done your duty, thegn. So wash away the blood and be proud that you have served your people.'

Osgar nodded and stood slowly. He trudged towards the river with his axe resting on his shoulder, the same river where hours ago thirty warships had rested along banks now empty of everything but the debris left behind by Forkbeard's men.

'He's a bloody madman,' said Wigs when Osgar was out of earshot.

'And not a mark on him, even after all that wild fighting without a shield,' Gis agreed.

'A good man to have beside you in a hard fight,' Beornoth added.

'As long as he doesn't cut your head off by mistake.'

Beornoth stared at his hands, wishing the shaking to stop. Wigs and Gis looked away out of respect, but they were as close to Beornoth as brothers, and he did not fear their judgement. His fingers curled in once more like claws.

'Maybe that was our last fight,' said Gis.

'Or the last time we *can* fight,' Wigs added, and was rewarded with a punch on the shoulder from Gis.

'I was worried that my strength would fail me,' Beornoth whispered. 'There was a time I could fight all day, and my shield and sword arm would not fail.'

'You fought as well as ever, lord. I saw you kill that big bastard who was with Forkbeard at the parlay.'

'I killed him, and I was spent afterwards.' Battle and fighting defined him and had done so since he was old enough to lift a blade. He had been raised to it, bred for it. Even in the dark days after his children had died and Beornoth had sunk into a pit of ale and misery, he had become a reeve, a man who punished criminals and hunted masterless men.

'You still have your experience, your battle cunning and your reputation.'

'What use is a king's thegn who cannot fight? Did we change anything here at Theodford? Would Ulfcytel have done things differently had we not come?'

'Who can say? Perhaps the Vikings might have retreated into the town, or perhaps they would have slaughtered Ulfcytel and his men. Maybe they would have sailed away peacefully or dug in and waited for the gafol payment we all know the bishops and the king would rather pay than fight. Forty thousand pounds of silver would cripple England for a generation. So let's assume we have played our part. We've saved the kingdom's silver and hopefully saved some lives.'

'Do we ride back to Brand and Stag Hall?' Wigs asked, frowning as a man wailed whilst a priest tried to set his broken leg.

'No, I ride for home in Cheshire. You are free of any oaths you have sworn to me. I release you from my service. Stay in the south, return to your old homes.'

'That's a fine way to reward us after a night of hard fighting.'

'You are both fine men and are, of course, welcome to accompany me north. Ealdorman Alfgar will find you service in his hearth troop in Cheshire, and you can live on my land.'

'Thank you, lord.'

'Your home is our home,' said Gis. 'We have nowhere else to go, unless Wigs fancies taking up his original calling and enters the Church. You'd make a fine priest, Wigs.'

'You'd make a fine pig herder.'

'I can just imagine you saying Mass, absolving the sins of common folk. Churls who have scrumped apples from a neighbour's tree. Forgive me, father, for I have sinned.'

'Keep it up and I'll kick you so hard you'll be wearing your arse for a helmet.'

Wigs and Gis had once served Robert de Warenne, a Norman granted the land upon which they lived by Lady Aelfryth, mother to King Æthelred. Wigs was the third son of a reeve and destined for the Church until one of his brothers had died and he had become a warrior in the service of the local thegn.

'Why not return to your old homes?' Beornoth asked.

'I have seven children there somewhere,' said Gis, sadness in his voice. 'But my wife is now married to another man, a cloth merchant last I heard, and my children barely know who I am. Better to keep it that way. What can I offer them? They have a home now, comfort, and a chance to live a peaceful life.'

'We could visit there on the way north?'

'Better to leave them as they are. They don't need me. Maybe I'll leave some silver for them at the village, but I don't want to disturb them and fill their heads with warriors' stories.'

'So we ride for Cheshire, then,' said Wigs.

Beornoth closed his eyes as the morning sun warmed his face. Once Theodford was back on its feet, he would return north to live beside Eawynn's grave. Forkbeard was gone, for now. England was weak, its king hiding behind Lundenwic's high walls, refusing to marshal the nation's warriors to challenge the raiders. So Forkbeard would come whenever he needed silver or to keep his warriors sharp with battle and their need for battle and glory sated. He would come with his warships and warriors, and there would be war once more, and Beornoth would be there to meet him.

PART II

1009AD

4

Five years after the fight outside Theodford, Beornoth sat astride his horse swathed in a heavy wool cloak. He waited atop a windswept hill, staring out at a rolling grey sea. He stroked the beast's mane and patted its muscled neck. A pang of sadness stung his heart as he remembered fondly his old warhorse Virtus, who had died three winters ago. A trusty companion who had carried Beornoth into battle countless times. Another friend lost in the long years of Beornoth's life. A magnificent beast, a horse trained for war, unafraid of the sounds of battle or the smell of blood. The horse he rode now was a placid but stout roan mare Beornoth had bought from Ealdorman Alfgar's stable to carry him south last summer when news came of the latest Viking threat. Thorkell the Tall had come to England's shores with a fleet and an army of Viking warriors.

'It's supposed to be summer,' said Wigs, pulling his own cloak close about his neck as a sea wind ruffled his short hair. 'It's colder than a witch's tit up here.'

Beornoth had led his two warriors up to the hills for a better view. There had been a parlay with the enemy, a meeting on the outskirts of Cantwaraburg led by a bishop sent by the king. No king's thegns or ealdormen had taken part, no warriors or men with experience or knowledge of the Danes, and now the enemy sailed away, unchallenged, full of heart, ships heavy with silver and hungry for more.

'How many ships can you see?' Beornoth asked, not trusting his fading eyes to make an accurate count.

'Sixty-five, maybe seventy,' said Gis. 'Perhaps a few more or less. It's hard to count them; they won't stay still.'

'Four and a half thousand men, and not one warrior lost in a year of raiding.'

'They don't look like they are going north, anyway. Turning south, looking for somewhere else to raid.'

'Thorkell has grown rich. How much did the king pay him to leave Cantwaraburg last week?'

'Three thousand pounds of silver, lord,' said Gis.

'I wish someone would pay me silver to do nothing,' Wigs replied.

'What are you talking about? That's exactly what Lord Beornoth does every week.'

'Cheeky bastard.'

'Come on.' Beornoth clicked his tongue and pressed his heel into the horse's belly to wheel the beast around. This time it would be different, he hoped. This time the warlords of England were ready. Beornoth had returned south from Cheshire a year ago, when Thorkell the Tall had arrived at Sandwich with an army of five thousand men. Seventy ships was a huge number. A vast fleet the famous Jomsviking leader had brought south from Norway and Denmark in search of riches. He had ravaged much of the area around Sandwich and marched on Cantwaraburg, avoiding the army of Kent and then retreating with wagonloads of silver to take his ships back to sea.

Beornoth and his companions left the south-east coast, and it took a week to reach Winchester. They travelled slowly, stopping frequently to shelter from blustery winds and frequent showers, but reached the ancient capital of Wessex and England's kings on a bright day where a low sun dazzled the eye and folk wore winter clothes on a warm day, caught between the seasons like sheep sweating in their heavy fleeces before spring shearing. Wigs and Gis rode five paces ahead of Beornoth to clear the road for the king's thegn, who rode beneath the dragon banner of Wessex. They carried ash-shafted spears, from which the banner fluttered in a light breeze, and churls and merchants moved their wains, goats and baskets to the roadside and bowed their heads at Beornoth in his byrnie chain mail, cloak, sword and war gear.

Gis tossed a small coin to a thin-faced woman, and she ran to pass him three apples, one of which he handed to Wigs. The people bowed because they saw the banner, but also because the three armed men occupied a caste above common folk. They were the fighters, the soldiers, all that stood between men and women trying to live in peace and raise their families, and the sea wolves who would take everything from them and leave their villages and dreams in bloody ruin.

'Apple, lord?' Wigs called over his shoulder.

'Maybe later,' Beornoth replied, worried that biting into the fruit might loosen another of his teeth, which at his age were as precious as diamonds.

'We'd better brush down our clothes and horses before we reach the city, lord,' said Gis.

'We'll do as we are.' Gis was right, of course, a man should look his best when meeting a king, but they were close to the city now and Beornoth did not relish the thought of climbing his old bones out of the saddle and then needing to be helped back in it again, so they would continue on.

'Lord Alfgar will be there, lord?'

'He will. At least there will be one friendly face amongst the ealdormen and thegns come to hear the king's orders.'

'What about Lord Thered?'

'He won't come. Thered will stay in Northumbria with his northern lords safe deep in the Danelaw.'

'Won't the king be angry if he doesn't come? I thought they had summoned every lord in the land.'

'What can the king do? Ride his army north whilst Thorkell lays waste to southern England? Thered must keep his people happy because many of them are settled Northmen just like Brand, and they wouldn't want to march south and fight their old countrymen. Thered will stay.'

They reached Winchester in the late afternoon, riding alongside the winding River Itchen, upon which boats filled with wool, ingots, furs and food waited to moor and unload their goods for sale. The king's capital city emerged from the rolling hills and farmland, grey, brown and formidable amongst the grazing meadows and farmsteads. Its wooden steeples and patchwork of thatch roofs rose above the city's walls and fighting palisade. Its fortifications included timber supports, beams and plinths added to strengthen the neat dressed stone left by the Romans, along with a deep ditch, bank and timber palisade on which spearmen peered along the worn, wagon-rutted roads reaching to north, south, east and west. A cloud of grey smoke hung above the walls, rising from hearths, forges and cook fires, and Beornoth sniffed at the familiar town smells of smoke and animal dung.

Crudely built market stalls clustered outside the walls where ruddy-faced women and men with straggled beards sold roasted meat, ale and the promise of clean whores. The gate guards noticed Beornoth's banner and his scabbard and waved the three warriors through into the city. A young steward met them inside, a thin man with protruding ears wearing the king's livery of the green dragon of Wessex.

'Welcome, lord,' said the man. He bowed deeply, and his eyes flicked nervously at the crowds of people packed inside the space between the gate and the city's wattle and daub buildings. Warriors in leather milled about the square, men sporting the sigils of Cheshire, East Anglia, Kent, Defnascir, Somersaete and all the shires of England sauntered between stalls selling trinkets and charms, others with skins of ale or mead, and more with steaming strips of meat, wooden bowls of broth and chunks of fresh bread. 'The city is busy today.'

'We need lodging for the three and stables for our horses,' Beornoth replied.

'You are late, lord. The king will speak this evening, and most people have already taken the available accommodation.'

'Find us a place to sleep, or I'll throw someone out of their rooms, take them for myself and leave you to deal with the consequences.'

'Yes, lord, of course, lord. Please, follow me.' He led them through the press of warriors and barked at a boy to take the horses.

'Brush them, and make sure they have fresh hay,' Beornoth said, and he pressed a piece of hacksilver into the boy's hand.

Once out of the square, the steward led Beornoth and his men through a tangled weave of narrow streets and muddy lanes, hurrying beside a mass of timber-framed houses and buildings with wattle and daub walls and thatched roofs. Some leaned precariously against one another along narrow, winding streets, whilst other, larger buildings boasted painted gables and carved window shutters. The stone church and hall within King Æthelred's palace rose above it all, grand and magnificent amidst the mud, wood and thatch. The steward found them a room to share above a tavern where a score of Kentish warriors sang drunken songs from low tables, and Wigs was inordinately pleased to have secured lodgings so close to a ready supply of mead and food.

Guards carrying spears waited at the royal enclosure, and they took Beornoth's sword and seax. Beornoth handed over their weapons without challenge, for it was customary not to bring weapons into a home or feasting hall, and certainly not before the king's presence.

'Wait for me at the tavern,' Beornoth said to Wigs and Gis. 'There will be a church sermon, and if the king plans to address the high lords of England, this thing could go on for hours. So wait for me there, and don't get into any trouble.'

'We shall save you some mead, lord,' said Wigs with a wink, and the two warriors hurried away, laughing and slapping one another on the back at the prospect of an evening in a busy tavern.

The steward bowed to Beornoth and left him with the guards, tall men in hard-baked leather breastplates and carrying leather-covered shields daubed with Wessex's grasping dragon. One of those men led Beornoth inside the royal enclosure, a place of rose gardens, Roman water fountains, clean stone and bustling servants. The king's hall rose tall, its doors oaken and as broad as five men, flanked by the old minster, an iron-grey stone cathedral from which the praying and song of priests lilted above the city's din. They passed through a side gate and into a bright courtyard filled with flowers and neatly trimmed bushes. A cobblestone walkway linked the buildings and meandered its way around bright plants and bushes, which smelled fresh in the late afternoon sunlight.

Beornoth had been in that courtyard before, once with the great Ealdorman Byrhtnoth and again with Alfgar, but now the place was empty with nothing but wind whistling through the leaves and old stone columns where carvings harked back to the glory days of Alfred and Aethelstan, great kings of Wessex's struggle against the Vikings. The guard led Beornoth up a narrow set of mottled steps and into a shadowed corridor. They emerged into the king's great hall, a vast space with high ceilings and ancient, smoke-darkened roof beams. Heavy tapestries hung from the walls, and a hearth fire crackled and spat at one end. The hall reeked of smoke and leather, and Beornoth sighed to see more than a hundred men packed into the hall. Men in finely woven jerkins with oiled hair, others in mail and leather, and yet more wearing the crow-black of the clergy. Men turned to note Beornoth's arrival. Some nodded in greeting; a few he recognised, but most were unfamiliar to him.

'Lord Beornoth,' said a voice, and Beornoth turned to find Ealdorman Alfgar grinning at him, hand extended in greeting. Beornoth shook his wrist warmly, glad to see the man he had known since he was a nervous boy, and who Beornoth had seen grow into a warrior, an ealdorman and a man to respect. His eyes shone, and his smile was both sincere and glad. Crow's feet creased his eyes, deep furrows lined his forehead, and the ealdorman's hair had grown thin, greying and wispy.

'Lord Alfgar, how is Mameceaster?'

'Home is as it ever is, old friend. Busy and bustling. Not as busy as Winchester, though. You have seen the enemy?'

'I have, lord.'

'Are there really five thousand of them?'

'Unfortunately, lord, yes.'

'Two eminent men together,' said a silky voice from beyond Beornoth's sight. He turned to see a tall, thin man wearing an elaborate coat of chain mail with silver forged into its links. He wore a gold chain around his neck. His golden hair was long and swept back from his face, and his beard was combed to a lustrous sheen. He had a long, clever face and strolled towards Beornoth with his thumbs tucked into a thick leather belt studded with gold.

'Lord Alfgar, ealdorman of Cheshire,' Beornoth said, 'this is Lord Eadric, once of Wessex, now ealdorman of Mercia and son-in-law to the king.'

'A pleasure,' said Eadric Streona, with a smile that could curdle milk.

Beornoth could not help but frown, his deeply lined wrinkles creasing the hard crag of his face even more than usual. Eadric had risen from obscurity to the position of head of the king's guard, had become ealdorman of Mercia two years ago, and by marrying Æthelred's daughter had become the most powerful man in England. The thought of the backstabbing, cunning, plots and conniving it had taken to make that incredible rise possible made Beornoth's scars and old wounds pulse. His shoulder ached, stomach knotted and his thigh throbbed. Too many wounds to remember. The cold stab of steel had cut at Beornoth throughout his entire life. Swords, axes, spears and arrows slashed and stabbed at him as he had hewed at the kingdom's enemies with his monstrous strength and savagery. Terrible wounds suffered fighting brutal Viking warriors come south across the Whale Road from the wild lands of

Jutland, Kattegat and the Vik. Whilst Beornoth fought the kingdom's enemies, Eadric had made himself wealthy and powerful, filling graves with good men and dead ealdormen and using his sly tongue to elevate himself high in the echelons of power.

'What news of the Vikings, Lord Eadric?' asked Alfgar.

'Thorkell the Tall has come with five thousand men to ravage our kingdom. He turned his forces away from Cantwaraburg, and God be praised that he did not turn that holy place to ashes. But where will Thorkell and his horde strike next? That is the question. But we have not been idle since Forkbeard's last attacks. This time, we are ready.'

'And we shall shortly hear these grand plans?'

'You will. All shall rejoice, and the kingdom shall be saved. The king is thrilled, very happy. At one time we relied upon the swords of strong men, like Lord Beornoth here, but now that Beornoth and Ulfcytel of East Anglia enter the twilight of their years, where are the warriors to replace them? Dead, or hiding behind stout walls. We shall use cunning and knowledge to defeat the invaders this time, my lords.'

'And what is this grand scheme, Lord Eadric?'

'All will be revealed; all will be revealed.'

'Thorkell may come to take Lundenwic,' Beornoth said, struggling not to grimace at the sound of Eadric's voice. Even his mannerisms made Beornoth feel like spiders crawled across his back and neck. He leaned in when he spoke, coming too close. As he spoke to Alfgar, Eadric had one pale hand on the ealdorman's arm, and another gently tapping his chest. Too close, too familiar. He spoke with confidence, never breaking eye contact, speaking with the silky, practised confidence of a travelling man who sells an oil or potion to cure all ills and must convince an entire village of his truthfulness before he disappears with all of their silver, leaving the mothers of simple-minded children, the wives of men with ruined backs, folk with terrible toothaches or the deathly, gnawing growths in their groins and bellies, all with a useless oil to rub on their loved ones' ailments.

'Oh, I doubt that, Lord Beornoth. We have high walls and stout warriors to defend the old city. Perhaps he will strike in the south or the west. Now, I must find the king so that we can make our address. Shall I ask a steward to find you a chair, Lord Beornoth?' Eadric touched Beornoth's elbow and spoke to him as though he were a toothless grandfather unable to stand or piss without help.

Beornoth twitched his arm away, and Eadric smiled at both him and Alfgar, and then slipped away into the shadows, sweeping across the floor rushes like a wraith.

'Thorkell attacked Lundenwic before,' Beornoth said to Alfgar. 'I know. I was there. I fought him on the bridge.'

'Why Lundenwic and not here, or another rich town on the coast?'

'Because the Thames is our widest river and he can sail his entire fleet to Lundenwic's walls. The river gives the owner of the city access to the sea, and trade between here and Frankia, the lowlands, the Holy Roman Empire of the Germans, and north to the Skagerrak, Jutland and the Vik. He can also defend its walls against us. With five thousand men, it could take us years to get the bastard out.'

'Why not come straight here and take Winchester, if Thorkell wants to conquer?'

'I doubt he wants to be king. He could call himself king now if he wished, for who would force him and his five thousand Vikings and his core of Jomsvikings not to? If a man wants to be king of England, he must take Winchester. If he wants to be rich and keep his army in silver, he must take Cantwaraburg, Lundenwic, York, Oxenforda, Gippeswic, Lincoln or Theodford.'

'Is that truly all he desires? Silver and to keep his men happy?'

'What do all men want?'

'Some of us just want to be left in peace, to hunt on a fine horse with a trusted dog, a wife who does not nag, a warm fire and mead to wash down our meat. But some men burn with desire for other things. Power.' Alfgar flicked his chin in Eadric's direction. 'Reputation in war, silver, warriors to serve him and make other men fear him, women under his control, slaves, and a name to be remembered when he is gone.'

'Thorkell is a Viking, and unlike Forkbeard, is a pagan. His gods demand war and valour, and if Thorkell desires to earn himself a place in Odin's corpse hall for the glorious dead, he must make himself a great warlord. Valhalla is no heaven for the faint-hearted.'

'Well, perhaps Eadric and the king have cooked up a plan to defeat Thorkell and his horde.'

'Maybe.' Beornoth watched as a gaggle of priests scampered about the hall, ushering men closer to a raised platform where the king would normally sit on feast days. They were all small, pale men with soft, ink-stained hands, shaven tonsures and quick eyes. Not godly men to tend to countryfolk and ensure their souls were made fit for heaven. These were the clerics, the politicians, men of God and men of power with quick minds. 'This hall was once home to King Alfred, King Aethelstan and the men who fought against Ivar the Boneless and Sigurd Snake in the Eye. Great men. Warriors. Now look at what we have become.'

Alfgar shrugged and allowed a priest with a pinched face to gently usher them both towards the hall's western pillars, where Beornoth found Ulfcytel of East Anglia.

'Still alive, Lord Beornoth?' he said with a warm smile. His face bore a long, deep scar inflicted during the fight outside Theodford. He wore a byrnie, like Beornoth, and cut a hard-faced figure amongst the ealdormen and courtiers in their fine cloth and soft cloaks.

'Just about,' Beornoth replied. 'Did you see Thorkell at Cantwaraburg?'

'No, but I brought five hundred men to oppose him at Sandwich.'

'Was there a fight?'

'No. No men came from Mercia or Wessex.'

'Nothing changes, then.'

'Something has changed. We have a fleet.'

'Ships?'

'Aye, that's what Streona wants to tell you all today. He's built fifty warships, employing shipwrights from the Danelaw to build them. Enough to match Thorkell and his bastards.'

Beornoth couldn't find any words. Fifty Saxon ships to counter the Viking threat. It was a radical change. It was action, a forward step, a blade with which to stab the Vikings and send them home bloody and fearful ever to come to England's shores again.

'Truly?' asked Alfgar, as astonished as Beornoth. 'How did the realm pay for such a staggering enterprise?'

'Such things are beyond simple soldiers, Lord Alfgar. But it seems that silver and power flow into our new ealdorman of Mercia's lap like rain from the clouds. A man who was the son of a lowly thegn of Wessex has risen to become an ealdorman. When has that ever happened before?'

The hall echoed with the murmur of hushed conversations as the great men of England leant into one another to whisper. Beornoth could not remember a time since he had been a king's thegn when so many great lords had gathered in one place to hear the king speak. Beornoth recognised Wulfnoth of Wessex, a powerful thegn, standing amongst other thegns of his shire along with his tall, broad-shouldered son Godwin, and other men he knew from old wars and half-forgotten battles.

'Never,' Alfgar allowed. 'So how did he accomplish such a feat?'

Ulfcytel glanced about him and leant into Alfgar and Beornoth, lowering his voice. 'He has great influence over the king. Our Lord Æthelred is sick. He grows weaker, and few men now have access to him. Eadric is never far from the king's chamber, and now he speaks with the authority of the throne. He killed Elfhelm, a northern ealdorman, with his own sword, and other men who have spoken out against Æthelred's rule have also met similar ends. Men complain of the king's lack of action, that the shires devolve into self-rule, that a great army of all England has not assembled to meet the Viking threat. But to give voice to such concerns is to invite the wrath of Eadric Streona. Many have met a knife in the dark, a robber band on the road, or a drop of poison in their mead horn. He wormed his way into the king's confidence by eliminating Æthelred's enemies, by endowing the Church with land and wealth, and by marrying the king's daughter.'

'A man to tread carefully around.'

Beornoth stiffened, imagining himself breaking Streona's neck like a rotten twig. Eadric wasn't a man to fear face to face, not like Thorkell the Tall, Skarde Wartooth, Palnatoki, Byrhtnoth or other brave men Beornoth had known in his life. He was a sneak, a back-stabber, a worm, but a dangerous man to have as an enemy.

A guard in the king's livery climbed up onto the raised dais and blew a series of short, shrill notes on a bronze trumpet. Every man in the hall fell silent, some standing on their tiptoes to get a better look. Guards stomped into the vast stone room, their boots echoing off the high roof beams, spears held perfectly in line as they formed a line before the dais. King Æthelred emerged from a dark door. He shuffled slowly, head bent and back bowed. He came with a tall golden-haired woman on his arm and, just as Æthelred kept his eyes on the floor rushes, she walked straight-backed, meeting the hard gazes of the prominent men in the hall without fear or apprehension. A youth followed behind them, a tall and well-made boy in a blue tunic and a circlet of silver upon his brow. His face bore the ravages of teenage spots, with large red patches on both cheeks and across his forehead.

The king's once lustrous auburn hair had turned as grey as a winter storm, and his tresses hung lank about his shoulders with a circlet of gold resting upon his head. His long, lantern-jawed face was ghostly white and seemed glossy with a coating of sweat or oil. His beard showed white at his chin, and he wore a large silver crucifix on a thick chain over a finely woven green tunic. He looked like a spectre, the spirit of a king drifting into the hall slowly, precariously, as if a gust of wind might topple him or if his lady did not prop him up, he might fall to the cold stone.

King Æthelred seemed weaker than ever, and Beornoth remembered the imposing figure of Thorkell the Tall and the strength of his axe hammering into Beornoth's shield on Lundenwic bridge. Thorkell had come to ravage and burn England like a marauding wolf, and the sight of King Æthelred made Beornoth shudder with fear for the fate of the realm.

5

'The lady queen?' Alfgar whispered, jerking his head at the raised platform.

'Aye,' said Ulfcytel. 'Lady Emma of Normandy, daughter of Richard the Fearless, count of Rouen. Her father's Norse kin also call him Jarl Rikard, son of William Longsword. A Viking who offered safe port to both Forkbeard and Olaf Tryggvason when they last invaded England. With them is Prince Edmund, heir to the throne.'

The king, queen and prince took their places on the dais, and every man in the hall bowed his head, including Beornoth. The king seemed ancient, though he was a younger man than Beornoth. He remembered seeing Æthelred for the first time, years ago, at Ealdorman Byrhtnoth's side. Back then, Æthelred's mother had ruled on his behalf, a hard woman who had killed old King Edgar's eldest son and heir by his first wife and placed her son Æthelred on the throne when he was but a child. Æthelred had always been a nervous man, no warrior and certainly not physically brave. He had led a long, strenuous life, ruling a kingdom split by the Danelaw, facing the return of the monstrous Viking threat his father had never endured, and the ever-growing power of the Church. He was now old and frail, and Beornoth glanced down at his own hands, curled with parchment-like skin spread thin across his bones. Did he seem as frail to others? Did men wonder how the once strong Beornoth had grown so weak? He hid his hands within the folds of his cloak.

Æthelred cleared his throat and raised his head. 'Welcome, my lords,' he said, and Beornoth had to tilt his head to hear. Æthelred spoke almost in a whisper, voice croaking as the queen gently tapped his forearm with a reassuring finger. 'Once again, we face a threat from the north. Thorkell the Tall has returned with a vast army and a fleet to fill the sea with their sails.'

'But we have not been idle!' called Eadric Streona in a loud, confident voice. He had interrupted the king himself, and Beornoth glanced at Ulfcytel in shock. The East Anglian shrugged as if to show it was tiresome but no surprise. Eadric bounded up onto the raised dais, and Æthelred smiled wanly, gesturing that Eadric should continue. Eadric inclined his head to the king. He bowed his head a fraction and placed a gentle hand on Æthelred's forearm as though he were a loving nephew greeting an ailing uncle. Eadric whispered something to the king, and Æthelred smiled and nodded, seeming to acquiesce rather than agree. Queen Emma stiffened, thin-mouthed and narrow-eyed, and she led the king to a high-backed chair towards the back of the platform. Eadric opened his arms wide as though welcoming the great lords to his own hall, and not the ancient hall owned by the kings of Wessex. 'For the first time in our history, we have a king prepared to fight back against the Viking threat. Our great king Æthelred, victor over Sweyn Forkbeard at Lundenwic, victor over Olaf Trygvasson and countless great Viking battle-kings, has built a fleet capable of meeting the enemy in battle.'

Men in the hall gasped and whispered to one another in surprise.

'We built this magnificent fleet on the south coast, deep within Wessex, so that word of our bold plan did not leak out on the tongues of Norse merchants and find its way to the Northmen's ears. Thorkell the Tall tries to cast our kingdom in flames, to strip us of our wealth and enslave our people. We shall not stand for it! Our fleet will sail out and meet this Thorkell in battle, and we shall prevail!'

The priests and bishops sat at the front facing Eadric erupted in clapping and cheering, and the rest of the hall followed, quietly at first, surprised at how it was possible to build such a vast number of ships without the rest of the kingdom knowing of it, or paying for it.

'We thank our brothers in the Church for financing this enterprise,' said Eadric, answering the question upon every man's lips. A loan from the clergy, repayment perhaps for the vast tracts of land Eadric and Æthelred had awarded to the Church across Wessex, East Anglia, Somersaete and Defnascir, lands rich in wheat, barley, cattle, sheep and rents. 'Command of the fleet is to be shared between the capable hands of Lord Wulfnoth, thegn of Wessex, and my brother, Brihtric. These brave men will sail out and meet the enemy on the open sea or in whichever river they choose to pour their malice. We encourage every brave man here to report to Sandwich, where the fleet will assemble, the greatest fleet our kingdom has ever seen. We go to war!'

Another half-hearted, surprised cheer rippled around the hall. Eadric Streona leapt down from the dais and went to his supporters, clapping men on the back, greeting others with his wide, disarming smile. King Æthelred allowed Queen Emma to lead him gently away from the platform, and Beornoth watched, astounded that the king had become so weak, and that Streona had become so strong.

'Don't look so angry, Beo,' said Alfgar, elbowing Beornoth playfully in the ribs. 'Isn't this what you have always wanted? If I had a silver coin for every time you have spoken to me of a need of an army of all England to fight the Danes, I would be a rich man.'

'Did you bring your men south?'

'I brought two hundred, yes.'

'Thered?'

'He can't, you know that. Half of his men would fight for Forkbeard or Thorkell if they asked.'

'An army of five thousand men to meet Thorkell's five thousand,' said Ulfcytel, mouth turned down appreciatively. 'Looks like we have ourselves a war, Beornoth.'

Beornoth nodded and took the East Anglian warrior's forearm and said his goodbyes. He left the king's palace and walked, half numbed by the surprising news, to the tavern where he found Wigs and Gis drinking mead with a band of warriors from Defnascir. He left them to their merrymaking and went to bed. His head swam at the sums of money required, and the skilled shipwrights and carpenters needed to build the new English fleet. The Saxons were not renowned sailors, and he hoped Eadric was right to put his faith in Wulfnoth and his brother. Beornoth went to sleep with dreams of war swarming his thought cage. Faces of men he had killed came to haunt him, his daughters came to make his heart weep, and his long-dead wife Eawynn seemed so real that he could almost reach out and touch her.

Morning came and Beornoth woke to find Wigs and Gis snoring like pigs and their room stinking of sour ale.

'Get up, you lazy whoresons,' he growled, and shook both of them awake. They groaned, clutching their heads, tongues clacking in dry mouths. 'We are off to war.'

Five days later, Beornoth and his companions arrived in Sandwich. They spent the last night of their journey in a warm monastery outside Cantwaraburg, where the monks fed them goat's cheese and glorious bread laced with honey. Sandwich perched on England's south-western corner, facing the Low Countries across the narrow sea from where the Vikings had launched so many of their attacks. It was a bustling sea town, busy with trade coming up the Wantsum Channel from Lundenwic before departing into the wide Whale Road. Beornoth found the town and its port overloaded with warriors and sailors, and its waters thronged with Eadric Streona's shiny new fleet.

'We aren't going to sea on one of those things, are we?' asked Gis as the three men paused their horses to look upon the town and the tangle of masts and rigging bobbing gently in the harbour.

'I'd rather stick my manhood in a wasp's nest than fight a battle on board a ship,' Wigs replied.

'The wasps wouldn't even notice.'

'You go on board then, sailor. I'd love to see you at sea, heaving your guts up at the first sight of a wave. You'd probably fall overboard and drown like a flailing pig before even getting close to the enemy.'

'We won't be sailing on ships,' Beornoth said. 'But if there's a fight on land, we'll be there.'

Beornoth urged his horse onwards, and the placid beast ambled towards the open town gates, outside which men had made makeshift camps. The smell of the sea mixed with the pleasant odour of fresh wood to drown out the stink of so many warriors and seamen in one place. Beornoth secured stables for their horses and found Alfgar and his warriors by the harbour watching as men loaded barrels and thick coils of rope onto the ships.

'Will you go to sea, lord?' Beornoth asked once he had greeted the ealdorman and his men, many of whom he knew from Mameceaster.

'Not me, Beo, I don't have the stomach for it. But half of my men must go, so they must find their sea legs quickly. We arrived here yesterday. What took you so long?'

'I don't move as fast as I once did, lord. Too many stops, and my horse goes slow, which suits me fine.'

'You miss poor old Virtus, eh?'

'Aye, a fine animal. A friend, just like Ealdorbana before her. Two stout warhorses, brave and trustworthy, which is more than I can say for most men, never mind horses.'

Alfgar laughed. 'The crews here are mostly fishermen. Or hired hands from Frisia and Frankia. They seem to know their business.'

'They'd better, because the Vikings certainly do. They are men born to the sea, raised to it just as they are to the blade. Many of them are born beside fjords and sail before they can walk. They have sailed as far east as a man can go, down fearsome rivers to the distant lands of the Rus, braving rapids like thunder and tribes with tattooed faces and barbaric gods. They have sailed so far west that men thought they would fall off the edge of the world, discovering new lands where ice, snow and fire exist alongside one another. Their shallow dragon ships can survive in wild seas where waves surge higher than this town's palisade. We wish to match them, to challenge them on the water with fishermen and warriors whose only experience with water is their monthly bath in a river.'

'Maybe we should use the fleet to frighten them off, or block them from entering our rivers.'

'Wulfnoth and Brihtric are in command?'

'Just as Eadric ordered.'

'Is Streona here?'

'He is. If you are lucky, you might see him ride past on his white horse. There is a council this evening where they will issue orders for departure. You should come with me. Ulfcytel will be there.'

'Aye. What news of Thorkell?'

'None. It seems he withdrew east across the sea, but doubtless he will return. Perhaps here, the Thames, or further south. Who knows? The meeting is in the hall by the water at sundown. Ah, there is our ealdorman of Mercia now.'

Eadric Streona came from a narrow street astride a startlingly white horse. He wore a jerkin of sea blue, and a russet cape flowed behind him. A dozen guards hurried to keep pace with their lord, and one slipped on a fresh pile of dung the horse dropped from its arse as Eadric waved to Ealdorman Alfgar and Beornoth.

'He looks cheerful,' said Wigs.

'So would you if you thought you were about to be the saviour of England.'

'Might be time to find somewhere for a drink before this meeting tonight.'

Beornoth watched the ealdorman on his horse and noticed the sour looks men cast in his direction once he had passed by. An unpopular man, but powerful. He pranced his fine horse along the quays, and men bowed as he passed. Eadric called to a sailor to fetch an oar for him to inspect, and from the back of his horse he made an elaborate show of eyeing its length and the smoothness of the ash shaft, though Beornoth doubted Eadric knew any more of seamanship than he did himself.

The sky brooded overhead, clouds low and heavy like a pregnant cow's belly, and a sea wind cut across the harbour to sting men's eyes. Hulls and masts stretched far beyond the harbour. The fleet moored as close to shore as possible, but it was too vast to get all within the safety of Sandwich's curved harbour. Beyond the mass of oak, pine and birch, the sea broiled dark and tipped with white, and Beornoth could feel a storm coming in his bones. He left Alfgar with the warriors of Cheshire and walked along the quayside, careful to give Eadric Streona a wide berth and avoid any awkward conversation.

The ships seemed to be made well enough to Beornoth's untrained eye: clinker-built in the Viking way with stem posts where the Northmen usually positioned their snarling beast heads. The Vikings gave their ships frightening names, like the *Shining Dragon*, the *Sea Wolf*, the *Seaworm*, or the *Fjord Bear*. The Saxon fleet bore more godly names. *Bread of Christ*, the *Holy Ark*, and other such nonsense, and Beornoth hoped that there were no bad omens in such names. To have a fleet that might challenge the enemy was a mighty achievement, even if Eadric had likely borrowed so much money from the Church that it would take three lifetimes for the nation to pay off. So Beornoth accepted the fleet in good faith, and hoped that it would be enough to prevent Thorkell landing again with his army five thousand strong. Perhaps even the sight of so many warships might make Thorkell turn his fleet around and return north.

Beornoth sat down to rest against a heavy piece of timber set into the quay, to which thickly woven hemp rope tied one of Eadric's warships securely to shore. The wind grew brisker, and the sea rolled, heaving and slopping against the shore. Boats creaked and groaned as they rolled on the swell, rigging taut, timber groaning as the sea pressed with impossible power against rivets and planks. He breathed in the fresh wood smell and observed that some vessels were unpainted. The Vikings painted their hulls and beast heads in startling colours to bring their ships to life. They loved their drakkars, karves and snekkes. The different-sized versions of their boats each capable of braving the deep, wild, open sea and sailing up shallow rivers to cut like a knife into a countryside where they could raid, ravage and plunder. Beornoth caught a waft of tar from the boiling cauldrons where men had stirred together hot pine tar, horsehair and animal fat, which they spread between the ships' timbers to make the boats watertight.

The ships were new, young, fresh, full of hope and expectation. If used properly, they could deliver a new age of freedom to the Saxon kingdom, enough ships to frighten the sea wolves – who only came to prey on the weak – and send them to other distant lands to sate their bloodlust. What Viking would come to England if he knew he must fight his way through a fleet of warships before reaching the lush green valleys, churches full of gold and silver plate, candlesticks, chains and crucifixes?

The wind blew strands of Beornoth's hair away from his face. He closed his eyes, the cool air fresh against his skin. The king had looked frail, too frail. Æthelred had aged rapidly since Beornoth had last met him. Back then, Beornoth had met the king alone, taking orders from the man himself. Æthelred had never been a strong, vital man. He had always been a thin and troubled king. Beornoth recalled clearly the problems with Æthelred's mother, Aelfryth, and how she had once tried to have Beornoth killed. He remembered meeting the king with Ealdorman Byrhtnoth like it was yesterday. His had been a hard life. Not hard in the sense of Beornoth's life. No brutal wounds from axes, swords or spears. The king had not lost his family to Viking raiders or watched as his sword brothers died beside the ebb tide at Maldon. But Æthelred had faced different pressures. His mother, who had killed Æthelred's half-brother to make him king; the Church and the battle to undo the changes his illustrious father had made to the power shared by the monasteries and the priesthood; the return of the Vikings and the challenges posed by his lords in the Danelaw who were more Viking than Saxon. The pressure of a kingdom and all the lives within it bearing down upon his narrow shoulders day after day, night after night.

It felt in that moment like the entire kingdom had aged. The age of the Saxons seemed bent-backed and grey-haired. The first Saxons had come across the sea once, hundreds of years ago, and had ripped the land from the Britons.

Those Saxons had come from the lands close to Forkbeard's own home in Denmark, had crossed the narrow waters from Frisia in similar ships and made landfall in Kent, East Anglia and Northumbria and there won themselves a kingdom from the folk who had lived in England since time began. The Britons had suffered and survived Roman invasion and domination, but that conquest had left the land improved, with great stone cities, aqueducts, grand villas and roads upon which a man could travel the length of the country on horseback. The Romans had brought law and order, foreign trade, bridges and countless other innovations to a people who lived in huts and worshipped old gods of land, sky, tree and wind. They had outlived the great Roman Empire, but the Britons had lost the war against the Saxon invaders. Beornoth and Æthelred's ancestors had beaten them and pushed them out of their homes into the mountains and dark places of Wales and Cornwall where they still spoke their ancient language and longed for the return of the place they called Lloegyr, the lost lands, or England as the Saxons now called it.

The ships shifting and rolling in the swell had once been trees. Acorns fallen from branches perhaps in the days of the Romans, grown to full, sprawling, sturdy oaks. Aged and weathered trunks and branches, which had seen great men, kings, queens and warlords come and go. Those trees had seen common folk born, married, bear children, grow old and die countless times down the long years. Beornoth realised that he and Æthelred were like those trees, like the land of England itself. They had seen eminent men come and go, battles to shake the very earth, sadness, glory, woe and happiness all wrapped up in their long lives. Beornoth opened his eyes and watched as a woman crouched in the lee of a market stall weaving a basket, making something new from something old. He pulled his cloak closer about his shoulders as an unwelcome thought seeped into his mind, infecting it like the lung sickness in men Beornoth's age. Perhaps the time of the Saxons was over, just like it had once been for the Romans and the Britons. Would the Saxons find themselves pushed back to the edges of the kingdom as the Vikings battered their way across England to forge for themselves a new kingdom made in their own image? If so, he would not be here to see it, and he had no children left alive on God's earth to suffer through that change.

The wind brought a shift in the world. Beornoth felt it in his aching bones. He fought for a land ruled by an aged king, a place that strong men from across the sea longed to make their own and would soak the valleys and fields with blood to do it. Were the younger men rising to power in England capable of fighting back those enemies? Beornoth could not imagine Eadric Streona in the shield wall or commanding an army, but he could imagine him pulling the strings in Winchester like a puppet master at an Easter fair. What of Æthelred's children, Beornoth wondered, were they prepared to take up their father's mantle once the king had left the mortal world? Aethelstan, Edward, Edmund. Young princes raised in the royal court in all its finery, fine food, soft clothes, the best horses. Royal weapons masters taught them to fight, but they had never fought in combat. Beornoth wondered how they compared to Forkbeard's son, Cnut, a young wolf already sailing to war, witnessing his father's decisions, strategies, spilling blood and getting a taste for battle and glory.

Beornoth stood, bones aching, muscles slow. He placed a hand on his shoulder and rolled the stiff joint. He was like Saxon England, he thought, creaking. Like his sword, notched by too many blades, Beornoth had witnessed too much blood, fought too many battles. He found himself assailed by time if not by his enemies. The wind grew stronger, and a squall at sea made the horizon bleak, as if the sky touched the water with grimy, dark fingers, ominous and powerful. Beornoth turned away from the fleet. It was time to prepare for the meeting in Sandwich's hall. There, the great men, the leaders of England, would meet and agree on how to meet Thorkell the Tall and his five thousand warriors. They would decide how to deploy the fleet, and Beornoth hoped that men who knew more than he about the sea could devise a strategy to keep the Vikings away, save the Saxon people more suffering, and perhaps rescue the kingdom from its doom.

6

Beornoth leaned against a timber post as the ealdormen, king's thegns, bishops and great men entered the open doors to Sandwich's hall. They shook rain from their cloaks, stamped their wet boots and warmed their hands on the hearth fire burning at the room's centre. Smoke swirled from the blaze and escaped through a smoke hole cut into the thatch. It gathered in the high beams like a storm cloud, staining the wood an even deeper black before escaping into the evening sky. Raindrops came through that hole to splatter and singe on the rocks surrounding the hearth fire, and thralls with bowed heads brought men spiced, warmed ale in wooden mugs.

'I don't think we should be in here, lord,' said Gis, moving to hide behind Beornoth's wide frame. 'There isn't a soul in this room who isn't a lord or a great man, except for Wigs and me.'

'I fancy myself a great man,' Wigs replied, brushing his cloak back and propping his elbow on his hip. 'I could pass for a thegn, at least.'

'And I could be the abbess of the convent at Ely.'

'You can both stay,' Beornoth said. 'Just keep quiet.' He enjoyed his companions' levity, a welcome distraction to his own world of war.

Beornoth nodded a greeting to Ulfcytel, who marched into the hall flanked by two warriors, one of whom, Beornoth was pleased to see, was Osgar. They came to stand beside Beornoth, but Ulfcytel said nothing. He inclined his head in greeting, but his hard face was taut and stern, and the East Anglian stood, arms folded across his chest, staring straight ahead. Eadric Streona and his brother Brihtric stood amongst half a dozen Mercian lords, each with the shire's sigil of a gold cross on a blue background on their scabbards. Those scabbards lay empty, as did Beornoth's, for all men left their weapons outside the hall, as was the custom.

'No axe this evening?' Beornoth said to Osgar.

'No, lord,' he said, 'I keep that for the Danes.'

Beornoth smiled. 'You fought well at Theodford. If it comes to battle again, I'll seek you out.'

'You honour me, lord.'

Beornoth clapped the warrior on the back and hoped there were more men like Osgar coming through the ranks of their lords' retinues, for the kingdom needed them.

'Welcome, my lords,' said Eadric Streona, stepping forth with his head high, searching the room and meeting every eye with confidence. His gaze passed over Beornoth but did not linger there. He paused on Ulfcytel, and then continued, smiling at some, inclining his head to others. 'We gather here to complete our plans to meet the enemy. You have now witnessed the magnificent fleet I have assembled, a fleet of our own for the first time in our history. History will remember us, friends. They will marvel at our achievements and the deeds we in this room have accomplished together. I give the floor to my brother, who will outline his plan to counter the Viking threat.'

Brihtric stepped forward and thanked his brother. He was shorter than Eadric, but older, with dark hair and a neatly trimmed beard. Brihtric wore a gold chain around his neck, and rings adorned his fingers. He wore a shining byrnie inset with silver links, just like his more illustrious brother.

'Do you know this Brihtric?' Beornoth whispered to Osgar.

The warrior shook his head. 'Not really. He came out of Wessex when his brother gained influence. He helped Eadric when they purged the king's court, before Eadric became ealdorman. Brihtric has been here ever since. He was captain of the king's guard after his brother. Now I think he owns a swathe of land in Mercia as a thegn. He has grown rich and powerful.'

Brihtric spoke, pacing across the floor. He praised his brother's achievements, King Æthelred's decisions, and spoke for too long about the process of building the vast fleet.

'How many men did they kill in the purge of Æthelred's court?' Beornoth whispered to Osgar, already bored by the speech.

'I am just a simple thegn, lord. Such matters are beyond my understanding, but many men lost their lives and new men, men beholden to Eadric for their power, came to court in their stead.'

'Can he fight?'

'I have not seen either brother in the shield wall, lord.'

A commotion at the rear door caused men to grumble as boots shuffled on the floor. Wulfnoth, the thegn of Wessex in joint command of the fleet, marched into the hall with his son Godwin. Grizzled men with rain-soaked cloaks followed their lord, and the men already in the hall stepped back from their determined entrance.

'Lord Wulfnoth,' Brihtric said nervously, glancing at his brother for support.

'You begin without me,' Wulfnoth said, his voice full of gravel and his eyes blazing with fervour. He wore black leather beneath a black cloak, hair and beard cut close to his skull to give him a granite, fierce appearance. Brihtric opened his mouth, but Wulfnoth raised a finger to silence him like a child who had spoken out of turn. Men looked at Wulfnoth with respect, and Brihtric shifted his feet nervously. 'Yet I come with news. Thorkell and his fleet plan to come across the narrow sea from Frankia. They gather on there on the coast, waiting for the right time to make the crossing. They plan to sail for the Thames, for Lundenwic, fifty ships and five thousand men coming to destroy the city and cast our kingdom to bloody ruin.'

'Then we shall sail to meet them,' said Brihtric, waving a fist as though he were a lord of war the Vikings should fear.

'Sail to meet them?' Wulfnoth said, and he took slow steps closer to Brihtric. Wulfnoth's hand flicked out. A slight gesture, but enough to still his retinue as he came to stand beside his co-commander of the fleet. Wulfnoth stood taller than Brihtric, not by much, but his demeanour, his confidence and experience made him seem enormous compared to his colleague, even though Wulfnoth was not a large man.

'Of course. We shall put out this very evening. We can board our ships and enter the Thames estuary, block their passage and meet them in battle.'

'Sail tonight?' Wulfnoth frowned.

'We are not afraid, and we are ready for this fight.'

'There is a storm outside. One does not take a ship to sea at night. Do you know whether the tide floods or ebbs?'

'Well... I...'

'I have men in my employ who have crossed the sea at significant risk to their lives to bring me this news. The Danes will not sail until the weather breaks, but then they will come quickly, they will come organised, and they will come to take everything we have.'

'I am not naïve about the Viking threat, Lord Wulfnoth.'

'I sincerely hope not.' Wulfnoth kneaded his brow as the men in the hall cleared their throats and whispered to one another. The air became cloying, and the room seemed to become smaller. Beornoth's cloak and mail felt heavier as he watched the two commanders face off when they should have already come up with a battle plan which every commander could get behind. Thegns and ealdormen had brought warriors south to join the fight. Lives were at risk. The very kingdom balanced on a knife edge as an army came across the sea. Wulfnoth sighed in frustration and seemed to master himself with a twitch of his neck. 'We can put to sea tomorrow on the flood tide, if the storm breaks. We must decide which men will sail aboard the fleet and which should march for Lundenwic's fortress. The fleet shall block the estuary, as you say, and if we do this right, we have a chance to present our ships to show the Danes our power. Thorkell will not willingly lead his fleet against ours. We are evenly matched. That battle would be a slaughter, and Thorkell is a warlord, leader of the Jomsvikings whose very existence depends on his ability to bring his forces to whichever king can pay him to fight. If Thorkell fights us in the Thames, even if he wins, he would lose so many men that his army and power would be crippled.'

'We should not delay.' Brihtric's tone had become pugnacious, his cheeks flushed red as he found himself demeaned by Wulfnoth's clarity, and by his experienced view on what should happen.

'We won't.' Wulfnoth smiled thinly, trying his best to be patient with his co-commander.

Both men paused, staring at one another. Eadric Streona took half a pace forward, thought better of intervening and stepped back. Ulfcytel looked sideways at Beornoth, and Beornoth raised his eyebrows to show he was as surprised as Ulfcytel to see the two leaders arguing in front of the great men of England. Beornoth had expected to hear a well-thought-out battle plan, but clearly Wulfnoth and Brihtric had not discussed a strategy before that moment. Wulfnoth looked across the hall as if he hoped someone might speak up to support him. All he had said made sense, of course. Wulfnoth was an experienced thegn, a man who had fought his entire life. Beornoth could have spoken up in support, but to give voice to either side in that moment would have made a man the enemy of the other.

'I shall lead the fleet out in the morning, then. I will take the ships to the Thames and arrange a blockade. You, Lord Wulfnoth, can command the land forces who march to Lundenwic to organise the city's defence.' Brihtric smirked, pleased with his quick thinking and his attempt to undermine the Wessex thegn. He glanced at his brother and ran his tongue across the inside of his mouth.

'Now is not the time to grasp for power like a crab trying to claw its way out of a bucket,' Wulfnoth said, and many inside the hall gasped at his curt response. 'We are at war. You have no experience, Lord Brihtric, I beg you and every man in this room to see sense. This is not a chance to seize power or to burnish one's influence bright. We have one chance here to defeat an enemy who has dogged our people for a century. Do not squander it.'

'Squander? Crab?' Brihtric spluttered. Eadric stepped forward and placed a hand on his brother's shoulder, but Brihtric shrugged him off and stepped closer to Wulfnoth. 'You are afraid. I propose a bold plan, and you wish to wait. Spies, you say? What spies? How can we be sure that you, Wulfnoth of Wessex, are not in the employ of Thorkell himself?' Brihtric was shouting, chest puffed out, face so red that a vein on his forehead stood out blue and strained. He raged, incensed at Wulfnoth's humiliating disregard of his plans.

One of Wulfnoth's retainers burst forward and pushed Brihtric away from his lord. Brihtric fell back, stumbling and shouting. A Mercian charged in and punched Wulfnoth's man in the face. Two of Eadric's burly warriors threw Wulfnoth's men backwards and Beornoth closed his eyes, heart breaking as the awareness dawned on him that these were not men capable of saving England. They were not men who could match the cunning or the ferocity of Thorkell the Tall.

'Stop them, lord,' said Gis, his face drawn downwards in horror.

'Why?' Beornoth said. His shoulders sagged, and he suddenly felt like taking to his bed.

'Before their disagreement ruins everything!'

'I am tired,' Beornoth said, and Gis stared at him open-mouthed as if he had cursed God. There was a time Beornoth would have charged into that fray, banged a few heads together until the bravado slipped away as men realised they could not challenge Beornoth's savagery. Brihtric and Wulfnoth's men hurled insults at one another, pushing and shoving like drunken men in a tavern. Beornoth turned away, head bowed. If all the lords and warriors of England only bickered about leadership and deployment instead of uniting against Thorkell, Beornoth would return home and live beside Eawynn's grave in peace.

'Wait,' said Wigs. He tugged at Beornoth's arm, and he turned, anger flaring that one of his men would touch him so. But then he relented, interest returning as Ulfcytel barged his way to where Brihtric and Wulfstan's men fought. Osgar hurled two men out of the way as if they were old rags. A Mercian tried to hit Osgar, but he caught the fist and headbutted the man with a sickening crunch. Men fell back from Osgar as the Mercian crumpled to the floor.

'Enough!' Ulfcytel bellowed, pushing the different factions apart. 'We must work together, my lords, I beg you!'

'He is a traitor!' Brihtric roared into the silence which followed Ulfcytel's words. He pointed a stubby finger at Wulfnoth. 'A traitor to his king and to all of us! He is in league with the Vikings!'

Wulfnoth's mouth turned in on itself, and his face slackened. He glanced from Brihtric to Eadric, and there was a momentary flicker of fear in Wulfnoth's eyes. It was a grave insult, a terrible thing for one lord to say to another before other ealdormen and thegns. Wulfnoth, however, offered no rebuttal or objection to that offence. He justifiably could have offered Brihtric the chance to defend his accusation in single combat. But Wulfnoth simply turned on his heel and marched out of the hall, closely followed by his son Godwin and his men.

The hall fell silent, men's faces ashen as they exchanged nervous glances, unsure what to do. Brihtric straightened his dishevelled clothes and smoothed his hair. Eadric's usual air of smiling confidence slipped to reveal a frowning, thin-mouthed face.

'Everybody out!' Streona bellowed, fists clenched. He spat some quiet words to his brother, and Brihtric opened his mouth to protest, thought better of it and flounced out of the hall.

'We can't just let this happen,' said Gis.

'Why not? What can we do about it?' Beornoth replied.

'You are a king's thegn, lord, men respect you. They will listen to you. Let us try to make peace between the commanders.'

Beornoth took a breath. Gis was right, of course. Beornoth had not left his home to ride south just to give up the fight when a gaggle of weak men fought over a pissing contest. He pushed through the gathering, easing around men who had formed small groups to discuss quietly the public falling-out, and the unthinkable charge Brihtric had laid squarely at Wulfnoth's feet. Beornoth used his bulk to push through the crowd until he found Ulfcytel.

'A sad day for our people,' Ulfcytel said, sucking his teeth in despair.

'We must try to reconcile them before things get out of hand. Wulfnoth's men crew more than half of the fleet, and Brihtric has the power to lay him low. We must find a way to resolve the disagreement tonight. If left to fester, those two will become mortal enemies.'

'No man wants Eadric Streona for an enemy. So many lords have died in dispute with him he does not even hide his methods any more. It used to be a knife in the dark, a fall from a horse, or a heart-clenching poison. When he killed Ealdorman Elfhelm, he simply slew Elfhelm during a hunt, setting his huntsmen on the poor man in front of everyone. When it was done, Eadric dragged Elfhelm's sons, Wulfheah and Ufegeat, to Cookham and blinded them. The king himself was at Cookham and gave no objection to the terrible deed.'

'Then it doesn't sound like there's much reasoning with the bastard if he and his brother have set their ire against Wulfnoth. Why did Eadric appoint Wulfnoth if he knew his brother would oppose the joint command?'

'How would the ealdormen and thegns respond if Eadric gave his brother sole command of the fleet? A man without experience or reputation? Would you follow such a man to war, Beo?'

'No. You have the right of it.'

'So Wulfnoth must return and make peace with the brothers, or men will melt away during the coming days and return to their homes. Before we know it, we shall have a magnificent fleet without warriors to crew it.'

'I am not one for fine words. Banging heads together, yes; a fight to resolve a dispute, certainly; but something more delicate is required here. We must find Wulfnoth and ask him to put his pride to one side before either he or Brihtric seeks to remove his rival and take overall command.'

'Come then. Let's go to Wulfnoth.'

Beornoth and Ulfcytel strode through the rain, boots splashing in puddles formed on the narrow streets. Wigs and Gis followed, as did Osgar. They marched in solemn silence, and Beornoth's heart pounded as though he marched to war. The entire campaign lay in the balance. Thorkell would make his crossing as soon as the storm broke, and then all hell would descend on England. They found Wulfnoth's quarters in the town's western quarter. A score of men in leather and armed with spears and shields stood guard in the rain, lined up before a large merchant's house above which flew the banner of Wessex.

The guards stiffened as Beornoth, Ulfcytel, Osgar, Wigs and Gis approached. They lowered their spears, faces stern as rivulets of rain ran down their cheeks.

'Make way,' Ulfcytel ordered, but the guards did not shift.

'We have orders not to admit anyone, lord,' said a guard with red hair and a flat nose. He kept his gaze fixed firmly ahead, not making eye contact with any of the visitors.

'I am Ulfcytel of East Anglia, and this is Beornoth. We are king's thegns, soldier.'

The warrior's eyes flitted to Beornoth, and he gulped, taking in his size and the king's ring upon his finger.

'Lord Beornoth, all men have heard of your legend. I...' He snapped his head back to attention and bit his lip.

'You have your orders,' Beornoth said. 'But Lord Ulfcytel and I are standing here in the rain. A king's thegn can command hospitality from any hall in England. Let us in, friend.'

'Lord Beornoth is not usually so diplomatic,' Wigs added. 'Stand aside, or you might find yourselves on the wrong side of his anger.'

The guard thought about that for a moment, likely bringing to mind the stories he had heard of Maldon, and the many other famous battles Beornoth had fought, and which bards and scops sang of at halls up and down the country. The guard shifted his grip on his spear and turned to the warrior next to him. 'Inform Lord Wulfnoth that the king's thegns are on their way to see him. The rest of you, stand aside.'

The guards made way, spears shifting to rest on their shoulders, and Beornoth led the small group through on towards the two-storey building. He strode across a courtyard covered in light shale and reached a narrow door, forced to duck under its low lintel to enter the house. Darkness had descended on Sandwich, and Beornoth found himself in a long corridor lit by rush lights set in troughs high on the walls. Beornoth didn't wait for a steward or guard to meet him and show him the way. He marched onwards, heavy boots stomping on the hard-packed earthen floor, cloak and mail dripping rainwater onto old straw cast across the ground. He followed the sound of men's voices until he came to a closed pine door. Beornoth pushed it open, discovering a dozen men crammed into a small room, gathered around a table that held untouched bread, a flagon of ale and a round cheese. Wulfnoth stiffened as the door opened, and beside him stood his son Godwin, tall and serious-faced.

'Lord Beornoth,' said Wulfnoth, warned of his coming by the wet-haired guard from outside, who stood at the thegn's elbow. Wulfnoth's black leather clothing creaked as he turned, hands on hips and face cast in a grave frown.

'I won't bandy words,' Beornoth said, speaking loud and clear, meeting the eye of every man in the room one by one. 'Thorkell the Tall comes across the sea with five thousand men. This fleet is our only way of stopping him from laying our country to waste. You must make amends with Brihtric and Eadric.'

'Must?' Wulfnoth laughed mirthlessly. 'I have one and a half thousand men here in this town. How many have you brought? Half the fleet is built from wood cut on my land. The wool for their sails came from my sheep, thousands of them from across Wessex, woven by churls and thralls in my hills and dales. Wool I could have sold, people who should have been sowing, reaping, weaving and making the land produce what it must to keep my warriors fed and my coffers full enough to pay men to defend it. After all of that sacrifice, after all I have done to serve my king and my people, I am branded a traitor and insulted by a back-stabbing son of a whore who five years ago was fit for nothing but plucking muck nuts from sheep's arses.'

'And yet we must fight Thorkell.'

Wulfnoth leaned forward, resting his fists on the tabletop. 'My little birds tell me Thorkell will strike at the Thames and try his hand at Lundenwic again. You were there to stop him last time, Beornoth, and all men have heard the song of how you fought Thorkell on Lundenwic bridge. He strikes at Lundenwic, not at Wessex.'

'The king has assembled an army of all England here at Sandwich,' added Ulfcytel. 'We have all come to defend our country, not just our own shire. For years, that is how we have thought. Keep our warriors at home to protect our own lands. The Vikings move fast. They can appear on any beach, or sail up any river, and our duty is to the people in our own shires. But how can we fight such a force of Vikings unless all the ealdormen and shires unite? The last time the Vikings brought an army that big to our shores, the sons of Ragnar led it, and the land they conquered remains the Danelaw to this day. Not a separate kingship any more, but still peopled by Norsemen, nonetheless.'

'Everything you say is true, and I respect you both. The men in this room are my oathsworn warriors. Men who risk their lives and fight for me, and in return I reward them with silver. It is my duty to protect their families and to ensure I make decisions in the best interests of Wessex. I came here to Sandwich in good faith. I brought the twenty-five ships built on my land, even though I have not seen one pound of the gold and silver promised to me by Eadric and his bishops. I came ready to fight, to put to sea and to make a stand against Thorkell and his famous Jomsvikings. But I will not sail out in a storm on the orders of a man who knows less than an onion about sailing or war.

'We are men here in this room. All battle-hardened. All men who shed blood and lost brothers to the blade. I have spent years building a network of spies throughout Frankia, Jutland, the Vik, the Skagerrak and the fjords of Norway. They are merchants who come to our shores from theirs, trading amber, pelts, ingots, wine and mead. They whisper to me of what goes on abroad, of how our enemies prepare for war, of how Forkbeard still fights to secure his dominion over Norway. I am no fool, and I know they also whisper to our enemies of what we plan, but I have been careful and kept our great fleet secret. But I know Thorkell is coming, and I know he wants Lundenwic. It is the gateway to trade and wealth, the link between our country and the rest of the world. Thorkell is already a wealthy man. He is Sweyn's man but not his oathman. He is a Jomsviking, and they are mercenaries who fight for pay. Forkbeard pays well, and Thorkell fought for him at the battle of Svolder when Olaf Trygvasson died and Forkbeard became the first king of both Denmark and Norway. Does he attack us because Forkbeard orders it? No. He comes to make himself impossibly wealthy.'

Wulfnoth paused, shifted his head uncomfortably and glanced across the room at the faces of his own men he trusted, and the visitors he barely knew. His lips turned in on themselves, and he shifted his feet. Wulfnoth stood straight and spoke freely.

'Thorkell comes because we have a weak king who has fallen under the control of a serpent, a grasping back-stabber who seeks to drain all the power and wealth in this country into his own coffers. Streona brings this country to ruin. He has become the ealdorman of Mercia! Once a great kingdom in its own right. The Vikings see that. They smell weakness, and so Thorkell comes to devour us. Perhaps he even dreams of making himself king. He has bound five thousand men to his cause and comes to do us great harm. Forkbeard wants to be king of England, but first he must pacify the wild Vikings of Norway and their thousands of islands, countless fjords and fortresses. Will I fight Thorkell? Of course, that is why I am here. But the Streona brothers have set their ire against me. What would either of you proud warriors do if Brihtric denounced you as a traitor before the great lords of England?'

'I would fight him for it,' said Beornoth, which was true.

'How could Brihtric, the useless bastard, stand against a man like you, Beornoth, or you, Ulfcytel, or me, dare I say it? Do you think he will accept if I challenge him to fight? No. A knife in the back would be my fate, or a tragic accident before we join battle. I cannot allow that. Perhaps Brihtric dreams of making himself ealdorman of Wessex? Perhaps those foul brothers planned this confrontation all along for that very reason.'

Beornoth's stomach sank, because everything Wulfnoth said was true. 'So what will you do?'

Wulfnoth sighed and shook his head. 'I must protect my people, my lords. I will think on it and decide tomorrow. We need the weather to change before we can make sail, anyway. You come to me and ask me to swallow my pride and make peace with Brihtric and Eadric Streona. Have you asked them to do the same?'

'No,' Beornoth conceded.

'Why not? Why should only Wulfnoth suffer their insults and give way to keep this army and fleet together?'

'Because you are a warrior, and a man of courage who understands what it means to sacrifice for his people and for his king.'

'Aye, as do you. But those weasel bastards do not. They see only their own betterment and would crawl over the corpses of every lord in England to achieve it.'

'So we shall talk again tomorrow?'

'Tomorrow.' Wulfnoth tucked his thumbs into his belt and looked at the floor, unable to meet Beornoth's gaze. 'Stay, have something to eat and drink, I beg you.'

'We shall go to our own lodgings, but thank you. I will return in the morning, and I truly hope all is not lost.'

Beornoth and his companions left the house and emerged into a night where the rain had stopped falling, but the town stank of wet thatch. They walked in silence, boots splashing in puddles. Lights still showed in the great hall, where Eadric Streona's meeting seemed still to be underway. Beornoth's mood was as dark as the sky. Hope had turned to fear. Everything Wulfnoth had said was true. He understood Thorkell's reason for risking his life and his army, risking his ships on the wild and unpredictable Whale Road, all to attack an England he sensed was vulnerable and ripe for the picking. But he was also right about Eadric and Brihtric. The dispute between Wulfnoth and the brothers, which had come from nothing but now seethed like a boiling cauldron, threatened to destroy Saxon England's chance to defeat the Vikings once and for all.

7

Morning came with bright sunlight and the caw of gulls bursting through Beornoth's window shutters. He woke with a start, dragged himself out of bed and pulled on his clothes and byrnie. Beornoth hurried from his lodgings and out into the fresh coastal morning air to resume his discussion with Wulfnoth. He did not wait for Wigs or Gis, nor did he break his fast with food or ale. It was early, the sun barely emerged from the horizon, fat, golden and hot in a red-tinged sky. Beornoth strode through the narrow lanes and streets still wet from the previous night's rain.

The only other people awake at that hour were fishermen in caps and trews cut above their knees, who went quietly towards their boats to seek the morning catch. Beornoth came about the timber church and out towards the palisade, slipping through the open gate and out onto the harbour. He stopped, stunned as though punched in the face. Beornoth's breath caught in his chest, and a great sorrow like a heavy anchor stone dropped into his empty belly. Half of the fleet was gone. Twenty ships rowed away from the quayside, thronged with the warriors of Wessex beneath their fluttering banner.

The dream was over, ripped away by an insult hurled by a man who had never fought in the shield wall. A great sadness overwhelmed Beornoth, a deep, cutting weight on his heart like the death of a loved one. Wulfnoth was gone, along with his men and half the fleet. The remaining ships were not enough to mount a serious challenge to Thorkell the Tall. There had been a whisper of a dream, a sliver of a chance to defeat the Vikings rather than suffer their depredations and then pay them off when the Danes had stolen enough treasure, raped enough women and burned enough villages. That chance had flickered like a candle in the wind. A plan, well-conceived and executed, to build a fleet and challenge the great enemy, and now ambition and petty squabbling had extinguished that flame.

It was a depressing way for it to end. No battle, no confrontation. No demonstration of Saxon strength to warn the Vikings to find other shores to raid, to make the jarls and warriors of the north speak of other countries to raid and plunder in spring. Just words, pride and foolishness. Wulfnoth was gone, taking his ships and his men home rather than face the treacherous ire of the Streona brothers. With him went hope, and Beornoth longed for the great men he had once known. England had become a country led by the weak and ruled by graspers. Beornoth wished for the warriors he had fought beside and respected. Men like Byrhtnoth, Aelfwine of Foxfield and Leofsunu of Sturmer who stood strong at Maldon even when faced with inglorious defeat.

Wulfnoth's ships eased out onto a glassy, still sea where the early sun glistened on the whitecaps like morning dew on spiderwebs. He had awoken before the dawn, boarded his warriors and was gone before even the fishermen had taken to the water. Beornoth thought of running along the quay and shouting to Wulfnoth, seeking one last chance to change his mind and avert a pitiful disaster. But it would do no good, and instead Beornoth turned back towards the town. He shuddered and pulled his cloak about his shoulders, because just as Wulfnoth had used the break in the weather to sail away from Sandwich, so Thorkell the Tall would awake to find a calm sea and bright sky. He would set sail and could be in the Thames any day. War beckoned, the crash and clang of the shield wall, the screaming, the blood, the agony and the glory of war.

Beornoth turned about the church, where priests brushed its stone pathway with brooms, and found Eadric Streona and Brihtric alone outside the great hall where last night's ill-fated meeting had devolved into farce.

'Is it true, Lord Beornoth?' asked Eadric, his usually perfectly combed hair and beard wild and unbrushed from bed. 'Has Wulfnoth betrayed us?'

'Wulfnoth has taken his ships and his men,' Beornoth replied. The sight of the brothers raised Beornoth's hackles. Anger flared inside him, anger for what could have been, and for the cost of that loss the people of England must now bear.

'I knew it,' Brihtric spat. 'A traitor, a betrayer, a turncloak.'

'Wulfnoth is a man of honour.'

'Honour? He has stolen our ships and a host of men. He has the honour of a penniless whore.'

Eadric paced back and forth, head shaking from side to side. 'If we put out now, we can head him off. Kill Wulfnoth and bring the ships back. What say you, Beornoth? Will you lead us out in pursuit?'

'Thorkell the Tall will leave Frankia today with five thousand men and seventy ships. I must go to Lundenwic and organise the defence of the city. You should take what remains of the fleet and sail with all haste to the Thames. Block the estuary so that Thorkell must engage you to pass. With luck, he may turn back from such a fight, a fight that would cost him many men, too many men to mount his campaign.'

'We sail to war, whilst you ride away?' said Brihtric, eyes narrowing. Beornoth could almost hear the wagon wheels turning in his small mind, could feel the next words forming in Brihtric's mouth, the same reckless insult he had tossed at Wulfnoth so easily. Beornoth flexed his hands. He wore his sword buckled to his belt and his seax sheathed at the small of his back.

'That's enough, brother,' Eadric warned. 'Lord Beornoth, you understand we cannot allow Wulfnoth to steal our ships? We must pursue him.'

'Then we leave the way open for Thorkell and his army.'

'Are you deaf?' Brihtric spat, arms flailing, face flushed red. 'We must stop the traitor. He must pay! Maybe you don't have the stomach for war? An old man like you should see out his days beside the hearth and leave the fighting to younger...'

Beornoth took three steps forward so that his chest touched Brihtric's own. Beornoth was much taller and broader than the newly minted thegn of Mercia. Brihtric stared up at the cliff of Beornoth's face. He smelled like a woman, as though he had some scented oil or powder in his hair. His face was soft, unscarred, and he carried no weapon.

'I go to Lundenwic to defend the city. Not for the first time. I advise you, my lords, to sail your ships into the Thames and block Thorkell's advance.' Beornoth spoke slowly, deliberately, fixing Brihtric with his cold killer's eyes.

'Lord Beornoth,' Eadric said, and placed a hand on Beornoth's forearm. He applied pressure as if to draw him away from Brihtric, but it was like a small child tugging at the arm of its father. 'My brother meant no insult. We find ourselves in trying times, faced with an enemy abroad and now an enemy at home. It falls to us to protect the kingdom, and our decisions must be made carefully and with determined surety.'

'He disobeys us!' Brihtric said, spittle in his beard. He took a step back from Beornoth and pulled at the cuffs of his jerkin, not wearing his byrnie that morning. 'We command you to accompany the fleet and punish the traitor Wulfnoth!'

'I am a king's thegn,' Beornoth said, keeping his stare fixed on Brihtric. 'I obey only the king. Not you.'

'Lord Beornoth...' Eadric began.

'Enough!' Beornoth shouted, and the two brothers jumped with fright. 'You accused Wulfnoth of treachery.' He pointed a thick finger into Brihtric's thin chest. 'A baseless charge against a man I have fought beside in battle. You have caused this woe, this failure of our one chance to fight back against our enemies.'

'How dare you raise your voice to me? I am in charge here. This is my...'

Beornoth placed a heavy hand on Brihtric's shoulder, and another on the hilt of his sword. 'You are what?' he said, as sudden understanding descended upon Brihtric, and his eyes grew wide in terror and his mouth turned down in fear. 'Do you feel in charge now?'

Beornoth pulled his sword a thumb's width from its scabbard.

'It's just us here,' Beornoth continued. 'We three men. Alone. No guards or warriors to protect you. I am not a young man any more. If you believe I am your enemy, then strike me down. There are two of you, and I am just one old man. Do you have the courage to back up the words of your mouth?'

'Lord Beornoth, this is not the time for...' Eadric began, until Beornoth turned to him with a snarl.

'I shall ride for Lundenwic. I advise you to bring the fleet to the Thames, but what you do with your ships is up to you.' Beornoth removed his hand from Brihtric's shoulder and let his sword slide back into its scabbard. He strode away, leaving the brothers in his wake. Brihtric spluttered and raged, but Eadric spoke softly to calm his pompous brother. Beornoth couldn't hear the exact words. His time in Sandwich and with the fleet was over.

Beornoth reached his lodgings shortly after, and found Wigs, Gis and Osgar waiting for him. Osgar carried his huge long-handled war axe resting on one shoulder, and all three wore their armour.

'The fleet,' Beornoth said.

'We know,' Wigs replied.

'How do you know? There is barely a man awake in Sandwich this early.'

'Follow me.'

Beornoth followed the three warriors around to the rear of their wattle and daub lodging. Five score warriors waited on an open stretch of grass behind a ramshackle stable, which leaned to one side. One of them, a young, fresh-faced lad on a dappled mare, carried the dragon banner of Wessex. He was familiar, but Beornoth couldn't quite place him.

'Lord Beornoth,' said Ulfcytel, marching from the lodging's back door in full armour with his helmet under his arm. 'Are we for Lundenwic?'

'Aye,' Beornoth replied. 'Who are these men?'

'Judging by your demeanour, I assume that you have learned of Wulfnoth's departure with twenty ships and the warriors of Wessex. This is Godwin, Wulfnoth's son. Wulfnoth has sailed away to protect himself from Eadric and Brihtric. Much as that sticks in my craw and scuppers any chance we had of beating the cursed Vikings in a fair fight, he has likely saved his family's life. Wulfnoth has placed his son and one hundred of Wessex's finest warriors under our command. They march with us for Lundenwic.'

'Then what are we waiting for?'

Beornoth led one hundred Wessex men away from Sandwich, along with Ulfcytel and two hundred warriors from East Anglia. Three hundred men rode west with heavy hearts, a solemn, silent column winding its way away from the harbour and its town. They wound their way along a steep path, sea wind at their backs and all hope of fighting Thorkell's army on an even footing whipped away like smoke in a windstorm. Beornoth and Ulfcytel paused on a steep headland to watch as Eadric and Brihtric rowed the fleet out of port, heading south in pursuit of Wulfnoth, and not towards the River Thames.

'They go to kill my father, when we should sail for the Thames together,' said Godwin. He wore a leather breastplate and carried a sword at his hip. 'Have we witnessed the end of our kingdom?'

Beornoth turned in the saddle to stare at the lad, who could not yet have seen eighteen summers. He was calm despite his father's desperate position.

There was a cleverness in his blue eyes, and Godwin tore his gaze away from the departing fleet.

'Maybe,' Beornoth replied. 'Your father has sailed away with his men and given himself a chance of survival. But Eadric will see to it that the king seizes your family's land in Wessex. He will brand your father a traitor to the crown, and there can be no way back from that.'

Godwin smiled sadly. 'My father has not taken the ships to save his own skin. He goes to get my mother and my sister before Streona sends men to kill them, burn our hall and kill our people. My father is a hard man, Lord Beornoth, but he is no fool, and he loves his family. The ships travel faster than any horse, so he will reach Wessex before Eadric and Brihtric's riders. Where will he go after that? I do not know. North into the old Danelaw, maybe? We have cousins there.'

'We lost a war because Brihtric accused Wulfnoth of treachery, without a ship making sail or the swing of a sword,' Ulfcytel said with a shake of his head. 'What must our ancestors think of us?'

Beornoth urged his horse away from the headland, heading west. He rode in his byrnie, with his shield and helmet tied to the saddle. Gis carried Beornoth's spear, and Wigs carried a pack with food and three skins of ale. It took five days to reach Lundenwic travelling slowly. Ulfcytel used the journey through his shire to collect as many hunting bows and sheaves of arrows as possible, and he commandeered horses from stables and breeding farms so that seventy of the three hundred men rode rather than marched to the old Roman city. Horses made it possible to send scouts ranging ahead and to the flanks of the marching column. They could forage and leave supplies on the road and return at regular intervals with news of what lay ahead.

On the third day, a scout returned on a lathered horse to report news of Thorkell's arrival.

'They are in the Thames, lord,' said the man, a sallow-skinned East Anglian with worried eyes. 'I have never seen so many ships. So many that I could not see the water, like a great snake of wood and oars sliding across the land.'

'When will they reach the city?' Beornoth asked.

'They pause on a small island beyond the estuary. If they leave today, they could be there late today or tomorrow.'

'One of us must go to the city and prepare its defences,' said Beornoth. 'I have fought there before against Thorkell when he came with Forkbeard.

There should still be a garrison there, though I do not know who commands it. With luck, the king remains at Winchester, but that means his royal guard is not at Lundenwic. We will have few men and long stretches of wall to defend.'

'If you could go back and fight that battle again,' asked Godwin, 'what would you do differently?'

'A fine question, young man,' said Ulfcytel, glancing at Wulfnoth's son with a raised eyebrow.

Beornoth thought about those grim days for a moment, of Robert de Warenne and his Norman warriors employed by the king to defend the city, of Pallig the Viking and his Norsemen also in the king's employ. A hard fight with many good men lost, but the old stone walls had held.

'The walls should remain in good condition,' said Beornoth, leaning forward to pat his horse's neck as he spoke. 'The Romans knew how to build, and we today cannot cut and lay stone as well as they. When I was there, they had repaired the high walls and gates with timber, and so we held them against the Vikings' ladders and attempts to climb. We did not defend every foot of wall. We simply defended where the Vikings attacked. They brought their ships into the river's widest sections and attacked from their boats and tried to attack the gates on each bridge. But if I were to fight them again today, I would leave a force across the river outside of the city. The Vikings must forage and cut timber from the surrounding lands for ladders, campfires and battering rams, and they obviously must seek a vast amount of food, ale or mead to keep their army fed. So I would harry them from across the river and give the bastards a headache. Attack them at night, kill their foragers, attack from the landward side whenever they launch an attack on the walls.'

'Then you should lead that force,' said Ulfcytel. 'Who better to kill as many Vikings as possible than the most famous Viking killer in all England?'

'I think my days of hunting Danes and sleeping wet-arsed beneath the stars are far behind me, Ulfcytel.'

'Horseshit! I saw you fighting Forkbeard's men at Theodford. You are as strong as ever. I shall go to Lundenwic and make sure the walls hold. You take one hundred men and all our horses across the river to harry the bastards and kill as many as you can. Take Godwin with you. Teach him how to fight a war.'

'Whilst you sleep beneath wall and thatch and rest beside a warm fire?'

'Rest? I am sure you spent many nights drinking and napping beside the blazing hearths whilst Thorkell and Forkbeard hammered at the city walls. You also probably enjoyed dealing with the city's powerful inhabitants, the merchants and folk who want to complain about every decision you made? And then there's the current garrison commander, whom I trust will be delighted to relinquish his command to a king's thegn from East Anglia?'

'Very well.' Beornoth grumbled his response because Ulfcytel was right. He had the most experience in fighting the enemy in the field. He had done it his entire life. Also, commanding Lundenwic's defences did present countless problems and headaches beyond stopping the Vikings from clambering over the walls and putting the complaining inhabitants to axe and sword. 'I'll go across the river and kill as many of the bastards as I can.'

'Which is what you were born to do.'

'Lovely,' said Wigs, riding just behind the leaders alongside Gis. 'We have so much to look forward to. Nights spent sleeping in the open, rain soaking us, damp rotting our clothes, not enough food to eat, no campfires for fear of alerting the enemy, waking every morning freezing my arse off whilst a badger licks my...'

'We get the idea,' said Gis, closing his eyes to banish Wigs' overly detailed description of what awaited them.

Godwin gulped at the prospect of accompanying Beornoth on his mission to kill as many of the Danes as possible. He was fresh-faced and new to war, but Beornoth saw a cleverness in the young son of a thegn. So one hundred men went to fight a dirty war against Thorkell the Tall, his Jomsvikings and an army of five thousand marauding Norsemen, and as Beornoth spurred his horse onwards, he hoped his body had enough strength to do what must be done.

8

Beornoth's horse whickered, so he stroked her ears and shushed the beast softly. The forest's smell of damp leaves and pine cones filled Beornoth's nose as he waited, one hand resting on the pommel of his sword, chain mail heavy about his shoulders and his helmet hot above its leather liner. Shafts of light shone through the boughs like beams from heaven to light the ferns and mulch, and many of the warriors behind Beornoth whispered prayers to God to keep them safe and guide their hands.

'Are they close?' Godwin whispered, and he licked at dry lips, eyes fixed on the glade ahead.

'They're close,' Beornoth replied, 'so keep your teeth together.'

He shifted in the saddle, stomach rumbling with hunger and his back aching from riding all day, for the tenth day in a row. It had been two weeks since Thorkell the Tall had sailed his vast fleet between the Thames' wide banks, and since that day Beornoth had seen no rest. He leant to the left to relieve the pressure on his bones, leather saddle creaking beneath his bulk.

A dozen figures picked their way carefully into the clearing, men with braided beards and axes resting upon their shoulders. A flame-haired man led a donkey by the halter, and behind it rumbled a wain on two squeaking wheels, freshly cut wood piled high and shaking as the wain rumbled over the uneven ground. It was late afternoon on a balmy summer day, and so the men came in jerkins, some stripped to the waist to reveal the elaborate tattoos of ravens, wolves and dragons sprawling across their chests and backs. They had worked hard, Beornoth thought, chopping firewood all day in the heat, and now they were on their way back towards the river and Thorkell's sprawling camp with wood upon which to cook their food and keep them warm through the long night. A score of warriors appeared behind the wain, these men in hard-baked leather breastplates and armed with spears.

Ten days ago, such foraging patrols had come cheerfully, singing rowing songs in parties of six or eight. Until Beornoth had started killing them. Now, they came in larger groups with armed escorts, wary of the force waiting for them in the woodland, behind hills, or crouching behind thick river reeds, hedges and hummocks. So these men marched carefully, eyes flickering to the surrounding woods, heads full of the stories drifting back to Thorkell's camp of the corpses found hacked to ruin, of men hung from stout branches to die without a blade in their hand and denied a glorious afterlife in Valhalla.

A warrior in Beornoth's war band coughed, and Beornoth turned to reward him with a scowl that could curdle milk. He put one hand over his mouth and raised the other in apology, and Beornoth turned back to the glade as the Vikings paused, pointing and whispering to one another. They had heard the cough, and their armed escort hurried forward to form a protective circle around the woodcutters and their wagon. They were alert to the danger, and ready to fight, but it didn't matter. Beornoth would kill them anyway.

'Loose,' Beornoth said, and flexed his hands, uncurling the fingers, open and closed, preparing them for what must come next, hoping they did not betray him, that his weakened hands could maintain a firm grip on his sword. Fifty bows creaked from within the trees and brush, and fifty goose-fletched arrows sang through the branches with a sound like the wind rushing through an open window shutter. A further twenty shafts came from the opposite side of the glade, and then the arrows fell like deadly rain. Some struck harmlessly into the wild grass and soft earth with a low thud; others hit the wain and its cargo with loud bangs. One even slapped into the donkey's rump, which made the beast bray and dash off in panicked pain. But some arrows struck home, iron heads slicing into flesh and bone to make the Vikings scream and shout in panic.

A Viking screamed like a frightened child, a bare-chested woodcutter with one arrow in his stomach and another through his cheek. He flailed and howled, and his comrades just stared at him, unsure how to stop his suffering, or when death might come for them.

'Charge,' Beornoth growled, dragging his sword free of its fleece-lined scabbard so that the iron scraped against the wooden throat. He held his blade aloft, and the warriors of Wessex in his war band shouted their war cry, a loud bark to set fear alight in a man's heart, and then they erupted from the trees with war fury. Most charged on foot, for fighting on horseback is a precarious business of unbalanced striking and unpredictable mounts, even when riding a trained warhorse like Virtus or Ealdorbana. Beornoth led ten riders from the trees onto the clearing's northern edge as a handful of Vikings tried to make their escape from the Saxons, who had appeared from their front and rear in a murderous ambush. Beornoth rode to head them off, and once his riders blocked the only way out of the trap, he slid from the saddle with a groan.

'Kill them all!' he shouted to his men. 'All but one. Leave me one to tell the tale.'

His men roared their understanding, and those who had charged closed on the enemy with the fury of warriors to defend a country under attack from men who would burn, rape and pillage every home and family in their path. Thorkell's men had assaulted Lundenwic twice, and Ulfcytel's defenders had beaten them back. The Danes had sent bands roving through the lands across the Thames in search of plunder and supplies, and they had found Beornoth waiting for them with all his pitiless fury.

'Mine,' he snarled as a burly Viking ran at Beornoth's line of warriors, axe in hand, teeth bared. He came in a wild charge, hair flowing behind as he ran.

'Odin!' the Viking shouted, calling upon his god to witness his bravery, and how he charged to earn his place in the corpse hall of the glorious dead.

Beornoth strode forward, muscles bunched, right hand firm about his sword's leather-wrapped hilt. The Viking came at Beornoth at full speed, running towards a man in full armour and dressed for war like a lord of warriors. Beornoth let him come, anger flaring within him, enjoying the familiar embrace of rage warming his body, strengthening it. The Viking swung his axe low in a sweep to disembowel Beornoth, and at the last minute he flicked his wrists so that the axe head came high at Beornoth's neck. It was a simple trick, and the Viking's eyes widened in anticipation of the blood to come, of a last triumph to carry with him to the afterlife. But Beornoth was no inexperienced warrior wet behind the ears, no fyrd man new to the ways of war. He had seen the blow coming as the Viking's wrists shifted about the haft of his axe and so Beornoth brought his sword blade up, holding it in front of him in two hands, edge in front of his eyes, and he met the axe square on, blade against the axe's wooden haft to protect the edge of his weapon.

The Viking grunted as his axe thudded into Beornoth's sword. He met the Saxon's implacable strength at a full run, with momentum behind him and violence in his soul. But he was a head shorter than Beornoth, slighter, and as their weapons crashed together the Viking stumbled backwards. He fell to one knee, surprise at his opponent's strength etched on his wind-burned face. The axe fell, and the Viking scrambled to pick it up. Beornoth stepped forward, lowered his sword and reached to the small of his back. He whipped the antler-hilted seax free from its sheath, and just as the Viking gripped his weapon and began to rise, Beornoth slammed his seax into the side of his skull. The Viking quivered like a landed fish, a length of steel as long as a man's forearm punched through skull and brain to burst out of the other side. Beornoth kicked him down, pressed one boot onto the man's dying throat and yanked his seax free in a spray of dark, iron-stinking blood.

'Kill the bastards,' he ordered his men, and so they did.

Since he had fought the Danes as a youth in the badlands of the north-western Danelaw, Beornoth had learned to treat them with the same brutality they brought to war. Beornoth lifted his seax, gore dripping from its broken-backed blade, and his men loped towards the fight imbued with courage, stepping over the dead Viking and his terrible wound. Beornoth marched with them, his pace slower, breathing heavier. The younger men hurried to the fight, carrying their shields and with their spears levelled. Wigs and Gis had led the charge from the far side of the glade, and their warriors tore into the Vikings with a crash.

Beornoth's men encircled the Viking warriors, just as Beornoth had taught them, and closed in for the kill. Young Godwin stood in the front line with his countrymen, shield and spear stout, and Beornoth frowned as the circle became ragged, men fell out of line to hurry towards the kill. They broke ranks, too eager to punish their hated enemy, and a Viking burst through their shields. He banged his shoulder into a shield and twisted through the gap. As he went, he spun and struck his axe blade across a Wessex man's skull with an audible crack. He stumbled, righted himself and lurched into a run, but instead of open grass and a sprint to freedom, he found Beornoth instead.

The Viking reared, axe in one hand and knife in the other.

'I am Kjartan Gormsson,' he said in Norse, proud of his name, bristling with the arrogance of a professional warrior. He wore a battered leather breastplate. He wore his hair in two long plaits and leg wrappings about his calves. His wrists jangled with warrior's arm rings, and he set himself to fight.

Beornoth flicked his sword at Kjartan's face, and the Viking danced backwards away from the blow. He smiled, and then launched an attack of his own, axe and knife coming one high and one low. Beornoth parried the axe with his sword and leaned away from the knife thrust. His comrades died behind him in a welter of spears and Saxon hatred, but Kjartan never took his ice-blue eyes off Beornoth's own. He came on again, and Beornoth shuffled backwards, feigning slowness, hoping that his foe saw his grey beard and came on recklessly to take advantage. Kjartan darted in, ducking low and sweeping upwards with his knife to cut at Beornoth's groin. But instead of an old, slow warrior, he found a wall of war-hardened muscle and a body calloused and made granite-hard by a lifetime of combat.

Kjartan's knife cut at thin air and Beornoth brought his knee up, smashing it into the Viking's face. He rocked backwards and Beornoth stabbed his seax into Kjartan's shoulder. He stepped backwards, grimacing at the pain, staring in disbelief into Beornoth's eyes.

'How many Saxons have you killed?' Beornoth asked him in Norse. 'How many women have you taken, how many children burned?'

Kjartan shook his head, blood seeping down his breastplate. He sagged to one side and dropped his knife to clasp one hand to his ruined shoulder. His breath became ragged and wheezy even above the din behind him. He let out a guttural roar and came on, axe swinging, desperation etched on his face. Beornoth sidestepped the wild attack and brought his sword down hard, back-cutting across Kjartan's hamstrings. He fell forward and scrambled from his back to his front, axe clutched to his chest, sensing death was close and desperate to die with his blade in his hand.

'Godwin,' Beornoth called. A moment later the young Wessex man appeared, his face sweaty. 'Did you kill anyone today?'

'No, lord,' he said, eyes flitting to his un-bloodied spear blade. His shield bore scratches and dents from battle. The lad was brave enough, but killing changed a man, and no leader of men could shirk from its horror.

'Then kill that bastard.' Beornoth pointed his sword at Kjartan Gormsson, who coughed and winced at the pain of Beornoth's seax still embedded in his shoulder. The fight around the timber wain dwindled. Beornoth's larger force had easily dispatched the Vikings. Some men now stopped and stared at Beornoth and Godwin, and the young Wessex man's face flushed red. 'His name is Kjartan, and he came across the sea on a drakkar warship to take everything from you. He'd kill your mother, enslave your sisters and butcher your father, burn your home and steal your silver. He'd do that and laugh about it, boasting of his bravery with his shipmates as he supped your stolen mead. To be a warrior, you must kill, so kill him now and blood your spear.'

'But, lord, I...'

'Do it now!' Beornoth shouted, startling Godwin.

Godwin swallowed hard and stepped forward. He held his breath as Kjartan grimaced and clutched his axe close. The Viking did not beg nor cry for his life. He set his jaw and prepared for what must be done. Godwin grimaced and rammed his spear forward. The first blow glanced off Kjartan's jaw, opening a gash from mouth to ear. Kjartan shook, arms folded about his axe, eyes clenched closed.

'Do it clean,' Beornoth said, his voice hard, 'and do it quick.'

Godwin brought his spear back and thrust again. This time the point rammed into Kjartan's gullet, gouging deeper into a pool of welling blood.

'God have mercy on him,' Godwin said as he pulled his spear free, the tip now bright with Viking blood.

'He had no mercy for any Saxon souls, so let the bastard die.'

Beornoth bent and yanked his seax out of Kjartan's dying body. He wiped the filth on Kjartan's sleeve and then slid the weapon back into its sheath. Beornoth placed his hand on Godwin's shoulder. Looking into those shocked blue eyes, he remembered Ealdorman Alfgar when he was of a similar age, afraid, callow, but determined enough to become what he must. Alfgar's father had entrusted his war education to Beornoth, and so he had learned how to fight and how to kill, and became a man prepared to do battle with the warriors from across the sea.

'It's hard to kill a man,' Beornoth said, softly this time. 'And so it should be. His face will haunt your dreams, his fetch will call to you from their afterlife, and you will never forget this moment. But steel yourself to it. When your father is gone, you have the right to his heriot and can petition the king to take over his mantle as a thegn of Wessex. We thegns must be ready to fight and to die for our people. That is our position. We have land and weapons, and men bow when we pass. The churls on our land pay us one tenth of everything they produce as our rightful render, and for that we must protect them. So do not look away from this dead Viking and do not flinch from the blood. Get used to it and be ready to kill them before they kill you. You are brave, lad, and now you know what it means to take a life.'

'Yes, lord, thank you, lord.'

Beornoth turned to his men. 'Are all the bastards dead?'

'All but this man,' said Gis, his spear pointing at a kneeling Viking with a bloody nose and a terrified expression tugging at his features.

Beornoth marched over the kneeling man and spoke to him in Norse. 'I am Beornoth Reiði. Tell Thorkell who kills his men. Tell him I wait for him here, across the river, if he has the courage to come and face me.' The Viking nodded his understanding and cast a belligerent look towards Beornoth, lip curled and defiant despite his war band lying dead around him. Beornoth sheathed his sword, turned his back, then paused and looked at Wigs. 'Let him go but first put out his eyes and cut off his right hand.'

The Viking's bravery melted away and was replaced by wild screams as the Saxons heated a blade and pressed its red-hot tip into his eyeballs. They cut off his right hand, sealed the wound with the fiery knife and sent him stumbling into the trees towards Lundenwic. Beornoth took no pleasure in such grim deeds, but the Vikings must learn to fear.

'Leave the corpses, take what wood we need from their wain and then burn it,' Beornoth ordered.

They marched away from the ambush, leaving thirty-one Viking corpses in a sun-washed clearing. Beornoth's men stripped the enemy of their weapons and anything of value and left them lying beside their burning wain. Beornoth rode away from the crackling fire and swirling smoke column as it twisted away into the pale sky to notify Thorkell the Tall of what had become of his foraging party. He imagined the wounded Dane limping to the Thames and men bringing the blinded cripple before Thorkell. Maybe, Beornoth wondered, the great Viking war leader might feel a twinge of fear at the thought of his old enemy. Certainly, Beornoth hoped, Thorkell would send a larger force into the countryside across the river from Lundenwic in search of the Saxon war band who had killed so many of his men. That took warriors away from the attack on the city walls and gave Thorkell a problem to distract him from his assault.

Beornoth's war band returned to their camp, set deep within the sprawling forest which stretched north beyond Lundenwic's walls. They moved camp every third night to keep them safe from any Viking trackers who might follow their trail. They had made a waist-high fence of briar and brush, which would provide some small protection for their temporary quarters, and slept beneath crude huts roofed with cloth and kept dry with layers of branches, bracken, sods and leaves. Wigs and Gis helped Beornoth out of his chain-mail coat, and he felt like a boulder was lifted from his shoulders as he slumped down to rest on an upturned log. He took a drink of ale and sat in silence as Gis made a campfire and Wigs prepared a meal of hard bread and dried beef.

'Another fine ambush today, lord,' said Wigs to lighten the mood. The rest of the camp was buoyed up as men cheerfully set about their evening meals, encouraged by their victory over the Danes, but Beornoth could not lift his sombre air. He grunted agreement and Wigs continued with his work.

The small skirmish had left Beornoth exhausted. In the heat of battle, he had felt as strong as ever, slower and more cautious perhaps, but capable of hefting his sword and shield to defeat his enemies. But that strength was fleeting, and even the brief fight with Kjartan had left him exhausted. Greater battles loomed, the reckoning that must come when Thorkell sent a larger force into the woodlands, and Beornoth feared how his body would hold up when he had to stand in the shield wall and trade blows with Thorkell's champions. He stared at the dancing flames, small, kissing the kindling as Gis bent and blew beneath the twigs to help the fire grow. He knew all too well the consequences if a warrior let his shield drop in the terrible crucible of battle. A warrior's shield protected not only his own body but also the unprotected sword and spear arm of the man to his left, and to let it fall left that man vulnerable to an enemy axe or spear. If two men fell when that shield gave way, it compromised the shield wall and gave the enemy a gap to charge into and carve Beornoth's battle line in two. Beornoth stared at his shaking hands. He closed his eyes and prayed silently. He asked God to let his strength hold, to grant his old body the power it needed to cast Thorkell and his horde out of the Thames and back out onto the Whale Road.

'Someone approaches, lord,' said Godwin, dashing across the camp.

'Friend or foe?' asked Gis.

'It's Osgar, lord. Come from Ulfcytel with news of the war. He has men with him, men from Northumbria.'

9

Beornoth reached the edge of camp and found Osgar talking to a handful of Wessex men, his monstrous long-handled war axe resting on one shoulder, his usual dour look making the hard slab of his face even harsher. Behind Osgar waited a large force of newly arrived warriors stretching back into the deep woodland, each man well-armed in leather, some with patches of mail on their chests and shoulders, and all armed with shields and stout spears.

'Osgar,' Beornoth called in greeting. 'You missed a fight today.'

'I have seen nothing but fighting since last we met, Lord Beornoth,' he replied, with cuts and bruises on his face and hands as proof of his hardship. 'Men came south from Northumbria to answer King Æthelred's call. They say they know you, so Lord Ulfcytel asked me to bring them to join your force.'

'Fine lodgings you have here, Beo,' said a short man with long moustaches and a thick neck.

'I left my hearth and hall for this,' said another, a well-built man in a shining byrnie and long straw-coloured hair tied at the nape of his neck. 'I hope you at least have meat and cheese.'

'Sigeferth and Morcar,' Beornoth said, and shook both men's forearms in the warrior's grip. 'I had not expected men to come from the Danelaw.'

'Ealdorman Thered received the king's summons and thought it best to send some northern blades south so that you soft southerners don't lose the war,' said Morcar, the smaller man.

'How many men march with you?'

'Two hundred spearmen,' said Sigeferth. 'Men from our own lands in the five boroughs of Northumbria. Good men.'

'Not all the warriors of Northumbria, then?' Beornoth replied.

'The men of Northumbria must protect their own lands, and those lands are far from Winchester and Lundenwic.'

'Aye, and half of Northumbria probably has kin still in Denmark and Norway.'

'We are here, and we've come to fight. Is there any ale in this godforsaken place?'

The men of Wessex welcomed the Northumbrian warriors to their camp, and shared food and ale with the warriors who had marched the length of the country to join King Æthelred's fight against Thorkell the Tall. After making sure the two Northumbrian thegns found huts to sleep in and hay for their horses, Beornoth met Osgar, Wigs and Gis to share a skin of ale.

'How did you find our camp?' Beornoth asked, waving the warrior down after Osgar attempted to rise from where he sat upon a log to greet him. 'We had thought it a secret until you arrived with two hundred men.'

'Ulfcytel sent me to look for you, lord. So I left the city through the eastern gate and crossed the marshes north-east of the river where the Danes do not patrol. I saw the smoke and marched towards it.'

'What if the smoke was a Viking raid?' asked Gis.

Osgar shrugged. 'I thought either Lord Beornoth was burning Viking supplies, or the Vikings had raided a village and Beornoth would be there to punish them.'

'Fair enough,' said Wigs, nodding appreciatively at Osgar's simple logic.

'Why has Thered sent men from Northumbria now?' Osgar asked.

'He sends a small force so Streona cannot say the ealdorman of Northumbria failed to heed the king's call when this is all over,' Beornoth replied.

'Men fear Eadric Streona,' Osgar said.

'Do you fear him?'

Osgar thought about that for a moment whilst he chewed slowly on a piece of bread. 'No,' he said eventually.

'Then why do other men?'

Osgar shrugged, and so Beornoth waved his hand to encourage him to speak more openly. Wigs laughed, and Beornoth, a man of few words himself, understood the irony.

'Powerful men fear Streona,' Osgar said. 'He does not bother with men like me, a simple war thegn with only a small landholding. Thered is an ealdorman, Sigeferth and Morcar hold vast lands in south Northumbria, touching on Eadric's Mercia. They should fear him. He can crush a man and see him dead with words alone.'

'You do not fear those words?'

'No, lord.'

'Why not?'

Osgar frowned at Beornoth, as though it were a question even a fool would know the answer to. 'If he crossed me, I would kill him.'

'Yes, I suppose you would.' Beornoth took a piece of bread of his own and saw something of himself in the brutal East Anglian warrior. Beornoth had seen things in simpler terms as a younger man, but now the world grew more complicated. Kingdoms were at stake, as were the lives of the folk who farmed and lived in the valleys and dales of England and depended on its warlords to defend them from those who would turn their existence upside down with fire and sword.

'There is news of Brihtric and Eadric. Is Wulfnoth's son still with you?'

'I'll fetch him,' said Wigs. 'Though I hope the news of his father isn't bleak.'

'He should hear it, bleak or no.'

'Fair enough.' Wigs hopped up and hurried into the tangle of small fires and groups of warriors to find Godwin.

'You have news, Lord Osgar?' Godwin said, arriving only a few moments later.

'Aye. Your father drew Brihtric and Eadric into a cat-and-mouse pursuit across the south coast. He even raided a few towns and took their silver.'

'To recover the money left unpaid after Streona's broken promises.'

Osgar stared at him for a moment, his flat forehead and stark cheekbones eerily still as though he did not care about Godwin's reasoning. 'Brihtric and Eadric used their larger fleet to surround Wulfnoth, but a storm ran their ships ashore, smashing them on sand dunes and cliffs. Wulfnoth closed in and attacked them. He burned Brihtric and Eadric's fleet and sailed away in his twenty ships.'

'So, my father lives?'

'He lives. Streona and his brother march to Winchester with their remaining men. A messenger came to us with the news yesterday.'

'The fleet is gone?' asked Gis.

'Gone.'

'What a jape our leaders are,' said Wigs. 'Only we Saxons could build a vast fleet to challenge the Vikings, argue over nothing, and then burn it ourselves in a spat over an insult.'

'Bloody Brihtric knows less than a turnip about sailing.'

'You can go to Wessex, if you wish,' Beornoth said to Godwin.

Godwin thought about that for a moment, his clever blue eyes narrowing in the evening firelight. 'My place is here, with you. My father will protect my family. I must prepare for what happens next.'

'Then get some rest, for tomorrow we'll go after the Vikings again.'

Godwin paused for a moment, staring glassy-eyed at Beornoth, and then down at his hands.

'It's alright, lad,' Beornoth said. 'You killed your first man today. It will stay with you forever. No one here will judge you for the sleepless night awaiting you, or the regret. But it had to be done. This is how we protect our people.'

Godwin nodded and turned away, shoulders slumped, to be alone with the ghost of the man he had killed.

'Smarter than a bishop stashing his silver hoard, that one,' said Wigs, 'with more cunning than a nest of weasels.'

Beornoth watched Godwin retreat into the camp. 'He's no fool.'

'Because he fights with us?' asked Osgar, brows knitted together in puzzlement.

'Because he thinks beyond today,' said Gis. 'Our young master there wonders what will happen to him when his father is dead, for dead he shall surely be after making an enemy of Streona and humiliating him with the destruction of his fleet. When the king confiscates Wulfnoth's lands in Wessex, the son may have cause to petition for forgiveness and return of those lands. Godwin can make his case to the king if he fights with us and proves himself a loyal subject rather than running away with his father and family.'

Osgar stared off into the distance and ate a piece of dried beef.

'He's not listening,' said Wigs.

'Was I not clear?'

'Clear, just boring. Like listening to a priest at mass. I nearly fell asleep twice whilst you droned on.'

'A pox on you, bastard.'

Wigs laughed, and Beornoth left them to their endless banter. He shifted seats to sit on a log beside Osgar.

'What news of Lundenwic's defence?' he asked.

'The walls hold, lord. The Danes attacked with ladders and twice tried the bridge gates. Just as you said.'

'Where are they now?'

'Their ships mass in the widest part of the river, lord. Ulfcytel believes Thorkell will throw everything at the walls tomorrow, or soon after. We should keep harrying them from this side of the river.'

'Can Ulfcytel hold the city?'

'He must.'

Beornoth clenched his jaw at the thought of the blood and struggle about to take place upon those high Roman walls. He had been there. Beornoth had seen men die as Vikings made the incredible, daring climb up rickety timber ladders. He had stood firm as they launched arrows, spears, fire, axes and whatever they could dream of up and over the ramparts to keep the defenders back from the edges so that the bravest men could gain a foothold and hack and chop at the Saxons with their sharp axes. Beornoth closed his eyes and recalled himself and Pallig splashed in blood, treading in gore as they strove to the edge of their sanity and strength, beating back the Vikings for days on end until brave men wept, crouched in alcoves, and young, untested boys fought like champions to defend a scrap of grey, cold wall with their lives.

He lay down beneath his cloak, listening to the trees creak and groan in the chill night breeze. The kingdom struggled under the weight of invasion and ate itself from within like a gnawing tumour killing it slowly. Beornoth twisted and turned on his rough bed of straw. His mind worried about his ability to fight and maintain his strength, then shifted to concern about Eadric Streona's increasing control and influence over the king. Then his thoughts pondered how to help Ulfcytel keep Thorkell from breaching the city's defences. It was a long night of stinging eyes, restless shifting, standing to stretch his aching back and shoulders, of strange thoughts, plans he dreamt up and then dismissed. Amidst the sweating, and in the deep of night, other more torturous thoughts came to plague him. Beornoth's mind told him he was a fool, an old man clinging to former glories. Were his men laughing at him behind his back as he flailed about with his sword like a mind-addled grandfather? Should he leave the fight and return home to die beside Eawynn's grave?

Morning came in a sliver of wan light above the trees, and Beornoth washed himself in a babbling brook winding its way around the roots and burrows of the deep forest. The cold water swilled the sleepless sting from his eyes and the grease of a night spent lost in his mind from his body. Beornoth dressed himself, the familiar weight of leather and iron bringing confidence and returning belief in what he was. A warrior.

They struck camp at first light, and Beornoth led three hundred men towards the Thames to harry the enemy. They marched south, following the steep banks of a tributary river flowing through the forest and out onto the meadows and pastures to the city's north-east, butting on to the swampy marshes and soft ground to the east where the great river became broader, shallower and much more tidal with vast grey slick silt banks at low tide. Beornoth heard the Vikings before he saw their ships. Drums beat in the distance, a constant, undulating thrum of deep war music, reverberating through Beornoth's bones. Great, shrill blasts from Viking war horns interspersed the thudding drumbeats with long, sonorous wails like beasts from the depths.

'What are they doing?' asked Godwin, cantering his mount until he came alongside Beornoth.

'Thorkell readies his men for war,' Beornoth replied. 'It takes courage beyond the understanding of normal men to stand in a shield wall. When bards sing of great battles, it can seem as though both armies line up and hurl themselves at one another in a glorious charge. The truth is that it can take all day for men to summon the courage to march into a wall of blades and shields where they know many will die and more will suffer painful wounds. Thorkell's men must climb the city walls, where Ulfcytel's warriors wait to hurl rocks and loose arrows at them, and for the brave few who reach the summit, they will find axes and spears there to greet them. So the war music stirs their hearts and drives them to do the impossible.'

'You have fought Thorkell?'

'I have.'

'Was he fearsome?'

'He was very brave.' Beornoth's shoulders shuddered at the memory of fighting the Viking monster.

'Are the Jomsvikings more fearsome than Forkbeard's Vikings?'

'I once killed their leader Palnatoki, he who was as a father to Olaf Trygvasson, king of Norway before Forkbeard slew him at the battle of Svolder. The Jomsvikings are a band of warriors for hire, and their home is an island fortress at a place in the far north called Jomsburg. They live for battle, permitting only the stoutest warriors to join their ranks. They allow no women inside their fortress, and men fear them for their skill and ferocity.'

'Can we beat them?'

'We've beaten them before, lad.'

The river appeared through a clearing where the tributary river poured into the Thames' vast brown waters. The drums grew deeper and the horn blasts louder, sweeping along the riverbank to make the very earth shake. Beornoth clicked his tongue and urged his horse out of the trees and onto a patch of grass above the riverbank. The Thames swept about in a wide loop around Lundenwic, and its walls loomed high and foreboding, grey, ancient and strong. Banners of East Anglia and Wessex flew from the summit, flapping in the morning wind, and sunlight glinted off the helmets and spear points of Ulfcytel's defenders.

'So many ships,' Godwin gasped, for Thorkell's fleet thronged the waters, countless ships rowing under oar, their hulls curved like a woman's hip and their beast heads snarling at the city like demons from hell. Godwin stared at the horde, mouth open and eyes watering as the wind and the sheer vastness of Thorkell's army took his breath away.

'Scouts return, lord,' said Wigs, pointing back to the trees where a warrior on a smoke-grey pony leapt from the saddle.

'What news?' Beornoth called to the rider.

'They attack the city on three sides, lord,' he said. 'They have crews on the banks carrying wood to make more ladders.'

'Show me.'

The scout leapt onto a fresh mount and cantered along the riverbank. Beornoth led his hundred mounted men behind him and left Osgar with orders to bring the rest of the war band on foot. Beornoth's horse threw up clumps of soil from its hooves, weaving along the bank, around trees, leaping over patches of rushes, and he kept his eyes fixed on the ships to his right. So many drakkars, enough to cast a kingdom asunder. Five thousand warriors had come across the North Sea like a plague, and from the ramparts, Ulfcytel's men loosed a wave of arrows. They flew downwards from the walls like a murder of crows swooping, but so few, so insignificant compared to Thorkell's vast fleet.

The drums boomed, and the horns sang. Beornoth's heart raced, and he led his riders onwards until he came to a low spit of land, a finger pointing out into the river and topped with deep green grass. A drakkar sat there, moored against the island, its warriors ashore, and Beornoth saw a chance to strike at Thorkell's army. Warriors walked to and from the warship carrying freshly cut tree trunks split into golden lengths for building more ladders to bring against Lundenwic's walls. For every ten ladders reaching the ramparts, Ulfcytel's men would throw five back into the river, and so if Thorkell's assault was to work he must overwhelm the defenders by casting yet more ladders against the walls or building a ram strong enough to smash open one of the bridge gates spanning the wide length of the river-facing walls.

'Spears,' Beornoth shouted to his men, 'then wheel and dismount to attack.'

His men understood the order, and had executed it a dozen times since their hit-and-run campaign against the Vikings had begun. Beornoth reached out, and Wigs leant forward from his mount and handed Beornoth his spear. The riders cantered towards the spit of land, and the Danes stopped their work and turned to look, alerted by the rumble of hoofbeats. The thunderous noise of one hundred horses so close drowned out even Thorkell's war drums and the shouts and cries of the unfolding battle further along the river. Beornoth led the riding column closer, waiting until they came within throwing distance before unleashing their barrage.

'Shield wall!' came the shout in Norse from the Viking shipmaster. His men dropped their logs and tried to run back to the grassy finger where their spears and shields lay in stacked piles ready for them to collect in case of an emergency. But it was too late; the emergency was already upon them. The shipmaster berated his men, pushing and urging them to hurry and arm themselves before the Saxons attacked. He was a long-faced man with greasy hair the colour of summer straw hanging in filthy lanks about his shoulders and a beard braided and tied with scraps of black cloth.

'On me!' Beornoth called to his men. He pulled on the reins and pressed his heel into the horse's flank. The horse veered, and as it turned, Beornoth flung his spear. The shaft flew in a low, flat arc and slammed into the back of a Viking who had turned to run. He fell, sprawling onto the grass with Beornoth's ash-shafted spear and its iron head between his shoulder blades. Beornoth saw no more of his men's spears, for he had brought his horse about in a circle and rode her twenty paces away from the Viking raiders. He slid from the saddle, almost losing his footing as he stood on the grass and the horse shifted away from him. He righted himself, pulled his helmet free from the saddle and pressed it down onto his head so that the metal of the boar-shaped nasal felt cold against his nose. Beornoth closed the cheekpieces, enclosing his skull in iron so that all the enemy would see of his face were two eyes staring at them from the darkness. The black horsehair plume flowed behind him, and he drew his sword with his right hand and grabbed his shield with his left.

More of his riders followed, and the Vikings shouted in alarm as one hundred spears threw the crew into panic. A score or more of the enemy lay dead or dying, and their shipmaster in his battered and torn byrnie roared at his men to bring their shields and spears to bear. Beornoth paused so that his riders could catch up and form a wall of attack. This would be no shield wall, no organised battle lines where his hundred would fight the Viking crew. It would be a slaughter, and Beornoth had surprise on his side. He strode forward, weapons in hand, and his men hurried to form loose ranks around him.

'Boar's snout,' he barked, ordering them into a spearhead formation, just like a boar's vicious nose, with Beornoth at its apex. The aim was to punch through any organised line the Vikings could cobble together in the time it took the Saxons to march towards their ship. Warriors ran into position around him, and Beornoth readied himself for battle. His breath came in a tinny echo from within his helmet, and he kept his eyes fixed on the enemy. The shipmaster placed himself at the centre, positioned between the Saxons and his precious ship.

Beornoth flexed his fingers around the wooden grip of his shield. The grip spanned the bowl behind the iron boss, and a leather strap, which ran across his forearm, made the shield more secure. It felt heavy, strong and familiar, and it must be strong because the Vikings raced to grab their spears, and all carried axes at their belts. Those weapons would batter at Beornoth as he charged them at the head of his hundred, slicing into them like an arrowhead to smash their force in two before his men turned and slaughtered them.

The Viking shipmaster glanced over his shoulder and then smiled at

Beornoth. He lifted his axe and called to Odin, and then Beornoth cursed under his breath because another Viking drakkar slid through the river water like a serpent, and grim-faced men with axes, spears and bright helmets glowered at Beornoth from its deck. He had raced to the fight with his horsemen to face a disorganised band of Viking foragers, and now another crew joined the fight, sixty men waiting to leap from their dragon ship to help their comrades slaughter Beornoth and his men. What had been a chance to kill the enemy and strike another blow against Thorkell had turned into a nightmare, but it was too late now. Beornoth's only option was to attack.

10

Beornoth led his men forward, slowly at first, cautiously marching with his shield braced before his left shoulder and his sword resting on its rim. He waited until he could feel Wigs' and Gis' shields pressing against his back, until the boar's snout formed tight and impenetrable. Then he picked up the pace. Boots stomped on the riverbank, Beornoth's men grunted with every step, their leather armour creaked and on the grassy spit of land the Vikings hollered at the new ship to hurry. Across the river, the attack on Lundenwic grew in ferocity. Five thousand Danes and Norsemen bellowed their war cries at the walls, and Ulfcytel rained down blocks of stone, spears and arrows from above. Ladders lifted slowly from Thorkell the Tall's ships, rising like a forest to rest against the cold stone.

'No mercy!' Beornoth called to his men. Ten paces away from the enemy, then eight. His breath had already become ragged. Hard to breathe inside the closed cheekpieces of his helmet, hot, strength sapping. His shield was heavy, and his shoulder screamed at him to let it fall. His thighs burned with the effort of moving so fast, but still he must press on. Five paces and he could see blue and brown eyes staring back at him as more Vikings rallied around their shipmaster. The new ship rose behind the disorderly enemy lines, its hull becoming huge, its prow beast painted and snarling. Three paces and Beornoth held his breath and tensed his body for impact, axes and shields waiting to hack into his skull, chest, heart and lungs and smash his body to bloody ruin.

Beornoth was the first of his force to crash into the enemy shield wall. His monstrous size and the momentum of his charge smashed two men out of his way. The impact thumped into his shield, and his shoulder drove it forward. He kept moving, not using his sword yet, pushing himself onwards. An axe swung at him, but the timing was off, and the haft struck his shoulder. A Viking then stabbed at him with a spear, which only scraped along Beornoth's shield and then across his chain mail. The shipmaster reared up before him, screaming like a demon with his axe raised to smash into Beornoth's forehead, but he stared into the depths of Beornoth's helmet and saw only darkness there, the eyes of a killer staring back at him, and at the last moment he tried to turn and run but Beornoth smashed him to the ground with his shield.

Three more steps and he was through them, stumbling onto the long spit of grass as all opposition disappeared. Beornoth sucked in a huge gulp of air, sweat streaming down his face, and then reeled as the new warship loomed up before him. Sixty men shouted and spat hate over the bows. Big men in armour and armed with sharp blades, they were still too far from land to leap from their deck and join the fight, and so Beornoth raised his sword to taunt them. They howled like dogs, and Beornoth turned, sword ready, as his men had already begun the slaughter.

Wigs ran an enemy through with his spear, and Gis caught an axe low on his shield and tripped his attacker with his axe stave and then stabbed down into his throat. Godwin stabbed at the enemy with his weapon, its iron tip already stained crimson with enemy blood. Beornoth's men had smashed the woodcutting warriors into disarray in moments. The brutal boar-snout charge had destroyed the Vikings' morale and stolen their will to fight, but it was too late for them to run. A dozen of them leapt into the Thames to save themselves and waded towards the oncoming ship, but that huge drakkar was under oars and with one more great stroke she reached the spit, her hull crashing into the souls in the water who sank beneath her curved, clinker-built timbers to drown in the murky waters.

'Bastard!' screamed the greasy-haired shipmaster. A Saxon warrior lay dead at his feet, blood spattered his armour, and he came to kill Beornoth with hate in his pale eyes. Many had tried before, but even now, Beornoth was a hard man to kill. The axe came in a wild swing, and Beornoth smashed it away with his shield. The shipmaster turned, caught off balance as his axe swung wide, and Beornoth stabbed his sword into the man's ribs, twisting the blade as it broke bone and slid into soft flesh and vital organs. The shipmaster gasped and reared like a leaping trout. Beornoth withdrew his blade and kicked the shipmaster into the water so that his body disappeared beneath the oncoming warship.

'Back!' Beornoth ordered. 'Form shield wall on me.'

He hurried away from the finger of land and back to the riverbank, chest burning with fatigue and legs as heavy as Roman columns. Beornoth turned and readied his shield as his men formed up around him.

'In it up to our bloody necks again,' said Wigs as his shield overlapped Beornoth's.

'Hold fast,' Beornoth replied.

Sixty men leapt from the warship, creeping over its sheer strake like demons from the underworld. Men in helmets, axes in their fists, armour scored by blades and arms strengthened by a lifetime at the oar.

'For Odin and Valhalla,' said their leader, and he banged his axe against his shield boss with a loud ring. He wore a helmet crested with raven feathers and a thick gold torc about his neck above a chain-mail byrnie. 'Spears,' he growled, and his men hefted their long weapons and formed up in two ranks.

'Brace yourselves,' said Beornoth, and no sooner had the words escaped his lips than sixty spears hurtled across the narrow space with vicious force. One spear smashed into Beornoth's shield, and its force was like being kicked by a stallion.

The Vikings stepped across the corpses of their slaughtered comrades and approached in organised, practised ranks. Their leader pulled a horn from his belt and blew three sharp notes. He removed the horn and offered Beornoth an evil smile and then pointed his axe at Beornoth in challenge. The Vikings held, and Beornoth fought the agonising desire to drop his shield and rest his throbbing shoulders.

'Why don't they attack?' asked Gis, shifting his own shield uncomfortably.

'They are waiting for something,' Wigs replied.

Beornoth searched the riverbank. Wigs was right. The Viking Jarl waited for something, for someone, for more men he knew were coming to join the fight.

'Lord!' Godwin called, and Beornoth followed where his spear pointed, and his heart sank to see another crew running from the woodland to the east, more Vikings, three score at least.

'We are outnumbered,' said a warrior further along Beornoth's shield wall.

'Hold,' Beornoth growled, his force outmatched, and beyond this skirmish on the riverbank Ulfcytel's war raged. More ships reached the walls, ladders rose and Vikings made the treacherous climb. The defenders cheered every time they thrust a ladder away from the ramparts to send Vikings falling with flailing arms through the air to splash into the deep waters, or crunch with murderous force into their ships.

The new enemy added their ranks to the ship's crew, joining their force so that Beornoth's men now faced one hundred and twenty warriors. He had come to the riverbank to harry Thorkell's forces, to distract them and keep Viking spears from the city walls. He had killed one crew and now faced more. Three crews that would not raise ladders against Ulfcytel's defenders.

'Let them come,' he said to his men, and he shook his head to banish the weak desire to rest. Beornoth braced his shield again and readied his sword. This was the life of a king's thegn. War, suffering, risking his own life to protect his people in service of the crown. He was ready to fight, and ready to die. His men were warriors, men of Wessex who understood the risks of a warrior's life.

The Viking jarl led his men forward. He placed himself at the centre of their shield wall, directly opposite Beornoth, and ever since he had blown his war horn that wicked smile had not left his lips. They came on as Beornoth expected they would, in perfect time, shields level, professional warriors trained and ready to kill. Beornoth shifted his feet for the charge he knew would come when the shield wall closed in, for the crash and crunch as shields came together, and for the screams and howls as blades found gaps in wood, iron and leather.

'Loose!' came a shout from Beornoth's flank. He tensed for a heartbeat, half expecting a barrage of enemy arrows to thump into his men. But the voice had been Saxon, a hard, unflinching voice. Osgar's voice. With an echoing twang, bows released from the west of Beornoth's line, and then a deadly hail of arrows whipped across the riverbank and slammed into the enemy with sickening force. Arrowheads tonked off shield bosses and helmets as others flew wide and into the water, but more found shoulders, thighs, eyes, arms, necks and the Viking approach faltered.

'Charge,' Beornoth snarled, opportunity and battle-luck rearing its head for him to take advantage. 'Kill the bastards.'

Beornoth's men roared, and the Saxon shield wall charged. He led them, and one hundred shields smashed into a Viking line reeling from arrow strikes. The smile fled from the Viking jarl to leave a face and lips quivering with sudden, desperate fear. Osgar led the Northumbrians and the rest of the unmounted men of Wessex in a wild charge from the enemy flank, and the Vikings, who had thought to have found themselves a slaughter beside the Thames River, instead faced a fight for their lives.

Beornoth made for the jarl, closing the space, his men tight around him, locked together, ready to kill, ready to die. The jarl ducked suddenly, crouching behind his shield, and Beornoth smashed into it at full force. The Saxons hammered into an enemy standing still, rocked by Osgar's arrow barrage, and Beornoth's men smashed them backwards, paused, and then used that space to strike at the enemy. Beornoth stabbed at the Jarl, but his sword punched into his opponent's shield with a bang. The Vikings closed the space, recovering, using their experience to reform and present a solid wall once more.

'Nithing!' the jarl shouted. 'Stinking Saxon whoreson!' He shoved at Beornoth out of sight, crouched behind his shield, strong, young and fearsome. Osgar's men hurled themselves at the enemy line to Beornoth's left, out of sight, but Beornoth heard their cries and the Vikings struggling to hold the attack on their flank.

Beornoth stabbed with his sword again, and the blade scraped across the jarl's shield rim. His men stabbed and were cut at in return. Beornoth adjusted his stance and raked his boot down the jarl's instep. The Viking shouted in anger and stood on one leg to relieve the pain. Beornoth banged him with his shield and stabbed again. The jarl caught the blow on his shield again, and his axe came low, the flat top of its blade hammering into Beornoth's stomach and the wind flew out of his body. He creased and took a backward step. The jarl crowed his victory and emerged from behind his shield, eyes blazing, axe rising to strike the killing blow. Then he died. Godwin's spear lanced over Beornoth's shoulder and punched into the jarl's mouth, slicing lips, breaking teeth and ruining his evil smile forever. The jarl stiffened and then slumped, and a great wail went up from his men, who crumbled as their lord died.

Beornoth stamped on the dying jarl's face and turned to give Godwin an appreciative nod. Godwin recovered into his shield wall position, ready to strike again. The Vikings in front of Beornoth folded, scrambling for their ship, and Osgar appeared in that space wielding his huge double-bladed war axe with wild ferocity. He cut the head from an enemy's shoulders, kept on moving, axe scything, lopped off a leg, battered a shield into splinters and behind him came Sigeferth and Morcar. The Northumbrians rolled up the enemy line, massing on the spit of land between the Vikings and their ship. Beornoth let his shield drop and waited as his men surged past him to complete the slaughter.

'Are you injured, lord?' asked Gis.

Beornoth had fallen to one knee, and Gis crouched beside him, worry etched on his face as the fight raged before them.

'No,' Beornoth replied, hands shaking uncontrollably.

'Rest, lord, recover.' Gis saw the struggle in Beornoth's eyes, understood what even a few moments of battle cost his fading strength and worn-out body.

Beornoth's head bowed. He took off his helmet and savoured the cool river breeze blowing through his sweat-soaked hair. The Vikings died as Saxon warriors hacked into them and washed the riverbank red with blood. A score of the enemy threw down their weapons and fell to their knees in surrender. Osgar stood before them, axe held in two hands and hundreds of baying Saxon warriors at his back. He lowered his axe and glanced at Beornoth. Beornoth shook his head, and Osgar butchered them with the pitiless savagery it took to win a battle.

'They had surrendered!' said Godwin, running to Beornoth and pointing at the massacre. He had taken a cut to the face, and his shield was battered and bent.

'They had.' Beornoth rose slowly, wincing as his joints objected. 'Would they have offered quarter had we thrown down our arms?'

Godwin swallowed and wiped sweat from his brow with the back of his sleeve. 'No, lord. But the warrior's code?'

'The warrior's code is fine for bards and stories of war. This is real battle. If we let these men live, what do we do with them? Leave them there whilst we continue the fight? Bring them with us and sacrifice forty men to guard them? Let them sail away on their ship only to fight against them again tomorrow?'

'I see, I...'

'You are learning, Godwin. The Vikings are a brutal enemy, and we must be every bit as fierce and ruthless. You fought well today and killed a jarl. Find his body. His weapons and his byrnie, his torc and his arm rings are yours by right.' Beornoth clapped Godwin on the shoulder, struggled against the urge to limp because his hips ached, and marched to Osgar. 'You came just in time.'

'We were here before we attacked,' said the big thegn.

'You waited whilst we fought?'

'Yes, lord.'

'To watch us die?'

'To win.'

That was the right answer, and Osgar had played his part well. He was a man of few words, but a fearsome warrior and a thegn who knew not just how to kill a man, but how to win a battle. Beornoth stared out over the river as myriad ladders rose and fell from the walls. The drums beat without end. Beornoth had killed three crews, but thousands of Thorkell's warriors remained.

'Come, we must find more of the enemy.' Beornoth returned to his shield, lifted it and sent Wigs to find his horse.

'Wait, lord,' said Wigs. 'Look.'

Beornoth turned back to the river. He squinted to sharpen his vision and thought for a moment that his eyes deceived him. The entire upper edge of Lundenwic's walls wobbled, shaking as though the earth shook its ancient foundations. Beornoth walked to the riverbank, where his men all stared out across the water. The walls' upper edge shook again, shifting back and forth like a rowing man's back. Helmeted Saxon warriors heaved at it, shoving at the stonework with all of their might from behind the walls. A cloud of dust rose from the stone like smoke, the city groaned like a giant awakening from slumber, and then an entire length of rampart crumbled and fell. The topmost yard of rampart collapsed in an avalanche of dressed stone and rock, and a great cry of terror erupted from the river below. That momentary howl of despair was suddenly cut short as a mountain of rubble smashed into Thorkell's ships with a crack like a hundred trees falling at once.

'May God have mercy on them,' said a Wessex man, and he made the sign of the cross.

Beornoth's war band watched in silence as a dozen of Thorkell's ships twisted and canted in the water. Hulls rose and turned upside down, mast posts sank beneath the brown water, and men drowned as their armour and weapons dragged them down to the muddy riverbed. At the sight of so much carnage, at so many ships smashed to ruin, the rest of Thorkell's fleet backed oars away from the city, abandoning their ladders in the water, and a cry of triumph went up from Ulfcytel's defenders.

Thorkell the Tall's attempt to sack Lundenwic had failed in an avalanche of masonry, and Beornoth watched as his vast fleet rowed away along the wide River Thames. A ship flying the Jomsviking sigil slid past where Beornoth stood on the spit of land, and at its steerboard platform stood an enormous man, a baleful figure in mail who turned to look at the Saxons peering at him from the riverbank. It was Thorkell the Tall, retreating from his attempt at everlasting glory.

Take Lundenwic, and skalds would sing the name Thorkell to the far reaches of the Whale Road, and men would remember his name long after his soul had ascended to Valhalla. But lose too many men and Thorkell must abandon his entire campaign. He was a Viking warlord abroad, risking everything to win himself everlasting glory. If a Saxon ealdorman lost a hundred warriors, he could call upon the fyrd. If the fyrd lost three hundred men, he could call upon the king or a neighbouring ealdorman to send more spearmen to his aid. Thorkell had only this army, and though it was five thousand strong when he left King Sweyn Forkbeard's service in far Norway, he had lost ten, maybe fifteen ships and a thousand men in his attempt on Lundenwic. A high price to pay, but had he won Thorkell would be the lord of Lundenwic, controlling all trade east to Frankia, Frisia, Norway, Denmark, Sweden, Saxony, Germany and beyond to the far reaches where Mussulmen made coins of pure silver and sold slaves by the hundred.

Beornoth raised his sword aloft, pointing its sharpened tip towards heaven, and then he slowly lowered the weapon until it pointed at Thorkell himself. The big man stared hard at Beornoth, and he clapped a fist to his broad chest and then inclined his head. Beornoth wondered if Thorkell recalled their fight on the bridge before this very city as vividly as Beornoth himself. A fearsome champion, a successful warlord and leader of the greatest fighting force in the world. Beornoth wondered if their blades would cross again, shuddered at the thought of his failing strength and stamina challenging the Danish giant and his implacable war axe.

Thorkell's ships sailed away, oars rising and falling like the wings of magnificent birds, powering their sleek keels through the water and towards its tidal estuary.

'Do they flee for good?' asked Gis, leaning on his spear, marvelling at so many ships sailing past as the warriors of Wessex and Northumbria stripped the dead and clambered on to the captured Viking ship to plunder its contents.

'No,' Beornoth said sadly. 'Thorkell dare not depart after such a defeat. He will find another place to attack, somewhere else to plunder.'

'So what do we do?'

'We find him, and we fight him.'

And so they did.

11

Weeks later, Ulfcytel stormed along the army's left flank, bellowing orders at men to close spaces and to check shields. He had spent an hour organising the East Anglian levy, the churls and thralls who came to fight because Ulfcytel had ordered it, and it was their duty to fight whenever he called in return for the right to live and make their livings on East Anglian land. Most carried mattocks, wood axes, scythes or clubs, but every man carried a shield, many of dubious quality and hastily made. They shifted on nervous feet, quiet and long-faced in their wool jerkins and threadbare cloaks.

'He's going to shout himself hoarse. God help them if Thorkell's men get amongst them,' said Wigs, standing beside Beornoth and Gis. They waited ten paces ahead of the centre, in full war gear, facing the ranks of Vikings who milled about the battlefield carelessly, drinking ale, laughing and seeming disinterested in the Saxon army preparing to do battle. 'Will the bastards fight today?'

'They'll fight,' Beornoth replied. He watched the banners fluttering above the Viking army, scraps of cloth painted with skulls, wolves, bears and ravens. Other war bands carried skulls on high poles, human and animal, and one even flew the yellowed skin of a flayed man on a spear.

'What makes you so sure, lord?'

'Because I'm going to pick a fight with Thorkell. Fetch my horse.'

'God help us,' said Gis as Wigs hurried off to fetch Beornoth's mare.

The Saxon army gathered on a swathe of open heathland, spotted here and there with patches of light woodland. It was common land, a vast open space owned by no man because the land offered no hope of raising crops or providing nourishment for animals with its dry and sandy earth. To the south and east lay the winding rivers and marshlands of the Breckon area, and Beornoth stamped his boot on the hard ground, content that it would provide a sound footing for the thousands of men who would soon try to hack one another to death and dung the heath with their blood.

Eadric Streona sat upon a white gelding in the space between the Saxon army and Thorkell the Tall's massed ranks. Three men, also mounted, flanked him. One was a bishop looking uncomfortable in his mitre with his shepherd's crook staff in one hand, and the other two were Æthelred's men wearing the dragon banner of Wessex upon the shields hanging from their saddles.

Thorkell had raided his way from the Thames to Sandwich and Thanet after leaving Lundenwic, just as Forkbeard had before him. Those towns had burned, as had many villages along the coast and rivers of south-eastern England. Thorkell showed no signs of returning across the sea and continued to lay waste to the entirety of East Anglia, and so Beornoth and Ulfcytel had marched in pursuit east before a horn of mead was drunk in celebration of the victory at Lundenwic. It had taken two weeks to send messengers across East Anglia and order its fyrd to assemble, but they had come in family groups of two and three, or as village war bands of ten or more accompanied by their local thegns who came in armour and with spears, axes, swords and shields.

Eadric Streona had met Beornoth and Ulfcytel on the road. He had offered sour congratulations for their victory at Lundenwic but mentioned nothing of the humiliating loss of the entire Saxon fleet. Wulfnoth lived. He had taken his family and his warriors and fled Wessex to escape the wrath of Streona and his brother. Brihtric was notable by his absence, and Beornoth assumed Eadric's brother had slithered back to Mercia in disgrace, so that his brother could pin the blame upon him, absolve himself of shame and maintain his vice-like grip upon the kingdom. Beornoth wondered what King Æthelred made of the fleet's loss. Had he berated Streona? Called him to Winchester to answer for the humiliation which had cost so many lives? He doubted it, judging by the king's last appearance before his warriors, where Eadric had led proceedings. Æthelred had seemed frail that day, led by his wife and controlled by Streona. Beornoth doubted there had been a reckoning at all, not even for all the silver lost in the fleet's construction, and in the opportunity to defeat the Vikings wiped away like shit from a baby's arse.

Streona leaned in his saddle and stared at Ulfcytel with a tight expression on his face. He said something to his courtly companions, who dutifully chuckled as Eadric shook his head. Streona wore a fantastically expensive byrnie, whose sleeves and neck were trimmed with golden links, and its body threaded with silver links through the iron to make it shimmer like starlight. Eadric had insisted on commanding the centre during the battle, should Thorkell bring his men to fight. It was the place of honour usually reserved for the best troops and the most experienced commander. Streona had placed his Mercian warriors and the shire fyrd in the middle, with his true warriors in the front ranks and the inexperienced levy in the rear. Sigeferth and Morcar had objected, but only after Eadric had moved out of earshot, whilst Ulfcytel and Beornoth had simply accepted the ealdorman of Mercia's command to avoid another spat and debacle like the fleet's unfortunate destruction.

Ealdorman Alfgar had returned north to his shire after the fleet's collapse, but had left five hundred warriors of Cheshire to help fight Thorkell. Those men formed the left flank, along with the Northumbrians and the warriors who had come from Defnascir and Somersaete. Four thousand Saxon warriors lined up on Ringmere Heath to do battle with Thorkell's horde. Beornoth and Ulfcytel had led their horsemen and three hundred men on foot deep into East Anglia to harry Thorkell's marching columns, and their raids had eventually pinned the Vikings down to a wide stretch of heathland at a place known as Ringmere, a low strip of flatland set between Theodford, the Abbey of St Edmund, a town close to the Little Ouse river known for flint and rabbit warrening, Elveden and Icklingham. Thorkell's men had already sacked and burned half of those towns and settlements and so moved slowly, pulling ox carts, wains and wagons loaded with plunder, food and mead.

Wigs returned with Beornoth's horse, and Beornoth stroked the beast's nose and patted its powerful flank. She had worked hard, a long week riding along riverbanks as Beornoth sought to manoeuvre his small force between the local towns and Thorkell's only route of retreat to his fleet. Ulfcytel's scouts had located Thorkell's ships lying north in the Wash, a vast tidal estuary on England's east coast. He had fortified a swathe of tidal mudflats, salt marsh fringes and shallow channels and left six hundred men to defend the ships.

Should a Saxon force approach the fleet, the defenders would retreat to the boats and simply sail out to sea to protect the drakkars from attack.

Thorkell had raided south from the Wash, following the Great Ouse, then the Little Ouse and the River Thet to strike deep into the heart of East Anglia. Beornoth had sent riders to summon the levies and forces gathered by Eadric Streona in the king's name and form them up on Ringmere Heath, so Thorkell had to do battle if he was to break through and return to his ships. Beornoth checked his horse's tack and took a moment to make sure he was ready to goad Thorkell to fight. The Vikings had delayed for a full day already, and the Saxons had spent a chilly night sleeping under the stars. Thorkell hoped that the Saxon force would wither and shrink as the fyrd slipped back to their homes and farms when hunger and fear gnawed at them, and he was right. If the wait for battle dragged on for another day, the Saxons would begin to squabble, and their men would whittle away in the night and leave them weakened, perhaps with no option but to withdraw. There had to be a fight, or Thorkell would slaughter his way across England unopposed.

Streona continued to stare with unhidden bafflement as Ulfcytel struggled to force the fyrd into something like an organised force. Ulfcytel was a powerful king's thegn and ruled East Anglia like an ealdorman. The last ealdorman of East Anglia, an old man named Aethelwine, had fallen foul of King Æthelred's mother, Queen Ælfthryth, in the dark days following the late King Edgar's death. Aethelwine had supported the dead king's oldest son and heir, Edward, and Edward had become king upon Edgar's death, just as the king had wanted. Aethelwine had long been a staunch supporter of King Edgar and his work to support monks over the Church and its bishops by stripping Church land and awarding it to the monasteries and abbeys across England. In the dark days following Edgar's death, Queen Ælfthryth had killed the newly crowned King Edward and had her young son Æthelred crowned in his place. Aethelwine had fallen foul of her wrath in his support of the slain King Edward and had died suspiciously shortly after his death.

Since that day no ealdorman had ruled in East Anglia, and as a king's thegn Ulfcytel had taken on much of an ealdorman's duties and powers. It had happened slowly, out of need, as Ulfcytel had stepped up to combat Viking raids, to fight Forkbeard and the other countless three-crew sea jarls who came looking for slaves and silver. Upon their departure from Lundenwic, Ulfcytel had sent riders east to raise the fyrd and every man in East Anglia heeded his call as though it came from an ealdorman, whilst Beornoth marched the men of Wessex, the Northumbrians and as many of the Lundenwic guard uninjured and able to fight following the great battle for its walls.

Beornoth stood before four thousand men on the wide, open heath and offered battle to the army of Thorkell the Tall. The fyrd made up half of the Saxon force, whilst every man in Thorkell's force was a fighter bred and trained for war. Thorkell had set out for England with five thousand men. Many had died beneath the walls of Lundenwic. Six hundred protected his ships, and so, as Beornoth stared across the heath, he reckoned Thorkell had three and a half, perhaps four thousand men. A fearsome prospect, but one that must be faced and fought if the war with the Norsemen was ever to end.

'We must have our war!' Eadric shouted suddenly. His white horse pranced and then turned in a circle. He clung to the saddle and then let the horse canter along the front rank. He probably imagined that the warriors would cheer him, that he could ignite their battle-frenzy with his presence, but the massed Saxons simply stared at him.

'The men have no love for Streona,' said Gis.

'He's like a man marrying a widow too soon after her husband's death, and the men are her children,' said Wigs with a shake of his head and his eyes closed as though he were the wisest man in East Anglia.

'What are you talking about? Are you drunk?'

'No. They don't like him. He's like finding a turd in the bottom of an ale barrel.'

'When have you ever found a turd in the bottom of an ale barrel? And for that matter, who would shit in the ale?'

'It's a saying, like two wrongs don't make a right, or a bird in the hand is worth two in the bush.'

'I swear to God, you have the cunning of a carrot and the sense of a rock.'

'You don't exactly have the mind of King Alfred the Great either, and you look like the bottom of a donkey's hoof.'

'That's enough,' Beornoth said, and he climbed slowly onto his horse, settling into the saddle with a long groan. 'I'm not listening to you two all day. Let's have this battle now.'

Beornoth urged his horse forward, cantering her towards Eadric and his companions. He turned and waved to Ulfcytel. A boy held Ulfcytel's horse, and the king's thegn left the fyrd, mounted the beast and hurried to join Beornoth.

'Are they ready?' Beornoth asked when he drew close.

'As they'll ever be,' he replied.

'We will win the battle on the right flank. Our best men are out there. If Thorkell strikes at our fyrd, or at Eadric's centre, we cannot hold.'

'The Mercians can fight, Beo. I've fought alongside them before.'

'Will they fight and die for Streona? He isn't a Mercian. Did they love the last ealdorman? What happened to his family when Eadric took control of the shire?'

'They loved Aelfhelm, and he was a good man, a stout fighter.'

'And Streona slaughtered him. He killed an ealdorman and blinded his sons, and King Æthelred allowed it, supported it even. How can the warriors of Mercia fight and die for such a man?'

'If the Mercians don't hold, then we are done for.'

'So we must win the battle from the right.'

'Ah, our great warriors, the victors of Lundenwic,' Eadric called as Beornoth and Ulfcytel drew close. Beornoth ignored him and kept riding on towards the Viking ranks.

'We should wait, Beo,' Ulfcytel said, half laughing at Beornoth's belligerence.

Beornoth ignored the warning, and when he came within twenty paces of the Viking army, Beornoth turned his horse and cantered along their front line, glowering at them in challenge. They bristled, some shouted curses and insults and waved their axes at him. Beornoth reached their left flank, wheeled his horse around and rode across the line again.

'Thorkell!' Beornoth shouted in Norse. 'Thorkell whoreson, Thorkell killer of children, slaver, and nithing. Where are you? Forkbeard's dog, lickspittle, trembler. I am Beornoth Reiði. You fear me. Your men shake when they hear my name. They shit their breeches and cower behind their shields like children.'

The Vikings were ever fond of the ritual insults before battle, and so Beornoth called out the foulest calls he could summon, and sure enough the monstrous figure of Thorkell the Tall came forth from his army, sitting high on a horse so grey it seemed almost silver. Half a dozen warriors flanked him, scarred men in chain mail and fur. Beornoth reined his horse in, and Ulfcytel joined him.

'Whatever you said, it did the trick,' he said.

'Let's have this cursed fight today,' Beornoth replied.

'I lead this army!' Eadric barked as he reached Beornoth. He had galloped the final distance to reach the parlay before Thorkell arrived, and now his horse would not stand still. It whickered, stomped the ground and turned in a half-circle so that he had to lean in the saddle to glower at Beornoth. Eadric sawed at the reins, and his horse shook its head. One of his men leapt from his own mount and grabbed the horse's bridle and whispered to it until the horse calmed. 'I am the commander, and I speak for England,' Eadric continued. 'That's enough,' he spat at the man holding his horse. 'I don't want Thorkell to think I can't ride well enough to master my horse.' The man bowed his head and remounted his own beast. Eadric continued to fuss with his mount until Thorkell came close, and then Eadric stiffened, sitting straight, shoulders back and chin raised.

Thorkell let his horse amble towards the Saxons, rocking slowly in time with the beast's movement. His forehead jutted out from his skull, brows flat over dark eyes and a long jaw. He wore an iron half-helm pushed down over the lank hair that hung about his face like seaweed from a rock. He wore a coat of mail fringed with fox fur, heavy boots and carried a double-bladed axe strapped to his back. The men flanking him came similarly dressed, bristling with a warrior's pride and arrogance. Their arm rings shone, as did the gold and silver at their necks. They were men made rich by raiding and war, fighters, men brave enough to cross the dangerous, wild seas in search of fortune and reputation.

'Have you come to surrender?' Beornoth asked in Norse, and the Vikings chuckled.

'You look like a corpse,' Thorkell said in his low, slow, rumbling voice. 'Are there any teeth left behind that grey beard?' The Vikings laughed louder this time.

'Forkbeard let you loose for a summer, did he? Gave his lover a chance to make a name of his own? You cannot win without King Sweyn. He is cunning and understands the ways of war. You are a big, dumb ox with a head full of rocks. Go, run back to Sweyn. His bed grows cold without you in it.'

'King Sweyn isn't finished with this country.' Thorkell set his jaw, small eyes gleaming with malice. 'I have come to soften you up, to bleed the dying corpse of this kingdom for any silver and wealth that yet remains. When I'm fat and happy and every man in my army is as rich as a jarl, I shall leave. But when

Sweyn returns, that will be the real reckoning. You think you know war? You sit there on your horses and pretend you are warlords? Sweyn Forkbeard is the king of Denmark and Norway, where dangerous men live, where every island and fjord is home to fierce warriors and proud sea jarls. He won those kingdoms with his axe and his daring. He defeated Olaf Trygvasson at the battle of Svolder. That was a battle. Not like this skirmish against your crusty half-soldiers and farmers. Olaf was a great man, a king, a warrior and a man to fear. If he fell to Forkbeard, what hope is there for your weasling king? How can you possibly hope to survive? So I'll bleed you, Saxon, I'll choke your country until my ships are heavy with gold and silver, and then King Sweyn will come, and then even I worry for the fate of your people, for he will be king here one day.'

Beornoth fought to keep his face still, not to show the shock in Thorkell's certainty that Forkbeard would return to claim England for his own. He forced himself to offer a retort, to counter Thorkell's words with threats and insults of his own, or else lose face in front of Thorkell and his companions and imbue them with confidence. 'You have a new axe. Though you needed one after the last time we met. I took your old one when you ran from the bridge. You still bear the scar I gave you, I see.' Beornoth pointed to the jagged scar above Thorkell's eye where his seax had sliced open the Viking's face during their fight. The Vikings did not laugh at that.

'Speak English,' Eadric hissed, his lips turned in on themselves. 'What did you say to him?'

'We insulted each other,' Beornoth replied. 'He wants to fight you in single combat here, before the army.'

Eadric swallowed and glanced to his right, where a baleful warrior with a flat nose and small eyes sat on a large mare. Beornoth had noticed the warrior with Eadric before, and assumed the man was his champion.

'I did not say that,' Thorkell said slowly, in heavily accented Saxon. 'But we can fight. If you wish.'

'Take your army, and leave England never to return,' Eadric said, once he had recovered from his surprise to hear Thorkell speak their language.

Thorkell laughed in a low rumble. 'I will leave, little man, if you pay me enough silver.'

'Leave, or we shall destroy you.'

Thorkell smiled, a half-growl that made his feral face crease with deep lines. He turned to Beornoth but continued to speak Saxon. 'Who is this pup who yaps at me? I know you, Beornoth Reiði, and you, Ulfcytel Snillingr, but not this preening pony. He looks soft, like a woman.' Thorkell gave Ulfcytel the byname 'the Bold', as he was known amongst the Northmen.

'Lord Eadric, ealdorman of Mercia.'

'Ah! The Grasper. A back-stabber. You have grown powerful with your silver tongue. Do you wipe the king's arse? Empty his shit pail? Or do you service his wife because he cannot?'

The bishop with Eadric gasped and made the sign of the cross, and the Vikings laughed so hard they almost fell off their horses. Eadric's eyes narrowed, and his face turned ashen.

'Thorkell insults you because it is their custom in the northlands,' Beornoth said. 'He insults you because he is afraid. He has lost to me already and carries my scar. He lost again at Lundenwic when we smashed his ships to driftwood. He mocks us because he trembles like a blind woman stumbling in the darkness.' Beornoth dug his heels into his horse so that she surged forward, coming close to Thorkell, so close that Beornoth could smell the leather and stale ale on his companions. They shouted and shifted on their own mounts, and Beornoth turned his beast savagely, and he snarled at them like a wolf. 'You are brave men when you kill churls, thralls, women and children. But you run and hide when it comes to war. Your ancestors are ashamed of you. When I killed Palnatoki, the Jomsvikings were fierce men, men who sought war and not rape and murder. What are you curs compared to those men? You shame your banner. You are imposters, robbers and thieves.'

'Bastard,' Thorkell growled. 'Snivelling old whore.'

'Fight us then! Show us your mettle, or scuttle away to your ships and leave our lands forever.'

'We shall fight, Beornoth. I shall seek you out on the field and take your head. I'll piss on your dead corpse and mount your skull on the prow of my ship.'

'You couldn't knock the skin off a barrel of skyr. Coward. Ready your men. You'll find me on the right.' Beornoth wheeled his horse around and cantered away.

'What are you doing?' Eadric shouted as he rode hard to catch up with Beornoth. 'We could have paid them off. The gafol has worked before.'

'Worked before? It's like a shepherd leaving meat out for a pack of wolves and wondering why they return every night to savage his flock. We must fight them and kill so many of the bastards that they must sail away broken and defeated.'

'I command here, Beornoth, not you. I decide whether or not we fight.'

'Then ride back to Thorkell and renegotiate. Otherwise, prepare your men and hold your line. Hold fast, Eadric, keep your shield wall steady and we can give the enemy a fight that shall ring down through the ages. But if you break, then we shall all die here today.'

'I won't break, Lord Beornoth. Worry about your own flank, and when the day is won we shall drag Thorkell to Winchester in chains.'

Thorkell the Tall rode along his men, holding his enormous axe high in the air. The sun glinted from its twin blades, and the Vikings roared their support for the famous Viking champion and warlord. Drums began to boom from behind their lines.

Boom, boom, boom ba boom.

The drums rolled over and over and the Vikings hurried themselves into organised ranks, their shield wall forming efficiently and bristling with spear points. The drum beats thrummed in Beornoth's chest, and he dismounted, giving his horse to a boy to lead away from the field. He pushed on his helmet and hefted his spear and shield.

It was time for war.

12

Beornoth smashed his shield boss into a Viking's face and stabbed his spear overhand, its shaft sliding across the shield rim to cut the ear from a warrior in the second Viking rank. Men pressed behind him, and the Vikings shoved from the front as Beornoth stood strong, pinned between both sides in the front rank where the dangerous men fought. The Viking with the bloody nose shoved back at Beornoth, snarling and spitting curses through his thick beard. Beornoth brought his spear back, wanting to rip open that face with its point, but had not the room to manoeuvre his shoulder and arm, and he instead stabbed at the enemy second rank again, seeking another Viking to kill or maim. The bloody-nosed man shook and twisted, but the struggling lines pressed him, and he could not move his axe because it was stuck between their two heavy shields.

Beornoth sweated inside his helmet. The sun, leather, iron and press of heaving, shouting, furious men around him made the air thin and cloying. The iron stink of blood mixed with the acrid smell of sweat, leather and death as two armies fought for supremacy. When the shield walls came together, it was impossible to see how the battle progressed further along the line. All Beornoth could see were the horrible faces in front of him, the tattooed arms, the combed beards braided with trinkets and charms, the golden hair, arm rings, axes, shields and spears of men who wanted to cut out his heart and push their sharpened blades into his belly, liver, throat and groin.

'Hold!' Gis called, standing beside Beornoth in line, a dead Viking propped in front of him, unable to fall as the armies pressed together.

'Backwards step!' a voice bellowed in Norse.

'Brace yourselves for...' Beornoth began, but not in time for his men to stop themselves stumbling forward as the entire Viking left flank took two steps back in perfect time. They created a gap between the lines, and suddenly the pressure on the Saxon front rank disappeared, but the push from behind remained. The Vikings struck with their axes, chopping at the faces and necks of the Saxons, who took a heavy forward step or lost their balance completely.

'Archers,' Beornoth called. 'Signal the archers now!'

'Yes, lord,' Wigs replied, calling from three ranks back. Beornoth couldn't see, but trusted his man to raise his spear, to which they had tied a scrap of russet cloth to serve as a signal to the men Beornoth had placed in a ragged copse of woodland twenty paces away from their flank.

Beornoth braced his knee against the bottom of his shield just in time. The bloody-nosed Viking hooked the blade of his axe over Beornoth's shield rim, his goal to yank it down so that a warrior in the second enemy rank could cut at his unprotected face and neck. His shield stayed firm, braced against his knee, and now Beornoth had space to move. He whipped his spear back, lifted his elbow and stabbed the point into the bloody-nosed Viking's eye, yanked it free with a wet, sucking sound and then pushed the leaf-shaped blade into the wounded man's gullet. Beornoth let go of his spear, reached behind him and drew his seax from the sheath at the small of his back. He kicked the dying Viking down, and when the next man tried to clamber over his body, Beornoth bent low beneath his shield rim and opened his thigh from knee to groin in a wash of hot blood.

A great wail went up on the Viking left as two hundred arrows whipped into their unprotected sides. Those men shuffled to their left, pushing, desperate to get away as another volley of arrows tore into their ribs, legs and shoulders. That movement pressed hard against the men facing Beornoth, fouling their shield wall as they came too close.

'Now kill them!' Beornoth roared, and he charged into the enemy line like a maddened bull. Three men down from him, Osgar used the gap between the shield walls to pull his monstrous axe free from his back. He dropped his shield, and Beornoth clenched his jaw with appreciation as the Saxon warrior smashed a Viking shield in two as though it were made of rotten wood. A

Viking stabbed a spear at Beornoth, and the point glanced off his shield and then his helmet with a loud ring.

Age fled from Beornoth like an old cloak, and he charged forward, battering the Vikings back with his shield. A big man reared before him, stabbing forward with a long knife. Beornoth swayed his head away from the blow and jabbed his seax twice into that man's armpit and then back-cut the broken-backed blade across another Dane's face. He was among them now, sensing Osgar's formidable wrath also forcing them back, and Gis followed, moving with professional efficiency, not attacking, just shuffling forward behind his shield. The rest of the Saxon line followed, and the Vikings fell back.

An axe chopped into Beornoth's shield, and he let go of its grip so that its heavy wood and iron dragged the axeman down. His bearded face stared at Beornoth in a moment of surprise, mouth open, suddenly come face-to-face with his mortality. He stared into the bleak black pit of Beornoth's full-faced helmet and saw nothing but death in the huge, baleful Saxon warlord. Beornoth rammed his seax into the Viking's mouth and ripped its gore-smeared blade free. He passed it to his left hand and drew his sword and laughed with mad joy as Osgar cut a Dane almost in two with his axe. The Vikings fought to get away from Osgar's crazed fury, and they died as the Saxons forced them backwards, stabbing and cutting to avenge the poor souls who had suffered their raids and depredations. Beornoth parried a spear thrust with his seax and stabbed his sword blade down into the spearman's thigh, twisting the blade so that the Viking howled in pain. Another enemy charged him, spear held in two hands and a feral look in his eyes. Beornoth twisted away from the weapon, but too late to stop it from scraping along his ribs. His chain-mail armour absorbed the blow, but it still felt like a horse had kicked his midriff. Beornoth bent almost double and tripped the charging Norseman with his sword. The Viking toppled, and Gis battered the back of his skull to a grotesque slop with the rim of his shield.

The Viking rear rankers turned and ran, and once men flee from battle, it infects the rest of an army like a plague. The entire Viking left flank crumbled, and the Saxons cheered their victory to heaven with bloody spears and wild eyes. Beornoth sagged; the strength he had found in his battle-rage suddenly fled from him.

'Oh, lord, no,' Gis said, pain in his voice.

Beornoth removed his helmet and understood his friend's concern because the Vikings had utterly destroyed the Saxon centre and left flank. Thorkell and his Jomsvikings were among the fyrd, their banner flying and their axes scything into the churls and their farm tools and littering the heath with their corpses. Thorkell the Tall strode amongst his enemies, unmistakable with his giant frame, towering over every other man on the field, his mighty axe scything through men like wheat. The Vikings who fled from Beornoth's Wessex men and Northumbrians veered away to join that slaughter, whooping for joy and hurling insults at the Saxons who had thought the battle won. Eadric Streona and his warriors formed a retreating shield wall, a half-circle moving carefully away from the battlefield, five hundred warriors leaving their countrymen to die as the Vikings left them alone to find easier pickings.

'We have to move,' Beornoth said, though he felt as though he could not walk three more paces without collapsing from fatigue. 'We must protect the survivors, the fyrd men, we must protect the weak. Gather the men; we march to support the fyrd's retreat.'

Beornoth tried to rise, but his body failed him, and he fell back to his knees. He coughed, a wracking, chest-wrenching spasm that shook his entire body. The coughing would not stop. It was as though he had lost control of his body. Beornoth tensed his muscles, acutely aware that his men saw the affliction he had, until now, sought to hide as much as possible. The battle was lost, Thorkell was loose amongst the fyrd, and any hope of destroying the Viking army spilled away with the blood of dead Saxon warriors. The coughing stopped, and a ragged, bloody spittle poured from Beornoth's mouth onto the grass. His insides burned, and the side of his midriff throbbed.

'Lord?' asked Gis, bending to help, but stopping short of touching Beornoth.

'Help me up,' he said, lifting his arm, swallowing his pride.

Gis grabbed Beornoth and pulled him to his feet. He stared at Beornoth with a gaping mouth as though he could not believe his lord had shown weakness. Beornoth wiped the blood from his mouth and stared out over the desolation on Ringmere Heath. He sheathed his weapons and held his breath, fighting to master his body even though it screamed at him to lie down. Another coughing bout tickled his chest and throat, and Beornoth forced it down. It seemed in that moment like the battlefield echoed the state of the kingdom – wretched, cut to pieces, sundered by a weak middle which folded under the pressure of Viking aggression. Beornoth's right flank had held; more than that, they had won their side of the conflict as the combined forces of Northumbria, Wessex and Cheshire and the warriors drawn from across the country had smashed the enemy into retreat, only to find that Streona's Mercians had crumbled, and the fyrd had inevitably fallen in the face of organised, well-armed soldiers.

'The men are ready, lord,' said Gis. Osgar stood beside him, slathered in other men's blood, huge and baleful with his axe held in two hands. Godwin leaned on his spear, his shield battered, its boards loose and broken, iron rim bent and buckled.

'We march around the heath,' Beornoth said. 'Put ourselves between the retreat and the Vikings. The men flee east into the marshes, and we must help as many as we can to escape the slaughter.'

'We lost,' Wigs said, voice dripping with despair and disbelief, his spear held low, tip resting on the grass.

'Thorkell won,' Beornoth corrected him. 'He brought his hardest men with him to fight our weakest point, Eadric's centre, and he crushed them like maggots under his boot. March. On me.'

Beornoth staggered forward, sword and seax in his fists, his head light, and for a moment he thought he might fall to the ground. Wigs and Gis sensed his sudden weakness and stood on either side of him, their shields close, bracing him so that Beornoth could march on.

'We've got you, lord,' said Gis.

Osgar marched with them, as did Sigeferth, Morcar and five hundred men from the right flank. Two hundred more formed a screening shield wall, marching behind Beornoth's force and facing towards the Viking army in case they tried to charge their rear. The Vikings whooped and cheered their victory; half of their force capered on the battlefield, banging their drums and going amongst the dead to claim anything of value from the dead and dying. The rest of Thorkell's army swept across the battlefield to kill as many of the retreating forces as possible. Eadric and his men had already left the field, disappearing into the shaggy, watery marshes to the east whilst the fyrd men followed.

Beornoth reached the men of the fyrd and found them bloodied, wandering in packs towards the marshes but fearful that the enemy might follow and kill them. They were leaderless and panicked, and Beornoth's heart sank to a deeper, despairing level when he found Ulfcytel between the arms of two farmers. A great rend in the shoulder of his byrnie showed blood and torn flesh, and the warrior's face was as white as morning ash.

'We are done for,' Ulfcytel gasped through clenched teeth.

'Thorkell won,' Beornoth agreed. 'All we can do now is get to safety and regroup.'

The ragged Saxon survivors retreated into the marshes as an organised war band following Beornoth's command. The Danes let them go, Beornoth's marching shield wall proving too formidable for the Vikings to attack when the battle was already won. Nothing lay between them and total freedom to ravage England, to bleed it dry and to make themselves masters of all before them.

* * *

The days following the battle were a grim, desolate haze of forced marches, nightmare-filled nights where each morning the Saxons awoke to find more of the wounded had died of their wounds in the darkness. Ulfcytel lived, but a Viking axe had inflicted a terrible injury to his shoulder and chest, and he could not use his left arm, so he had to lash it to his body with a cloth bandage.

Beornoth struggled. Every day, a fog of pain and struggle against his fading body and the weight of defeat weighed heavily on his mind. The survivors left the marshes and turned north, marching through East Anglia until they reached a hall where the folk took Ulfcytel in and brought a priest to tend to his wounds. Word came of a great gathering at Sandwich to which Eadric Streona had summoned the great men of East Anglia, and its closest shires, and so Beornoth rode there with Osgar, Godwin, Wigs, Gis, Sigeferth, Morcar and fifty men. To Beornoth's surprise, they found the Viking army camped outside the town with Thorkell's fleet moored in the harbour and off the coast. Saxon guards stood at the gate and admitted Beornoth, Osgar, Sigeferth and Morcar, but forced the rest of their war band to remain outside the walls.

Inside the town, Beornoth walked into a bizarre mix of Viking jarls and shipmasters drinking in taverns and wandering the streets in an uneasy peace with Mercian warriors, who patrolled the narrow lanes and formed a protective ring about the main hall. It was a stunning thing to take in; men who had fought a bitter battle now mingled and drank in the same taverns like old friends.

'This place feels wrong,' said Morcar, twisting his neck uncomfortably. 'There is ill work afoot here.'

'The Vikings have won,' said Sigeferth. 'Or our leaders have surrendered.'

'Streona's work,' Beornoth said. There was something off about the town, a foul humour, something of the underworld, cloying and claggy like the slime left as a slug slithers across the land. Beornoth's jerkin and mail sat heavy about his shoulders, as though the air in Sandwich tried to drag him down. It was like the feeling after a nightmare on a hot summer night – uncomfortable, a film of sweat needing to be washed away with fresh water.

Beornoth led his companions towards the great hall and was stunned to see Thorkell the Tall striding towards him with a smile splitting his face. He came in a fine wool jerkin and a green cloak with his thumbs tucked into a thick leather belt studded with silver stars. He wore a gold chain coiled twice about his thick neck, and nicks and cuts from Saxon blades marked his face and forearms, and yet he walked about the town as though he owned the place.

'Beornoth, you are still alive,' Thorkell called cheerfully in Norse. Six of his warlords trailed him, similarly dressed like rich country lords rather than the brutal killers they were. The insults exchanged before the recent battle forgotten.

Beornoth stopped and stood still, unable to find any words to greet his enemy, still rocked at the incongruous sight of Thorkell amongst the Saxons to whom he had brought so much suffering.

'Is there peace between us?' asked Sigeferth, also speaking Norse after he had waited for uncomfortable moments for Beornoth to speak. He was a Northumbrian and the descendant of settled Vikings and so was as familiar with the language as Beornoth.

'There is,' Thorkell said cheerfully. 'Lord Eadric and King Æthelred have agreed to provide me with the silver I require to pay my men for our voyage.'

'How much?' Beornoth asked, his voice coming as a raspy croak.

'An appropriate sum. Forty-eight thousand pounds of silver, which, I am told, is the most you Saxons have ever paid to end a war.'

It was an enormous amount of silver, twice what the king had paid Forkbeard and Olaf Trygvasson to leave after they had almost brought the kingdom to its knees. Beornoth could not imagine how Streona and Æthelred planned to find such a sum.

'It will take time to find and deliver so much silver,' said Sigeferth.

Thorkell shrugged, his mouth turned down at the corners, and he waved a dismissive hand at the Saxons. 'There is no rush. I won't be going anywhere for a while.'

'But the gafol payment?'

'That is for my men.' Thorkell smiled and winked at Beornoth. 'You haven't heard the news, Lord Beornoth? We are to be brothers of the sword, comrades. We shall stand together and do battle with the enemies of our king.'

'Our king?' Beornoth said, almost as a whisper, the news spilling out of Thorkell's mouth taking him into a waking nightmare.

'Yes! Ealdorman Eadric and I have come to an arrangement. My men and I fight for King Æthelred now. Half of my warriors will return home. I have released them from their oaths. Those who wish to stay will swear an oath to King Æthelred this very week. We are enemies no more.'

'Enemies no more,' Beornoth repeated in a wan voice.

'We shall stand in the same shield wall when Forkbeard comes to conquer England. We can burnish our reputations even brighter. What army could stand against Beornoth and Thorkell?'

'Forkbeard will come to make himself king?'

'He will. Sweyn likes this place. Rich soil, wonderful land. Half of the place is populated by our people, anyway. Sweyn is a dangerous man, Beornoth. He always wants more.'

'Don't all Vikings?' The words came out of Beornoth's mouth, and he could hear them as though another man spoke and he were listening. He seemed outside of his own body, rocked to the core by Thorkell's revelation and new role as a protector of the throne.

'We do.' Thorkell laughed raucously, as did his men. 'There is so much silver in the world, so many women, and infinite glory. Sweyn is different, though. He is already the first king of both Denmark and Norway, and now he would add England to his... What is the word?' Thorkell clicked his fingers, searching for the phrase. 'Empire. That is what he craves. Like Charles the Bald or the Romans. He wants an empire to leave to his children. He might come next year, or in three years' time. Who can say? But come, now that we are on the same side, we should share a horn of ale, you and I. We can remember our great battle together on Lundenwic bridge and drink to the future. What say you?'

Beornoth turned away from Thorkell, unable to organise his churning thought cage enough to offer a coherent response. Thorkell's men shouted in outrage that Beornoth had turned his back on their leader, but the noise drowned out into a continuous mess of noise, like the sea sighing and shifting behind him.

'Where are you going?' Godwin asked, hurrying to catch up to Beornoth.

'I must speak with Eadric.'

'Can it be true? Thorkell has become our ally?'

Beornoth stopped and turned to Godwin. 'Thorkell is many things, but he is not a liar. You should look to your own safety now, as should we all. You can stay with me until your father's problems are resolved, one way or another. The rest of the thegns should go home. The war is over.'

'Shall I wait here for you, lord?'

'Go to Wigs and Gis and prepare to leave. We return to Ulfcytel to protect him.' Beornoth stepped closer to Godwin and lowered his voice. 'We are in dangerous times. Tread carefully. Tell Sigeferth and Morcar to return to their lands. We shall guard Ulfcytel. Eadric has unfettered power. He decides for the king, so any men he perceives as enemies are in mortal danger.'

Beornoth turned on his heel and marched towards Sandwich's great hall, his boots stomped on the pathway as he brushed past the press of people in every lane. Men grumbled as Beornoth's bulk shouldered them into the wattle houses and low-hanging thatch. It was as though he had stumbled through a dream, everything paling into a dull haze as his mind swam. People, buildings, Saxons, Vikings, churls, thralls, pigs, chickens, dogs and children all blurred into nothingness as the fate of England seemed all but sealed.

Beornoth had spent his long life at war, fighting for his family, for his people, to avenge his dead brothers, to preserve the Saxon kingdom. It was his duty as a thegn, just as it had been his father's before him. His blood had soaked into battlefields across the country, and now at the end of that painful, savage journey, weak leaders and powerful enemies sundered the kingdom, slicing it slowly like killing a man with a thousand cuts.

The country, and people, Beornoth had sacrificed so much to protect quivered with a blade to its throat. So Beornoth went to talk to Eadric Streona to reason with him: to try to defend an England in its death throes.

13

Beornoth reached Sandwich's great hall, a long, low wattle building with a cross set above its twin pine doors and greying thatch hanging low from its gable ends. Two guards stood on either side of the doors. They bore long spears held resting on the floor, points towards the sky. Shields bearing Mercia's sigil of a gold cross on a blue background rested against their legs. They offered Beornoth a tired, lazy-eyed stare from beneath their pot-shaped half-helms and stiffened as he drew closer.

'I wish to speak with Lord Eadric,' Beornoth said.

'The ealdorman is not receiving visitors, lord,' said the eldest of the three. He spoke with a lisp, and his beard showed a patch of pure white around his chin.

'I am Beornoth, king's thegn, and I wish to speak with Lord Eadric.'

'The ealdorman is not receiving visitors.' The guard repeated himself, talking slowly this time as though he spoke to a small child or someone with a dull mind.

'Go and tell Eadric that I am here, and that I wish to speak to him urgently.'

'The ealdorman...' the guard began after a long sigh.

Beornoth stepped closer to the man, towering over him so that the guard had to look up to meet Beornoth's angry eyes. 'Open the door and bring me to Eadric. Or you and I are going to have a serious disagreement.'

The guard gulped, turned and opened the door with a long creak. He slipped inside, and Beornoth followed, ducking beneath the lintel and into a wide hall with no corridor or rooms before the meeting space. A fire crackled at the centre, and rush lights lit the long space which smelled of damp floor rushes and old smoke.

'Lord Eadric,' the guard said after clearing his throat.

'What is it?' barked Eadric, sitting on a high-backed chair close to the fire. He waved a dismissive hand towards the guard, and a girl sitting on his lap giggled as he tickled her.

'Lord Beornoth wishes to speak with you, Ealdorman Eadric.'

'Tell him I am busy.' Eadric tickled the girl again, and she laughed raucously, and slopped mead from the silver embossed horn in her hand.

'The kingdom is in peril,' Beornoth said loudly, so that his voice echoed around the high rafters. 'We must talk.'

Eadric threw his head back at the sound of Beornoth's voice and rubbed his tired eyes as though weary. He pushed the serving girl from his lap, snatched the mead horn from her hand and pushed her away. She was a small woman with blonde hair tied up high on her head in two thick buns. She wore a low-cut dress, which she straightened, bowed to Beornoth and Eadric with flushed cheeks and hurried to the hall's far door.

'Lord Beornoth,' Eadric said in greeting. He stood slowly, took a long drink of mead and tossed the rest into the fire. The droplets hissed on the flames, and he turned to face Beornoth, one hand on his hip and the other clutching the empty horn. 'I had told my guards that I was not receiving visitors until later.'

'I can see you are engaged with urgent matters, yet I have come far to see you.'

Eadric's eyes narrowed. 'Return to your post,' he said to the guard with narrowed eyes. The man shuffled his feet, bowed, and then hurried through the front door, closing it behind him to leave Eadric and Beornoth alone. 'Well? Now you have my full attention.'

'We have new allies?'

'We do. Thorkell and his Jomsvikings are now in the king's service. They shall fight for us against our enemies and use their ships to protect our coast.'

'Thorkell the Tall, who has ravaged our country, killed its people, burned its villages and sacked its churches. He will now protect us from our enemies?'

'Yes. Better to have him as an ally than an enemy.'

'And when his master Sweyn Forkbeard arrives in spring, which Thorkell has assured me he will, to make himself king of England as well as Norway and Denmark? What will your friend Thorkell do then?'

'I don't think I care for your tone. I would remind you I am the ealdorman of Mercia.'

'And I am a king's thegn and answer only to the king. I am surprised King Æthelred would have Thorkell as an ally. Feed his army, house them through winter, pay them, run the risk of them returning to their old ways.'

'You are surprised? Know the king well, do you?'

'Not as well as you, I am sure.'

'The king has given me full authority to make this arrangement, and he supports it wholeheartedly as the best strategy to defend our country.'

'And the gafol? Forty-eight thousand pounds of silver? Where shall the kingdom find such a sum? Where will Thorkell's force live and spend winter? Who will feed them? Who will fight them when they break their oath and renew their attacks on our people?'

'I do not answer to you, Beornoth Thegn.' Eadric's voice became low, his body tense.

'I have not come to argue with you, Eadric. I have come to reason with you. To try to make you see sense and rescind this arrangement with Thorkell and cast him out, cut him out like the pirate he is.'

'Reason with me? You? We are speaking plainly here, you and I. You seem to think it's perfectly acceptable for you, a warrior, to come here and challenge me on the things I do to keep our kingdom safe. I am not sure if you remember, Lord Beornoth, but we lost the battle of Ringmere Heath. We lost, and Thorkell won. Without a victory on the field, what choice did we have but to come to terms with Thorkell? Should we run away, ignore him, let him continue to use our country as his plaything? Should we let him march on Winchester, or attack Lundenwic?'

'I fought at Ringmere, my body still bears the marks of it. I fought on the right flank and we did not break.'

Eadric clenched his jaw and threw the ale horn across the hall, where it clattered loudly in the shadows. 'You fought on the left, great Beornoth, warrior of legend, survivor of Maldon and countless other battles where many brave men died. You were on the left, and yet Thorkell and his champions came against the centre where I met him with my Mercians. We could not hold out against his numbers and strength. That is what you are insinuating, isn't it?

That I gave way whilst you stood strong like the pillar of bravery and courage you are? I ran, and you stood. Well, congratulations, Beornoth. You emerge triumphant with your reputation and esteem intact, and yet we lost. So I have taken action to stop Thorkell's attacks, and I did not need your approval to do it.'

'You demanded to take the centre, insisted on it. Even though Ulfcytel and I warned you that was where Thorkell would attack with his picked champions. You wanted the glory for yourself. You craved it, to add a warrior's fame to your name.'

'How dare you talk to me like this!' Eadric shouted, fists balled, teeth showing.

'I dare because I have earned it. You have agreed to pay Thorkell the largest amount of silver ever paid to a Viking, and now invite the fox into the henhouse? Rethink it before it's too late.'

'Earned? Have I not earned my rank, Lord Beornoth? Everything I have I earned with this.' He pointed at his head, tapping his forehead and sneering at Beornoth. 'How many sons of low-born men do you know who have risen to become the ealdorman of the most ancient and largest shire in England? When I was a boy, I lived in a hovel, going hungry for days, waking in the winter with ice in my hair. Now I am the son-in-law of the king, and my children shall marry royalty. My descendants will rule nations, and all my power and influence I won with my mind. So do not talk to me of earned. I have achieved what no man has before, and I am not done yet. Why do we need Thorkell, you ask? We need his ships, and we need his men. Or when Forkbeard returns, England shall become a Viking kingdom. The northern half of our country is already half Viking, full of men of dubious loyalty, descendants of invaders themselves. What would they do if Thorkell marched north and rallied them to his banner?'

That at least was true enough, but Beornoth could get no sign from Eadric that he understood his arrangement with Thorkell was like inviting a wild boar into a feasting hall and expecting it to sit peacefully in a corner. 'I have not come to Sandwich to argue with you, Lord Eadric. We want the same thing. Thorkell cannot be trusted. It is not too late to change your mind. Pay the bastard his silver and send him away, or better still, cut his throat and kill his army of marauding whoresons whilst they least suspect it.'

'Really? The honourable Beornoth would slit throats and stab men in the back? What would Ealdorman Byrhtnoth think? What would the people think when they hear that the great Beornoth is a cut-throat? You would tarnish your legend forever.'

'I care little for legends or reputation. We have not come so close to losing everything since King Alfred hid in the marshes whilst the Great Heathen Army almost destroyed his kingdom forever. He fought back from that, and so can we.'

'Danger? The war is over. Thorkell is at peace. There is no more danger, Beornoth. We have won without our swords. Diplomacy and discussion have led to victory where spears and shields could not.'

'There can be no peace with Thorkell, or Forkbeard or any Viking.'

'I know them as well as you, Beornoth, so do not lecture me on the Northmen.'

'They are butchers, brutal men who live for war. Their hands are filthy with the blood of our people. I have watched them hack my friends and brothers to pieces with axe and sword. Men I loved like brothers destroyed by axe blades with not enough of their bodies left to fill a shit pail. Vikings killed my daughters and cut my wife's throat. I have fought both Forkbeard and Thorkell. I saw Forkbeard come from the sea dripping with bloodthirsty malice to cut down the flower of our warriors and march in the blood. Thorkell stays because you have paid him. Do you think he will fight for you against Forkbeard, a man he respects and fears?'

'I know the face of war, Beornoth. You speak of the brutality of the Danes, but are you not such a man yourself? The Vikings call you Beornoth the Wrathful. You famously cut the arms and legs from a Viking jarl and left him a trunk-like horror to be wheeled around by them, and so their warriors knew what Beornoth the Saxon was capable of. You killed Robert de Warenne, even though he was Æthelred's man. You rode across England after Maldon and butchered any man you believed had not fought with honour. You believed! Not the king. Yet Æthelred tolerates you because of your legend and because the Vikings fear you. It was he who wanted to recall you from the wilderness in Northumbria to meet Forkbeard's threat, not I.'

Beornoth closed his eyes and fought for calm. 'Men died at Ringmere and at Lundenwic, good men. Ulfcytel himself lies grievously wounded. Now Thorkell strolls through our streets like a Saxon lord. He has an army at his back, and now the wealth to rally more Viking jarls to his banner. Forkbeard threatens to return for a third time to destroy us. Now is the time to be strong; now is the time to protect ourselves. We have made mistakes, but they can be fixed. It's not too late.'

'Mistakes?'

'The sundering of our fleet. Your brother's pursuit of Wulfnoth. Our strategy at Ringmere. The truce with Thorkell. We find ourselves at a crossroads. Put aside ambition and do what is best for the kingdom. You have the power and influence, Lord Eadric, use it to make a decision now that will save us all. Cast Thorkell out, and I will stand at your side and see it done.' Beornoth stared hard at Eadric, resisting the urge the sigh and seek a chair. He was a man of few words, a warrior not a poet, so to summon such a plea, to speak with such care to a man he loathed and could kill in a heartbeat, taxed his mind and body. Eadric had clawed his way to the very summit of power, had become an ealdorman despite lack of noble birth, seemed to control King Æthelred like a steersman leads his ship, and had killed and slithered his way across the great and good of England to find himself responsible and in control of its survival.

'You imply I am responsible for losing the fleet and the battle?'

'Your brother lost the fleet when he falsely accused Wulfnoth of treason, and you should have allowed Ulfcytel and me to hold the middle with the Wessex men and the Northumbrians. Cast Thorkell out now and we can salvage something from this campaign.'

'Wulfnoth got what he deserved, and don't think I haven't seen his whelp following you around like a puppy. Who do you think you are, soldier, to come here and talk to me as though we are equals? What gives you the right to lay these defeats at my feet?'

'I've earned the right with blood. Listen now, I beg you.'

'You should beg, for it is men like me who win wars in this new world of ours. Look at you, a haggard old warrior. The last of a generation of fools who believed a sword can solve everything. You warriors and your honour. Relics of a bygone age. The world has changed, Beornoth; it has moved on. This is the age of agreements between nations, of the possibility of advancement by intelligence, not just by birth. The world has turned, just as it did when the Romans came, when they left, and when our people first came to these shores to wrest it from the Britons. I am the victor and the peacemaker. I am the man who can save our country and make it great. Not you, and your sword, and your grey beard. You come in here like a blind old dog in a village street barking at the moon, and I do not care for your advice. It is neither wanted nor sage. I will send for you if it comes to war, if we need a brute to stand in the front rank and trade blows with our enemies. You are dismissed.'

'The world is not so different.' Beornoth stepped closer to Eadric, and the ealdorman of Mercia gasped and took a backwards step. Beornoth smiled. 'You are not in danger from me; there is no need to be afraid. Your friendship with Thorkell will fail, and Forkbeard will return. I will await that reckoning in East Anglia with Ulfcytel, and when it comes to war, we shall be ready.'

'I should call my guards and have you clapped in irons for your impudence.'

'You can try. How many guards do you have? Will it be enough?'

Eadric's mouth turned small with anger, and his eyes blazed. 'You dare threaten me. I am the ealdorman of Mercia!'

'I am not your enemy, Eadric. Our enemy walks the streets of Sandwich, and his men drink in its taverns. Beware the Vikings. I shall wait in East Anglia, but heed my words and prepare for war.'

'Get out! The king shall hear of your impudence! Guards!'

The doors swung open, and two warriors stormed into the hall, spears ready. Beornoth stalked towards the open door. His anger drowned in sadness as the fate of England in Eadric's hands broke his heart. The guards' eyes shifted from Eadric to Beornoth, and they shifted their feet nervously. Eadric gave no order, though Beornoth felt the ealdorman's anger seething like the pressure a man feels in the air before a thunderstorm. Beornoth walked between the guards and out into the town.

He thought of riding straight to the king to make his case, to plead with Æthelred to listen and to cast out Thorkell before the Jomsviking was granted land and even more wealth from the kingdom he had savaged so badly. A cough burst from his mouth, so violent that Beornoth had to lean against a house wall to brace himself. A series of bone-shaking coughs rattled his body until he tasted iron in his mouth and gobbets of blood spat onto the path. He sucked in huge breaths and closed his eyes to recover. His body trembled, and Beornoth wiped the blood from his mouth with a scrap of cloth he now always kept on him for that very purpose.

His bouts of severe coughing had increased, and Beornoth felt something dark growing, looming in his chest like a shadow. But there was no time for rest, no time to take to his bed and try to recover. He had told no one of his affliction, though Wigs and Gis had witnessed the bouts on more than one occasion. To bring his concerns to Æthelred was folly, Beornoth realised. The king would not go against Eadric's wishes, not after the actions he had stood by and let Eadric kill ealdormen, thegns, and seize wealth and power, not after the expense of building a fleet and losing it because of a foolish insult.

All Beornoth could do was prepare for the war he knew must come. So he sent Sigeferth and Morcar back to Northumbria and sent the men of Cheshire home to warn Alfgar of the dark events in the south. The Wessex men returned home, but Godwin remained with Beornoth as he rode to East Anglia to help Ulfcytel prepare for the invasion of England by its greatest enemy. Because Forkbeard would come again, and this time he came to make himself king.

PART III

1013AD

PART III

14

The riders came on a balmy August afternoon, as Beornoth and Ulfcytel ate a meal of bread and cheese outside in the sun. Beornoth had spent the last four winters at home in Cheshire beside Eawynn's grave, cold months wrapped in furs, holed up beside a warm fire as his body suffered, coughing, shaking and forcing him to his bed for weeks at a time. Each spring, when the snowdrops and daffodils brought an end to snow and frost and the sight of lambs signalled the end of the long, dark days, Beornoth, Wigs and Gis rode south to East Anglia to Ulfcytel to prepare for Forkbeard's invasion which had not come.

Beornoth wore a light jerkin and watched as Ulfcytel's men walked horses around a paddock set within a pleasant meadow.

'Fine beasts, lord,' said Wigs, sipping cool ale.

'You barely know the difference between a donkey and a pony,' said Gis, throwing a heel of bread at his friend.

'At least I don't ride like a sack of cabbages. I pity your horse. Your belly has grown so fat you need to put new holes in your belt.'

'This is muscle, I'll have you know.' The companions laughed, and Ulfcytel stood and limped over towards his animals.

'That one looks as though it's favouring its left foreleg,' he said, grumbling as he went.

'His leg's not improved any,' said Gis.

'Ringmere hit us all hard,' said Beornoth.

'Who knew that of the wounds he took that day it was the minor cut to his leg that would leave him so crippled, and not that terrible gash in his shoulder.'

'He's a fine host, bad leg or not.' Wigs took another long pull at his ale, so much so that it ran down his beard and dripped onto the table.

'Keep drinking like that, and you'll fall asleep before the afternoon wanes.'

'And why not? What else is there to do?'

Beornoth growled at that. They had spent a month drilling and training the fyrd and warriors of East Anglia, just as they had for the last four years. But after a month of shield-wall manoeuvres and no sight of the enemy, Ulfcytel had sent his men home to their farms and villages.

'I hate to say it,' said Wigs, sidling away from Beornoth before he finished his sentence, 'but Thorkell has kept the peace these last years.'

'Let's pray that remains the case for years to come,' Gis replied, and touched the wooden table for luck.

Beornoth wheezed and swallowed a cough lurking in the back of his throat. He took a sip of ale and stood slowly from his chair. Standing seemed to help with his bad chest. It distracted him, where sitting still for a long time seemed to bring on the pain and the coughing, which he had grown to despise. Winter was worse, dark months where Beornoth felt he flitted between life and death and went to sleep on frosty nights not expecting to wake up again. But life clung to him like a limpet to a rock, and Beornoth came to East Anglia every spring expecting Forkbeard to arrive with his fleet and his ambition, only to return to Cheshire in late autumn, riding through a country at peace.

'I'm running low on honey,' Beornoth said, his voice raspy. He rubbed his chest with his hands, which had become more like claws with every passing winter. 'Can you find some from Lord Ulfcytel's hives?'

'Aye, there's more by the orchard to the west of his hall. The beekeeper's daughter isn't half pretty as well,' said Wigs, hopping up from his seat.

'I'll go, you stay here and rest,' said Gis, standing and giving his friend a gentle push backwards.

'Ha! She won't look at you, not with that belly.'

'We'll see about that.' Gis set off at a run, and Wigs chased after him. Beornoth had found that a drink of warm mead and honey soothed his chest and brought respite from his ailments if he drank it three times a day.

The riders came as Beornoth walked slowly around the paddock, stretching his legs. Six horsemen cantered across the flatlands where Ulfcytel's lands swept westwards in a swathe of wheat fields, orchards and pastures. They came in mail, with shields and helmets tied to their saddles, and a banner tied to a long spear snapping in the light wind.

Ulfcytel came to stand beside Beornoth. 'They come from the north,' he said, scratching beneath his beard. 'They fly the banner of East Anglia.'

Beornoth squinted but could not make out the East Anglian sigil of three gold crowns on a blue background. He could see the riders, but not their faces, arms or legs, only blurs on horseback, and the sigil to his eyes was just a scrap of cloth on a spear. 'Your men then?' he said.

'My men. It's Osgar.'

The horsemen reached the paddock, and Osgar climbed down from his horse. Beornoth smiled to see the big warrior and noticed his double-bladed war axe strapped to his saddle. Ulfcytel had set scouts and beacons atop every stretch of coastal hills across East Anglia, and they had watched dutifully for four years without sign of any Viking ships in the narrow sea between England and Frankia. Every Viking attack in recent memory had begun in East Anglia, and so Ulfcytel had prepared his shire for the attack they knew must come. The Danes had always crossed the sea and sought to begin their invasion with attacks on Sandwich or other towns close to the coast and where they could establish a base close to wide rivers where their ships would be safe as they struck inland. Those rivers also offered a fast retreat into the sea should their attack on England turn sour, and enabled them to flee with their plunder across the water to Frankia, where friendly ports could provide succour before any journey home to the north.

'What news, Osgar?' Ulfcytel called and greeted his man with a warm grip of his forearm.

'Greetings, my lords,' Osgar replied in his deep voice, and Beornoth took his arm in the warrior's grip.

'Your men look weary from the road,' said Ulfcytel. 'Send them to the hall, and my people will provide food and drink, and hay for the horses.'

Osgar ordered his men to the hall, and they bowed to Beornoth and Ulfcytel and then rode their mounts slowly towards Ulfcytel's long hall. Osgar followed the two king's thegns to the table where they had taken refreshments, and Ulfcytel offered Osgar a wooden cup of mead, which he drank deeply.

'The Vikings have finally come, lord,' Osgar said after he had drained the cup and set it down on the table.

'Forkbeard?' asked Beornoth.

'Aye.'

'Where?' Ulfcytel said, eyebrows creased. He ran a hand down his iron-grey beard.

'The beacons are lit?'

'No, lord. No beacons. Forkbeard is in Northumbria with six thousand men.'

'Northumbria?'

'Aye. Sailed straight there. News came to us three days ago. The Northumbrian lords have joined Forkbeard, as have every ealdorman and thegn in the Danelaw. They march south and will reach Oxenforda this week.'

The news struck Beornoth like a slap across the face. 'Ealdorman Thered marches with Forkbeard?' he asked in disbelief.

'Aye, as do Lords Sigeferth and Morcar.'

'Ealdorman Alfgar of Cheshire?'

'I do not know, but most northern lords are with Forkbeard. I have seen their army with my own eyes, lord. Messengers came from the king summoning every thegn and ealdorman to Lundenwic, and I bring that message to you.'

'If the Vikings are already at Oxenforda...' Ulfcytel began.

'Then they can take Winchester before the month is out,' Beornoth finished. Winchester was the ancient capital of Wessex power, and the traditional home of England's kings since the country had become one in the reigns of King Alfred's children. Capture it and the Vikings all but sundered Æthelred's rule over his country, just as Guthrum had done a century before when Alfred had fled to the marshes and begun his legendary campaign to win back his kingdom.

'The king is in Lundenwic?'

'He is, lord, as are Eadric Streona and the men of Mercia and Lundenwic's guard.'

'Eadric bastard Streona,' Ulfcytel growled, and kicked a chair over, wincing at the pain in his bad leg. 'This is of his doing. He taxes the northern lords savagely. It is they who have paid Thorkell the Tall's gafol silver. Word of unrest has circulated these last years, a whisper of rebellion, rumours of discontent.'

'I know Ealdormen Thered and Alfgar well,' said Beornoth. 'They would not align themselves with Sweyn Forkbeard. I have not been in Northumbria these last four years. Ealdorman Alfgar of Cheshire suffers the taxation bitterly, and his people hate him for the collections, but I do not believe he would side with the Vikings. We fought them together; his father died fighting them. Ealdorman Thered rules a land peopled by the sons and daughters of Viking settlers, and of them I am not so sure. Thered fought beside me countless times against the Northmen, but his people certainly despise Streona and his taxes. They might see Forkbeard's coming as a liberation, rather than an invasion.' Beornoth thought of his old friend Brand, and even though Brand had saved Beornoth's life after Maldon, it would take much to persuade him to join Forkbeard's army and rebel against Streona's rule.

'Eadric does not rule England. We still have a king, the great-great-grandson of Alfred, no less.'

'We do. But where is that king? The edicts demanding more render than a man can afford bear Eadric's name above the seal of the crown. Æthelred lives, but Streona rules.'

'Osgar, summon the thegns.' Ulfcytel set his jaw. 'We march for Lundenwic.'

* * *

Three weeks later, Beornoth crossed the Thames and entered Lundenwic at the head of eight hundred East Anglian warriors. He rode with Wigs, Gis and Osgar, whilst Ulfcytel led the column on a night-black warhorse and his banner flying proudly from a stout spear. Their hooves clattered across the wooden bridge, and Beornoth rode through the high gate to find the city crammed with warriors. Men thronged the main thoroughfare, lounging against the old Roman walls, hurrying to make way for the horsemen. They carried their spears and shields; some carried skins of ale, and others handfuls of food. More peered down at Beornoth from the ramparts and the windows of wattle houses leaning against each other in the ancient cobbled streets. Ulfcytel led them along the road, and Beornoth saw the sigils of Mercia, Wessex, Defnascir and Somersaete on men's shields.

'Place stinks of shit,' Wigs said, wrinkling his nose at the foul city smell.

'It always does,' Gis replied, 'but I've never seen the place this busy.'

They reached a wide square where Ulfcytel called a halt. He signalled to Beornoth, and the two king's thegns dismounted.

'We'd best find Eadric and the king,' Ulfcytel said with a grimace at the prospect.

Beornoth marched through the narrow lanes he knew so well after his defence of the walls against Forkbeard and Thorkell the Tall, a fight which seemed like a lifetime ago, and yet every street brought familiarity. A market stall reminded him of a dead comrade, a stone arch of an enemy face, a wooden door arch of an enemy ship in the river.

'You were quiet on the road. Even by your standards.'

'The thought of Forkbeard with the Danelaw behind him worries me,' Beornoth replied, vastly understating the sorrow he felt for the kingdom and the peril into which it had fallen. Every waking moment, visions of fighting against men he loved like brothers plagued his mind. Of Thered and Brand standing across from him in the shield wall, of what he would do if he came face-to-face with them in the height of battle. Dark worries, a sadness which kept Beornoth awake at night as he coughed and rolled beneath his blanket, the shadow in his chest pushing and aching at his insides.

'Aye, well. It worries me too. It all worries me. The king is old and sick. You and I are older and sicker. What will become of the kingdom when we are gone?'

Beornoth offered no answer to that question, for it worried at his soul like Níðhǫggr, the serpent Norsemen believed gnawed on the corpses of the dishonourable dead on the corpse shore of their underworld. Beornoth knew their beliefs just as he knew their language. He had grown up beside the men of the Danelaw, fought to uphold their laws, lived amongst them cheek by jowl. Now those same men marched south with a dangerous Viking coming with an army to make himself king of England. Beornoth offered no answer, because deep in the corners of his thought cage he feared England could not stand against such a force. A decade ago perhaps, but now the country did not feel like a kingdom. It felt like a collection of ealdormen and thegns struggling under Streona's oppressive taxes and his malignant influence over the king. Would the great men of England's southern shires rally behind Streona and risk their lives in battle? Beornoth doubted it, and that made his headache like the morning after a Yule feast.

They pressed on through the busy streets, shouldering through men in leather and padded linen armour. The warriors talked among themselves, and

Beornoth listened as he walked. They spoke of the king, gossiping about the state of his health.

'The king is as dead as my old granny,' said one man sitting in a nook between houses, wagging a long finger at a dozen men who listened to his drivel. 'Streona rules, keeping the corpse to prop up at windows and balconies so we think he's alive, whilst that snivelling bastard lives like a king.'

'Whilst we eat slop!' cut in another man.

'A lad from Mercia told me Streona is the son of a thrall and a whore. Imagine that.'

Beornoth lost track of their conversation as he wound around a bend in the road and onto a wide thoroughfare leading to the city stronghold. Guards admitted Ulfcytel and Beornoth into the stone building, and both men surrendered their weapons at the entrance to the royal enclosure, as must all men other than the king's guard. They followed a steward along a corridor lit by window openings cut high into the Roman stone and into a small chamber with two stools, and a small pine table upon which lay a silver platter with bread, cheese and ale.

'Please wait here, my lords,' the steward said after a deep bow. 'The king and his advisors are extremely busy with matters of the utmost urgency, as I am sure you can understand. But I will notify them of your arrival.'

An evening downpour battered the city with a wash of heavy rain, and the sound of rumbling thunder woke Beornoth from his nap. After hours of waiting, Beornoth had fallen asleep with his back against the wall, sitting on a low stool with a belly full of bread. Ulfcytel sat opposite him, kneading at his bad leg.

'You've slept for an hour or more,' he said.

'The older I get, the more I need to sleep and piss,' Beornoth replied, and rubbed the sleep from his eyes. He stood slowly, shoulder, back and legs as stiff as dried wood.

The door swung open on its iron hinges. Two warriors in chain mail stepped under the low lintel and stood on either side of the door. Then Eadric Streona slid through the opening. A tall, thin man, Eadric now carried a paunch about his midriff, and his once lustrous golden beard had grown thinner. He wore his hair long, and had tied it at the nape of his neck with a strip of leather. Eadric had a long, clever face which now bore deep lines across his forehead and beneath his eyes. He stalked into the room, without a bow or greeting to Beornoth or Ulfcytel, one hand resting on the golden pommel of the sword he wore belted at his waist, a privilege he had continued from the days when he was commander of the king's royal guard.

'Winchester has fallen, and Forkbeard comes next for Lundenwic,' he said in his silky voice, but this time tinged with a seriousness which lessened his usual arrogant air. Eadric stood straight and examined the king's thegns. He stared with barely concealed contempt at Beornoth's travel-stained cloak and boots and did the same at the mud Ulfcytel's boots had left upon the stone floor. Eadric himself wore soft leather slippers, palace shoes. He wore heavy gold rings on both hands and a gold crucifix about his neck on a gleaming silver chain.

'God save us,' Ulfcytel said, stunned at the news.

'Was the city defended?' Beornoth asked. Winchester, the seat of Wessex kings, and England's crown. Beornoth had visited Æthelred there many times; it was a hallowed place, a sacred place of kingship and royalty. He had talked with the king in fragrant gardens, visited there alongside Ealdorman Byrhtnoth. Alfred and Aethelstan, both great kings, had ruled from its hallowed ground. Now Forkbeard's growlers drank ale and rolled like drunken boars in its corridors and courtyards.

Eadric met Beornoth's gaze. His right eyebrow raised a fraction, and he ran his tongue beneath his top lip. 'The Danes hunger for Lundenwic and its access to the sea, its trade. Take the city, and you have the Thames, and that river gives you all the trade flowing from our valleys and dales and out to Frankia and beyond, and the trade coming in. He who controls that trade can tax it. We decided it was impossible to defend Winchester against Forkbeard's vast army, and so we defend these walls instead.'

'We?'

'I see you have lost none of your bluntness with age, Lord Beornoth. The king's advisory council decided.'

'You and Thorkell?'

'Happily, I do not answer to you.' Eadric smiled, but his eyes narrowed as both men recalled their last meeting, and a stare of barely concealed enmity passed between them, so awkward became the air in the chamber that Ulfcytel cleared his throat to disturb it.

Another figure stooped beneath the door lintel, but this man was not thin and languid like Eadric. He was hugely tall and broad across the shoulder.

'The war ravens come on the eve of battle,' said Thorkell the Tall, speaking in heavily accented Saxon. He shook both Ulfcytel and Beornoth's forearms in the warrior's grip and grinned as though they were old friends reunited at a cousin's wedding, or Easter celebration. 'Did you bring warriors?'

'We did, the men of East Anglia have come,' said Ulfcytel. 'Eight hundred spears.'

'Good. Then we have five thousand men to defend the walls.'

'How many men are in Forkbeard's army?'

'Two hundred ships and eight thousand men.'

'So many!' Ulfcytel's eyes widened and his jaw dropped.

'This is no raiding force,' Eadric said. 'This is an invasion bent on conquering England. So you see why we could not offer a defence of Winchester.'

'King Sweyn moved fast,' Thorkell added. 'He didn't raid until he came south of Watling Street.'

'Keeping his allies in the Danelaw happy,' said Beornoth. 'He has the north on his side.' King Alfred had determined that everything north of Watling Street should be the Danelaw in his peace with the Vikings, and the old Roman road still served as the border between Saxon lands and the lands settled by the Danes. They had ruled there for many years, until the reign of Æthelred's father, King Edgar, and the death of Eric Bloodaxe.

'The folk in the Danelaw are not unhappy to see a Dane on the throne,' said Thorkell with a shrug.

'Traitors,' Eadric spat. 'Turncloaks who seek their own survival over their oaths and duty to the king.'

'We live in hard times,' Beornoth said, not taking his eyes off Eadric. 'Perhaps the folk in the north have suffered too much.'

'Suffered? What do they know of suffering up there with their sheep shit and mountains? It is in the south that war rages unfettered. They shall be punished. There will be a reckoning, I tell you. A reckoning!'

'Maybe you should tax them.'

Eadric's lip curled, and he shook his head, seeming to win an internal battle with his own anger. 'I have missed you these last four years, Lord Beornoth. At our last conversation, you expressed a concern that our great friend and ally Thorkell would betray us and that his alignment to the king offered nothing but danger to the kingdom, did you not?'

'I did.'

'And yet we have had peace these last four years. No raids, no death, no Saxon folk enslaved.'

'They fear Thorkell and his Jomsvikings, so the Vikings seek easier prey on different shores.'

'So you were wrong, then?'

'We'll see.'

'You doubt me, Lord Beornoth?' asked Thorkell, a gleam in his eye and an amused half-smile creasing his broad face.

'I think you are a brave man, and you and your men fight well. But your allegiance has already shifted once, and it may do so again.'

'Will Forkbeard remain at Winchester?' asked Ulfcytel to change the subject before things got out of hand. 'He could wait for us to march out and face him?'

'No,' said Thorkell. 'He won't wait. Hard to keep an army that size together. He cannot be king of England unless the old king submits to him, or…'

'So he will come to Lundenwic and try to kill the king,' said Beornoth. 'Or force us to surrender.'

'Just so.'

'Then we organise the defence and fight him here.'

'That is the plan, Lord Beornoth,' said Eadric. 'We are not new to the ways of war, Thorkell is feared and respected across the seas and can hold these stout walls against Forkbeard, no matter the size of his army.'

'The city walls are twenty feet high and ten feet thick,' said Thorkell. 'We have reinforced every gate, Aldgate, Bishopsgate, Cripplegate, Newgate, Ludgate and Billingsgate by the river.'

'The walls looked repaired close to the main bridge,' said Ulfcytel.

'After you toppled them onto my ships?' Thorkell laughed as though it were a great joke. 'Yes, my men have repaired the walls.'

'When will he arrive?'

'Perhaps by the end of the week.' Thorkell shrugged.

'Do we expect more men?'

'Speaking of traitors,' said Eadric, and then yawned extravagantly. 'Your friend Godwin, son of Wulfnoth the bastard who cost us our fleet, arrived yesterday with five hundred men of Wessex.'

'Godwin is a good man, and loyal,' said Ulfcytel.

'He wants his father's lands restored.'

'Wulfnoth lives?'

'Oh, dear God, no. My brother caught him and killed him two summers ago, wife too, I think.'

Beornoth had to close his eyes and swallow his rage. Eadric's company had become impossible to bear any longer. His aloofness, his disregard for life or honour, made Beornoth's blood boil. 'Do you need our help to organise the defences?' he asked.

'Beornoth and I have both held Lundenwic before,' said Ulfcytel.

Thorkell nodded and was about to speak when Eadric raised a single finger to silence him. 'No. Lord Thorkell has it under control. You can both rest assured that he knows his business. Go rest. I am sure you are both tired. After all, war is no place for the elderly.' He glowered at Beornoth one last time and strode from the chamber with his hands clasped behind his back.

'The fighting will be hardest at the main bridge of the Thames,' said Thorkell with an apologetic half-smile. 'We shall need your men there. Where we fought, Lord Beornoth, you and I, remember?'

'I remember.'

'And now we fight as friends. Take your men to the bridge and join with Godwin of Wessex.'

Beornoth and Ulfcytel left the chamber and marched along the night-darkened corridors of Lundenwic's great stone keep.

'Eadric is not very fond of you, Beo,' said Ulfcytel once they were out of earshot of Eadric's guards.

'Nor I of him.'

'We shall take our men to the bridge and fight there. Thorkell knows his business, so we must trust him.'

'Trust?' Beornoth chewed on the beard below his bottom lip. How could he trust a Dane like Thorkell? By his very nature, he was a pirate, an adventurer, the jarl of the Jomsvikings. Thorkell had fought for Sweyn Forkbeard for a decade, had helped him become king in Denmark and Norway. How could Beornoth resign himself to complete trust of a man like that, a man he had fought against outside this very city?

'Lord Beornoth?' came a voice from the shadows, startling Beornoth. He reached for the sword he had surrendered at the gate and then relaxed. It was a woman's voice, and a tall, broad-hipped lady stepped from the shadows.

15

'Queen Emma,' said Ulfcytel, and bowed deeply. Beornoth recognised King Æthelred's wife, as tall and straight-backed as he remembered. She wore her blonde hair tied up in coils above her head, and her face bore a grave expression.

'Please, my lords. A moment.' She gestured into a small room behind her, and then turned into the open door, her gown long and swishing about her feet.

Beornoth glanced at Ulfcytel, who shrugged and followed the queen, and so Beornoth went after him. They found themselves in an empty room, walled and floored in cold stone, with no furniture, so that their footsteps echoed around the small space. The door creaked and closed, and a young man appeared from behind it. He pushed the door closed with a loud bang and then turned to face the queen and the king's thegns. He was as tall and well-made as his mother, perhaps eighteen years of age, with the pockmarked scars of youthful spots across his cheeks and forehead.

'My lord,' said the queen, 'may I present Prince Edmund.'

'Lords Beornoth and Ulfcytel,' said the prince, 'it is an honour to meet you both. The city is safer now that you have arrived.'

'You are too kind, lord prince,' said Ulfcytel.

'I saw you enter the keep from a window, and I just...' said Queen Emma, wringing her hands. 'I apologise for my nervousness, but if Lord Eadric saw us talking together...'

'My father grows frailer by the year,' said Edmund. He walked to his mother and placed a reassuring hand on her forearm. She smiled at him and hooked her arm through his. 'His rule has been... influenced in recent times by his councillors. Now we find ourselves in a situation where our noble northern ealdormen would rather side with our enemy than defend their king.'

'The country has suffered, lord prince,' said Beornoth, 'the great northern lords have paid much of the gafol owed to Thorkell. Eadric agreed to it, and they have paid for it. The southern shires had already paid vast sums to the Vikings in recent years, and their well of silver had run dry. So it fell to the Danelaw to find Thorkell's forty-eight thousand pounds of silver.'

'Lord Eadric is the reason I have brought you into this quiet corner of the keep.'

'Be careful,' warned Ulfcytel. 'Royal walls have ears, and Eadric is not a man to cross lightly. So, choose your words carefully, my prince.'

'I thank you for your concern, and I will speak plainly, for we do not have much time. There are some who would like to see Eadric removed from influence at court. Without Eadric, perhaps our northern nobles would reconsider their support for Forkbeard?'

'I doubt their loyalty to our king falters even now,' said Beornoth. 'But men need to see the king and hear him speak. It seems to them that Streona rules England and not Æthelred.'

'There are men loyal to my father, and to me, who would curtail Eadric's influence. Can I count on you both, on your reputations, to join us?'

'You have my sword, Prince Edmund,' said Ulfcytel, 'but these are matters best discussed after the defence of this city is over, hopefully after we have been victorious. And even then, this is a delicate matter. Eadric has spies everywhere. Every servant, thrall, lord, priest or bishop could be his spy, who would gladly run to him to whisper your secrets for a handful of silver or the promise of advancement. What do you think Eadric will do if he finds out that you plot against him?'

'He will kill you,' Beornoth added. 'He will declare you traitors and have you butchered. Do not doubt it.'

'I am young, but no fool, my lords. Can I count on your loyalty?'

'Of course. I would fight to the very last for you and your father. I took an oath when I became a king's thegn to protect the king with my life, and I would sooner die than break it.'

'Then we wait for the right time. We fight Forkbeard, and we band together and pull my father away from Eadric's influence.' Edmund extended his hand to Beornoth and stared deep into his eyes. There was strength there, and conviction, a strength Beornoth had not seen in the king. It stirred him, gave him hope for what might be. He took the prince's forearm, and Edmund's grip was strong. He nodded to Beornoth, and shook Ulfcytel's arm in the same determined way.

'And now for another delicate, but necessary matter,' said Queen Emma. 'Whether or not Forkbeard takes Lundenwic, my son and I shall sail for Frankia and the court of my brother, the duke of Normandy. The king may follow, for we cannot hope to defeat Forkbeard in battle, not as things stand.'

'If the king flees, my lady, then Forkbeard will declare himself king.'

'He will. But we shall return. My husband will return. When that happens, we shall need an army to win back the throne. Can we count on your support?'

'The king cannot flee, my lady.' Beornoth could not hide the desperation in his voice. If the king left, he would never return, and the war against the Vikings would be over. England would become Daneland and Forkbeard would be king. Everything Beornoth had fought for, everything his family and friends had died for, would go up in ashes, wasted, lost in the mists of time as though they had never existed at all.

'Do you believe Eadric and Thorkell will stay true to my husband once it becomes apparent that the kingdom is doomed? Will they protect our king when Forkbeard asks for their surrender and promises that they may keep their land and titles if they only swear allegiance to him?'

'We cannot simply run away, my lady.'

'Should we stay here locked up inside this keep whilst our lords desert us one by one? Do we watch from shuttered windows, waiting in fear for the day warriors march into these very corridors to take our heads? To take my son's head? If we go now, we do so to live and fight again another day. We do not run. We shall regroup, organise, plan, and return. My brother is Duke Richard the Fearless and did not earn that name by running and cowering from battle. He will offer us sanctuary in Normandy. I am the granddaughter of Vikings; their blood flows through my veins. I do not fear conflict, Lord Beornoth. I may be a woman and a queen and so cannot stand in the shield wall as you do. But a woman can be as brave as a man. A queen can have the same courage as a warrior. I must fight to protect my family and for my husband. My weapon is my mind, just as yours is your sword. I will not cower here and wait for men to come and kill my husband and my son. If we defeat King Sweyn here at Lundenwic and he sails away to Denmark, then we need never talk of this matter again. But if he stays, even if we win, then I will take my son across the sea and prepare to retake our country. Forkbeard has the Danelaw, and now much of the south as well. We need soldiers to win, and ealdormen who will support us and bring their men to fight.'

'But we must have allies here in England,' said Edmund. 'A base from which we can build and rise again. We need loyal, brave men we can trust, and who the people trust. The northern lords who join Forkbeard do not do so out of hatred of my father or rebellion against his rule. They do it because they despise Eadric. If we can remove Eadric, men will return to my father's banner, especially if they see heroes at my side and at my father's side. Who better than Beornoth and Ulfcytel, the great Viking killers, to show them the way?'

'We are loyal, lord prince,' said Ulfcytel, and he raised hands and clasped them together like a man praying in church. 'I understand the need to protect the heir to the throne, but the king cannot leave these shores.'

'Sweyn Forkbeard will declare himself king if Æthelred leaves,' Beornoth said, cutting to the point but trying to soften his hard voice as much as possible. 'He is a Christian, just like us, and the bishops and priests will endorse his rule. They will say he is God's anointed king and crown him at Winchester. He will be king, and your family will be little more than exiles relying on relatives abroad for bed, food and safety.'

'We shall only take to the sea if Forkbeard remains in England after this battle is over. If he sails home, then we shall stay. If Forkbeard dies during the fighting, we shall stay. If the defence of this great city fails, we shall leave and protect the crown. All I ask of you is your loyalty, and I believe we have it.'

'To the very end, lord prince,' said Beornoth.

'I thank you both,' said Queen Emma, and she smiled sadly. 'Now, you should go. Eadric's men will notice if you tarry any longer. Go, and I wish you luck in the battle to come.'

'Thank you, lady. One last question before we go. Can you arrange an audience with the king? Perhaps if I can meet him, I could talk to him of Eadric and the danger he faces?'

'Regretfully, my husband the king is not a well man. He spends much of his time in his chamber, and Eadric's men guard that room.'

Beornoth sighed and took his leave. He and Ulfcytel marched out of the keep's labyrinthine corridors, and Beornoth's neck itched. It was as though eyes watched him from every shadowed corner and every door. A strange feeling, like feeling eyes upon you in a crowd and catching a stranger's eye just as they look quickly away.

'This war is like an onion,' Ulfcytel whispered, 'with too many layers to peel back.'

'I am no man for back-stabbing and courtly intrigue,' Beornoth said, still glancing about him along the dark corridors. 'I am a warrior. Give me a battle and a shield wall to face any day, but not whispering behind closed doors.'

'I agree, old friend. But the queen and prince have the right of it. We live in dangerous times, and I do not disagree with their reasoning.'

'Let them decide what they wish, and I will support the crown.'

Ulfcytel chuckled, and the sound was a relief after the strained discussions with Streona and the queen. 'If only all men were as straightforward as you, the world would be a better place.'

Wigs and Gis had commandeered a house left empty as its residents had fled the city when news of Forkbeard's advance filtered down to the common folk. Beornoth sat down on a high-backed pine chair, his bones aching after a long evening spent listening to scouts' reports. Eadric and Thorkell had not consulted the two veterans on their battle plan. Orders came down through one of Eadric's captains. Scouts came to Beornoth and Ulfcytel out of respect rather than because Eadric wished them to have any information of Forkbeard's movements. They ate a small meal of hard bread and fish caught that day in the river and drank ale from horn cups.

'So we fight for this city again,' said Gis, after what seemed like an age of silence. Beornoth was not in the mood for small talk, even less so than usual. His mind churned, going over and over Eadric's words, and the pleas of Queen Emma and Prince Edmund. Too many problems weighed the kingdom down, buckling it like a wagon filled with too much cargo.

'This isn't even our home,' Wigs replied. 'It stinks. The river is browner than runny shit, its people are thankless, and I swear the place is haunted.'

'Haunted?' Gis almost spat out his bread.

'Fetches. Ghosts. Whatever you want to call it. I can hear them whispering in the night. I hate this bloody place. I don't want to die here.'

'It's the wind catching in cracks in the walls, not ghosts.'

'I've wind coming out of the crack of my arse, but it doesn't sound like the fetches of dead Romans.'

Gis laughed so hard he banged the table. 'Where do we fight, lord?' he asked, catching his breath when he noticed the lack of humour on Beornoth's hard face.

'On the bridge,' he said.

'When will they come?'

'Tomorrow, the scouts say. So don't drink too much. We rise before the sun and secure the bridge.'

'We don't fight on the walls or above the gate?'

'Not this time. We hold the bridge.' Beornoth coughed, a dry, burning cough that shook his entire body. He bent double and coughed again, wheezing this time, clutching at the pain in his chest.

'Take a drink, lord,' said Wigs, kicking out his chair and surging to his feet.

Beornoth spat a horrible gobbet of blood and sat back against the wall. He sweated and trembled, the shadow in his chest pushing at his insides like a fist. He let Wigs and Gis help him to the cot they had prepared with straw and his cloak for a blanket. Beornoth lay down and closed his eyes and worried about the horror awaiting him on Lundenwic bridge, and if his strength would hold when Forkbeard's growlers came with their axes and spears and hearts full of malice.

16

Beornoth stomped his feet, boots banging on the bridge's wooden slats as he tried to keep out the cold. Frost clung to the timbers and walls, and a mist steamed above the river like dragon's breath despite the summer season. The sun sat low in the sky, barely a wan, pallid glow in a grey death-coloured sky. He peered over the bridge, and the river ran black beneath the two hundred men Beornoth and Ulfcytel had brought to defend it. The men of East Anglia, warriors they had practised and drilled all summer to meet the dreaded enemy in the shield wall, now prepared to protect a long, wide bridge from Viking warships who would come and disgorge brutal warriors bent on hacking the way over the bridge and battering through the gate to enter the city, where pillage and treasure awaited as a reward for their savage bravery.

'Do you hear that?' Ulfcytel growled, cocking an ear to the sky.

Beornoth listened, and above the flow of water and the grumbles of men woken from their beds came the creak of oars, the groan of timber and the whispered, guttural voices of men heaving at oars as they splashed in the water. The Vikings were coming.

Beornoth rested his hand on the worn haft of his spear, and with the other he pushed his helmet onto his head and closed its cheekpieces. He took a breath of damp air and thought a silent prayer, asking God to keep his pain away, to still his coughing and give his old body enough strength to do what must be done. The bridge was the heart of the city's defence. First built by the

Romans in the echoes of time and reinforced by lesser artisans over the long years, its oak beams were thicker than a man's chest. It stretched from one bank to the other, its piles driven deep into the riverbed. Silt rose slick and dirty on each bank, and the waters rose high against the walls because the tide was in flood. The estuary further east was much more tidal where it flowed wide and muddy through marshland and bogs, and that tide still affected the river here where it flowed alongside the stone walls.

'Prepare yourselves,' Beornoth barked at the men. 'Stoke the fires and ready the oil and water. Spears and shields to the front.'

Men busied themselves with the preparations, and Ulfcytel marched to the far bank with one hundred men to defend that side of the bridge. The river ran nine hundred feet wide beneath the bridge, vast and as loud as a summer thunderstorm.

'It's our job to stop them here,' Beornoth said as men formed up around him. 'We hold them so that they cannot bring their ships past this point. We don't have enough men to defend the entire length of the city walls, but hold them here and our men will punish them from the walls above. If we let them through, their ladders will overwhelm our walls and the city will fall. Our king is within, and the folk who depend on us for their protection. Two hundred ships come to destroy us and to destroy our kingdom. But they can only bring two dozen ships to bear against us at one time, the rest of them must wait or risk sailing beneath us as we loose our arrows at them, as we pour boiling oil upon their heads and drop masonry through their decks. So hold them here, kill the bastards and trust that the men on the walls will do the rest.'

Gates of heavy oak barred entry to the city, and towers rose above them where the city levy waited behind piles of rock to hurl at the enemy should they reach the gateway. The bridge's rail served as a fighting platform, a timber parapet from where Beornoth and his men could look down upon the river and hurl death into the faces of their enemies. The city waited, the stubborn jewel of England, which had held firm against so many Viking attacks. Its Roman walls still stood high and hard, though time had gnawed their stones and Saxon timber-work repaired the structure because men no longer possessed the stonemasonry skills of the long-gone legions. The streets sat cramped and stinking beyond the walls and the gate tower. The houses were a mix of wattle, daub, timber and thatch, but its people were proud and the city levy had taken up spear and bow to defend their hearths.

'Steady,' Beornoth said to his men, who shuffled nervously as they listened to the sounds of an approaching enemy, of men who came to kill them. These were the warriors who would do the hard fighting, who would stand and do battle beside Beornoth. Above on the walls stood the common folk, the butchers, weavers and smiths all called to the city's defence. They stood and peered over the battlements with frightened faces alongside boys with slings and old men with rusted mattocks and spare shields. Lundenwic's souls prepared to defend their homes with their lives.

'A not so friendly face, but a welcome one,' said Wigs as Osgar's monstrous frame sidled through the men to stand beside Beornoth.

'Why aren't you with Ulfcytel?' Beornoth asked.

'I was,' he replied in his deep, slow voice. 'He ordered me here.'

'Why?'

'To fight beside you, lord.'

Beornoth frowned. Ulfcytel had sent the baleful warrior and his enormous axe to protect Beornoth, to mind him when the blades came just in case Beornoth's strength gave out. He did not object, though it was another nail in the coffin of his warrior's pride. He understood that if he fell, if Beornoth the Viking killer died in battle on the bridge, the army's morale would plummet, so he suffered Osgar's presence in silence. In truth, death was not an unwelcome prospect. His years grew long, and most of the people he had loved were dead. Beornoth stiffened and rolled his neck. Better to die in battle, as a warrior should, than coughing up blood in a sweat-soaked bed.

The first dragon-prowed ships appeared through the mist. Their snarling beast heads loomed, painted in red and gold, dragons, bears, eagles and wolves, and their oars beat in perfect time. A great wail went up from the city walls, and to Beornoth's right, Ulfcytel's men shouted in unison as they came to attention, ready to kill.

'Here they come,' Beornoth said, and his men shouted a curt salute as they formed ranks around him. 'Ready the pitch and water. Wigs and Gis, see to it.'

'Yes, lord,' both men replied, and slipped from the east-facing side of the bridge to help the men behind prepare the cauldrons boiling on fires, set in between piles of masonry brought out from the city in preparation for battle. Ships beyond count came into view, and a Viking war horn sounded an undulating tune, after which eight thousand voices bellowed their war cries. The sound was enough to shake the bridge and the river beneath, and Beornoth's heart quickened, his palms became sweaty, and he steadied himself. So many of the enemy came it appeared the river had become a shifting mass of timber, oars, spears and shields.

'Archers!' Beornoth shouted.

The bowmen stepped forward, bows creaked, arrows nocked, faces pale in the grey dawn. All along the battlements, archers appeared, leaning over to point their iron-tipped missiles at the enemy fleet. The ships came on, Forkbeard's banner flying proudly from mast posts. Beornoth searched for any sign of Ealdorman Thered's sigil, of Brand, Sigeferth or Morcar, but saw none in that tangle of hulls, rigging and steel. A cry went up from a Viking ship, and the enemy roared as one, and it was as though the world shuddered beneath their fury. Spear points and mail glinted in the faint light, and as the ships came closer, Beornoth could make out bearded faces. It was time.

'Loose!' Beornoth ordered.

Arrows darkened the sky. Shafts hissed through the clearing mist down into the packed ships, thudding into shields, punching through leather and skewering flesh. A man toppled from a prow with an arrow through his throat. Another wailed like a child with a shaft buried in his groin. The Danes replied with their own arrow storm. Missiles rattled against Saxon shields, and Beornoth crouched behind his own as arrows slammed into the wooden bridge and skittered off the stone walls. A young warrior let out a grunt and folded over, a shaft in his belly. He screamed and then fell face first into the Thames.

'Here they come!' Beornoth warned, and the first ship struck the bridge. Its hull smashed against the oak piles stuck into the riverbed, and snarling Vikings leapt from the deck with grappling hooks and axes, their iron points biting into the bridge's timbers. They hauled, straining to drag themselves closer as more arrows rained down from the second line of ships to keep the Saxons behind their shields. 'Kill them!' Beornoth roared as the first face appeared above the fighting platform.

Beornoth surged from behind his shield and smashed his heel into the Viking's face, feeling nose and cheekbone crunch beneath his heel. An arrow whistled over Beornoth's shoulder, and another enemy appeared beneath him. Beornoth grabbed a fistful of the warrior's hair and yanked his head down towards the bridge. He wrestled the axe from the Viking's fingers and chopped it down hard into the back of the man's neck. The head came away after the second blow, and Beornoth threw it onto the closest ship's deck.

'Three of the bastards are through,' he growled, and turned to Osgar. 'Hold them here whilst I send the others to the bottom.'

Osgar hefted his war axe, its double blades shining in the wan morning light, and Beornoth turned away from the fighting, leaving Osgar to take his place on the fighting platform. Beornoth hurried to where Wigs and Gis waited beside the broiling cauldrons and the piles of rocks set at intervals in between the cauldrons and their smoking fires.

'It's ready, lord,' Gis shouted above the now cacophonous din as a Viking army howled and roared its anger from two hundred warships rowing along the Thames towards Lundenwic bridge, and as the defenders on the high walls roared their defiance down at their hated foes. Gis stood on a ladder, half leaning away from a large iron cauldron as he did his best to peer over its edge and check its condition without burning his face off in its foul-smelling steam.

'Then burn them, throw the cauldrons onto their decks and destroy them,' Beornoth said.

Gis leapt down from the ladder and joined Wigs and two dozen men as they lifted the cauldrons from their fires using long wooden staves. Beornoth paused and peered down between his feet and through the bridge's timbers as a drakkar warship glided underneath the bridge. A bearded face looked up at him and grinned. A man with a broad brow and a beard the colour of summer straw licked his lips like a hungry wolf closing in on its prey, and Beornoth bent to pick up a flaming log from the fire upon which the cauldron had boiled.

When Forkbeard had attacked Lundenwic before, he and Thorkell had attacked the bridge and the walls simultaneously, aiming to overwhelm the defenders. Thorkell himself had launched an all-out attack on one section of wall, using hundreds of ladders to secure a foothold on the battlements and sweep the Saxons away. Both attempts had failed, and Beornoth had been there with a bloodied sword. This time Forkbeard had come with a vast army, men from far shores across the sea, hard warriors from the Skagerrak and Kattegat straits, from Jutland, the Vik, and the myriad fjords and islands of distant Norway where men grew big and strong on fermented whale and shark meat, along with them came the half-Saxon warriors of the Danelaw. With his superior numbers and his deep cunning, this time Forkbeard wanted to stretch the defenders. The Roman walls covered one thousand eight hundred feet along the river, rising in sheer stone from the silted banks, and Forkbeard knew the Saxons had not the numbers to defend its entire stretch effectively. He wanted to attack along its length, to take the bridge and the walls and conquer the famous old city which had for so long eluded the Vikings' vicious attacks.

Beornoth reached over the cauldron and touched the flaming log to the pitch, and its contents whooshed as it caught fire. He stalked along the bridge and lit four more. Forkbeard wanted his ships to pass beneath the huge bridge and stretch his force far along the fortifications, and Beornoth would stop him.

'Now,' he said.

Three Viking warships emerged from the far side of the bridge, and once their curved hulls glided clear – when their mast posts which the sailors had removed to lay lengthways along the ships' decks poked through the edge – Wigs and Gis tipped the first flaming cauldron onto the Viking ship. The burning pitch stank, stinging the inside of Beornoth's nose. It dropped slowly at first, then the Vikings screamed in terror as the heavy iron cauldron slammed into their precious ship. Its weight crushed the clinker-built timbers, and the fire roared as the sticky, horrendous pitch burned men's faces, arms and hair. The Vikings tried to beat the flames from their bodies with their bare hands, and their skin sloughed away as the fire roared, devouring shields and furled sails. The boat lurched as its shipmaster abandoned the steering oar and along the bridge Beornoth's men repeated the action, pouring boiling, flaming pitch onto the enemy. Others poured boiling water onto the foe and then cast the heavy cauldrons over the side to crush ships' timbers like a boot through rotten wood.

Vikings leapt overboard to escape the flames. The ships canted as water surged through broken timbers, and the Thames swallowed them into its murky depths.

'Kill them!' Beornoth roared, sword aloft.

His men loosed yet more arrows into the defenders, and as those first ships fouled in the water, more drakkars came behind trying to push them forward like sheep in a pen. Ulfcytel's men fought the same battle further along the bridge. Two ships had broken through there, but the shipmasters backed oars in open river water, staring back in horror as their comrades burned, drowned and died beneath the horror of Lundenwic bridge.

More ships came on. They crowded the river, oars thrashing, prows crunching into the bridge piles and into the ships in front of them. Vikings tried to clamber up the bridge from the floundered warships, and Wigs skewered a Dane through the throat with his spear. More came on and died as the defenders waited for heads and chests to appear before skewering them with their blades. Viking jarls roared orders at their men trying to organise a counter-attack against the initial Saxon victory at the bridge. Some of Forkbeard's fleet had reached the walls before the bridge and ladders rose shakily like old men's fingers to rest against the walls as Eadric and Thorkell's men hurled down rocks, spears and arrows at the Vikings below.

Ladders also touched the bridge platform, and Beornoth left Wigs and Gis to continue the slaughter at the western edge of the bridge where Danes still tried to escape the ruined boats. On the east side, the enemy swarmed up their ladders set against the bridge. These were the dangerous men, the brave ones who fought with reckless abandon and came to burnish their warrior reputations bright with the slaughter of Saxon defenders. They came with axes in their fists and hate in their eyes. A Dane caught a spear thrust and used the strength built into his shoulders and arms from a lifetime at the oar to drag the Saxon over the fighting platform to fall onto his ship's deck where the man would die in a welter of blades. The Dane roared like an animal, tried to swing his axe at another defender and then died as Osgar appeared and hit the warrior so hard with his axe that he almost cut him in two from shoulder to groin.

More Vikings came up those ladders like spiders scuttling across a web to catch their prey. Another enemy gained the platform and swung his axe at Beornoth, but he dodged the blow and jabbed his sword point into the warrior's gut. He shoved, felt it rip through leather, and the Viking's eyes went wide as Beornoth kicked him back into the river. The fight raged along the bridge. Arrows hissed from ships and walls. A man next to Beornoth died as an enemy threw his axe over the bridge and it struck the Saxon like a meat cleaver into his face. Smoke from the burning ships coiled across the water, and the air stank of pitch, blood and sweat.

Still they came on. Forkbeard wanted the bridge, needed to get his ships through the gap because, if he took it, he could overwhelm the defenders all along the vast stretch of walls beyond the bridge and take the city. His men rowed with fury, oars hammering the black water, their angry shouts drowning out the cries of the wounded. But the ships came on too fast and too determined and crashed into the vessels already caught beneath the bridge. Another three made it through and wallowed in the water, waiting for others to join them. More canted in the water, pressed together as shipmasters bellowed curses at each other across the bows. Saxon archers poured arrows into them, threw rocks onto their decks. Men died, shields splintered, and Beornoth searched the water for any sight of Forkbeard himself but found none.

'Keep them back!' Beornoth shouted to his men. 'Hold the bridge!'

The warriors roared in response. So many Vikings had died on the platform that blood washed its timbers slick, but still more of the enemy came to die as Beornoth's men stabbed and tore at them with spears, axes, knives and seaxes. Hours passed. Attack after attack came at the bridge. The sun climbed, turning the mist to gold and then smoky ash as more ships burned. The Vikings came on in vast numbers and with unthinkable bravery, but the bridge held, and along the walls the defenders thrust ladders aside and crushed enemy skulls.

By midday, the river had become choked with wrecks. Broken ships bumped against the piles. Bodies floated past the bridge like gruesome fish with wounds washed clean by the water. Seagulls wheeled overhead, shrieking, already scenting death. Beornoth's strength waned. He let Osgar and the younger men lead the slaughter as he leaned on a spear and gave orders, sword sheathed in its scabbard. Murder rained down from the high walls, and Thorkell prowled there with axe in hand, his colossal figure unmistakable as he hacked at ladders and led King Æthelred's Saxons in their defence against his countrymen and former comrades.

Wigs had suffered a spear wound across his arm, and he crouched beside Beornoth as a warrior bound the injury with a clean scrap of cloth. Wounded men lay all about them, groaning and writhing in agony as the battle raged across the water. The three ships that had passed the bridge had wallowed there under fire from the walls until their shipmasters had abandoned assaulting the western stretch of wall with just their ships alone and had tried to return under the bridge. The wreck of their ships joined the rest as Ulfcytel's men battered them with missiles and sundered their hulls with broken masonry.

The Viking war horn blared again, sonorous and undulating, and Beornoth was certain he could hear Sweyn Forkbeard's voice bellowing through the chaos, urging his army on to one more push. And push they did, coming on in one last furious assault. They screamed their oaths to Christ, Odin and Thor and attacked the bridge and the walls. And the defenders broke them. Spears thrust, axes hewed, rock and brick smashed and hammered at the Vikings, and they could not prise Beornoth and his men from the oak beams of the bridge.

At last the enemy war horn blew once more, a deep, mournful note. The Vikings backed oars, churning the blood-red water, and slowly, grudgingly, the enemy fleet retreated downriver. Lundenwic bridge stood, and the defenders roared and wept at their triumph and the sheer joy of survival and victory over an enemy who had come to kill them. A voice called across the water, and Beornoth shuffled through his men, his limbs exhausted, and his strength spent. There, on a Viking drakkar, stood Brand Thorkilsson. A Viking, a savage warrior who had saved Beornoth's life after the slaughter at Maldon, and for whom Beornoth had risked his own life to defend Brand's family against a Norman war band. Brand stood in the stern with his hand raised in greeting. He wore a byrnie and wore his long hair in two braids, there was grey in his beard and he smiled, like they were two friends greeting one another in a crowd rather than enemies across the field of battle.

A wave of sadness overwhelmed Beornoth in that moment, to see Brand facing him, knowing that Thered and other men from the Danelaw he knew were with an enemy who had come to make Sweyn Forkbeard king of England. The sheer madness of it cut at Beornoth, that after his long life of constant warfare it had come to this, men of England fighting each other, split by Streona's taxes and his malign influence over the king. Beornoth suddenly felt his years. He waved to Brand and then fell back. Only the spear kept him on his feet. The shadow inside his chest throbbed and pushed at his insides. Beornoth staggered, and Wigs surged up from his treatment to catch Beornoth's arm.

'Are you alright, lord?' he said, but his voice sounded muffled and distant.

A cough burst from Beornoth's throat like a bear's roar, followed by another. His body shook, and a gout of dark, filthy blood fell into his beard. Darkness came in slow blinks, and Beornoth slipped away. He fell and did not feel himself land.

17

Light shone as bright as gold, warm like a mother's embrace. Beornoth heard a woman's voice.

'Eawynn?' he whispered, hoping, wondering if he had reached heaven and his wife and beloved daughters welcomed him.

'He's awake,' said the woman, but her voice was unfamiliar.

Beornoth opened his eyes. The light blinded him for a moment and then he could make out shapes before him.

'Lord, can you hear us?' said Gis.

'Don't get too close,' said Wigs, 'he doesn't want to smell your arse breath when he wakes up. Give him room to breathe.'

'Where am I?' Beornoth croaked, his throat as dry as a sun-parched river.

'In the keep, lord, at Lundenwic.'

Beornoth looked down to find himself in a bed covered by a long fur blanket and wearing a woollen jerkin. 'How long since the battle?'

'Three days, lord.'

'I have slept for three days?'

'We thought you were dead at first, but then a priest felt a whisper of breath from your mouth, so he brought you up here and you're alive!'

'Idiot,' said Gis as he clouted Wigs around the head. 'Drink this, lord.' He handed Beornoth a wooden mug of his honeyed drink, and Beornoth drank it thirstily.

'Where is Forkbeard?'

'Gone west, lord. To take the rest of the shires.'

'Help me.' Beornoth lifted himself on his elbows and tried to rise.

'You are supposed to rest, lord.'

'Help me up, I said.' It was bad enough to need help, never mind asking for it twice like a cripple.

Wigs and Gis helped Beornoth stand. They objected to him dressing in mail and his heavy belt until Beornoth threatened them with violence, and so he left his sickbed dressed as a warlord. He marched on unsteady feet, using the cold walls to brace himself at first and then striding more confidently as his boots pounded the keep's corridors.

'Where is Ulfcytel?' he asked.

'I'll show you, lord,' said Gis, and he hurried past Beornoth to show him the way.

The two warriors exchanged nervous glances, and Beornoth chewed his beard, wondering what further bad news they were holding from him. The city had held firm. Forkbeard was still on the loose, but he had surely lost many of his men in the attempt on Lundenwic. Beornoth resisted the urge to ask Wigs or Gis, preferring to get whatever the news was from Ulfcytel, blunt and to the point rather than listen to his loyal companions dance around it for fear of upsetting him.

They found Ulfcytel in the keep's hall, a long stone room with a fire burning at one end and a figure sitting hunched before it on a stool. Beornoth approached, and Wigs and Gis waited by the door. His boots crunched the floor rushes, and Ulfcytel's hunched figure half turned his head, and then turned back to the fire. Its orange light danced on the links of his chain mail, and he sat straighter as Beornoth approached and waved to a steward by a distant table to bring ale.

'Lord Beornoth,' he said, in a distant, detached tone. 'Up and about?'

'Just about,' he replied. 'What news?'

'News.' He spoke slowly with a shake of his head. Ulfcytel took a cup from the steward, as did Beornoth. Ulfcytel stood and walked to the fire. He placed one hand on the wall beside the hearth and stared into its blaze.

Beornoth drank his ale to give Ulfcytel a moment to gather himself, but the mood was ominous, and after he had drained the cup, Beornoth moved closer to the East Anglian warlord.

'What has happened?' he asked.

Ulfcytel snapped out of his melancholy and clapped Beornoth on the shoulder. 'Much and more, old friend. Thorkell the Tall has betrayed us and taken his ships and his men to join with Forkbeard. The queen and prince left yesterday for Normandy, and the king will follow today. We won the fight for Lundenwic, but the realm slips away from us like sand through our fingers.'

'Thorkell? Why leave us after defending the city against his old master?'

Ulfcytel shrugged. 'He left the day after. Said not a word. He simply marched his men out of the city, went to his ships and sailed west. Word came of his betrayal days later. Perhaps he could smell defeat on us and wanted to get on the right side before it was too late.'

'Bastard. I'd wager his ships could barely float with all the silver he took from the kingdom.'

'The gafol has been a curse on our nation since it was first paid. You have spoken out against it many times, as have I. Those cursed payments serve only as a lure on a fishing pole, bringing hungry Vikings to our waters to bleed us dry.'

'Aye, better to fight to the last and deter any future raids than to make the wolves rich. We must raise an army and meet Forkbeard in the field.'

'What army? Without the king? Godwin has marched west with the Wessex men to defend their homes as best they can. It's just us, Beo, and my East Anglians. The king's guard will go east to Normandy with the king, and the Lundenwic guard and its levy must remain here to protect the city. We have no army.'

'Streona?'

'Still here organising the king's passage to Normandy.'

'He goes with Æthelred.'

'Of course he does. They have plans to return with an army of Norman warriors to wrest the kingdom back from Forkbeard.'

'So they believe the kingdom is lost?'

'They do. They have all but surrendered and flee for their lives.'

'If the king has not yet departed, perhaps there is a chance to dissuade him? If he stays, he can retreat into East Anglia with us. He can be a beacon for men to rally around, just like when King Alfred fled into the marshes.'

'You can try. But you will need to see the king to persuade him to stay. Eadric keeps him hidden in his sickbed. I must prepare my men to march. East

Anglia lies unprotected whilst we remain here, and what if a new force of Vikings arrives, smelling the stench of our kingdom's rotting corpse and coming to feast upon its remnants?'

'Wait for me at the east gate.'

Beornoth stalked from the hall, and Wigs and Gis followed. They pounded along the corridors as Beornoth breathed slowly to keep his anger at bay. The city walls stood firm, but whilst he had slept, laid low by his affliction, everything within had crumbled. They found a steward, and Beornoth asked him where he could find the king. He looked at Beornoth, terrified by his size and countenance, and pointed a shaking finger along a winding corridor. Beornoth followed his direction, and the steward ran away with his soft slippers stroking the cold stone floor.

Two guards holding spears stood before an ancient oak door, its timbers blackened and its iron hinges showing rust at the edges.

'I am Beornoth, king's thegn, come to speak to the king,' he said in a commanding voice.

They said nothing but stood aside, which surprised Beornoth because he had expected them to refuse his demand. Beornoth pushed the door open and stepped inside to find Eadric Streona waiting for him, sitting in a high-backed chair, lounging like a lord at rest. The steward who had pointed Beornoth to that room stood halfway through a rear door, a frightened look on his pale face. He turned and ran away, and Beornoth faced a grinning Eadric.

'Surprised, Lord Beornoth?' Eadric said, and crossed his long legs. 'Looking for someone else?'

'I came to see King Æthelred,' Beornoth said, unable to stop his lip from curling at the sight of the man he blamed for the kingdom's downfall.

'I heard you were at death's door. I prayed for you.'

'Where is the king?'

'Sick. Very sick. But we depart for Normandy shortly, and the sea air will do him good. I would offer you a berth on the royal ship. But we are full, I'm afraid.'

'If the king leaves, Forkbeard will have himself declared king. All will be lost.'

'We shall return with an army and restore the king to his throne. It is a matter of time and troops, that's all.'

'Time? A Viking is about to take the throne of England, and we must fight!'

'Fight with what? Should you and I ride across the valleys and fight the foe in glorious combat? We can raise what, eight hundred men, perhaps a thousand? Sweyn Forkbeard has eight thousand men, perhaps seven after the assault on Lundenwic, but more of our nobles flock to his banner every day. He has Thorkell's men and ships, and we are doomed if we stay. So, we must withdraw, regroup, and fight again when we can.'

'Thorkell betrayed you.'

Eadric laughed and shook his head. He rose and yawned as if there were nothing at all wrong with the world.

'All men betray. All men lie. Except for you, is that what you want me to believe, Lord Beornoth? Have you never made a mistake, never broken an oath, told a lie?'

Beornoth thought of his descent into drunkenness following his daughter's death, of how he had lived as a reeve and the dark deeds of those distant days. 'We are none of us saints. But you forced the northern lords to pay Thorkell his forty-eight thousand pounds of silver, leading them into Forkbeard's lap. Thorkell himself battered our country into submission before he joined you and took our silver. He softened us up for the kill, and you drove the Danelaw to Forkbeard.'

'I must leave you now, Lord Beornoth, though I wish we could continue this pleasant conversation.'

'I will see the king.'

Eadric turned, the pretence of aristocratic arrogance falling from his face to be replaced by a taut snarl. 'You will not!' he shouted, face reddening. 'I decide who sees the king. Go back to your sword and your horse. You march around this keep with your hard face and your scars and play at lordship? You think to come in here and tell me what is what with the kingdom? You think like a child. What do you know about the politics of this nation? The king can barely think for himself. Who do you think has run this land since his body and mind failed him?'

'You have, and look where we are, Eadric Streona.' Beornoth gave Eadric the name folk used to mock him behind his back. He wanted to kill Eadric in that moment, and it would be so easy. One snap of the neck and his poison would be gone from the land forever. But he held himself.

'The Grasper. I have heard that name before, Lord Beornoth. Is that what you are reduced to? Hurling insults like children fighting behind a pigsty? They tell me you fought well on the bridge. Well enough for a grey-haired old fool, anyway. You almost died from the exertion. Better that you had, I think. Your time is over. The time of Byrhtnoth, the age of heroes, of bards and songs of warriors is over. The world has moved on. We must learn to live and trade with our foreign neighbours, to think beyond England and its petty squabbles. There are empires out there, and we are fighting over scraps of mud and sheep shit.'

'We fight for our king and for our families.'

Eadric sighed and laughed, rubbing his eyes. 'I leave for Normandy. The king is already aboard his ship. It is arranged. Goodbye, Lord Beornoth, I truly hope we never meet again.'

Beornoth stepped forward, closing the gap between them quickly. He loomed over Eadric, casting the slender man in shadow, and Streona stumbled backwards to get away from Beornoth's imposing figure.

'Guards!' he called in a curiously high-pitched voice, and two burly warriors burst into the room.

Beornoth smiled at Eadric's fear, and the ealdorman of Mercia slid between his men and hurried out of the door.

'I thought you were going to kill him,' said Gis when the big men had gone.

'Maybe I was,' Beornoth replied.

'Maybe you should have,' said Wigs.

They went to the city battlements and found Ulfcytel there with his captains. A dozen men stood on Lundenwic's walls, where they had spilled blood and seen good men die. They watched as three ships flying the king's dragon banner eased away from the city under oars, heading east towards the narrow sea. Smaller ships worked to drag the debris of burned and crushed ships from the water, and so the royal ships moved slowly, rowing between the skeletons of ruined Viking warships.

The stiff wind tugged at Beornoth's hair and drew a tear from his eye as he watched the king of England abandon its shores to Sweyn Forkbeard, shores where men had given everything to keep the Viking threat at bay. Weak men had gained power and control over the realm and now left it to fend for itself.

18

Winter came to East Anglia, and the land became like iron. Frost sheathed in the furrows, and the marshes became white beneath still, pale skies. Even the birds seemed hushed, their wings heavy with cold, their voices stilled by a season that showed no mercy. Beornoth, Wigs and Gis spent the cold months with Ulfcytel in his East Anglian hall, retreating there after the defence of Lundenwic, and after the king had fled across the sea like a scolded hound. Forkbeard had declared himself king shortly after, yet no Dane had come to East Anglia demanding surrender, oaths or tribute. Winter was the time to stay indoors beside a warm fire, eating supplies gathered over the warmer months. It was a dark season of stories by the fire, of animals brought indoors for warmth, of cold, death and waiting for the promise of rebirth in spring.

Osgar patrolled the borderlands with Ulfcytel's warriors, riding all along the Thames estuary and sending scouts back with reports of enemy movements. Men said that Forkbeard planned to have himself formally crowned when the swallows returned and men could make the journey to Winchester to witness the formal ceremony when a bishop would place the crown of England on Sweyn Forkbeard's head and anoint him as God's representative on earth. Forkbeard, like his father Harald Bluetooth, was a Christian, and the powerful bishops would have few qualms about the coronation once the new king allowed them to keep their vast lands and opulent lifestyles.

No Dane had come to East Anglia, and yet Beornoth and his companions had waited. Long, dark evenings spent listening to bards and skalds sing of old battles and dead heroes with one eye on the hall door waiting for the messenger to come and demand surrender. Or for armed men to come for their heads. Fear gnawed at the men's bellies, melding with the terror of the unknown to keep the Saxons afraid and whispering of what might come to pass and how the kingdom would change with his new Viking king.

Beornoth struggled through the cold months. Something bit at his bones, growing inside him, something dark, dragging him towards the end without ever pulling him under. He coughed and sweated beneath fur blankets, wiping away the blood from his mouth, praying to God for forgiveness of his many sins. Beornoth waited for death, but it never came. He woke each morning, cold, stiff and clinging to life as if some final purpose awaited him, as though God was not ready to welcome him to heaven until his old body had completed one last task.

East Anglia in winter was a hard land. The fens spread wide in a shifting wilderness of water bound by ice and snow. A man could walk across the waterways and wet marshes where in summer he would drown, and a horse might stumble and slide where once a boat or coracle had rowed. Rivers became slow with ice, the meres froze silver like moons, and frost made the rushes stiff and brittle. Here and there, the black stubble of last year's harvest jutted like tufts of hair from snow-whitened fields, and the trees became stark bones against the iron-grey sky. Alder and willow, oak and ash stripped bare, and their limbs creaked in the wind like the masts of dead ships. Deer had fled deeper into the bleak woodlands and wild geese still haunted the meres, but their cries were fewer, muted like distant war horns. Wolves became bolder, hunger driving them close to settlements, and their tracks trailed the village around Ulfcytel's hall like ghosts.

Beornoth and Ulfcytel spent their evenings talking with Wigs and Gis, waiting for news from Osgar and his scouts. Their spears and swords leaned idle against the timber and wattle wall within Ulfcytel's hall, though Beornoth polished his blades each morning. The warriors of East Anglia had gone home before the cold sank its teeth into the land, save the men who rode with Osgar. The warriors huddled in the halls and homes along with the churls and thralls, watching the skies, waiting for riders to come with news of war, kings, princes, shields, spears and shield walls. When the waiting became too long and men craved news of the Danes and of King Æthelred, they made the journey to

Ulfcytel's hall wrapped in furs and with frost in their beards. They drank warmed mead by the fire and left despondent when neither Beornoth nor Ulfcytel could tell them if Sweyn Forkbeard was now their king, or if the true king would return to fight for his kingdom. They left, trudging home with bowed heads and heavy hearts, grumbling, asking what use was courage when kings fled and a Dane was to be crowned?

February came, the coldest month, and on a pure white day where the air was still and icicles hung from the thatch in long glassy fingers, folk crammed into Ulfcytel's hall to be together and keep warm by his fire. They brought whatever remained of their winter stores, and Ulfcytel's stewards and slaves prepared a meagre feast of dark bread, a broth thin with turnips and wrinkled vegetables, and hocks of ham which had hung in ceilings to cure and dry. Hearth smoke clung to the rafters in slow, sullen wreaths, and a wind picked up as night came early, finding the cracks between the timbers, though the fire roared bright and warm in a central pit wreathed with stones. Men and women sat close together, pressed for warmth, their faces made gold by firelight and those who had the talent sang of elves, dwarves, giants and kings of old who had fought to make the land Saxon and wrestle it from the Britons who were the first folk to live amongst its groves, rivers, dells and meres.

Beornoth sat with Wigs, and Gis sat across from them cuddling up to a wide-hipped widow he had grown close to. Wigs shook his head with dismay whenever Gis tickled or showed affection to the woman, who beamed with rosy cheeks, and he complained when a slave brought him a meagre bowl of boiled turnips and barley bread. Next came a pottage of beans thickened with a knuckle of old bacon, which went down without complaint, and both Wigs and Beornoth grew more content with the fayre when Ulfcytel broke open a barrel of strong ale he had kept for just such a gathering. Stewards dipped horn cups into the barrel and passed it around. It was sour and heavy, but it loosened the tongues of every visitor and dulled the worries of kingdom and war. A keg-paunched thegn had brought a small barrel of honey mead and doled out the fine drink sparingly in half-size wooden pots. The people drank and laughed, though the laughter was brittle. All feasts held in such times were acts of defiance, a claim that they were still there, still Saxons and still free. Beornoth wondered how Thered, Alfgar and Brand fared in the distant north. Brand and Thered had fought with Forkbeard, and Beornoth wondered if they truly celebrated his victory, and if they even cared in their stout northern bastions that one king had replaced another in the south. Perhaps they were content to be rid of Streona and his taxes, or perhaps they had simply done what was best for the many people in their charge.

The fire crackled and spat as one of Ulfcytel's men hung a haunch of venison over the flames, the last from the autumn hunt. Its fat dripped into the blaze, sending up sparks that whirled in the smoky gloom. A woman plucked at a small harp, its strings thin and mournful, and a weathered-faced grandfather sang the lay of Sigurd and the monster. Children huddled in the floor rushes, eyes wide as he told of beasts and dragons, of flame and treasure and the hero who slew the wyrm and bathed in its blood.

Beornoth drank little. He watched and listened as men spoke in hushed voices. They spoke of Sweyn. Always Sweyn. Some said he would bring law and justice, that better a strong Viking king than no king, or a weak king ruled by a man like Eadric Streona. Others spat into the fire and swore that no Dane would ever rule them. Beornoth said nothing, and Wigs glanced at him constantly with frightened eyes, worried that Beornoth would roar and bellow at the men who knew little of war and yet spoke of the enemy as though they were as familiar as lovers. Beornoth just stared into the flames, for he had seen Sweyn Forkbeard and Thorkell the Tall fight, had crossed blades with them, had seen Forkbeard's vast fleet gliding on the Thames, the dragon prows like wolves on the water, sails black against the sky. He had fought and killed the Danes, iron-clad and hungry for silver. A man like Forkbeard could never bring peace. He was a battle-king, a conqueror, and a lover of battle who could never satisfy his savage thirst for ambition.

As men grew mouldy with ale, and Wigs fell asleep with his head bowed upon his chest, the hall door slammed open in a crash that made men cease their songs and chatter. Wigs jumped as he woke, and a gust of snow whirled into the hall. The fire guttered, and folk stared at the door with gaping mouths. A man staggered in, a big man in a ragged cloak heavy with frost, his face whipped raw by the wind. He leaned upon a thick-shafted spear, panting, his breath smoking in the firelight. He removed his hood. It was Osgar, and the warrior searched the room with his flint-hard eyes.

'News,' he gasped. 'News from Winchester.'

All was silent but for the crackle of burning wood. The hall was a held breath.

'Sweyn Forkbeard is dead.'

The words fell like stones into a frozen pond, sending cracks into the silence as men hissed and whispered.

'Dead?' Beornoth said, his voice loud and deep as hope welled within his chest.

Osgar nodded, eyes growing wide with the wonder of it. 'A sickness took him, lord. He is gone. Forkbeard is gone.'

The hall erupted. Some cheered, pounding tables with their fists, their voices ragged with joy. Others muttered in disbelief, believing it to be a Viking trick, for how could the great warrior die so easily? Women crossed themselves and kissed their children, whispering prayers, and Ulfcytel's eyes met Beornoth's across the crowd, a question in his warrior's eyes. What now?

Beornoth picked up his ale and drained the cup. The flames called to him, burning, eating at the wood within. Beornoth saw a hall burning, recalled his first meeting with Forkbeard where the Danish king had challenged him to a contest of riddles, he saw his friends screaming and dying at Maldon and Forkbeard coming from the water, axe in hand. He saw Skarde Wartooth snarling at him on the battlefield, he saw the bridge of Lundenwic and Thorkell the Tall and his monstrous axe. He saw arrows falling like rain on a river thick with longships, and an army commanded by the fierce-minded Cnut, son of Forkbeard. Sweyn Forkbeard had been like a storm given flesh, a man who it seemed could not die save by sword or axe, and yet he was dead. It was as if the sky itself had cracked. Beornoth thought of Æthelred, the king in exile, cowering in Normandy, and Eadric Streona, hated by his people and mocked by his foes. Would the king return now, summoned home by the death of his great enemy? Or would another Dane rise, perhaps Thorkell, or Cnut, Forkbeard's fierce son, to claim his father's crown?

Outside the wind howled across the frozen marshes and snow rattled against the window shutters. The wolves were circling. Beornoth closed his eyes and felt his chest rise and fall. He could almost feel the warriors stir, the brave men, the dangerous ones who fought always in the front rank, the lovers of battle who heard the same news in halls across the land and took their axes and swords down from their walls and sharpened edges for the war to come. For there must be blood. A war-king had died, a man who had subdued the fearsome warlords of Denmark, Norway and England. Warlords smelt blood, sensed opportunity in Forkbeard's death, a chance to seize power, a chance to win glory through chaos, to garner reputation, silver, women and glory. A wolf age loomed, a sword age, a time perhaps for a king to return, or a new one to rise from the ashes of Forkbeard's conquest.

Voices rose in argument, and song, hope and fear twisted together like smoke. The hall was warm, the fire was bright, but beyond its walls the land lay cold and uncertain. Sweyn Forkbeard was dead, war beckoned, and Beornoth had to find the strength to fight again, to don his armour and swing his sword once more.

19

Lent came, and with it King Æthelred returned from Normandy, chasing the rumour of Forkbeard's demise. With Lent came hunger as winter stores dwindled to scraps, a little barley, some turnips, dried peas and onions strung from the beams like shrivelled skulls. Men came to Ulfcytel's hall, drifting in alone or in groups of three, four and five. They came in cloaks and furs, with shields on their backs and spears in their fists to find out if the word on the wind was true, that the old wolf had died and that their runaway king had returned to reclaim his throne. These were the thegns of East Anglia and their retinues. They were the farmers whose duty it was to rally to Ulfcytel in time of war and fight for him in return for their right to hold their lands and farms.

The new arrivals gathered in the hall, slept in its corners, and in the stables and byres. Osgar had ridden out in search of more news of the Viking army and of the king's return and everyone, including Beornoth, waited impatiently to discover what would become of their country, who would rule and if the war horns would call to them once more.

'My belly thinks my throat's been cut,' grumbled Wigs as he ate a piece of fish. His face contorted as though it were a lump of dung. 'How much longer until Lent is over?'

'Ten miserable days,' said Gis, similarly chewing on his fish with little enjoyment.

No cheese, no butter, no milk. Cows stood lean in the byre, their udders shrunk and their bellies hollow from winter's poor pasture. The hens laid no eggs, for cold gripped the land too tight. Any eggs the hens managed to lay were scrumped away by dirty-faced children to eat in secret in the orchards without the priests discovering their crime. The Church forbade all but fish and bread. It was the season of sorrow, as Ulfcytel's priest, Father Eadric, insisted on reminding them every day.

'Pray, my children,' he said, sweeping through the hall and making the sign of the cross above the heads of men who poked and picked at their fish. 'Remember now, kneel and pray, give alms to those who are in need. Welcome the suffering!'

'Alms?' said Wigs. 'He's lost his mind. We've got nothing to eat ourselves. What could we give? Rocks?'

The Thames and the smaller rivers that ran through East Anglia like veins gave the people eels, and the sea gave them herring, but it was never enough. And even Beornoth, whose mind was elsewhere, caught up with the worries of king and country, was weary of the stink and taste of fish.

'A warrior's belly is meant for beef,' Wigs continued, 'for pork roasted and dripping fat, not for dried herring and barley gruel. How are we supposed to fight the Danes with nothing but herring in our bellies?'

Father Eadric continued his journey amongst Ulfcytel's guests, a smear of ash still on his brow. He preached of Christ in the wilderness, fasting for forty days, and told them they too must fast to break the body and humble the soul. Ulfcytel marched into the hall, limping, searching across the huddled men with keen eyes. He saw Beornoth and beckoned him outside with a jerk of his head. Beornoth rose and, flanked by Wigs and Gis, he left the hall and emerged into a sun-drenched but cold morning where the frost steamed on the fences and byres, and where two men waited beside thin ponies.

'They come from the coast,' Ulfcytel said. 'There is news.'

'Ships are in the sea, lord,' said the first rider, a small man with greasy hair and a thick lisp. 'The king's ships.'

'We saw the banner, lord, the dragon of Wessex, just like that.' The second man pointed to the dragon on Beornoth's ring. He wore a tarnished and thin silver ring in his ear, the mark of a sailor who wore such earrings in case they fell afoul of the sea's fury and drowned in its watery embrace. A man who found the sailor could use the silver to bury him properly, so that his drowned soul could find peace and make its way to heaven.

'How many ships?' asked Beornoth.

The two men looked nervously at one another, and the smaller man swallowed hard.

'Forgive us, lord,' he said, 'but we are simple men and cannot count like lords. A score, maybe more?'

'Æthelred returns with his family and his retinue,' Ulfcytel said to Beornoth, a fire burning in his flinty eyes.

'They have Norman-built ships, lord,' said the fisherman, 'small, fat-bellied things built for the short crossing. We came straight here to warn you, Lord Ulfcytel, just as you commanded. The wind is against them, but the crossing takes but a day. They'll be here before dark, at Sandwich, lord.'

'You did well,' said Ulfcytel, and he fished two small coins from a pouch at his belt and handed one each to the riders. 'Go inside and get some food before you leave.'

They bowed, grinned at one another and hurried off to the hall.

'We should march for Sandwich,' said Ulfcytel, clapping Beornoth on the shoulder.

Beornoth glanced at the hedges still whitened with frost. Ice still clutched the meres, though by day the sun softened their edges and the water lapped at its freezing prison. Hoar-frost clung to the alder trees, and his breath clouded the air even though the sun dazzled his eyes. 'It's still cold to march out, but you should summon your men. Many are here already, but we'll need more. The king will come ashore at Sandwich, just as the Danes have since the time of our fathers' fathers. It's the closest port to Normandy, and from there he sails his fleet up the Thames to Lundenwic. What news of Cnut?'

'None. A merchant came two days again, you remember, the man with the amber and the beads?'

'I remember.'

'He had been in Lundenwic after Forkbeard's death. The jarls and champions of Sweyn's army have raised Cnut up as their new leader. He will be king of Norway and Denmark, and of England. But his position is precarious, and he is away from Lundenwic, demanding hostages from the ealdormen of the great shires, hostages as surety for their loyalty should any uprising occur.'

'This is a dangerous time for Sweyn's son. He must act with speed, certainty and violence. There will be men in his army who fancy themselves as king material, men like Thorkell perhaps, who can command thousands of men of their own. There could be a dozen such wolves across Denmark, Norway and in the Viking army here in our land. Ships will have slipped away from Lundenwic as the hungry jarls return to Jutland and Skagerrak to seize more power and more land for themselves now that the great war-king is dead. If Æthelred is to strike at Cnut and the Danes, then it should be now, whilst confusion reigns and whilst loyalties are thin and tested. It's cold, but we should march. We haven't lingered here all winter just to delay now.'

Beornoth took Ulfcytel's forearm in the warrior's grip, suddenly feeling taller, stronger and younger at the prospect of change, at the chance of victory.

'The king has returned!' Beornoth shouted, rousing the warriors in and around the hall. 'We march to meet him at Sandwich. Bring your spears and your shields.'

The warriors let out a thin cheer, like men convincing themselves they had reason to rejoice.

'They want to fight for our country,' said Gis as he quickly saddled his and Beornoth's horses. 'But they don't want to fight for Streona. The king is weak, dithering and uncertain, and all winter men have worried at the nails, craving the fight to expel the Danes, but fearful of whom they would fight for. Why fight if all victory accomplishes is exchanging Forkbeard for Streona and his taxes?'

'Well,' said Wigs, tightening the cinch beneath his horse's belly, 'we can't crown ourselves king. Better a Saxon king than a bloody Viking. A kingdom without a king is like carrion on the field waiting to be picked clean.'

They rode and marched from Ulfcytel's hall to make the short journey to Sandwich. Osgar met them on the road with fifty men at his back and news of more making their way to join the king and witness his return. They crossed East Anglia's cold plains, through villages huddled in the shadow of winter. Smoke rose from every hall, the thatch white with frost, the cattle thin-ribbed in their byres. The common folk watched as the warriors passed by, their eyes hollow and cheeks pinched. Men in leather and iron called to them of the return of the king. They lifted their heads, and in those worn faces Beornoth saw the glimmer of hope.

They reached Sandwich at the turn of the tide. The sea rolled iron grey, foam white upon the shingle, and gulls wheeled screaming above the surf. They arrived just as King Æthelred walked cautiously and slowly along a gangplank from a Norman cog to a timber jetty. Streona held his arm, and just as

Beornoth's heart lifted to see his king back on Saxon soil, it dropped like a stone to see Eadric still holding, still controlling Æthelred like a puppet master at a summer fair. The king shuffled and then stopped, swathed in a russet cloak trimmed with fox fur, his face lined and thin, his beard white and straggled.

The warriors shook their weapons and cheered the king. They shouted his name and raised their swords, seaxes, spears or axes in salute and cried thanks to God for his return. Beornoth kept his own sword sheathed, even as Ulfcytel, Wigs and Gis joined the rest in the acclamation. Beornoth did not see a saviour, he saw a man who had fled, who had run from the Vikings like a dog and only returned now because mighty Forkbeard had died in his bed. It was not a victory. It was a sneaking, snivelling return. But it was an opportunity, a king returned to his kingdom cloaked in promises and a chance to restore that which was lost.

Beornoth went to bow before the king, though Streona kept Æthelred at a distance, high on a platform whilst the thegns and lords waited below to renew their oaths. Prince Edmund stood tall and broad-shouldered on the platform, dressed in a coat of chain mail and with a sword strapped to his belt. He stood away from Streona, beside his proud mother, Queen Emma, and there was a fierceness in his face, the look of a warrior and lord men could follow. Beornoth whispered the words of his oath, though they tasted like ash in his mouth as he felt Eadric Streona gaze upon him, drinking in the warriors on their knees, as though they knelt to him and not the decrepit king whom he propped up by his thin arm. Eadric eased the king into a chair, and he addressed the gathered warriors, talking to them of the need to be bold and strike towards Lundenwic with all haste whilst Cnut was absent from its high walls. Eadric spoke of messengers riding across the shires to rally men to march and join the king's grand army. He promised thousands from Mercia, spears from Wessex, Somersaete and Defnascir. The warriors cheered and let hope run away with their senses, and Beornoth wanted to hope with them. He wanted a victory just as much as they. He wanted the kingdom restored, not for Streona or even for Æthelred, but for his dead brothers, so that when his long life ended, the kingdom they had all fought so hard to preserve would remain a Saxon one, whole and unconquered.

Beornoth prepared for one more campaign, one more fight for king and country. He knew what he had to do but did not know if his failing body had the strength to do it.

20

Cnut had left three hundred men to guard Lundenwic as he rode out into the country to secure its lords and cement his fledgling leadership over his father's army and supporters. Those men fled the ancient city as news of Æthelred's approach ran along the Thames faster than his ships could sail. The guards left Lundenwic unprotected, and so the Saxons accomplished with a few hundred men what Forkbeard had failed to do with eight thousand, and took Lundenwic without a drop of bloodshed.

Godwin arrived four days later with a thousand warriors from Wessex. More followed from East Anglia as word of Ulfcytel's summons spread across the shire, and within a week an army assembled outside the high Roman walls. Men came alone and in war bands. They came from across the southern shires with battered shields and rusted spears. Men of the fyrd came with their mattocks and reaping hooks to fight for a king they had believed gone, and for a country they had believed lost. Beornoth and Ulfcytel camped with the warriors and did not seek an audience with the king, not whilst Eadric Streona remained at his side.

Prince Edmund came from the city each day and practised weapons with the men. He stood in the shield wall flanked by his royal guard and worked through manoeuvres of advancing, retreating and wheeling to left and right. Edmund laughed with them, drank with them and came to talk to Beornoth and Ulfcytel of strategy and to hear tales of old fights. He was, Beornoth thought, a man to lead and for men to follow, but he spoke no more to Beornoth of his discontent with Eadric and all men inside and without the city prepared for war.

After two weeks of mustering and practice, the army marched north under the dragon banner, led by Eadric Streona and Prince Edmund. Ulfcytel led the men of East Anglia, and Beornoth, Wigs and Gis split their time riding with Ulfcytel and Godwin.

'You have grown stronger,' said Wigs, squeezing Godwin's shoulders as they camped on the first night. Godwin had grown a hand's breadth taller and was now an imposing man with a thick chestnut beard and a serious face.

'Really?' he said, glancing down at his arms and shoulders.

'No.' Wigs laughed and skipped away as Godwin tried to slap him around the head.

'Careful,' said Gis. 'He's a lord now, and you are a simple shield grunt.'

'Not a lord, still just me.'

'So who rules your father's lands then?'

'I do, but only because I took upon myself to do so. I have not sworn my oath to the king, nor been asked to do it. My men follow me because they were loyal to my father. No other man has been appointed in my place, so...' Godwin shrugged.

'And your father?' asked Beornoth.

'Killed by Streona and his brother. Branded a traitor but still loved by his men.' There was anger in Godwin's voice, but a steely expression on his youthful face.

'The people must love you if a thousand have come from Wessex to follow a man without land or title.'

'If we fight well, perhaps the king will restore my title.'

'Hold on,' said Wigs, enjoying a cut of pork now that Lent was finally over. 'So you just live in your father's hall and pretend you're a lord and the people simply pay up their render and the warriors do what you say?'

'Something like that, yes. My men know I am my father's son.'

'Maybe I should do that. Find a hall without a lord, stroll on in there and say I'm the new one. Get myself a cloak trimmed with fur, a fine sword, and live off the fat of the land.'

'Maybe you should.' Godwin smiled, taking the banter well. Godwin had been young and pimply when he had fought beside Beornoth and his companions before. He had suffered cruelly at the hands of Eadric and Brihtric, men acting with impunity due to Eadric's influence over the crown. But Godwin fought on, clinging to his lands, seeking restoration of title and Beornoth hoped that one day he would bring Brihtric to justice. Godwin now looked every inch the lord and a thegn to command respect, but he had been around Wigs and Gis for too long to take their playful jokes as any more that what they were, and he lacked the arrogance to take insult.

'Who would follow you?' asked Gis. 'Godwin at least looks like a lord; you smell like a pig farmer, look like a goat herder and have the mind of a bashed-up onion.'

'I could be the ealdorman of Wessex with my looks and cunning.' Wigs pranced up and down, and the men laughed, Godwin hardest of all.

'Don't you want to be avenged on Eadric and his brother, for what they did to your father?' Beornoth asked once the camp had returned to quiet and Wigs and Gis had gone off to find firewood to keep their blaze going through the night.

Godwin smiled and ate his ration of pork. 'Of course, Lord Beornoth. But I owe it to him to hold our lands, to reclaim his title and to continue our name. That is my duty. I am simply one of many wronged by Streona in his rise to power. Will it serve my purpose to whisper and plot behind his back?'

'No. He is the master of whispers and the lord of shadows.'

'Certainly. Better to win our battles and fight well. No?'

'You have your head right, young Godwin. There are many thegns and ealdormen who went over to Forkbeard. Some are friends of mine. I worry what will become of them if we win this fight against Cnut.'

'Nothing. We need the lords and ealdormen of the north. They will be pardoned; Prince Edmund assures me of it. We will welcome them back into the fold. They will swear new oaths, and all will be as it was.'

'Prince Edmund?'

'Aye. He is a good man, I think.'

'And none too fond of Eadric.'

'No, he is not.'

'But we must defeat Cnut first, and he has Thorkell the Tall with him. We must not underestimate Cnut. Any man who can command the loyalty of Viking jarls and warriors is a man to fear and respect. The ravens must have circled when Sweyn died. Men will have challenged Cnut's right and ability to lead. He has emerged as their overlord, the master of the most warlike and dangerous men in the world, and that says something about the man.'

'And we must crush him.' Godwin spoke those words with a tinge of fear in his eyes. He had fought the Danes, Beornoth had seen him do it, and he understood what awaited them in the shield wall – the horror, the blood and the blades.

'We must drive him from the field. Cnut's grasp on his father's legacy is loose and slippery. If he is to be king of Forkbeard's three kingdoms, he needs warriors and an army. Men will rebel, especially those defeated by Forkbeard in his wars of conquest. Suffer a crushing defeat here, and his lords will doubt his battle-luck. They will cast him aside for another warlord, perhaps Thorkell, or perhaps another. So maybe we don't need to destroy him, just kill enough of the bastards to strike worry and fear into Cnut's heart.'

'Let us hope so.'

They marched west, following Cnut's forces. Folk pointed the way. The farmers, thatchers, woodsmen and shepherds bowed before the king's banner and to his warriors and showed them where the Vikings had passed along the Roman roads and wagon-rutted pathways. Spring thawed the land, and the marshes swelled. The fens became a silver maze, and the waters from the Thames spread wide, dotted with floating rafts of reeds. Geese returned, filling the air with their cries, and deer came shyly from the woods to gaze upon the army that marched whilst its king waited behind the walls of Lundenwic. Men ploughed again, toiling bent-backed in fields where the mud stank of thaw. Rich fields that would soon bloom fertile and green, rich enough that men would come across the sea and slaughter a kingdom to own their bounty. They rode along muddy tracks, past towns rebuilding from fire, alongside fields where the bones of men still showed through the dark earth. These were lands where Thorkell and Forkbeard had raided without mercy, the heartlands of England whose people had borne so much. Thegns and their retinues joined the marching column, coming from distant shires to heed their king's call to arms. And so the army arrived at green meadows outside Oxenforda, three thousand men come to do battle, and they found young Cnut unprepared, his ally Thorkell too far north of the battlefield with his men seeking to pacify reluctant lords, and so the Saxons met the Danes on equal terms and with equal numbers to do battle for England's throne.

The Vikings came to the field beating their war drums and blaring war horns as they marched beneath banners bearing wolves, bears, eagles' wings and yellowed skulls on high poles. They came with painted shields, braided beards, iron helmets, and Cnut rode before them on a chestnut mare waving his sword and the Vikings shouted and roared their anger at finding themselves caught without their full force. Streona waited behind the Saxon lines in a great tent with bishops at his side, and royal banners snapping in the wind. He knelt as the holy men chanted their prayers and blessed him.

Beornoth donned his byrnie and strapped on his sword. He pushed on his helmet, and beneath a spring sky heavy with thick clouds the colour of a swan's wing, Beornoth stared at his shaking hands. He had risen early that morning and taken himself away from the camp to take deep breaths, to await the coughing fit he knew came at every dawn. It came, driving Beornoth to his knees, and when he rose, leaving spots of blood on the leaves and grass, he worried that his old body had not the strength for battle. He walked through the camp, agonising, struggling to come to terms with the inevitability of age and decay. He feared his shaking hands and the endless coughing and what it meant for his ability to fight. So when the shield wall formed, and for the first time in his life, Beornoth took a place in the rear ranks. He left the front-rank fighting to the younger men – to Osgar, Wigs, Gis and Ulfcytel.

'Follow the battle,' Ulfcytel had said when he saw Beornoth at the rear. 'Use your experience to organise the men of the fyrd and tell us what we cannot see, how the battle unfolds. If they attempt to outflank us, if the centre breaks or folds.'

'I should fight beside you, old friend,' Beornoth managed, though he could not meet Ulfcytel's eyes. His hands had grown even more curled and twisted over the winter, and Beornoth could not trust his ability to hold up his shield, the shield which must protect his neighbour's left side in the shield-wall fight.

'A selfish man stands in the wall when he is sickened. It risks the very battle itself. What you do is a thing of courage. What would happen to morale if our men saw mighty Beornoth fall in battle? What if the Vikings broke through our line if your shield failed? Only fight if your body has the strength to do it. You have met this challenge head-on, and I respect you for it. You are a man of honour, Beo, and you have fought and bled enough. It's written all over your face how much this hurts you. Time comes for us all, even where blades and enemies have failed.'

'Fight well. And live, Ulfcytel.'

Ulfcytel left to take his place at the front, and Beornoth felt men's eyes upon him, judging him, the shame of their eyes piercing his body like blades. But the long years had robbed him of his old strength and vigour, and Beornoth watched as Edmund rode again along the battle line with his sword held aloft while the warriors acclaimed him, roaring their hate for the Vikings as they worked themselves up to march across the field to meet their enemies on the field where many of them would die, and more would suffer terrible and painful wounds.

Beornoth went among the fyrd and the rear rankers who gazed up at him in awe. They saw a huge man clad in iron, a legend about whom they had heard stories and songs for years. He adjusted a man's grip of his shield, checked a spear, adjusted the space between ranks and told the men to stay strong and fight together. Their chests swelled at each comment, and for the first time Beornoth's words rather than his sword influenced a battle. He was uncomfortable, forcing himself to encourage and help, keeping his eyes away from the front line where he really wished to be, where he was born to be. The familiar shuddering in his chest forced Beornoth out of the rear rank, and he hurried to a patch of scrub and thorn bushes on the edge of the wide plain. Beornoth coughed and hawked up a gobbet of thick blood. He wiped his mouth and beard on the scrap of cloth he carried for that purpose and tucked it behind his byrnie. He stood, straightened his armour and caught Eadric Streona staring at him from under the cover of his tent.

Eadric smiled and shook his head, a lopsided, piteous smile that made Beornoth's shoulders shudder with anger and shame. Streona turned and said something to the guards behind him, and they laughed. Beornoth wanted nothing more than to rip his sword free, march the twenty paces to Eadric's tent and cut him down. But today was about the battle, about winning the fight. Not about Beornoth's pride and shame. The Saxons had caught Cnut in the field without Thorkell the Tall and with reduced numbers. If there was to be a victory, then let it be today, and let them drive Cnut and his Vikings from the field and back across the sea.

Prince Edmund rode across the line once more with his sword raised, bellowing his rage, and the army responded with wild cries of their own. War horns blared from the Viking lines, and their war drums beat the sound of their advance. They came on, heavy boots thumping on the grass, thousands of men coming across the plain to fight and to die. Their spears shook above them like a great forest moving of its own free will. Edmund leapt down from the saddle and took his place in the line of battle, but Eadric remained in his tent, watching events unfold as he sipped ale from a curved horn.

Bows creaked as Saxon archers drew their yew staves, stretching the string to their right ears, and then the sky darkened as the missiles rose above the battlefield like a murderous rain. It was the battle song, the din of war. It let off a palpable air, and Beornoth breathed it in as though it were the last time. Men feared battle. They feared the wounds, the blood and the death, but war had been Beornoth's life. His secret pleasure. Where some feared the clash, the dangerous men like Beornoth, like Forkbeard, Thorkell, Byrhtnoth, Palnatoki and Skarde Wartooth, loved it and craved it like other men craved a beautiful woman or the inebriation of alcohol. There was guilt in that for a Saxon and for a Christian, but not for a Viking. Their gods encouraged them to war, rewarding death in battle with a place in their glorious afterlife. Beornoth closed his eyes and listened to the shouts, to the bows, to the footsteps, the drums and the horns, and felt a great sadness that he was there only as a bystander, that other men would fight and experience that inexplicable joy that comes when a man faces life-threatening danger, that heightened state when things move slowly and a warrior moves fast to take the life of an enemy who has come to kill him.

The shield walls came together with a sound like thunder shaking the sky. The ground trembled beneath Beornoth's feet, and the battle to decide England's fate began.

21

Cnut's army left the battlefield in an organised retreat. They did not flee across the hills like desperate men. After the first push against the Saxon shield wall, they simply disengaged and retreated across the field in dressed ranks, shields facing forwards. Streona railed at the army to advance and slaughter the enemy, but Prince Edmund took Beornoth and Ulfcytel's advice and allowed Cnut and his men to return to their ships. The Saxon army hailed Edmund as the victor. They raised him and chanted his name, for the prince had fought bravely and bore the marks of battle on his armour and face. Men named him Ironside after that fight in honour of his bravery, and Beornoth was proud to see the brave prince so lauded.

Streona slipped away after his advice went unheeded, riding away bitterly with his guards to carry news of the victory to Æthelred at Lundenwic.

'Short but brutal,' Ulfcytel said, describing the battle to Beornoth when the Vikings had gone and men began to drink and celebrate the victory. 'The shield walls came together, and we held them. Osgar hewed at them with his axe, and the prince fought valiantly.'

'A man we can all follow,' said Gis, raising his horn of ale in the prince's honour.

'Once they did not break us in the first clash, they withdrew.'

'Cnut needs his men,' Beornoth said. 'Our numbers were even. To win the battle would have cost him the war, and he must secure crowns in three kingdoms.'

'He ran!' said Wigs, guzzling ale like it was water, his eyes still blazing after the chaos of battle. 'He saw our blades and our shields and ran, the young pup.'

'Maybe he saw you and became stricken with terror,' said Gis.

'Maybe he did.'

'Or perhaps a gust of your breath filled Cnut's nostrils.'

'We should chase him,' Wigs said, laughing off Gis' banter. 'Follow the young cub and finish him once and for all.'

'He has too many men,' said Ulfcytel. 'Cnut did not rout. He retreated. Just let him go.'

'What's the point of beating him and letting him get away?'

'What if we catch Cnut and he turns like a cornered wolf and defeats us? What if Thorkell has already marched to join his forces to Cnut's and we find ourselves outnumbered? Let him go and fight his other battles and leave us in peace.'

'Cnut has shown himself to be no fool,' Beornoth cut in. 'As long as he lives, the danger to our kingdom remains.'

'Hopefully the bastard dies in Norway or Denmark. Perhaps an ambitious jarl will put a knife in his belly to make himself king.'

Ulfcytel, Wigs and Gis all bore the grime and sweat of battle visible on their leather and chain-mail armour. Their pale faces showed the shock that affects every man after the fearsome shield-wall clash, and spatters of other men's blood showed where they had hewed at their enemies. When the fight was over and the men had returned to camp carrying the injured and cheering the victory, Beornoth had removed his helmet and stood shamefaced as the heroes streamed past him and he bore not a mark on his fine byrnie and sword. Better to have died in battle, he thought, than feel like an imposter dressed up for war.

Men spoke of Osgar's fearsome strength and bravery, and as Ulfcytel, Wigs and Gis talked of the deeds they had done and witnessed in the battle, Beornoth went to find the big warrior. He found Osgar sitting on a log whilst a priest cleaned and bound a gash on his arm.

'Lord,' Osgar said in greeting as Beornoth approached. His long-handled, double-bladed war axe rested against a wagon, its steel not yet cleaned of enemy blood and gore.

'I hear you broke them,' Beornoth said.

Osgar shrugged. 'I just fought.'

Beornoth smiled at the simple brutality of the big man. He saw a younger version of himself in the warrior, a man born and bred for one purpose. War. He didn't waste time thinking about the machinations of great and ambitious men. Osgar did his duty, and when it was time to fight, he did so with astonishing ferocity.

'Lord Osgar,' said a cheerful voice, and Beornoth saw Prince Edmund striding towards them with a smile splitting his youthful face. 'Well done today, well done indeed. I swear you fight like a demon from hell with that axe. Thanks be to God that you are on our side.'

'I am not a lord, my prince,' Osgar said slowly, and winced as the priest tied his bandage tight.

'You are now. I shall see to it that you are made king's thegn after all you have done for the realm. Just like Lord Beornoth here, a hero worthy of the king's service.'

'Thank you, my prince.'

'Congratulations, lord,' Beornoth said to Edmund, and was surprised when the prince reached out and shook his forearm warmly in the warrior's grip.

'A first victory, but not a final one, I think.' The prince wiped a dark smear of mud mixed with blood from his cheek. 'We must all return to Lundenwic to celebrate the battle. We shall send messengers to the lords north of Watling Street and ask them to come and renew their oaths to the king.'

'You'll forgive them for fighting with Forkbeard?' Beornoth could not hide the surprise in his voice. Ealdormen like Alfgar and thegns like Brand had fought in Forkbeard's army when he had ravaged southern England and attacked Lundenwic. That army had driven Æthelred to Normandy and made Forkbeard king.

'I do not believe they fought against my father. They did not rebel against the crown. They fought against Eadric. You know it, Beornoth, just as every man on this field knows it.' He waved greeting to a group of warriors chanting his name. 'Forkbeard went north to gather them to his banner, and I imagine it took little persuasion. Those men deserve forgiveness. Let them know Cnut is defeated and my father has returned.'

'What does Eadric say about it?'

'He is the ealdorman of Mercia, not the king of England.'

***

Four weeks later, the great men of the realm gathered at Lundenwic to celebrate the victory over Cnut's army. Beornoth rode with Wigs and Gis whilst Ulfcytel and Osgar rode with the thegns of East Anglia. The city smelled of smoke and roasting meat as Beornoth and his companions approached from the east. They rode through fields where spring had begun to win over the damp earth, and Beornoth's horse kicked up mud onto his cloak and shield.

Lundenwic's walls rose from the wide grey Thames, the Roman stone black with age and patched with timber and daub where the Saxons had mended what Rome had left behind and the Vikings had sundered in their brutal attacks. Banners snapped in the wind, hanging long and bright between towers and gates, cloth bright as blood against the pale blue sky. Lundenwic was dressed like a bride. From Aldgate to the river, royal stewards had hung garlands of pine and holly woven with the first blossoms of spring. Beornoth rode beneath a gate draped in cloth of red and gold, and above the stone walls crucifixes gleamed in the pale sun, polished and new, and between them flew the king's dragon banner. Priests in new robes stood beyond the gate to bless those who entered, whilst others swung censers heavy with smoke. The air was thick with it, incense and pitch mingling with the sharp, foul stench of the river beyond the walls.

'Bit of a difference since the last time we stood on this bridge,' said Gis as their horses' hooves left the wooden timbers and clattered upon the cobbles of Lundenwic's stone road.

'Turns my bloody stomach coming back to this place,' said Wigs. 'We bled on this bridge. I almost died. Twice! Nobody thanked us for it. We don't even bloody live here.'

'You'll be thanked today,' Beornoth said, reining in his horse so that she wouldn't crush a group of thegns carrying the banner of Defnascir who scuttled across his path. 'More food and ale than you can eat or drink.'

'That's a lot of food and ale, lord,' said Wigs, and even Beornoth laughed.

The bridge was alive with people, and just as Wigs and Gis grimly remembered, it was the same bridge where they had thrown back Forkbeard's fleet and risked their lives for Lundenwic and its people. The bridge spanned wide enough for two carts to pass, and today wooden booths lined the platform where Beornoth and his men had hacked at Forkbeard's Vikings. Women leaned from those booths, shouting blessings to the lords and warriors as they sold trinkets, bread and honey mead for pennies and scraps of hacksilver. Children ran along the bridge and through the streets. They tossed handfuls of rushes onto the road as they swerved between the men in armour and helmets. The river beneath the bridge foamed against its piers and beyond it masts swayed as merchants and visiting ealdormen's ships thronged the wharves.

Men rode and marched in a long line, their mail bright and their banners proud. Common folk cheered as Beornoth and his companions passed, throwing flowers and waving in celebration. The air shook with sound, bells clanging, traders shouting, sheep bleating as men herded them off the road to make way for the lords and thegns. Beornoth would have preferred to ride to the king's feast without the pageantry, but the warriors had earned the respect and thanks and so he endured it for their sake.

Beornoth searched the crowds for any sign of Thered, Alfgar or Brand but saw none. He glimpsed Morcar turning a bend in the road and so knew that some of the northern lords at least had come to make their peace with the king. Beornoth longed to see Brand, his old friend and sword brother, a Viking who fought like a bear and found peace in Northumbria as a thegn of Ealdorman Thered. He had seen Brand in the water aboard one of Forkbeard's drakkars, a fleeting glance, and thankfully they had not come close enough to trade blows. Beornoth could not imagine fighting the man who had saved his life after the battle of Maldon, and to see him here at Lundenwic with all old allegiances forgiven would gladden Beornoth's old heart.

The streets twisted and narrowed, and timbered houses leaned in so close that their roofs almost met above like the eaves of a forest. Smoke curled from thatch, and the smell of cooking fish and roasting pork swirled with the stink of tanners' pits. Children continued to laugh and run as they tossed rushes onto the path to hide the city's mud and filth, and ribbons fluttered from high poles. Stewards in the king's livery stood at every corner shouting praise for King Æthelred, who had driven back the Vikings to preserve God's land, and for Lord Eadric, who had won the great battle at Oxenforda.

'Bloody simpletons don't know that Cnut is a Christian just like his father,' grumbled Gis as they trotted slowly by another such crier.

'Eadric won the battle?' said Wigs incredulously. 'Bastard didn't even swing his sword. He hid in a tent and came here to claim the glory. Miserable turd.'

They passed Cheapside, where the market bustled even amidst the celebrations. Men stopped to spend their silver at stalls heavy with meat, fish, bread and honeyed cakes. Alehouses spilled red-faced men onto the road. They raised their cups high and shouted acclaim to Prince Edmund Ironside, to God, and for their victory over the enemy. Beyond the market, the procession turned south, riding towards the river again, and there on a gentle rise above the wharves stood the king's hall. Its walls were made of high oak planks, darkened by smoke and age. Fresh thatch spanned its steep roof, and gilded dragons curled at its peaks. A stout palisade encircled the structure with its gates wide open and guards in mail standing tall, spears glinting as the great men of England passed by.

Beornoth, Wigs and Gis dismounted and handed their reins to stewards who led the horses away. The sound inside the yard was deafening. Ealdormen in silver and gold stood alongside thegns and champions in mail, their cloaks bright, their weapons polished and their chatter as thick as smoke. More stewards went amongst them to take their swords and seaxes and place them in empty barrels to be collected after the feast. Horses stamped, dogs barked and slaves hurried amongst them towards the hall carrying barrels and baskets of food and drink. Beornoth and his companions followed the crowd to the hall's grand entrance and passed through its oak doors carved with serpents and saints, iron-bound and heavy.

The hall ran long and high, a forest of twinkling light, beams blackened, rafters alive with banners, shields, axes and trophies of war. Rush lights and torches burned in iron sconces as their flames danced, and great fires burned in pits running the length of the hall. Smoke curled into the roof, where holes in the thatch allowed it to escape. The light inside was golden, flickering on polished shield bosses hung upon the walls beside thick tapestries, on cups of silver, on chain mail and gilded helms.

Benches ran the hall's length beside low tables, and rushes lay thick on the floor. Lords and thegns sat according to their rank. A steward recognised Beornoth's ring and beckoned him towards the front. He followed whilst Wigs and Gis took their seats with the East Anglian thegns towards the rear. Eadric's Mercians took most of the front benches, and beside them sat the men of Wessex. Godwin waved to Beornoth, and he nodded to return the greeting. Kentish men roared as loud as gulls, drinking with the warriors of Defnascir, and Beornoth caught sight of some Northumbrians but was forced to look away as a thegn from Somersaete clapped him on the shoulder in greeting. There was laughter, boasting, hands and forearms clasping, the clash of mugs on wood, and Beornoth wondered why there had never been such a celebration before? He had been part of many greater victories, where the Saxons had slaughtered thousands of the enemy, and were rewarded with little but curt thanks for their duty performed.

The king's seat sat upon a raised dais, where Æthelred himself sat with a gleaming crown upon his head and a cross lying against his breast. He leaned in as Eadric Streona, who sat alongside him, whispered in his ear. The king's beard was now white and grizzled, his face thin and drawn. Queen Emma sat straight-backed on his left, her Norman beauty pale and proud, her shoulders square. Edmund Ironside sat beside his mother, offering waves and smiles to men he recognised in the hall. He caught Beornoth's eye and grinned broadly, and Beornoth bowed respectfully.

Beornoth sat between Ulfcytel and Osgar at a table where other king's thegns sat, and he felt pleased to see the big warrior among them.

'A fine display,' Ulfcytel said after clasping Beornoth's arm. He glanced around at the banners and flowers with a grimace.

'Will there be a sermon?' Beornoth asked, watching as a gaggle of priests fussed around a tall bishop, straightening his robes and vestments.

'Undoubtedly. Best get comfortable.'

Osgar cleared his throat and pulled at the jerkin beneath his mail. He drank a cup of ale and mopped sweat from his brow.

'You won't have to say anything,' Beornoth said to calm the warrior. 'Edmund or the king will call your name. They'll announce you as king's thegn and give you your ring and sword. Just bow and come back to your seat.'

'Don't turn your back on the king, though,' added Ulfcytel.

'And don't fall over.'

Osgar's head snapped around to stare at Beornoth as though he had not considered such matters, and an unknown fear unlocked behind eyes capable of facing ruthless Viking warriors on the battlefield.

'You'll be fine,' said Beornoth, and clapped Osgar on the shoulder.

Thralls hurried between the tables with jugs of ale and mead, and with platters of bread, butter, cheese and roasted fowl. Once that course was over, they brought whole salmon from the Thames, roasted swans stuffed with apples, oxen carved and dripping fat, great hams glazed with honey, and trenchers of rye bread piled high to mop up the glorious meat juices or to toss to the dogs, who snuffled and whined at their feet.

Beornoth ate and scanned the room for any signs of his friends but saw none amongst the many tables. The smells of roasted meat, hot bread, honey and herbs made Beornoth's stomach growl, and he tore into a piece of soft pork, its juices running into his beard. Osgar drank foaming ale, and his knee shook beneath the table as he glanced towards the dais and contemplated the moment he would receive his honour. Pipes and music rose, and a harp played as a skald sang of Alfred and Athelstan. Men roared their approval at the mention of great battles and heroes. They slammed their cups and shouted toasts. It was a hall of triumph, and Beornoth wondered if Streona and the king believed they had won an ultimate victory over the Vikings. It had been a standstill rather than a crushing victory, a mutual but unspoken truce.

Beornoth drank mead and ate bread smeared with the honey that helped his cough and with the pain in his chest. He watched Streona as he continued to babble to the king, smiling his snake's smile, his cup always raised, his tongue always smooth. The music stopped, and the skald bowed. King Æthelred sat back and, to Beornoth's surprise, rather than Eadric, it was Edmund who stood to address the gathering. Eadric sat back in his chair, not a flicker of surprise on his face, but a look of barely concealed malice in his eyes as he listened to the warlords acclaim Edmund Ironside with raucous cheers.

Edmund waved them to quiet, and though still a fresh-faced lad, he spoke confidently and without fear even though the men gazing up at him owned vast swathes of land, and commanded hundreds of spearmen in war. He spoke eloquently about the battle, and how God had granted the army victory over the enemy. He praised his father for returning to England and the lords of the north who had made the journey south to heal old wounds. Edmund, Beornoth noted, omitted Eadric Streona from his praise, and the ealdorman of Mercia seethed upon his seat, a false smile splitting his face.

The prince called up men to be honoured one by one. Amidst much applause, they announced Godwin as the new ealdorman of Wessex, making him the ruler of England's richest and most powerful shire. The role surpassed that of his father Wulfnoth, and Beornoth felt pride for the young man who had done so well to navigate Streona and his brother's wrath and exceed his father's power. Eadric clapped along with the crowd, and Beornoth wondered how Prince Edmund had achieved the promotion from his father without Streona's intervention. Æthelred sat quietly, neither clapping nor smiling. He simply sat in his chair with a blank face, whilst Queen Emma held his thin, pale hand.

Osgar took his turn, walking slowly and carefully towards the dais as men stood and roared for the great warrior. He accepted his ring and sword, swore an oath to serve the king and returned to his chair. He let out a gushing gasp of relief and downed two horns of ale. Then came the lords of the north, and Beornoth's heart soared because Thered and Brand stood with Sigeferth, Morcar and the other eminent men of the Danelaw and were forgiven for siding with Sweyn Forkbeard.

The bishop followed Edmund's speech, and Beornoth fell asleep twice as he spoke in a low, rumbling voice, admonishing the guests for their sins and encouraging them to greater godliness. When the talk was done, the feasting resumed, and Beornoth was about to rise and seek Brand and Thered when a steward bent between Beornoth and Ulfcytel and summoned them to a meeting with the prince. A meeting away from the hall, a secret meeting, a dangerous meeting. Osgar went with them, and there in a dark corridor without light or torch waited a group of men, and with them were Brand and Thered.

22

'Lord!' Brand shouted. The Viking ran along the corridor and embraced Beornoth with the warmth of a long-lost brother. Brand laughed and clapped his old friend's wide back.

'The last time I saw you, I thought I might have to kill you,' Beornoth said.

'You are so old I doubt you could lift a sword to do it.'

'There's enough strength left in these arms to handle you, don't worry about that.'

They laughed, and Beornoth asked Brand about his wife and children, and Brand talked effusively of his sons fighting, hunting and riding and of his beautiful wife and daughters. 'By the gods, it does me good to see you. And we are on the same side now!'

'I have missed you, old friend.' Beornoth could not keep the smile from his face. Brand stood not as tall as Beornoth but was thick across the shoulders and chest. He wore his long golden hair in two braids, and a raven tattoo crawled up the side of his neck. 'Ealdorman Thered.' Beornoth bowed his head, and the ealdorman laughed, shook his head and embraced Beornoth just as warmly as Brand had.

'Don't give me that,' said Thered. His hair had turned grey, and his face carried new wrinkles, but he looked well. Holding him brought back memories of long-dead friends, of brothers, and of great men lost to the horrors of war. Thered was as scarred as Beornoth, with the marks of Maldon slashed into his face, his missing fingers and the sadness deep within his eyes. He had ever struggled with the terrible nightmares war had left upon his soul. He was a good man, a gentle man at heart, who had forced himself to become the man his position required.

Thered and Beornoth had been enemies once. Thered's father, the old Ealdorman Oslac, had tried to have Beornoth captured and killed inside York's great hall. Ealdorman Byrhtnoth had saved Beornoth's life that day, along with Leofsunu of Sturmer, Aelfwine of Foxfield and the rest of the ealdorman's old hearth troop. All dead now, slaughtered at the massacre at Maldon. After Thered's father met justice, Thered had joined Ealdorman Byrhtnoth's hearth troop as a hostage. He had fought well, and Beornoth and Thered had eventually become brothers of the sword. An unbreakable bond, even for men who had stood in opposing armies.

'Is Alfgar here?' Beornoth asked.

'No. He did not join with Forkbeard,' Thered replied. 'Old Alfgar is as cunning as a fox. He has kept to himself these last years, minding the business of Cheshire and keeping out of the wars. We had little choice when Sweyn came north and requested our oaths and our warriors. How could we stand alone against his army when so many of our people wished to join him, anyway?'

'Which is why I have asked you men to join me here for a brief conversation,' said Prince Edmund. He came from the shadows and strode purposefully through the men before opening a heavy oak door. Inside lay a wide room full of dust, broken benches, bent candlesticks and a floor covered in bird shit.

A score of men filtered into the room, and Edmund closed the door behind them.

'Welcome, my lords,' said the prince. 'You are loyal, and brave. I have picked the most famous among our nobles, our champions and heroes of battles gone by. Lord Beornoth is here, Osgar, Ulfcytel, Godwin now ealdorman of Wessex, and our northern lords, Ealdorman Thered, Sigeferth and Morcar, and others amongst who have reaffirmed their oaths to my father. The realm is in peril, lords, and not only from Cnut and his Vikings. We have a plague eating us from within, a shadow corrupting the kingdom and eating away at the heart of our homeland. It was that plague that turned our northern brothers against us and into Forkbeard's arms. Not traitors, but men who had had enough of crippling taxes and senseless gafol payments. Men forced to do the right thing by their people. We have gathered here and must be able to trust each other, and so I will speak freely. I shall give name to the shadow, to the plague that threatens to drive deeper wedges between our shires and sunder everything my forefathers fought so hard to build in this glorious land of ours. Eadric, ealdorman of Mercia, is the shadow and the plague. He is the growth that gnaws upon my father like a demon, pouring honey into his ear, sucking up power and influence for himself. His ambition knows no bounds, and yet he does not have the courage to lift a blade on the battlefield. His curse must be cut out, it must be removed before it is too late.'

'Then why not cut the bastard's throat?' asked Brand, and the men in the room gave throaty approvals to that suggestion. 'Do it tonight whilst he sleeps. Or out there at the feast. I'll do it myself.' Brand shrugged as if it were the most obvious thing in the world.

'Eadric has power and influence. We must tread carefully. I wish it were that simple.'

'Why? You are the prince, and your father is the king. We could march out of here now, up onto that high platform and put a blade in his heart. You are the law. I'll cut his heart out if you want or take his head. Doesn't matter. That's the way we do it in the far north across the sea where only the strong rule.'

'We are not in Norway or Denmark, friend Brand, we are in Lundenwic, England. We have the rule of law here, and if our crown is to be legitimate, we must abide by those laws.'

'Your grandmother didn't care too much for those laws when she had your father's brother killed to make Æthelred king,' said Beornoth, and men winced at the harshness of his honesty.

Edmund met Beornoth's stare and did not flinch from the truth. 'We have all done things of which we are not proud. Today was about celebrating victory, and forgiving decisions made under duress. I cannot change history, but I can do the right thing now.'

'Eadric has done his work well,' said Godwin. 'Streona is a dangerous adversary. He has been thorough, careful, and his web has spread far. Eadric is the ealdorman of Mercia, risen to that position from nothing. He did away with the old thegns, the ancient aristocracy of that shire which was once the most powerful kingdom in Britain, and appointed his own men in their stead. Men loyal to him, dependent on him for their power and wealth. His brother holds vast swathes of land, and Mercia can raise close to a thousand spears all on its own. He has allies here at court, powerful churchmen beholden to him for their land grants and their silver. Streona is married to the king's daughter. He is your brother-in-law, Prince Edmund. His children will have a claim to the throne. He has the king's ear, and the power to sign edicts and royal commands. With all due respect, he is not an easy man to kill. He has guards with him every waking hour and protecting his bedchamber all night.'

'And yet he must be stopped,' said Prince Edmund, 'or our rule will not survive when Cnut returns with Thorkell the Tall and his entire Viking army.'

'Are you sure he will return?' asked Morcar, and some men mumbled agreement with his question. 'I hear there are problems in Norway and Denmark, merchants and traders whisper of rebellion.'

'He'll return,' said Edmund. 'A new king cannot easily stomach a defeat in his first battle. Vikings rule based on their strength, and as our friend Brand said, they do not suffer defeat easily. He has already sent a signal of his intent. Do you remember the hostages Cnut took when he came to power? Saxon hostages taken from our nobles in case we should rebel against his rule? Before he crossed the sea, Cnut cut the hands, ears and noses from those men. A warning.'

'Savage,' spat a lord at the back of the room.

'He took the hostages to assure the nobles' good faith,' said Brand, brows knitted as though he could not understand the man's point. 'They rose against him. That's the point of hostages. What was Cnut supposed to do, release them with a packed meal and a skin of ale, a pouch of silver and a pat on the back? His own men would kill him. He did what he did to those hostages because that is what a leader must do.'

'He'll come back,' said Sigeferth. 'He must. His jarls and champions will demand vengeance for the defeat. But let me show you the other side of this sword, and forgive me, lord prince, for speaking plainly. We in this room have much to lose, not least our lives. If Streona gets a sniff that we conspire against him, what do you think will become of us? Do you think he holds the same compunctions as you about cutting his enemies' throats? I can assure you that he does not. He has done it before; he killed the old Mercian ealdorman to pave the way for his ascension to that title. So whatever we do, we must do it swiftly and without mercy. We cannot fight a ruthless man with manners and honour. Any fight with Eadric Streona is like two drunken brawlers rolling in the mud.

It is a fight of biting, scratching and gouging, a fight for survival where anything goes.

'Going beyond the issue of Eadric Streona, there are still many folk north of the Danelaw who do not care if a Saxon or Danish king sits on the throne. They are not traitors, but what connection do they have to the throne? The realm and the folk within it continue with their daily lives no matter who wears the crown in Winchester. Do you think the thegn on the borders of Pictland who fights constant battles against raiders and roving bands of masterless men cares who is his king? Or the man who ploughs a furrow beside Bebbanburg's high crag, or the woman who weaves baskets beyond the River Mersea? More than that, many of them are descendants of Norsemen and Danes. You all know this. That is why clever old Forkbeard came to the Danelaw to raise his army during his last campaign, and why he never raided north of the Danelaw. Cnut is his father's son, and he won't survive without Forkbeard's cunning, his savagery and willingness to make war. So when Cnut comes we must fight him as one, and I can tell you now that the northern fyrd and its warriors will not muster if they believe they fight for Eadric Streona. That bastard has bled us dry to pay Thorkell's gafol. Bled the north dry!'

'Thank you for your honesty,' said Prince Edmund, with no anger in his voice, understanding plain on his face. 'I agree with everything you have said. And so we return to the problem at hand. What do we do about Eadric Streona?'

'Can you and the queen keep your father away from Eadric?' asked Godwin. 'Only you and Queen Emma have that power. Keep Eadric from his ear and the king might listen to you. Brihtric has retreated into Mercia, but I will hunt him. He killed my family, and for that there must be a reckoning.'

'He will listen, but my father is very ill, my lords. He grows frail and can barely put his hand to royal decrees. But I will try.'

'Then the rest of us must prepare our shires for war,' said Godwin, his clever eyes blazing. Men listened to him despite his youth, and he stood beside Prince Edmund, and two young men faced a room of grizzled veterans and commanded respect. 'We must tell our men that they do not fight for Streona. They fight for the kingdom. Tell them the truth. If Cnut is victorious, he will replace every lord and every thegn with his own men. Tell them they fight for their families and their land and they should make ready to march when Cnut returns.'

'Aye,' agreed the room, and Beornoth smiled to see how Godwin had grown since they had first met beside the royal fleet when he was little more than a spotty lad standing in his father's shadow.

'Remove Streona from the king's ear,' said Beornoth, 'rally the shires. When Eadric does not have the power to issue royal decrees and condemn men as traitors, then we can strike at him.'

'We have a plan, my lords,' said Prince Edmund, and he set his jaw with determination. 'We few are the key to the future of this country. Keep our strategy secret, friends, and keep it safe. Streona has eyes and ears everywhere. Perhaps there are even men in this room who are under his sway, and we do not know it. We must return to the feast now, before his spies notice we are missing. But we act now.'

They waited, returning to the hall in ones and twos so as not to raise suspicion. Beornoth spent the rest of the night drinking and eating with Brand, Thered, Wigs, Gis and Ulfcytel. Old friends and good friends. Beornoth relished every moment, every memory they discussed over good mead. If this were to be the last time he was in their company, it was a good way to say farewell. As time grew short for Beornoth, he could feel the shadow spreading deep within him, malignant and creeping, sapping his strength and filling his body with poison. But there was hope in that room. Men laughed, felt comradeship, and they believed in Edmund's strength, and that gave promise of his kingship when he succeeded his father's throne.

Hope swept across the hall, and its lords felt better than they had in years, because it was as though the thrashing rain had stopped, and a rainbow of dreams lit up the kingdom in bright colours, promising what might wait for them in the future. Men drank and were forgiven for siding with Forkbeard. They had sworn new oaths, and fresh allegiances were forged with the prospect of a powerful prince and a bright future.

But in the morning, the storm came anew to cast men's hopes asunder. A raging, bleak and malevolent storm to crush dreams and cast the kingdom into the fires of treachery and death.

23

'Lord,' said Gis, shaking Beornoth's shoulder to wake him. 'You must come quickly.'

'What's going on?' Beornoth croaked out of his parched throat. Too much mead drunk at the feast had robbed his body of every scrap of moisture. His head throbbed, and his eyes felt like pissholes in the snow.

'Prince Edmund has summoned you, lord. Come, you must dress quickly.'

Beornoth sat up and thought he might vomit. 'Drinking is a young man's game. When I was a lad, I could drink all night and fight all day and be none the worse. I feel like a horse has galloped across my head. Get my byrnie.'

'Yes, lord.'

'And Gis?'

'Yes?'

'Water. Lots of water. Not ale.'

Minutes later, Beornoth strode along the corridors of Lundenwic's keep. His chain mail and belt buckle chinked with every step, and his heavy boots thumped on the ground. Beornoth had drunk an entire jug of water, and it felt like he had drunk nothing at all.

'Where's Wigs?' he asked.

'Good question,' Gis replied, trailing Beornoth, also dressed in his leather armour. 'Last time I saw him, he was leaving the feast in the arms of a red-headed serving girl.'

They found Prince Edmund, Ulfcytel, Thered and Godwin waiting outside a chamber. Two guards in full armour and armed with spears guarded the room's door. A window opposite cast a shaft of sunlight, which lit the timber walls, and motes danced in its brightness before disappearing into the gloom beyond.

'What has happened?' Beornoth said, taking in the grim countenance of each man.

'Look inside,' said Edmund, a great sadness in his voice, but anger in his young eyes.

The other men looked away in disgust, and Beornoth suddenly felt afraid of what lay behind that door. Was it Wigs left for dead in a maid's bed? Had Brand tried to carry out his threat, and found himself slaughtered by Eadric's guards? He put a hand on the door and then paused.

'What room is this?'

'Eadric Streona's chamber,' said Edmund, and ran a hand down his fledgling beard.

Beornoth pushed the door open. Its black hinges creaked, and the first thing to hit him was the iron stink of blood. Beornoth held his breath and stepped inside. It was a dark room with a pallet bed at one end, a table and chairs knocked askew and two dead men sprawled across the ground, their blood seeping in dark pools across the timber floor. Light shone in through a half-open window shutter, and at first Beornoth did not recognise the two bodies because their heads were a mass of blood and blue swollen flesh. Thick crimson matted their hair, and sword blows to their faces and necks left their heads half severed. They wore mail, expensive armour, and Beornoth recognised them.

He inhaled sharply, and his stomach turned over.

'Sigeferth and Morcar,' Beornoth gasped. 'Who could do such a thing?' He knew the answer, of course, but the words escaped his lips before his mind had the chance to keep them back.

'Streona,' said Prince Edmund, coming to stand alongside Beornoth.

'I received an invitation to these chambers this morning to discuss urgent matters,' said Godwin. 'But I did not attend. Too much ale last night and too much suspicion kept me in my bed.'

'It's only mid-morning,' said Beornoth. 'He must have summoned them at the crack of dawn. Why did they answer his call?'

'The summons came not from Streona. It came from Prince Edmund.'

'Bastard,' Beornoth growled. 'He knows. Someone in that room last night went to him like a cur and told Eadric our plans. They told him who was there. We are all in danger.'

'These men are lords of Northumbria,' Thered shouted, his anger sudden and surprising. 'My men. Butchered like cattle. Where is your rule of law now?'

'This is an outrage,' Edmund replied, voice calm. 'And there will be retribution.'

'I march for the north to raise my army and prepare for war.' Thered turned away and marched down the long corridor. Beornoth noted his friend did not say against whom his army would fight.

'It ends now,' Beornoth said. He brushed past the others and ducked under the low door lintel.

'Where are you going?' Godwin called after him.

'To get Brand.' Rage had taken hold of Beornoth. In his later years, talk had taken the place of brutal violence, and he suddenly realised that talking got men nowhere. The only thing men like Eadric understood was brute force, the sword, blood and death, and so Beornoth would show him what violence really was. Brand was right, and Beornoth knew no better man to help him put Eadric Streona in his grave.

'Lord Beornoth!' Prince Edmund shouted.

Beornoth stopped in his tracks but did not turn around. He had already made up his mind.

'Eadric is no longer at Lundenwic,' Edmund continued. 'He left with his retinue shortly after this abomination. He has issued an edict that Sigeferth and Morcar were traitors who joined forces with Forkbeard and now conspire with Cnut of his return.'

'Where has he gone?'

'I do not know. Mercia, perhaps? Or north to claim Sigeferth's and Morcar's lands. They border Mercia and Northumbria, do they not?'

'They do,' said Godwin, standing beside the prince.

'Then I will see the king,' said Beornoth. 'Now.'

Beornoth strode away with the prince, Godwin and Gis running to keep up with his long strides. He was a king's thegn, and his oath was to King Æthelred, so Beornoth would have his audience with his lord now that Eadric was not there to intervene. Streona had gone too far. Murdering two of Northumbria's greatest lords and not even bothering to conceal his crime was beyond the pale, beyond any of the terrible deeds he had committed in his life of grasping, climbing, treachery, politics and ambition.

'Wait!' Edmund called, but Beornoth would not be stopped.

He wound his way around the corridors, up a set of wooden stairs until he came to a set of rooms where two big men in mail and armed with spears barred the way.

'I am Beornoth, king's thegn,' he said. 'Come to see the king.'

'No visitors,' said a guard as tall as Beornoth. His nose was bent and broken from some distant fight, and blue eyes peered out from beneath his helmet.

'Stand aside. There will be no other warning.'

'Piss off, grandfather,' said the second man, shorter but wide across the shoulders and with a thick neck like a bull.

Beornoth punched the bull-necked man in the stomach, grabbed the taller guard's spear and butted him hard in the face, breaking his nose anew. He grabbed the bull-necked guard's head and drove him backwards, smashing his skull into the wooden wall so that he slumped like a sack of onions. The first guard spat blood and turned on Beornoth, spear levelled and teeth bared. He came to kill a man who attacked the king's royal guard, and Beornoth readied himself to meet the spear. He would not be stopped. Beornoth had to speak to the king about Eadric Streona and the grievous damage he had done to the realm and to Æthelred's already fragile reputation.

'Hold!' shouted Prince Edmund, bounding up the stairs with his hands raised.

The guard turned, confusion in his eyes. He looked from Beornoth to Edmund and stood aside, casting a murderous look in Beornoth's direction.

'Stand down,' Edmund continued, and placed a calming hand first on the guard's arm and then on Beornoth's.

The prince moved to the door, knocked once and entered, beckoning for Beornoth to follow. Beornoth took a breath to calm his anger. A cough rattled in his chest, brought on by the sudden exertion. It burst forth, shaking his body, and Beornoth leaned against the wall. Gis hurdled past the guard and ran to Beornoth's side. He used his sleeve to wipe the blood from Beornoth's mouth and helped him stand upright. Beornoth cursed his age and his affliction. He straightened and ignored the mocking grin on the tall guard's face. For a fleeting moment, Beornoth had felt like his old self.

Strong, implacable, a force of nature capable of shocking violence. Rage fuelled that strength, uncurling his crooked fingers, imbuing his old bones with power. Now that the fight was over, it fled from him like a squall blowing from a stormy sea.

Beornoth followed Edmund into the room, a vast chamber with lavish furniture and a fire on the gable wall where a small blaze spread warmth throughout the room. A side door opened, and Queen Emma burst in wearing a long sea-green gown, which scuffed the timbers beneath her feet. She stood by the bed with her arms folded across her chest and a strong-boned face like thunder.

'What is the meaning of this?' she said, frowning at Edmund and then at Beornoth. 'How dare you burst into the king's presence like this?'

Only at that moment did Beornoth realise that King Æthelred lay in the bed, his wan, pale form propped up on a soft pillow. Beornoth saw him lying there with his eyes closed, his face thin and skull-like, and he understood why few men were allowed to see the king in such a sorry state.

'I apologise for the intrusion, my lady,' Beornoth said. 'But a heinous crime has taken place within the keep. Eadric has lured two Northumbrian lords into his chambers and had them murdered in the king's name.'

Queen Emma peered over Beornoth and Edmund's shoulder and gave a small shake of her head. Edmund turned and closed the door so that they were alone in the room.

'Eadric grows ever more powerful, so much so that he now acts with impunity. He had taken command of the king's seal, assuming power in his name, and so now signs edicts and issues proclamations. If he feels he can kill noblemen in the heart of this royal keep, then he truly believes that he rules the realm. Seize him.'

'He has gone,' said Edmund.

'Then you must ride out. Go among the people, gather spearmen and powerful lords to your cause. Bind them to you, for war is coming, a civil war fought between our own people even as Cnut and his Vikings muster their warriors to return and take the crown by force. You must build an army just as Eadric builds and adds men and warriors to him like so many pebbles on the seashore. Eadric must be removed by force, and only war can do it.'

'We shall leave today,' said Edmund.

'Can I talk to the king?' Beornoth asked respectfully, and walked towards the bed. Queen Emma opened her mouth to object but kept her silence as Beornoth reached the king's bedside. 'My king?' he said. 'It is I. Beornoth.'

The king lay still, as pale as milk and almost unrecognisable in his old age. He was a younger man than Beornoth, and Beornoth wondered if that would be his fate, to die whittled away to nothing by age and sickness until he was little more than a skeleton on a pillow. Breath came from the king's lips in a thin rasp, and Beornoth felt uncomfortable approaching the man in this weakened state.

'Can you hear me?' Beornoth asked one last time.

'Beo?' Æthelred said, his voice quiet and thin. His head turned, and his pale eyes flickered open and fixed upon Beornoth's.

'Yes, lord king, do you remember me?'

'I do. I do.' The king smiled. 'Did we win a battle? Is Byrhtnoth with you?'

'No, lord.' Beornoth glanced at the queen, who just stared flatly at Beornoth, letting him take in the state of Æthelred's health for himself. 'Byrhtnoth is resting; he fights hard to protect your realm.'

'He does. As do you. Such bravery.' Æthelred wheezed and winced at some hidden cramp deep inside his body. Beornoth swallowed a lump in his throat, a sudden wave of sadness washing over him. Not because the king was ill, but because of the time that had passed, the men who had died and the enemies who had tried to destroy them. Such men. Such heroes. Now it appeared everything waned, that wars were being fought in the shadows by lesser men rather than between champions on the battlefield. The kingdom crumbled and decayed, cut and slashed by too many blades, drained of blood by too many enemies from within and without, just like Beornoth and Æthelred. They were the last of the old guard, of those who remembered Olaf Trygvasson, Palnatoki, Byrhtnoth, Aelfwine of Foxfield, Leofsunu of Sturmer, men who seemed like giants compared to Eadric Streona and young Cnut.

'The crown is in danger, lord king, and we need your help.'

'Summon Byrhtnoth, my *dux bellorum*. Bring him to me, Beo.'

A memory scythed into Beornoth's consciousness, unwanted and unwelcome. The great ealdorman's golden-hilted sword crashing into the churned foulness, the mud, blood, piss and shit-soaked earth beneath the shield wall at Maldon. Olaf and his Jomsviking drengrs had come for the ealdorman. Olaf's picked champions had formed a swine-head wedge and encircled Ealdorman Byrhtnoth and cut him down in a welter of blades and fury. He also remembered King Æthelred as he was, with his shining auburn hair, a circlet of silver or gold on his brow and how men had bowed to the descendant of Alfred the Great.

'I cannot, lord king; it falls to us to fight this time.'

Æthelred smiled wanly. 'My days of riding with the army are behind me. Who is this enemy? A Dane? A Norseman?'

'No. An Englishman. A man who has seemed like a friend to you, almost a son. Eadric, the ealdorman of Mercia.'

Æthelred gave a subtle shake of his head. 'Eadric is dear to me. He is no enemy.'

'He killed two of your lords this morning in this keep. Eadric killed Wulfnoth of Wessex, and he taxes your northern nobles so fiercely that they rebel. He is your enemy, my lord.'

Æthelred tried to move, but his frail body trembled. He shuddered, and Queen Emma bent to wet his lips with a cloth soaked in water.

'That's enough,' she scolded Beornoth.

What she didn't say was that she had only allowed Beornoth to speak to the king to show him how far Æthelred had fallen. That he was incapable of ruling, that his mind wandered, laid low by age and sickness. But there was too much peril, too much to lose for Beornoth to give up now.

He leaned in to the king, bringing his scarred face close to the king's ear. 'I have given so much for your crown, my lord. I have lost everything. My wife and children, my brothers. My body is cut and stabbed to ruin by your enemies, and I am still fighting though death beckons to me, teasing me with the last embers of life and the fights yet to be won. I have never asked you for anything, nothing in return for my sacrifice. It was my duty, my oathsworn responsibility. But I ask you now, rescind your support for Eadric and instead support your son. Let Edmund rule in your stead. Empower him with the royal seal and do not allow Eadric to rule the land we all love so much.'

Æthelred winced and bit his lip. 'Eadric is my son-in-law. A good man. He brings me honey and pears.'

Beornoth realised then that any plea to the king was like shouting into a deep well and expecting a response. He stood, bowed to Æthelred and to Queen Emma.

'Leave us,' the queen called, and they all turned to leave.

'Not you, Lord Beornoth.'

Beornoth waited until the door closed and faced the queen. She stood, broad-hipped and square-shouldered, strong with her chin raised and her face calm.

'Now you understand,' she said. 'My husband is not himself. Streona must be stopped. He all but rules, and that cannot be.'

'Edmund rallies. There is strength in him; I see it.'

'There is. But he must fight. Edmund must raise an army and do battle with Eadric. There must be war so that we can have peace.'

'A war between our own people?'

'It must be so. We cannot outmanoeuvre Eadric at court. He has grown too powerful. I am the daughter and descendant of Viking warlords, Lord Beornoth. Rollo is my grandsire, he who carved out the dukedom of Normandy with his sword and his ships. My father and brother are great warriors, and I understand when battle is necessary. I want you to help Edmund. Advise him. Assist him in raising the army he needs. Sigeferth and Morcar are dead, and Ealdormen Thered and Alfgar are your friends. Help Edmund rally the men in Sigeferth's and Morcar's lands, bring the northern lords to his banner and bring Eadric and Mercia to war. It will take strength and courage. Many men will die. But if Edmund fails in this task, then Cnut will return to find a fractured kingdom ripe for the taking. He will take Winchester, just as his father did, and put himself on the throne. The reign of the Saxons will end, and the dawn of Viking rule shall begin. So help Edmund, Beornoth, lend him your strength and experience.'

'Yes, my lady.'

Beornoth bowed to her and gave King Æthelred another glance. The queen had the right of it. They had skirted the issue, looking for another solution, but war was the only way. So war it must be. Beornoth left the king's chambers and marched along the wooden corridor and out into the morning. He found Edmund and Godwin waiting for him on Lundenwic's high battlements, their faces long and pale.

'What is it?' Beornoth asked, the sense of foreboding palpable on the wind.

'Cnut has returned with a vast fleet,' said Edmund. 'He sails for Sandwich with Thorkell the Tall and the entire Viking army.'

24

1015AD

Ulfcytel returned to East Anglia to defend his lands against Cnut's grand army, which appeared like the Norse god Loki's monster brood, descending on the world on the day of Ragnarök. They had arrived with a fleet of two hundred drakkar warships. Slithering across the narrow sea from Frankia with their snarling beast heads and sails daubed with wolves, bears, eagles, foxes and skulls to land at Sandwich, just as they always did. Cnut loosed Thorkell and his Jomsvikings on the East Anglians with a vengeful fury, and they burned, raped and savaged the folk of the fens and marshes. For months Ulfcytel fought a dirty war to keep them at bay. He led his warriors along the secret marsh paths, striking at the Vikings from the mist and reeds, attacking at night, killing and retreating into the myriad islands and secret pathways known only to the marsh men to recover and hit again.

Beornoth, Wigs and Gis rode north with Prince Edmund and his hearth troop of one hundred warriors taken from the Lundenwic guard, the king's royal bodyguard, and the best of Godwin's Wessex men. They rode to raise an army in the north to fight Eadric Streona, just as Cnut came to bite and rend at a land at war with itself. Eadric himself had retreated deep into Mercia to raise an army of his own. He rallied his loyal lords to his cause, and so the shires of England became a place preparing for war on an unprecedented scale. Folk laboured to make sheaves of arrows, they cut spears from pollarded woods, they gathered supplies, forged blades, crafted leather breastplates and marched to join the lord to whom they owed their oaths.

Beornoth and his warriors rode across the land, summoning men and preparing for war. All the while they sent riders for news of Cnut and Ulfcytel's resistance, and news came back to say that the East Anglians held, and that Ulfcytel believed Cnut would dig in and remain in East Anglia for the winter, ready to strike anew at Lundenwic and Winchester in the spring. Thered and Brand met Beornoth, Edmund and their forces on the borders of Northumbria with the promise of a thousand spearmen, and Alfgar sent word that he would send five hundred warriors east to join their cause. Godwin had returned to Wessex to raise an army, and messengers had gone to Defnascir, Somersaete, Kent and all the shires to test men's loyalty and rally them north to support Edmund's war. Edmund had made camp outside a monastery deep in lands which had belonged to Lord Sigeferth, and there he had married the dead thegn's daughter and proclaimed himself earl of the East Midlands, a move which openly challenged Eadric who ruled the vast shire of Mercia on its borders.

'Men are coming from the hills and valleys in their hundreds,' said Gis as they watched a band of spearmen practise shield-wall manoeuvres on a wide grazing pasture.

'And thousands,' added Wigs. 'God help us, but the northerners hate Eadric Streona more than I hated my first wife.'

Edmund had raised his first banners along the River Trent where Sigeferth's and Morcar's lands, known as the Five Boroughs, had long guarded the frontier with the old Danelaw, stretching back to the days of uneasy peace between King Alfred and the Viking hordes of Ivar the Boneless, Sigurd Snake in the Eye and Guthrum the Unlucky. The army camped beside Snottingaham, a burh on high ground above the fast-flowing river. Just as it had in Alfred's day when he had ordered such burhs built to protect the Saxon people from their Viking enemies, a stout palisade ringed the fortification, complete with a well-kept ditch and bank. Timber towers rose at the gates, and wattle houses lined the streets beside high-gabled churches and merchant yards where the descendants of Vikings and Saxon traders mingled easily.

Beornoth stared out at the Midlands plain, a land of rivers and dark woods, of pasture and ploughland broken by the smoke of hamlets and villages, crawling now with makeshift tents and campfires as the army of Edmund Ironside gathered for war. The River Trent flowed wide and sluggish, its waters gleaming dull brown as winter approached. Boats rowed with the flow, laden with grain and ale to keep the army fed. To the north and east lay the flat fenlands and fertile fields of Lindsey; to the west, the rougher hills of ancient Mercia.

The land about them was stripped bare, no longer even stubbled with harvest. The air grew sharp with chill, and the changing season stripped the trees to black bones. Roads grew hard with frost, rivers swelled with the rain, and Edmund's banner of the white cross flew proud over Snottingaham as he tried to make his new wife comfortable before the battle began.

Beornoth took his drink of honeyed mead, which Gis prepared for him each day to help keep the wracking cough at bay. They shared a simple meal of black bread and thin gruel, and Gis stood up from his plate as Prince Edmund approached from the town riding a roan mare and flanked by six of his retinue.

'Looks like news,' said Wigs, standing to join Gis and offering a bow to the prince.

Beornoth groaned and rose slowly, bones aching as his byrnie sat heavy on his broad shoulders.

'That big bastard riding beside the prince looks like Osgar,' said Wigs.

'That is Osgar,' Gis replied. 'He's got his axe strapped to his back.'

Beornoth held up a hand in greeting to see the stout warrior approaching, but fearful of what his arrival might mean.

'Lord Beornoth!' Edmund called cheerfully from the back of his horse. The riders reined in, and Osgar raised a hand to return Beornoth's gesture.

'What news of East Anglia?' Beornoth asked.

Edmund turned to Osgar, but the big man remained silent.

'Ulfcytel still holds and Cnut has not advanced,' said the prince after it became clear that Osgar did not intend to repeat the message he had delivered to Edmund before coming to meet Beornoth.

'Then we can fight Streona before winter, and meet Cnut in the spring,' Beornoth replied.

'It looks that way, so we must march south with all haste and offer battle. Eadric has declared me a traitor and issued a decree that I am in open rebellion against my father.'

The prince spoke as though he passed news at market, rather than the terrible declaration that he was now an enemy of the crown.

'There's no time to waste then.' Beornoth turned to Wigs and Gis. 'Find Brand, Thered and the rest of the commanders and give the order to strike camp. We march south with all haste.'

'It's time, Beornoth,' said Edmund. His horse felt the prince's excitement and whickered; its forelegs scraped the grass, and the beast turned in a half-circle. 'Time to teach Eadric a long-overdue lesson. We'll have his head!'

Edmund rode back towards the burh and left Beornoth alone. He sat again and watched as thousands of men cheered the news of battle. They hurried to collapse their tents, put out their fires and load wains and wagons for the journey south to meet the foe. He slid his sword from its scabbard and touched the cold blade. The sword had been his tool, how he had made his living, and now the blade felt heavy in hands spotted with age. He sighed and glanced up at the sky, hoping that Eawynn and his daughters Ashwig and Cwen waited for him in heaven. He must join them soon, he knew. This would be his last battle, for his body could surely not bear the labour of another winter, or another shield wall. A single tear rolled down his cheek as he thought of the life cruelly snatched from him by the Viking raiders who had killed his children.

Beornoth closed his eyes and smiled as he remembered running through fields chasing his giggling daughters, of their soft hair and how their smiles made his hard heart warm. Then the sight of their burned bodies, shrivelled and shrunken in his burned house, and of Eawynn ravaged with her throat cut, but still alive. Beornoth sucked in a breath of chill air and banished those thoughts.

Was there enough strength left in his old body? There must be, Beornoth knew, for he would not wait in the rear this time whilst the brave men fought. If his curled hands and withered body could not fight, then he would die in battle as a warrior should, not coughing himself to death. But he would not endanger his men. If Beornoth could not hold his shield steady, he would charge the enemy and die in the welter of blades which had come at him his entire life. He was ready. He was tired. Streona must be stopped so that the kingdom could heal and fight the Viking threat as one unified force.

So Beornoth rode south beside Prince Edmund Ironside. Thered left his men under Edmund's command and returned north to his shire, long since done with the horrors of battle. Brand rode with the army, and so did Osgar.

Wigs and Gis rode with Beornoth, and an army of three thousand men marched south to do battle. Beornoth camped with Brand each night and listened to stories of his children, and of his wife Sefna. Good nights by warm campfires spent with friends. Beornoth savoured every moment with them, staying up late even when his aching body screamed at him to lie down and sleep. He woke early, as the aged do, and would watch Brand, Wigs and Gis sleeping. He walked the paths of his memories and remembered those lost to him. Whilst the marching army slept, Beornoth watched the sun rise each morning, it warmed his face, and he practised with his sword and shield, trying to add what strength he could in the short time before battle.

The army followed the Fosse Way, using the old Roman road for the wagons full of supplies. They crossed Watling Street and within a week came within a day's ride of Lundenwic, and so they made camp and sent riders to seek Eadric and offer battle. The first messengers returned as Beornoth and Brand sat beside a babbling brook to take a drink of ale as men prepared camp. Wigs came rushing from Prince Edmund's tent, running so fast that he tripped and rolled on the grass. He righted himself and stopped before Beornoth, red-faced and panting.

'Dark tidings, lord,' he said, eyes flitting to Brand and then back to Beornoth.

'Out with it, then,' Beornoth urged.

'Eadric Streona betrays the king. He has joined forces with Cnut and Thorkell.'

'Bastard serpent!' Brand shouted. 'Nithing! We should have cut the bastard's throat at the king's feast.'

'This happened a week ago when he had news of our army marching against him. But worse, he has gone and struck at Ealdorman Thered.'

'Eadric Streona attacked Thered?' Beornoth repeated, too stunned by the news for it to settle in his thought cage.

'Yes, lord.' Wigs gulped and ran a hand down his beard. 'Eadric knew the warriors of Northumbria were with us, leaving Thered unprotected. He knows Thered supported Prince Edmund and rode there to punish him. Ealdorman Thered is dead. Streona killed the ealdorman and his wife and hung their naked corpses from Thered's own walls.'

'Eadric killed Thered, and his wife, and hung their naked corpses from his walls?'

'Yes, lord.'

A deep, dark rage broiled within Beornoth. Eadric had killed and dishonoured his friend, a man who had saved Beornoth's life more than once. Eadric the Grasper, who was now a traitor and turncloak who had taken his warriors to join Cnut's invading army.

'And there's more. The prince is summoned to Lundenwic by the queen. King Æthelred's health worsens. The entire world feels like it's on fire!'

25

The bells of Lundenwic rang at dawn three days later.

At first, Beornoth thought it the usual call to prayer, the clang of a pious priest dragging Lundenwic from its bed for the first of the day's observances. But these were slower, heavier bells, each strike hanging in the air like a hammer blow against iron. One, then silence, then another, each echoed and drifted over the smoke-stained roofs, the stinking river, and over the narrow, filthy streets. Beornoth had barely slept. The horror and outrage at how his friend Ealdorman Thered had died swirled in his mind, torturing him as though Thered's ghost haunted him, imploring him for vengeance.

Beornoth mourned Thered terribly. Another friend gone, killed, slaughtered as the land fell further from its old glories into a murderous pit of betrayals and treachery. Thered's was a hard loss to take, and the manner of it left Brand a brooding, vengeful companion.

The bells rang out again, and Gis came from the stable into the yard of their lodgings where Beornoth stood brushing his horse.

'Do you hear that?' Gis said, mouth agape.

'The bells?'

'Aye. That's no usual prayer. They ring for death. Not some nameless monk neither, someone greater.'

The bells multiplied, and Beornoth's heart sank. Could there be yet more dark news for the people to bear in these grim days? The bells increased, and one great bell rang from St Paul's, its voice deeper and stronger than the others. From the east, the smaller churches added their clamour until the entire city throbbed with grief.

King Æthelred was dead.

Men came running through the streets shouting the news, and soon it was on every tongue. The king was gone, dead in his bed with the prince and his queen at his side. Some shouted that he had died of sickness, others of despair or a broken heart for how far his realm had fallen since the days of his illustrious father, King Edgar. Beornoth walked into the street with Wigs and Gis at his side, and beside them a mean-faced man in a mud-stained cloak spat on the roadside.

'God's judgement, that is,' he sneered to his big-bellied companion. 'For his failings. For letting the Vikings ravage us and then paying them fortunes to leave, only for the bastards to return every summer for more.'

Gis drove them off before they could say any more. Brand came outside and walked with Beornoth into the streets. The smell of Lundenwic wrapped about them – piss from the gutters, smoke from the hearths and the salt reek of the Thames. Folk stood in knots, staring at the churches as if the towers would tell them what came next. Women crossed themselves, and men muttered of dark omens, and the bells tolled slow and measured.

They walked to the bridge where a group of old women wept, and the streets became crowded as word spread. Traders, beggars, warriors and thralls all pressed north and west towards St Paul's, where they said that Prince Edmund would speak to the people.

'Æthelred held his kingdom with great toil,' Brand said in Norse, 'and great hardship for the length of his life.'

'Aye,' Beornoth muttered. 'His mother made him king over the corpse of his own brother, an ill omen if ever there was one. But he was not an evil king, just a man easily influenced. And a king must be strong.'

They passed by the gate to Lundenwic bridge, the same bridge where Beornoth had fought so hard for his king. Its timber roadway was already thick with carts and men. The Thames rolled black beneath its timbers, made sluggish by the tide. Folk muttered in hushed tones, some kind and mourning, others harsh and judging. Over them all rang the bells.

Beornoth, Brand, Wigs and Gis followed the paths as they narrowed with timber houses leaning like drunken men above the busy street. Folk lit rushes in their doorways in mourning, and priests sang sad dirges at every crossroads. At last the road opened onto the wide ground before St Paul's. The church stood proud on its hill, a vast timber structure, its western front hung with black cloth as priests in dark robes chanted at the doors.

And there before the steps was Prince Edmund.

He was bareheaded and wore his chain mail, tall, strong and proud. He bore a golden circlet upon his brow, and Queen Emma stood behind him dressed in a long black mourning gown with a veil hiding her face. The crowd pressed close to Edmund, surging like a wave towards shore. Warriors at the front raised their spears and banged their shields and a great cry of 'Ironside! Ironside!' rang out.

Brand went first as Beornoth and his companions forced their way forward until they stood in the front ranks of warriors and thegns. Edmund's eyes swept the crowd, and he inclined his head slightly to Beornoth and his eyes burned with the fire of battle, and suddenly Beornoth's sorrow for Æthelred and Thered vanished and was replaced by a surge of loyalty, of hope, and the hunger for vengeance.

A bishop raised his hands and called for silence.

'Pray for your king,' he cried out, voice cracking. 'Pray for the soul of Æthelred, son of Edgar, who is gone to God's mercy.'

A few warriors muttered at those words, for mercy was not the word many would have chosen for the man who had fled from Forkbeard, who had abandoned his people time and time again. Yet still they bowed their heads. Whatever his failings, he had been God's anointed, and now he was dead.

Edmund stepped forward and addressed the crowd, a sword strapped to his hip. They listened with open mouths and hope in their hearts.

'My father is gone,' he said, his voice carrying strong over the heads of the crowd. 'But England lives. Will you stand with me? Will you fight with me against the Vikings, against Cnut, who would steal our land and make this kingdom a Viking one?'

A crashing roar answered him. Shields clashed, swords rattled against spears. Women cried out and raised their fists, and for a moment the very air seemed to blaze with defiance. Beornoth drew his own sword and raised it up high.

'Ironside!' he roared, his voice raw with the emotion of a dead king and a slaughtered friend in the far north. Thered and his family, butchered like animals. Their deaths had sparked something deep within Beornoth, rage stirring the last embers of his strength. Around him, men bellowed until the entire square shook with it.

Lundenwic mourned Æthelred that day and night with vigils and prayers, but it was not grief that filled the streets. It was resolve. The people did not look back at the king who had failed them, but forward to their new warrior prince who promised to stand and fight where his father had not. Fires burned at every corner, and men swore oaths over ale. Women sang laments, and war songs drifted from taverns like the wind.

The following morning, Edmund had a bishop crown him king. It was a ceremony that would normally wait until a grand celebration could take place on the hallowed ground at Winchester. But there was no time to wait for pomp and ceremony. Beornoth and every thegn and warrior in the city swore fresh oaths to their new king, and then they went to war against Cnut Sweynsson, Thorkell the Tall, Eadric Streona and their vast Viking army come to conquer a kingdom and end Saxon rule forever.

26

1016AD

King Edmund Ironside's army marched until they met Cnut's forces in lands that had once belonged to the kingdom of the East Saxons and now served as the battlefield to decide the fate of Saxon kings forever. For weeks they followed the Vikings west of the Thames, manoeuvring, withdrawing, advancing and flanking as both armies vied to find a field, valley or riverside where they were prepared to stand and fight.

Godwin brought the warriors of Wessex to swell the king's ranks, and on his march eastwards Godwin had cleverly positioned his force between Cnut, Thorkell and their fleet, which sat moored in a wide bend of the River Thames. King Edmund joined Godwin with most of the army, and Ulfcytel arrived with Osgar and the warriors and fyrd of East Anglia so that nine thousand Saxon warriors mustered on a hill known as Assunden, the hill of ashes. Beornoth stood on the summit and watched Cnut's eight thousand warriors milling at the hill's base. Warriors in leather, chain mail, iron and furs, with long braided beards and hair beneath conical helmets, shuffled to stand beneath their banners. Strips and squares of cloth showed bears, wolves, eagles and dragons, whilst other banners were simply an eagle's wing on a pole, or a yellowed skull on a spear. One grisly standard fluttered in the wind, a thin grey length of flayed skin complete with flapping arms.

It was a chilly, damp October morning, and the ground beneath Beornoth's boots was heavy with mud. Trees about the hill stood stripped of their leaves by brisk, icy winds, and men shivered and watched their enemies gather for what would be a monstrous shield-wall battle. They had fought many skirmishes across the weeks of pursuit, foragers and scouts engaging in woodland or valleys, and both now faced off in a battle to determine the future of England. The Thames estuary lay to the south, and salt marshes fringed the land. Around Assunden's heights, the country rose in a series of low rolling hills cut by streams and thick with woods of oak and ash. Dawn had come grey and raw, a thin mist curling in from the low marshes to reveal the distant hills like the undulating back of a monstrous serpent slithering across the land, like the shining coils of Jörmungandr, the world serpent which the Vikings believed would swallow the world on the day of Ragnarök.

The Saxons stood cold and hungry on the hilltop, warriors and fyrd men huddled in groups sharing scraps of bread and whatever skins of ale remained to an army low on supplies after so long in the field. They had taken the higher northern ground, which forced the Vikings to attack uphill, if they chose to attack. King Edmund's army waited on slopes which served as rough pasture, a land of scrub and sparse woodland. At its crest stood a bare crown of brown ground where King Edmund would make his stand and defend his kingdom.

'Can we win?' asked Ulfcytel, standing beside Beornoth in his byrnie and with his helmet tucked under his arm. He looked thin after a summer spent fighting Cnut in the marshes of East Anglia.

Beornoth sniffed and flexed his curled fingers. He had woken early to massage his hands and wrists to loosen them. He had walked around the hill to get his legs and hips moving, and to expel the usual bout of wracking coughing. Wigs had tied strips of cloth around Beornoth's knees and rubbed oil into his old shoulder injury to get Beornoth's old, broken body into condition to fight.

'We have the numbers,' Beornoth replied. 'But half of our men are of the fyrd, where all Cnut's men are warriors.'

'We have the hill. We just need to get the bastards to attack us.'

'We do. Even then, we must stop Cnut and Thorkell from reaching the fyrd. That's how we lost when the Mercians broke.'

'We face Eadric's whoresons today, so let's hope they break again. You look like you are going to fight?'

'I will make my stand in the front one last time.'

'Many of us will die today, Beo.'

'Aye. So will many of them.'

'Can you see Streona down there?'

'No, but he's there somewhere.'

'Is it true about Thered?'

'It's true.'

'He was a good man and a fine ealdorman. He did not deserve to die like that.'

'He was my friend. All will be settled with Eadric Streona. One way or another.'

'We should find the king, advise him how to draw the enemy to battle. We will not find a better place than this; we have the high ground.'

They marched through the massed ranks, and men nodded or lifted their spears in salute to the two famous old warriors. Beornoth left his shield and helmet with Wigs and Gis as they waited for him with the champions forming the front rank, where the bravest and most fearsome champions of every shire prepared for battle. Beornoth and Ulfcytel found King Edmund bent on one knee as his Bishop Eadnoth blessed him and made the sign of the cross above the king's head. Edmund rose, crossed himself and thanked the bishop. He turned and smiled at Beornoth, and Beornoth's heart swelled with hope for the young king, who stood magnificent in a byrnie polished to a sheen with gold links on the sleeves and hem. Edmund wore a gold circlet on his brow and stood tall and straight-backed. He was a man to follow, a king men could love, and he was about to fight for his life and his ancestors' legacy.

'Battle looms, my lords,' Edmund said, leaning one hand on the hilt of his royal sword. Godwin marched to the summit and took Beornoth's arm in the warrior's grip.

'Streona is down there,' he said bitterly. 'I saw his banner.'

'We shall have the fight today,' said the king. 'All this marching around the dales has left our people starving. Both armies have taken too much from them, too much food, most of their winter surplus. A quarter of the fyrd men have melted away to return to their families.'

'They swell our numbers,' said Beornoth, 'but they cannot stand and trade blows with the Danes, anyway. Keep them in the rear, lord, with their wood axes and scythes. Let the warriors do the fighting; that is what they are oathsworn to do.'

'Just so, Lord Beornoth, just so. But how do we get Cnut to attack uphill? He is no fool and has spent weeks searching for a land of his choosing. He's not likely to attack us here.'

'His ships are behind us, lord king,' said Godwin, 'that's why he musters. He cannot lose his fleet, or his jarls will panic. The ships are their lifeblood, as precious to them as their wives. Without them, they cannot return home. We have the advantage.'

'Send riders towards the river, lord king,' said Beornoth. 'Give two hundred men of the fyrd all our horses and send them riding down the hill towards the Thames and let Cnut see them do it. We'll walk down the hill to have the exchange of insults the Danes love before battle. Goad Cnut and Thorkell, and the riders will panic them. We'll have our fight.'

'Very well,' said Edmund, 'that is what we shall do. What advice do you have for the battle, my great lords of war?'

'Warriors to front, fyrd to the rear. Arrows as they march uphill, then stand and kill the bastards.'

Ulfcytel and Godwin grinned at Beornoth's laconic reply, but could add nothing to it.

'Then may God bring you luck and keep our shield wall strong.'

'God protect you, lord king,' said Godwin, and they went to prepare the army.

* * *

An hour later, Beornoth rode down the hill to meet the enemy. He rode beside King Edmund, with three men of Edmund's royal bodyguard behind, flying the royal dragon banner. Beornoth went in case the enemy spoke Norse. Ulfcytel and Godwin remained with the army along with the other commanders, organising the warriors into ranks, the archers behind them, and the fyrd men on the summit. Riders came from the Viking army. Cnut himself, Thorkell and Eadric Streona. Six Viking growlers accompanied them: enormous, baleful warriors whose bulk made their horses look like foals.

The enemy leaders reined in five paces away from each other, and Beornoth stared at Eadric Streona. He looked like a Norseman with his straw-coloured hair and beard, both combed to a lustrous sheen. Eadric returned Beornoth's gaze, his long face serious and his mouth smirking slightly on one side. He wore mail with a sword belted at his hip, and Cnut also wore a byrnie and a crown of silver and gold upon his head. Thorkell sat huge upon a black stallion, axe strapped to his back, and his wide face showed no emotion.

'You should bow to the king of England,' said Eadric, gesturing to Cnut. 'The witan of England elected Lord Cnut as king at a gathering two weeks ago whilst you scrubbed in the forests looking for mushrooms and toads.'

'The witan? What council of lords and warriors did you gather, Grasper? A king crowned by traitors and cowards is no king at all,' Beornoth replied. 'The true lords and warriors of the realm wait atop the hill.'

'I was saddened to hear of your father the king's death,' said Thorkell the Tall, and bowed his head in a respectful gesture to Edmund.

'As was I,' added Cnut, both men showing a warrior's honour. 'I prayed for his soul and had my priests hold a vigil in his honour.'

'Thank you,' Edmund replied solemnly.

A sound like thunder shook the hillside, and Beornoth could not hide the snarl from his face as two hundred Saxon riders left the hilltop. He had come to pick a fight, not to exchange pleasantries in the morning air.

'They ride to burn your ships,' Beornoth said in Norse so that only Cnut and Thorkell could understand, more to annoy Streona than for any other reason. 'We'll burn your fleet, trap you here, and slaughter you all to the last man.'

Thorkell shifted nervously on his horse.

'Speak our tongue,' Eadric spat.

'Men will forget your names,' Beornoth continued in Norse. 'They will laugh for a few weeks at the fool who had himself crowned king in a muddy field by crusty traitors and turncloaks. Cnut the Stupid, they'll call you, the lack-witted son of a great warlord, and Thorkell the Nithing, who fights for the man with the heaviest purse. The fires will burn before noon, and your ships shall warm the hands of our churls and thralls as they drink and laugh at your foolishness.'

'Bastard!' Thorkell snarled, fighting with the reins of his horse as it skittered beneath his anger.

'What did he say?' Eadric said, his face flushing red in frustration.

'I said that you are a cowardly turncloak. That they dishonour themselves taking the field beside a man like you. You are a shirker, a trembler, a backstabber and not worth the shit on my boot.'

'Old fool! Look at you. Greybeard. How dare you talk to me as an equal?

Thegn! Dog! I killed your friend, the ealdorman of Northumbria, with my own blade. His wife moaned like a whore as my huntsmen ravaged her. I made Thered watch and then killed him as he wept like a dog. Then I stripped them both and hung them on their own walls like thieves.'

'Your life of dishonour is almost over. I shall look for you on the field,' Beornoth replied. 'Though I doubt I'll find you there.'

'We can have peace, you and I,' Cnut cut in, addressing Edmund directly. 'Swear allegiance to me and I will grant you lands in the north where you can live with honour. You can save many lives with a simple oath. Renounce your kingship, and you can live out your days in prosperity. I will spare your lords and your warriors, I swear it.'

'We can have peace,' Edmund agreed. 'If you take your army from the field, return to your ships and leave my country forever.'

'That cannot be. I am and shall be king of this place, and so will my sons after me.'

'Then it must be war. We shall burn your ships and mount your heads on the gates of Lundenwic.'

'I'll fight you now!' Beornoth suddenly roared, hate and rage simmering inside him as he gazed upon Eadric's smug face. Beornoth urged his horse forward, lurching her so that she bullied Eadric backwards. 'Fight me now!'

Eadric gasped at Beornoth's anger and almost fell off his horse. Beornoth wheeled his mount around until he faced Cnut and Thorkell, eyes bulging with anger, teeth bared in an animal snarl.

'I curse you both to Nástrǫnd,' he shouted in Norse. 'To the corpse shore reserved for thieves, traitors and cowards. When you die, your old gods will despise you for worshipping our God. They will cast you naked onto Nástrǫnd Strand, where Níðhǫggr, the death serpent, will gnaw on your corpses for eternity.'

'You shall have your fight,' said Cnut coldly, and he turned his horse and cantered away as Eadric struggled to recover his balance and wheel his horse around.

'Now we must win,' said Edmund as the Vikings rode away to join their army.

'We have to, lord king,' Beornoth replied. 'We cannot hide behind the walls of Lundenwic forever. If the witan has crowned Cnut, then it is worse than we thought. Many of the shires have already sworn him in as king. They must be the lesser shires and lords, for all the great houses are with you. But you must have a victory, lord, or flee across the sea like your father.'

'And what if we fail? What if they break us and the battle is lost?'

'Then the kingdom is lost, and we shall all die today.'

Edmund nodded and gulped. For a heartbeat his face turned bone white, and he suddenly looked a youth dressed up like a warrior. 'I am afraid, Beornoth,' he whispered, gazing out at eight thousand Viking warriors with axes, spears, shields and knives all come to end his reign and kill every remnant of Saxon lordship.

'So am I. So are they. Any man who doesn't fear battle has no knowledge of it. Bravery is overcoming that fear, lord. So master it and win this battle.'

'What if we cannot withstand the storm when they charge at us?'

'I am the storm. You must become the storm. We are warriors. There is strength in you, lord king. Men will follow you to the bitter end. Stand and fight and defend your kingdom.'

Colour returned to Edmund's face, and he set his jaw firm. Beornoth met the king's eyes with a hard stare, a look of trust and belief, and then he rode to take his place in the front rank, where he knew he was about to fight his last battle and perhaps take his last breaths before Viking blades came to hack his body to pieces.

27

War horns blared and eight thousand Vikings marched up Assunden Hill in ranks so thick that it was as though a sea of iron and wood advanced on the Saxon army. The enemy came on hunched behind their shields, eyes glaring over the iron-shod rims like bleak, shining raven's eyes, helmets gleaming, blades sharpened for the kill. They chanted a rowing song as they came, so loud that their voices rose like thunder. They came to protect their ships and to kill a king, and Beornoth hefted his shield and took his place between Gis and Osgar.

'So many,' Wigs whispered, standing behind Beornoth with his shield ready to catch any high blows coming at Beornoth's head above the shield wall.

'They will tire as they climb,' Beornoth said loudly so that all the men about him could hear. 'They must strike up at us, whilst we cut down at them. Watch for the low blow beneath the shield and hold fast.'

Men shuffled together, overlapping shields to form a solid wall of linden wood. In the rear ranks, a fyrd man vomited, and the smell of piss where men's fear had got the better of them mixed with the stink of leather and iron. Men drank ale for courage, others whispered prayers to God for their safety, and every warrior gazed down upon the horde approaching up the slopes of Assunden Hill. Cnut and Thorkell marched at the centre of their line, whilst Eadric's Mercians formed the left flank. They shouted and roared their defiance as horns blared and warriors ran out of their lines to offer challenges for single combat and threaten their Saxon foes. Nobody met those challenges, and the leaders along the Saxon lines urged their men to stay calm, and to stand strong when the charge came.

Edmund rode from the right flank on his horse, his sword held aloft, and a great cheer rippled along the Saxon army like the crashing of the sea. His horse reared, and the king wheeled the beast around.

'Warriors of England!' Edmund roared, and the men fell silent as behind him the horns sang and Vikings came on. 'These men come for our lives, they come for our wives and children and to make our land theirs. They are pirates, raiders and savages, and they come to take everything from you! So fight! Stand and fight and kill, protect your families and fight for your king!'

The army roared and shook their weapons, and Edmund rode along the length of the shield wall, repeating his rallying cry and staring into every man's soul.

'Who do you fight for?' Beornoth roared, his voice like a great bear growling over the din.

'Ironside! Ironside! Ironside!' came the reply from seven thousand men.

Beornoth's heart pumped, and he forgot his age and his weakened body. He pushed on his full-faced helmet so that the black plume fell down his back, and hefted his shield, hands unshaking and ready to hold it firm.

'Whatever happens here today,' Beornoth said to Wigs and Gis. 'It has been my honour to fight beside you. If I die, take my body north and bury me beside my Eawynn. There is silver in a chest beneath my bed. Whatever is there is yours to keep. Fight well, my brothers.'

'No, lord!' said Wigs. 'You are going to live. We are all going to live!'

'The honour has been ours, lord,' said Gis, and for a fleeting moment Beornoth thought he saw a tear in the warrior's eye.

'Archers!' came Ulfcytel's unmistakable voice to shatter the moment. 'Draw!'

The Danes came close, so close that Beornoth could make out their tattooed faces and the beasts painted on their shields. They roared with gaping maws and killers' eyes, and Thorkell the Tall strode like a giant in the enemy front rank, opposite Beornoth, marching towards him like a baleful god of war. He came armed like Osgar, without a shield and with his long-handled, double-bladed war axe held in both hands. He wore a helmet crowned by a hawk's wing, and he came to kill.

'Loose!' Ulfcytel called, and a hail of arrows sang over the Saxon warriors like a deadly gust of wind. The arrows flew low, sailing down the slope to thump into enemy shields and any exposed legs, faces and arms. Hundreds of men fell, and the screaming began. The Vikings loosed a volley of their own, but many of the shafts fell short. An arrow slammed into Beornoth's shield, and another tonked off the helmet of the warrior two men down from him. Men shuffled closer and braced themselves. A man howled in pain somewhere in the rear ranks, and still the armies exchanged volleys. Suddenly the deadly rain stopped, and Beornoth peered over his shield just in time to see Thorkell the Tall leading his men into a charge.

The Vikings were barely ten paces away now, screaming their defiance as they lurched into a run. They needed momentum to carry them uphill into the Saxon line, to hammer into the shield wall, to crush, cut, slice, hack and cut their foes to bloody ruin.

'Brace yourselves!' Beornoth said, and the champions around him tensed, mastering their fear, preparing themselves for the unspeakable horror of the shield wall.

The Vikings arrived in a wall of linden wood, crashing into the Saxon line with impossible force. A shield thundered into Beornoth's and drove him back a pace. He lowered it and felt a knife scrape along its bottom rim. Beornoth raised his right arm so that his spear tilted and stabbed hard downwards but struck only a hard shield. The Danes cursed and spat and pushed, and the Saxons heaved back at them. Blades probed between the gaps, seeking soft flesh to rend and tear between wood, mail and leather, and men howled in pain. Beornoth struck again, and this time he struck man and not wood. He felt the enemy jerk on the end of his spear, and he twisted the shaft savagely.

An axe thumped into Beornoth's shield, and a hand grabbed his ankle, trying to pull him down. Beornoth let go of his spear, stamped on the hand and reached behind to draw his seax from its sheath at the small of his back. The hand came again, and he rammed his shield down hard onto the wrist. As the shield lowered, the axeman struck again, and now Beornoth caught sight of him, a thick-necked, one-eyed brute with a mangled nose. Beornoth stabbed his seax into the brute's single eye the colour of a summer sky. He rammed the blade so hard that the point punched through the back of the Viking's skull, killing him instantly.

The warrior beside Gis died with an axe in his throat, and all along the battle line men churned Assunden Hill with their boots, blood, sweat, shit and piss as the dead voided their bowels, and the living fought for their lives. Thousands of men pushed and hacked at one another, and Beornoth lost all sense of time. All he could see were the two men on either side and the enemy in front, though the sound of so much chaos and carnage thrummed in his ears as though he were underwater. He did not know how long they struggled like that, only that his muscles screamed and he fought to keep his shield up and his seax stabbing.

It was Osgar who broke the shield wall first, just as Beornoth had done himself many times in battles long ago. Beornoth ripped his seax into a Viking's gullet, and the man thrashed to get away from the blade. He jumped sideways, fouling the shield of the enemy next to him, dragging it down, and suddenly where there had been two howling Danes there was space. Osgar's great axe scythed into it, cutting a Viking's head clean from his body in a spray of bright blood. Osgar barged into that gap, teeth bared, and he battered another Dane in the face with the haft of his axe. Beornoth followed, pushing with his shield and driving the enemy backwards.

For a glorious moment, it was as though they could carve right through the enemy and break their centre in two. A glimmer of victory tickled Beornoth like a feather, and then Thorkell the Tall appeared like a demon to block out the sun. He caught Osgar's axe with his own, and the clang of those mighty weapons coming together was like the bell of St Paul's at King Æthelred's funeral. Beornoth struggled to get to the Saxon champion, but enemy shields pinned him back.

Osgar swung again, and Thorkell swayed away from the blow. He surged forward and tried to headbutt Osgar, but the Saxon dodged his helmeted forehead and cracked the haft of his axe into Thorkell's face. Thorkell reeled, blood spurting from his split nose. Their axes whirled, twin-bladed weapons slicing and chopping into the men around them as they recklessly fought with impossible strength and skill. Thorkell overstretched with a backswing and stumbled into another man's shield, and Osgar roared, bringing his axe around overhand to kill Thorkell with one sweep. But Thorkell had feigned his stumble, and Beornoth cried out to warn Osgar, but it was too late.

Thorkell parried Osgar's axe with the bottom third of his axe haft and drove Osgar's weapon wide. He let go of his axe and whipped a knife from his belt and stabbed the blade upwards, his strength driving it through the links of

Osgar's mail and into his belly. He ripped at Osgar like a butcher, and the huge Saxon champion sagged as his blood soaked Thorkell's arm to the elbow. The Saxon lines moaned in shock and the Vikings roared their champion's glory as Osgar fell dead to be stamped and crushed by the boots of his enemies.

'Bastard!' Beornoth bellowed, horrified to see the great East Anglian champion slain. A man he had fought beside and respected, a warrior of few words and a man he counted as a friend. Beornoth let go of his shield and drew his sword.

'No, lord!' Gis cried out, but Beornoth was already into the gap, facing Thorkell with his sword in his right hand and his seax in his left.

'Come to die, Beornoth Reiði?' asked Thorkell, blood in his mouth and smeared across his face, and victory blazing in his eyes.

'Die now, bastard,' Beornoth snarled, no longer old and weak, feeling strong and full of rage.

Battle surged across the hill as the two shield walls pressed against one another, but in that small space men shifted aside and the fighting lulled as two famous champions faced each other: Thorkell the Tall, lord of the Jomsvikings with his axe and his skill, and Beornoth the Wrathful and his famed savagery. Thorkell picked up his axe and held it aloft, and his warriors cheered their support, and as the giant grinned with a feral look on his hard face, basking in the prospect of a fight to burnish his reputation even brighter, Beornoth charged.

Thorkell flinched in surprise as Beornoth came for him with alarming speed, seax stabbing low at his groin. Thorkell lowered his axe instinctively to parry the blow, and Beornoth stepped in. He knew he did not have the strength to stand and trade blows with the famous Viking. Beornoth had perhaps a few moments of power in his aged body before the anger-fuelled strength deserted him, and they must count if he was to avenge Osgar's death. He crashed his helmeted forehead into Thorkell's face, mashing his already cut nose to a pulp. Thorkell yanked his face away and tried to raise his axe, but Beornoth was too close, and he sawed his sword down Thorkell's skull, slicing off his ear in a spray of hot blood. Thorkell roared and pushed Beornoth back, but Beornoth slashed at his outstretched hand with his seax and cut two fingers from Thorkell's left hand.

The surrounding Vikings groaned and pressed in, trying to bully Beornoth with their shields, and the Saxons charged at them in retaliation, and so the shield-wall press joined again. Opposing shields pushed Beornoth and Thorkell together, and the gigantic Dane roared at his men to get back and give him space to fight. But there was no space, and Beornoth crashed into him again, butting him over and again with his helmet, feeling gristle and bone crunch beneath hard iron, and shields battered him from every side. Thorkell let go of his axe and drew his knife, the same knife he had used to kill Osgar, and he stabbed it twice into Beornoth's thigh. Beornoth kept Thorkell close, slicing at Thorkell's ribs and arm with his seax but unable to use his sword in the tight press. He could smell garlic on Thorkell's fetid breath as the bigger man tried to jerk his ruined face away.

The pain in Beornoth's thigh burned like fire, and Thorkell's knife came up and stabbed at his midriff, but Beornoth's mail held the blow. Beornoth leant in again and bit Thorkell's cheek like a war dog, lost his grip and then bit Thorkell's lip, ripping soft flesh from his face in another spray of blood. Thorkell howled in pain, and Beornoth brought his seax up and drove the point into Thorkell's armpit, twisting and grinding the blade deep into his insides. Thorkell slumped into the shields behind him, his face a mask of blood, exposed teeth and ruin. He stared at Beornoth with frightened eyes, terrified of Beornoth's brutality, and Beornoth had a yard to swing his sword. He swung the sword in a narrow arc, using the small space to cut Thorkell's throat with a half-swing, opening his windpipe in a wide red gash.

Thorkell the Tall died sheeted in his own blood, and his men howled with sorrow and anger. A spear flashed forward and sliced Beornoth's cheek open. A sword punched through his mail and opened a deep cut in his shoulder. His strength faded as the elation of Thorkell's death became a fleeting, dull joy. Hands grabbed Beornoth from behind and yanked him deep into the Saxon shield wall, and he fell to the ground exhausted as Wigs and Gis hauled him to the summit. Scores of men lay there, dead or writhing with terrible wounds as priests tried to bind and clean their wounds.

Bishop Eadnoth himself rushed to Beornoth, his vestments foul with blood and his face drawn taut with the horror of battle.

'Where is the king?' Beornoth gasped through the pain.

'Fighting at the front,' Eadnoth replied, 'like a hero from legend.'

'The flanks?'

'They hold. Lord Brand keeps the right steady with the men of Northumbria.' Eadnoth turned to his priests. 'Fetch me water and a clean cloth. Now!'

'I thought you were a dead man, lord,' said Gis, bending to help the bishop as he struggled to remove Beornoth's byrnie.

'Leave it!' Beornoth spat. 'Get me up. My place is in the front rank.'

Eadnoth put a hand on Beornoth's chest and met his gaze with firm eyes. 'Let me bind you, Lord Beornoth, or you will bleed to death.'

Beornoth cursed and lay back as the battle raged out of sight. They removed his armour and washed his wounds, the cuts on his shoulder, arms and legs bleeding freely. The bishop bound his cuts and gashes tight, and Beornoth ordered Wigs and Gis to pull on his bloody byrnie once more.

'Let others do the fighting now, lord,' Wigs pleaded. 'You have more than played your part.'

A great wail went up from the shield wall, and the warriors parted to let two burly warriors through, and between them they carried King Edmund. The young king held a blood-soaked sword in his hand, and his armour and face bore the marks of battle, but a wound in his side had torn his mail open and blood seeped there dark and wet.

'See to the king!' Bishop Eadred bellowed, and every priest on Assunden Hill rushed to help Edmund.

The Saxon line retreated up the slope, disheartened by the king's wounding and withdrawal. The Vikings followed, seething up the hill like the tide rising inexorably, pushing the Saxons towards the summit. Ragged and wounded, the Saxons gasped and shuffled backwards. Ulfcytel marched from the front to order the fyrd men into the shield wall to fill the gaps, and when he heard that order, Beornoth suddenly felt heavy and tired.

'Get me up,' he said.

'I beg you, lord, no,' said Gis.

'Get me up! If the fyrd is all we have left, we are done for.'

They helped Beornoth stand, and he took up his sword, and Gis took a shield from a dead warrior. Wigs pushed on Beornoth's helmet, and he limped towards the shield wall, battered, bloody, weakened and ready to die for his king. Ulfcytel followed him, silent and grim-faced. They pushed their way to the front where the battle raged, and as a Saxon warrior fell with a spear in his chest, Beornoth took his place. He overlapped his shield with the man's shield next to him and met the Viking press, holding them, grinding every ounce of strength left in his old body.

Cnut stood in the third rank, urging his men on to the slaughter, and

Beornoth took backward step after backward step as the Vikings pressed them upwards. The fyrd weakened the Saxon line, whilst every man in Cnut's army was a professional warrior and a trained killer. Beornoth stabbed his sword into the stomach of a warrior with the banner of Mercia on his shield, but he could not see Eadric Streona where the champions fought and died in a welter of horror and steel.

Ulfcytel killed a tattooed Dane with his sword. An axe hooked over the rim of Ulfcytel's shield and yanked it down, and then another axe swiped into the space and opened Ulfcytel's neck with such power that it almost severed his head. The great man sagged and toppled forward, his enemies howling in triumph, and Beornoth fought on, numbed to the terror, his emotions banished as sadness overwhelmed him like a fog. So many men died, hacked and crushed to death as the battle soaked the hill in blood and filth. A sword smashed into Beornoth's helmet, stunning him, and a knife cut across his chest. The man beside Beornoth fell with a Viking spear in his face, and Gis stepped into the space with his shield and spear. An axe hammered at Gis' shield, and Beornoth killed that enemy with a stab of his sword, and a huge Viking with golden hair and a fox head atop his helmet filled that gap. He carried a bright sword, and its point snaked out and punched through leather and bone and pierced Gis' heart. Beornoth screamed in agony as Gis fell, his body falling on top of Ulfcytel's corpse, and the Saxons moved further back, shaken by grief, battered by blades.

Wigs leapt at the Viking swordsman, vengeance in his heart and tears upon his face at the loss of his great friend. Beornoth tried to stop him, tried to push him backwards, but Wigs hammered at the Viking with his spear and the leaf-shaped blade stabbed deep into the enemy warrior's leg. Wigs drove them back with tears streaming down his dirty cheeks. He stood astride his dead friend, protecting his body like a wolf before her cubs. Beornoth tried to pull him back, but an enemy axe hammered his shield and drove him backwards. A Viking snapped Wigs' spear stave with his sword, and Wigs died as another warrior chopped his axe into the Saxon's neck.

Beornoth wept as he fought. He cried like a child as he pushed and stabbed and tried not to stand on the bodies of his dead friends. He had loved Wigs and Gis like brothers, just as he had loved his sword brothers who died at Maldon, and the sorrow was crushing, more painful than any flesh wound, and yet the battle raged on. Time passed, and Beornoth found himself falling backwards, pulled there to join the injured once more. The king rose and charged into the fray, and then Beornoth slipped into darkness. Sadness and loss of blood took him into shadow, and he hoped his time was done. He waited for Eawynn to come and walk him into heaven with her smile and her shining hair. But there was just darkness and sadness, blood, pain and devastation.

28

King Edmund Ironside and Cnut agreed to a truce after the battle of Assunden. The two kings met on a hilltop reeking of death and struck a grudging peace amongst the slaughter and dead champions. Rain came as evening closed in, a drizzle that turned the ground to mire and washed the blood into dark rivulets running down the slopes. After too many men on each side had died and warriors had paused in exhausted horror, the two kings agreed to end the slaughter. They stood together amidst the sharp tang of iron and voided bowels, the sour rot of opened guts and the cloying sweetness of flesh left for crows. They agreed to divide the realm. Edmund would hold Wessex, his father's heartland. Cnut would have Mercia and the north, rich and wide. When either died, the survivor would take all.

Beornoth awoke in Lundenwic, and the priests told him of the peace. Then, two weeks after the battle, as Beornoth's wounds healed, bells rang out from St Paul's and a thin-faced priest came to Beornoth with tears upon his cheeks. King Edmund had died of his wounds, and Cnut was king of England. A Viking king. The age of the Saxons was over.

Coughing, sweating and pain kept Beornoth in a half-life after that. He woke on soaking sheets, scratched at scabbed wounds, and then drifted again into darkness. Priests prayed for him, fed him and poured water and ale across his dry lips.

Beornoth lay in a straw-filled bed, clinging to life though he wished for it to end. Death refused to take him, or God refused him entry to heaven, Beornoth knew not why his wounded grey body yet drew breath after everything and everyone he had known and loved had died. Each day, a priest came and offered Beornoth sips of ale from a wooden cup.

'You should eat something, lord,' the thin-faced priest would say. But Beornoth turned away from him, wanting nothing but an end to the crushing sorrow for all that was lost, and what could have been.

He woke one morning to find his window shutter open, and a figure sitting next to him on a low stool.

'A bright but cold day,' said the man, speaking in Norse.

Beornoth turned but could not make out the man's face because bright sunlight from the open window blurred his vision.

'Close the window shutter a little and leave us,' said the man. A figure in black followed his orders and closed the creaking door behind him.

'Who are you?' Beornoth croaked.

The man took a cup and leaned across Beornoth to give him a drink of cool water. Beornoth gulped it down and rubbed his eyes. He blinked, and jerked backwards in his bed, for the man sitting beside him was Cnut, king of England.

'Don't be alarmed,' said Cnut, his young face smiling, a lurid red gash on his left cheek the only reminder of the horror of Assunden on his smooth skin and combed hair. He wore a green tunic and a gold circlet on his brow. 'Edmund's men brought you here after the battle, to heal, though many thought you might die.'

'I should have died. Everything I knew is gone. Family, friends, country and king.'

'Edmund fought well, a son greater than his father. You killed Thorkell. I had the tale from a skald after the battle.'

'What do you want with me?'

'You are a great warrior, Beornoth Reiði. Your time on this earth is almost over. I know you wish to join your loved ones in heaven. But before you go, there is one task remaining. One more thing you must accomplish. A matter left unresolved, an injustice needing remedy.'

'I do not serve you.'

'No. If I had more men like you in my service, I could become king of all the world. I have made Godwin the earl of Wessex, and he has sworn an oath to me. He is a good man, a brave man. But this matter is a service to dead King Edmund, to your friends Ealdorman Alfgar, Morcar and Sigeferth, for Ulfcytel Snillingr.'

'Godwin?'

'He did not betray anyone. He fought well at Assunden. I have offered many of Edmund's men forgiveness, and many have kept their former lands and titles.'

'What of Edmund's mother, the queen?'

'I shall marry Emma, and she will be my queen. The land will heal. Our people shall become as one. But we must cut out the poison to heal. We must remove any remaining bitterness.'

'Speak plainly.'

'Eadric Streona is here. Come to Lundenwic to celebrate my coronation and seeking his reward. I want you to give Eadric the reward he deserves, if you have the strength to do it.'

'Reward?'

'He is not a man of honour, not a drengr who follows the warrior's code. A traitor like him must not prosper. I heard what he did to Ealdorman Thered. Such things cannot go unpunished.'

'You want me to punish him?'

'If you have the strength for one more fight?'

'I'll bloody find the strength. Where is he?'

'Here. There will be a feast this evening. After that, I will deliver him to you. For justice. A warrior's justice. Godwin lays down his own vengeance tonight; he will send Eadric's brother Brihtric to the afterlife.'

'Why do you do this?'

'My father respected you. I respect you. Let this be a noble end to the song of Beornoth the Wrathful. Eadric is a plague, and there is no place for him in my kingdom.'

'Then bring him to me and I will end it.'

'Good. There is a man here who will help you prepare.'

Cnut stood and bowed to Beornoth and walked to the door.

'Lord king,' Beornoth said, and Cnut turned to face him. Beornoth was confused. He wanted to thank Cnut for this last chance to kill the man who had laid England low, but it seemed wrong to thank an enemy, and the words died on his lips.

Cnut smiled as though he understood. He left, and Brand entered after him.

'I've come to help you, lord. One last time,' he said, smiling sadly as he took in Beornoth's wounded state.

'Your family?'

'Safe and well. My son Vigdjarf asks about you all the time.'

'Good. Take care of them, keep them close.'

'Of course. I am sorry, lord, for Wigs and Gis.'

Beornoth could not speak about his dead friends. It was still too raw, too painful to contemplate. 'My armour?'

'It's here, along with your weapons. I'll help you dress for battle.'

Brand helped Beornoth wash and dress. He wrapped Beornoth's healing wounds tight with clean strips of white linen. Beornoth drank a cup of ale and ate some bread and cheese, but a wracking coughing fit burst open the stitches on his shoulder, and a priest had to come and close the wound again.

'Can you fight, lord?' Brand asked after he had pulled on Beornoth's boots and helped him tie his hair back at the nape of his neck.

'I'll kill Streona,' Beornoth replied, wincing as his body screamed at him to lie down and rest. But he didn't want to rest and had no intention of recovering.

'And then?'

'Then I need one last favour from you, old friend.'

'Name it, and it is done.'

'Take my body north and bury me beside my Eawynn.'

'What if you live?'

'My time is over. Everyone I knew is gone. The realm is no more. I have no place here. You are a Viking, so you can thrive under Cnut's rule. Take care of your family and do this last favour for me.'

'Why does Cnut give Eadric to you? Forgive me for saying it, lord, but you might not have the strength left to kill him.'

'Because sometimes there must be justice. Cnut is a Christian, just as Forkbeard was. But deep down they remember the old ways and the old gods, your gods. They remember drengskapr, the warrior's code, and I thank Cnut for this chance at revenge, for what Streona did to Thered, and to others. I'll find the strength.'

'And I will take you home when it's done.'

'Thank you, Brand. For everything.'

Brand clapped Beornoth on the shoulder, shaking his head. 'Enough of this soft talk, time to get you ready to kill.'

* * *

It was dark when one of Cnut's men led Beornoth to an open courtyard behind Lundenwic's great hall, where men sang and shouted as they drank and feasted to celebrate Cnut's coronation.

'Are you ready?' Brand asked, his teeth chattering in the cold.

'I am,' Beornoth replied. 'Pass me my helmet.'

Beornoth had grown stronger as the day went on. The coughing subsided, his wounds stopped aching and throbbing. His aching joints felt normal, and his curled-up, grandfather's hands felt supple. He wore his byrnie, still torn from Assunden, but clean and shining. His heavy sword sat in its scabbard at his hip, and his seax in its sheath at the small of his back. Beornoth stood in the shadows behind a row of timber pillars, above which a wooden roof provided cover for the royals on hot days. He stood tall, ready for one last task before the end.

An icy wind blew through the courtyard, and Beornoth shivered and pushed on his helmet. Brand stood back. He wore his own chain-mail armour with an axe in a loop at his belt and a knife on his left side. Snowflakes drifted down from the black sky, dancing on the wind, too few to stick, white specks fluttering precariously to land and melt on the grass and stone within the courtyard.

Loud voices laughed and talked raucously beyond the open space. A door opened, and a steward wearing royal livery emerged carrying a burning torch to light the way. Five men followed, four of them burly and in mail, and the last in a fine wool jerkin and a cloak fringed with fur. It was Eadric Streona, his men armed like royal bodyguards.

'Too many, lord,' Brand whispered urgently. 'They have swords and knives.'

'Not enough to save Streona,' Beornoth replied. Four guards would not keep him from his vengeance, not against the man who had betrayed and killed his way to power, a coward and a traitor who had to die, no matter the odds.

Beornoth waited for the men to come closer, the iron of his helmet cool against his nose and neck and his chain mail heavy on his shoulders. Cnut wanted to rid the kingdom of old ties, and Beornoth realised he was part of that. A warrior famed for killing Vikings had no place in the new kingdom, and so he had sent Eadric to face Beornoth with enough men to ensure Beornoth did not survive. The new kingdom must not be encumbered by the old.

The steward slipped backwards through the door and closed it behind him, taking his torch so that all that lit the courtyard was moonlight and spluttering rush lights at either end of the open space.

'You there?' Eadric called after the steward, voice slurred by mead, indignation heavy in his tone. The sound of Streona's voice made Beornoth shudder with hate. 'We need the torch. Bloody fool.' He sighed, belched and waved his men onwards. 'Come on, it's too late to go after him now.'

The five men trudged across the grass, through the flower beds ringed with rock. Beornoth emerged from the shadows, huge and baleful in his armour and helmet.

'Hold,' barked one of Eadric's men, and the group halted, staring with surprise at Beornoth's sudden appearance. 'Name yourself,' he said, hand moving to the hilt of his sword.

'It's time for justice,' Beornoth growled, his eyes fixed on Eadric. The ealdorman of Mercia stared back, and he saw a warrior clad in iron and steel, head clasped in a full-faced helmet so that only Beornoth's vengeful eyes shone in the darkness.

'Beornoth?' Eadric whispered, mouth agape, leaning to stare at him through the gloom.

'You killed Thered, Morcar, Sigeferth and many more. I've come for you.' Beornoth slowly drew his sword so that the blade scraped on the scabbard's throat, all threat and intimidation in the sound.

'Stop him!' Eadric said to his men, his voice high-pitched as he stepped backwards.

The four guards stepped forward, hands on the hilts of their swords, and the first one died as an axe came hurtling from the shadows. Brand's axe, turning head over haft in the moonlight, to slam in the first man's chest with a sickening thud. Brand came running into the courtyard, knife in hand, keening his Viking war cry like a Norse demon from the depths of Niflheim.

Two of Eadric's guards came at Beornoth, and he met them. The first guard fumbled with his sword, mead making him slow, and he only had his weapon half drawn when Beornoth tore his throat out with the tip of his sword. The second man came on, broad-shouldered and square-jawed. His sword flashed from its scabbard, and he roared a challenge as he came at Beornoth, lunging with the precision of a trained warrior. Beornoth parried the stroke, and they fought, blades clanging in the cold. Skilled warriors trading blows beneath the cold night sky. Beornoth blocked an overhand cut and grabbed his seax. He tried to stab the guard, but the man caught Beornoth's wrist with his left hand and drove his knee hard into Beornoth's groin. Beornoth gasped and stepped backwards. The sword came for him, and he parried it, but the strength in his arm failed. He coughed, vomiting up a stream of thick congealed blood.

'Old bastard,' the guard sneered, and he came at Beornoth, pitiless, swinging his blade to cut Beornoth's head from his shoulders. Brand fought with the remaining guard, weapons clanging, grunting as each struggled to kill the other. Beornoth lifted his arm, and the guard's sword crashed into his blade and drove it down. He stood, and the guard kicked him savagely backwards. Beornoth tried to summon his strength, but it would not come, left on the blood-soaked field of Assunden with his dead friends. The guard feinted high and then stabbed low. Beornoth tried to parry the cut, but he was too slow, and the guard's sword pierced his torso just beneath his chest. It felt like a punch, hard and hot, and Beornoth fell backwards. The guard yanked his sword free, and blood slopped from the wound.

The guard smiled and raised his sword for the killing blow. Beornoth waited for it, for the end, bitter that Eadric had survived but ready for death in battle. The guard's face sagged and stood stiff. He fell to his knees and toppled forward with Brand's axe in his back.

'Lord!' Brand shouted, and ran to Beornoth, staring at the terrible wound. Behind him, Eadric had run to the door, and he hammered on it, screaming for help.

'Get me up,' Beornoth uttered, and Brand helped him rise to his feet. More blood slipped from Beornoth's open gut, and his breath came in short, quick gasps. 'How many times have you saved my life?'

'Too many, lord. You have suffered the wounds of a dozen heroes.'

'Remember, take me home, take me to Eawynn.'

'Yes, lord.'

Beornoth pushed himself away from Brand, seax in his right hand and his left holding the sword wound closed. He stumbled across the courtyard, bleeding, lurching, struggling to remain upright. He shuffled past the dead guards and shadowed flower beds until he reached Eadric and the door Streona hoped would open and save his life. But it remained closed.

'Look at me,' Beornoth snarled.

'Wait!' Eadric said, turning with his two hands raised. 'We can come to an arrangement. I did what I did for the realm, for the good of the...'

'Treacherous murderer.' Beornoth advanced with his seax raised.

Eadric shuddered with terror, and at the last moment his pretence of fear slipped, and he whipped a dagger from his belt and came at Beornoth snarling like a wolf. He took Beornoth by surprise, and the dagger stabbed deep into Beornoth's side, breaking the links of his byrnie and punching into his body. Beornoth let out a whoosh of air and gasped in pain. He grabbed Eadric's face with his bloody left hand. Crimson smeared Eadric's mouth, nose and cheek, and he twisted the blade in Beornoth's ribs.

'Die!' he spat. 'Die, you grizzled old bastard!'

'You first.' Beornoth brought his seax up and pushed the tip into Eadric Streona's gut just above his groin. 'For Thered. For Wigs and Gis. For Edmund, Osgar. For them all.'

With the last drops of his warrior's strength, Beornoth ripped the blade upwards. He roared a kingdom's hate into the traitor's face and dragged his blade, tearing it through Eadric's body like a scythe through wheat. He opened Eadric from navel to neck and left his body quivering on the ground. Eadric Streona, the scourge of England, a man of malice, pride, treachery and cruelty, was dead.

Beornoth fell, landing heavily on his back. Soft flakes of snow landed on his face, cooling him. He felt no pain and heard no sound. Streona was dead. It was over. Time for his old bones to rest. Faces came to him, dead friends and old enemies he had known in his long, brutal life. A life that could have been different, should have been a tale of fatherhood and happiness, but was instead a life forged and lived amongst war and warriors. A father and husband had become a warrior and protector, and now it was time. Brand appeared over him, veins bulging in his tattooed neck as he called for help that would not come.

Beornoth's eyes closed, and suddenly he heard laughter, bright and warming. He smiled. It was the sound of Ashwig and Cwen, his small, beautiful daughters, running through the fields of his long-ago home. He felt Eawynn's warm touch against his skin, and it was over. It was time to go to his family, for peace, for the age of the Saxon had ended, and the age of the Viking kings of England had begun.

* * *

MORE FROM PETER GIBBONS

Another book from Peter Gibbons is available to order now here: https://mybook.to/ChroniclesArthur4

HISTORICAL NOTE

The *Saxon Warrior Series* deals with events up to and following the historical Battle of Maldon. It is a crucial period in English and British history, where the Saxon kings clashed with Viking kings of Norway and Denmark to decide the fate of England. In *Brothers of the Sword* we saw the events of Maldon unfold, including the death of Ealdorman Byrhtnoth. In *Sword of Vengeance* Beornoth exacted his revenge upon Godwin and others who led the great ealdorman and his war band to their famous doom. The Battle of Maldon itself is well documented in the poem of the same name, as I have summarised in the previous books in this series. The series is also the story about the portentous events during King Æthelred's reign, and how the age of Anglo-Saxons shifted to the rule of Viking kings. A number of different historical texts exist to help try and build a picture of those events, which include the *Anglo-Saxon Chronicle*, *The Lives of St Oswald and St Ecgwine* written by the monk Byrhtferth, the *Book of Ely*, and the various Norse sagas.

In *Enemies of the Crown,* Beornoth witnessed the St Brice's Day Massacre in 1004, and Sweyn Forkbeard's subsequent attacks came as vengeance for the deaths of so many Danes in England's north at King Æthelred's order. Sweyn's sister was amongst those slain on that fateful day. Forkbeard returned and put England to the sword. The battles in which Beornoth participates in this novel took place after the king of Norway and Denmark landed at Norwich, which he put to the torch, before advancing inland to Thetford. Ulfcytel, an East Anglian thegn, met them in battle and inflicted substantial losses on the Viking army. Sweyn returned to Denmark due to lack of supplies, and because a famine struck much of western Europe. This novel can feel as though Beornoth faces one battle after another, but every battle featured is historical. We can only imagine how the people of England suffered as first Thorkell, then Sweyn Forkbeard and then Cnut ravaged the land for food and supplies for their marauding armies.

Eadric Streona features heavily during the latter part of King Æthelred's reign. He was the main force behind a palace revolution in 1005–6 when various powerful men were executed, as in this book. Streona meant 'the Grasper', and various diplomas and edicts issued at the time imply his role in the sweeping changes at court. Writing Eadric is complex because his levels of treachery, back-stabbing and his swift rise to power can seem unbelievable. He moved quickly to first place amongst the thegns, leapfrogging many more senior figures in the process, and was eventually appointed ealdorman of Mercia. He married Eadgyth, one of the king's daughters, and rose to first amongst the ealdormen, a position he enjoyed until King Æthelred's death. We cannot now know for sure how Eadric managed to secure such influence over the king, but he certainly looms large in those dark days and in all the historical texts.

The episode in this novel concerning the great fleet gathered to oppose Thorkell the Tall in 1009 is factual. King Æthelred ordered that a warship be built for every three hundred hides in his shires to combat the Vikings' superior mobility, who could strike and depart seemingly at will. The fleet gathered at Sandwich, which was the Vikings' natural first port of call, lying immediately across the channel from the Low Countries, along whose coast the raiders sailed on their way to Britain. The Saxon fleet gathered but, before the Vikings appeared, the English forces unravelled. Just as I have described in this book, Eadric Streona's brother, Brihtric, accused Wulfnoth of Wessex of treachery. Wulfnoth doubted his chances of a fair trial and so left with twenty ships, Brihtric followed with the rest of the fleet and unexpected storms cast his ships ashore. Wulfnoth burned Brihtric's ships and so ended any chance of defeating Thorkell before his fleet came ashore.

Thorkell arrived in 1009 with eight thousand men, landing unopposed at Sandwich, and put much of England to the sword. He ravaged East Anglia,

Essex, Middlesex, Oxfordshire, Cambridgeshire, Hertfordshire, Buckinghamshire, Bedfordshire, Kent, Sussex, Hastings, Surrey, Berkshire, Hampshire and Wiltshire before Ulfcytel met him in battle at Ringmere Heath. Eadric Streona arranged a payment of forty-eight thousand pounds of silver to Thorkell, which he accepted and entered into the service of King Æthelred, fighting for the king when Sweyn Forkbeard returned with his son Cnut in 1013.

Forkbeard's return in 1013 saw him rally the Danelaw to his side, including the lords of the Five Boroughs of Northumbria, Sigeferth and Morcar. As I have described in the novel, the northern lords of the Danelaw were open to Danish rule due to their ancestry, and because they had suffered most during the palace revolution of 1005 and the tax raised by Eadric Streona to pay off Thorkell the Tall. Sweyn Forkbeard captured Winchester, but his attempt on London was repelled by Thorkell and King Æthelred's defenders. Facing defeat and the loss of every major city other than London, Æthelred and his family fled to Normandy, leaving Forkbeard to declare himself king.

The great Sweyn Forkbeard died on 3 February 1014, having ruled England for only five weeks, and was succeeded by his young son Cnut. Sweyn was the first Danish king of England, and also king of Norway and Denmark. Forkbeard's death opened the door for Æthelred to return, raise an army and drive Cnut and his forces from England, but only temporarily. Edmund Ironside rose to prominence during this period and raised forces in open rebellion against Eadric Streona. As I have described in this novel, Streona murdered the two powerful lords of the Five Boroughs, Sigeferth and Morcar, in his own chambers, and so Edmund quickly married Sigeferth's widow and rallied the men in those northern lands to his banner. Edmund began a rebellion against Eadric, whilst his father lay sick behind London's walls.

Cnut returned to take advantage of the civil war raging between Streona and Edmund, and arrived once more at Sandwich in August 1015 with two hundred ships. Cnut conquered most of England and, sensing defeat, Eadric Streona entered into Cnut's service with all the Mercian warriors under his command and so Edmund retreated to London to join his father. King Æthelred died on 23 April 1016 in London, having ruled for thirty-five years. His reign was marred by constant Viking attacks, and we cannot doubt the hardship endured in England at the time, nor the extreme difficulties he faced as king.

Edmund was crowned king in London, and at the same time a witan gathered at Southampton elected Cnut king. The two young warriors fought a series of skirmishes, and Edmund earned his epithet Ironside, and the young kings eventually met at the Battle of Assunden on 18 October and fought themselves to a standstill. Cnut and Edmund negotiated a peace dividing the country between them. Edmund received Wessex and London while Cnut took Mercia and Northumbria. Edmund died, perhaps of his wounds, some sources suggest by poisoning, on 30 November 1016 and Cnut became king of England and remained so until his death in 1035.

Beornoth plays his part in the great events of this period, and crosses paths with young Godwin who becomes the ealdorman of Wessex. Godwin would go on to become one of the most powerful earls in England under Cnut, and was the father of Harold Godwinson, the king of England who fought and lost at the Battle of Hastings in 1066.

In this tale I have Beornoth deliver justice to the odious Eadric Streona, and it was Cnut himself who ordered that Eadric be put to death on Christmas Day 1017. Eadric's body was tossed from the walls of London and left to rot unburied. The *Encomium Emmae Reginae,* an eleventh-century Latin encomium in honour of the English queen Emma of Normandy, states that Cnut gave the order to execute Eadric because he (Cnut) knew Eadric to have been deceitful, and to have 'hesitated between the two sides with fraudulent tergiversation'. The *Encomium* also says that Cnut ordered a Viking Earl Eric Haakonsson to 'pay this man what we owe him'. Eric chopped off Eadric's head with an axe.

I have omitted some elements of Eadric Streona's life of betrayal, purely because to weave them into this tale would leave the story unbelievable to the reader. Eadric did in fact change sides again and lined up to fight alongside Edmund Ironside at the Battle of Assunden. That turned out to be yet another devious ploy. As Cnut attacked, Eadric withdrew his forces from the field and left a gaping hole in the Saxon shield wall and allowed Cnut's forces to advance on to victory. Much of Eadric's life leaves us wondering how he could convince enemies and allies alike of his trustworthiness after so many examples of betrayal, and we can only marvel at his powers of persuasion.

I hope the reader will forgive me for replacing the Earl Eric Haakonsson with Beornoth to make sure Eadric received the appropriate reward for his life's work! I also hope the reader has enjoyed reading this series as much I have enjoyed writing it. Beornoth is a grim beast and hard man, made that way by the times in which he lived. But he is also a great character to write, and I will miss his adventures.

Beornoth is at rest, and his sword is sheathed forever.

GLOSSARY

Aesc spear – A large, two-handed, long-bladed spear.
Burh – A fortification designed by Alfred the Great to protect against Viking incursions.
Byrnie – Saxon word for a coat of chain mail.
Cantwaraburg – Canterbury.
Danelaw – The part of England ruled by the Vikings from 865 AD.
Defnascir – Devon.
Drakkar – A type of Viking warship.
Ealdorman – The leader of a shire of the English kingdom, second in rank only to the king.
Exanceaster – Exeter.
Eoten – A supernatural being, like a troll or a giant.
Gafol – The Danegeld, or tax raised to pay tribute to Viking raiders to save a land from being ravaged.
Gippeswic – Ipswich.
Grimseby – Grimsby.
Heriot – The weapons, land and trappings of a thegn or other noble person, granted to him by his lord and which becomes his will or inheritance.
Hide – An area of land large enough to support one family. A measure used for assessing areas of land.

Holmgang – A ritualised duel common amongst Viking peoples.
Jomsvikings – Viking mercenaries based at their stronghold at Jomsburg who followed a strict warriors' code.
Jörmungandr – The world serpent, a child of Loki. So large that its coils encircle the world. Jörmungandr will battle Thor at the end of days.
Lundenwic – London.
Mameceaster – Manchester.
Nástrọnd – The afterlife for those guilty of crimes such as oathbreaking, adultery or murder. It is the corpse-shore, with a great hall built from the backs of snakes, where the serpent Níðhöggr gnaws upon the corpses of the dead.
Níðhöggr – A serpent or monster who gnaws at the roots of the great tree Yggdrasil, and also gnaws upon the corpses of the dead at Nástrọnd.
Nithing – A coward, villain or oathbreaker, not worthy of the glorious afterlife.
Njorth – The Viking sea god.
Norns – Norse goddesses of fate. Three sisters who live beneath the world tree Yggdrasil and weave the tapestry of fate.
Odin – The father of the Viking gods.
Oxenforda – Oxford.
Ragnarök – The end-of-days battle where the Viking gods will battle Loki and his monster brood.
Reeve – Administer of justice ranking below a thegn.
Seax – A short, single-edged sword with the blade angled towards the point.
Seiðr – A type of Norse magic.
Skuld – One of the three Norns who sit at the great ash tree Yggdrasil and decide the fates of men.
Somersaete – Somerset.
Snottingaham – Nottingham.
Thegn – Owner of five hides of land, a church and kitchen, a bell house and a castle gate, who is obligated to fight for his lord when called upon.
Theodford – Thetford, Norfolk.
Thor – The Viking thunder god.
Thruthvangar – Thor's realm in the afterlife, where he gathers his forces for the day of Ragnarök. Similar to Valhalla.
Týr – The Viking war god.
Valhalla – Odin's great hall where he gathers dead warriors to fight for him at Ragnarök.

Vik – Part of Viking Age Norway.
Whale Road – The sea.
Wyrd – Anglo-Saxon concept of fate or destiny.
Yggdrasil – A giant ash tree which supports the universe, the nine worlds including our world Midgard.

ACKNOWLEDGEMENTS

Thanks to Caroline, Claire, Nia, Ross, Gary, and all the team at Boldwood Books for their unwavering support and belief.

ABOUT THE AUTHOR

Peter Gibbons is a financial advisor and author of the highly acclaimed Viking Blood and Blade trilogy. He originates from Liverpool and now lives with his family in County Kildare.

Download your exclusive bonus content from Peter Gibbons here:

Visit Peter's website: www.petermgibbons.com

Follow Peter on social media here:

- facebook.com/petergibbonsauthor
- x.com/AuthorGibbons
- instagram.com/petermgibbons
- bookbub.com/authors/peter-gibbons

ALSO BY PETER GIBBONS

The Saxon Warrior Series

Warrior and Protector

Storm of War

Brothers of the Sword

Sword of Vengeance

Enemies of the Crown

Death of a Kingdom

The Chronicles of Arthur

Excalibur

Pendragon

Camelot

WARRIOR CHRONICLES

WELCOME TO THE CLAN ✕

THE HOME OF
BESTSELLING HISTORICAL
ADVENTURE FICTION!

WARNING:
MAY CONTAIN VIKINGS!

SIGN UP TO OUR
NEWSLETTER

BIT.LY/WARRIORCHRONICLES

Boldwood

Boldwood Books is an award-winning fiction publishing company seeking out the best stories from around the world.

Find out more at www.boldwoodbooks.com

Join our reader community for brilliant books, competitions and offers!

Follow us
@BoldwoodBooks
@TheBoldBookClub

Sign up to our weekly deals newsletter

https://bit.ly/BoldwoodBNewsletter

www.ingramcontent.com/pod-product-compliance
Ingram Content Group UK Ltd.
Pitfield, Milton Keynes, MK11 3LW, UK
UKHW041329050226
10531UKWH00038B/405